I Want Us

By: Jessica Terry

I WANT US

First edition. March 9, 2024.

Copyright © 2024 Jessica Terry.

ISBN: 979-8990176904

Written by Jessica Terry.

I'm so appreciative of my son Langston, for shooing me away from the computer during my late-night writing sessions so I could get some rest.

My sister Jennifer for sharing my posts, and giving me feedback on my manuscripts (when I can get her to sit down and read them). lol

The rest of my family; my mother Barbara, nieces Lace and Alex, brother-in-law Tony, for showing up for me and hyping me up.

My friend Desmond for the constant cheerleading and encouragement.

My church family for being so proud of me. Friends that show support in any way, shape, or form. My Wordmakers, Black Writers Collective tribes, and my Sunday author group for the calls (where I do a good amount of venting), write-ins, collaborations, camaraderie, and encouragement. Not to mention the laughs.

And of course, the readers. I *so* appreciate every purchase, page read, review, and share. I don't take it for granted and I hope I can keep entertaining you for a long time. :)

Chapter 1

"Rome. Love ya, buddy, but you have lost your mind."

"What you mean??"

"What you just said. It was blasphemous and I refuse to co-sign that."

"Stop playing. You just hate to admit when you're wrong. Jazlyn *always* has to be right, huh?"

"Go outside right now and ask three random people and I *bet* they'd agree with me. Cinnamon Toast Crunch is better than some damn Coco Puffs."

"I doubt that."

"Seriously??" Marco, Jazlyn's boyfriend, exclaimed as he stood looking at her in disbelief. He'd just walked into the room and wasn't thrilled that she was still on the phone, as she had been for the past hour. And he was even less thrilled since he knew who she was on the phone with, yet again.

Jazlyn glanced over at him, then sucked her teeth. "What?"

"I need your help with something. I'm sure your boy won't mind."

With a slight roll of her eyes, Jazlyn turned her attention back to the phone. "Hey Rome, let me call you back."

"Aight. Hit me up."

After ending the call, Jazlyn pushed her bushy reddish-brown natural hair away from her face and looked at Marco. "What do you want?"

"I'm trying to take this picture but can't get the right angle with the tripod."

"Really? *That's* what you had me get off the phone for?"

"Oh, my bad. I didn't realize helping your man came second to a debate about some damn cereal."

"That's not *all* we were talking about, Marco, stop." She slid off the bed and walked barefoot towards him, eying him expectantly when he made no move out of the room. "Well? We taking this picture or what?"

He stood with his arms folded, a deep frown in place. "I'm not feeling how much time you spend on the phone with another man, Jazlyn."

"Ugh, not this again," Jazlyn groaned, stepping around him and heading to the other bedroom where Marco kept his lighting equipment. He was a fitness influencer and had taken over the space for any shoots he wanted to do at home. Jazlyn often got roped into being his slightly-unwilling photographer at times. "We've already talked about this, Marco. Rome is my boy, that's it. There's nothing for you to trip over."

"When I have to beg for your attention because you're giving most of it to him, I'd say that's something to trip over."

"You're exaggerating. Again."

"I'm not." Marco removed his shirt and grabbed the tub of the protein shake he was being paid to post about before taking a seat on the stool in front of the white backdrop. "You're always saying you and Rome are just friends when everybody knows that's impossible."

"Who is everybody?" Jazlyn clicked on the ring light.

"*Everybody*. It's a well-known fact that men and women can't just be friends. Especially when it involves a woman as sexy as you are. Eventually the man is gonna try something."

"That's stupid."

"Nothing stupid about it. Get over here so you can shoot me from below," Marco instructed, pointing.

Jazlyn wordlessly moved to the spot, kneeling in the position she knew he wanted so she could get the shot right the first time. She wasn't in the mood to do multiple takes like she often ended up doing when he was never satisfied, or just wanted a bunch of shots to choose from. Thankfully she'd done this for him enough that she had a good idea of what he liked.

"I'm just saying, baby, I think Rome is interested in more than just being buddies with you," Marco commented in between snaps. "No man in his right mind can be around a hot woman so much and it *never* cross his mind to try something. No *straight* man, anyway."

"Marco, we have had this conversation too many times," Jazlyn droned, standing and showing him the camera so he could view the shots she took. "Rome and I have been friends for years and nothing has popped off. And as cute as he is, *I* haven't thought about going there, either."

He glared at her. "You didn't have to say that part."

"Whatever. I just think it's a little ironic that you're so worried about me doing something with Rome when you haven't been a choir boy during our relationship, yourself. Remember that model you got a little too familiar with last year?

His eyes turned regretful. "You know I'm sorry about that. It didn't mean anything."

"Yeah, right. But I forgave you."

"Why'd you have to bring that up?"

"Because even after you stepped out on me, I have trust for you. And you need to trust *me*. Rome isn't thinking about me like that, not to mention he has a whole girlfriend himself. You're being paranoid. And frankly," she breathed a sigh of relief when he nodded his approval of the shots and stood, "I'm a little tired of having this same discussion with you."

"Well, maybe if you'd respect my wishes – hell, respect *me* – we wouldn't have to keep having it."

Jazlyn frowned. "How the hell have I disrespected *you*? And what wishes? I know you're not trying to say you want me to stop being friends with Rome. Because if you are, get ready to get *real* upset."

"I wasn't saying that but it's good to know what you'd say if I did."

"Marco," she sighed as she stuck both hands in her hair. "Do I trip when you talk to your women friends? No, I do not. You and I have been together for two years now; we should be past this nonsense."

"Jazlyn." He reached for her, pulling her to his muscled body by the waist. "You know I love you, right?"

"Uh-huh." She tried not to get temped by the oiled-up tattooed brown muscles staring her right in the face. Marco got on her nerves but he was sometimes distractingly hot. "Your point?"

"I'm not trying to lose you."

"I'm not going anywhere, Marco. I'm still here, putting up with you."

"You might not see it, but I'm telling you what I know. I see how Rome looks at you sometimes. Even if he hasn't done anything about it yet, that doesn't mean he isn't attracted to you. And I don't want him trying to take what's mine. 'Cause then I'll have to kill him and you'll *really* be pissed at me."

"You know I don't like when you say stuff like that."

"I'm just playing. But I *would* beat his ass."

"Marco." She pulled his face down for a kiss then gave him a semi-light pat on the cheek. "Shut up."

Jazlyn extracted herself from his arms and strode out of the room. It was the same thing at least once a week, and she was over it. Marco had a problem with her friendship with Rome from the beginning, even though she and Rome had been tight years before Marco came into the picture.

Which he wouldn't be in much longer if he kept bugging her.

• • • •

"HEY JAZLYN, I THINK your ridiculously cute friend is here."

Jazlyn was at Clipped, the salon where she worked as a manicurist, and lash and brow specialist. She was just finishing a set of acrylic nails on a customer and glanced up to see Rome heading towards her, all smiles and carrying a bag of something delicious.

"Hey, big head," he greeted, leaning down to give her a light hug. He nodded politely to her client, earning a flirty grin in return.

"Hush." Jazlyn smiled up at him. "I didn't know you were coming by here today."

"My consultation cancelled so I had some time. Figured I'd bring you lunch since you said you had a full schedule today. And you usually don't eat when you're busy like that."

"I meant to bring something but I forgot."

"That's what you always say."

"Well, you know I don't cook much."

"Yes, I know you don't do anything in the kitchen but pour drinks and make spaghetti." He set the bag of what she knew to be her favorite meat loaf dinner near her workstation. "Which is sad, considering how much you watch the Food Network. You'd think you would've picked up something else by now."

"I watch that for entertainment, not education."

Rome waited patiently while Jazlyn wrapped things up with her client, then obliged when she motioned to follow her outside. Even though Rome had visited her at work a thousand times over the years and was cool with her coworkers, they had a tendency to be a little too nosey at times.

"Thanks for bringing my lunch," Jazlyn told him once they were outside. "I love you for that."

"Love you back. You know I got you."

"Sometimes, though, I wonder if you do that for me or because you like being ogled by my coworkers and clients."

"I don't know what you're talking about," he replied, trying unsuccessfully to hide his smile.

"Uh-huh." Jazlyn grinned at him. She knew his big brown eyes, long lashes, splattering of freckles and straight, white teeth endeared a lot of women to him. Despite his mustache and goatee, he still looked a few years younger than his age of thirty-four, a fact that he had a love/hate relationship with.

"What you doing when you get off? You wanna hang?" Rome asked her.

"Yeah but I probably shouldn't. Don't want Marco to start acting up again."

"What?"

"He's not thrilled with the amount of attention I give you. I keep telling him we're just friends and not thinking about each other like that but he's just *so* sure that something is gonna happen eventually."

"For real? I didn't know he was insecure like that."

"He doesn't believe men and women can be just friends. It's bullshit."

"Doesn't he know I have a girl?"

"Doesn't matter, let him tell it."

Just then, Rome's phone buzzed in his pocket. He fished it out and smiled at the screen. "Speak of the devil..."

"Is that Nell?"

"Yep." He answered the FaceTime call. "Hey, baby."

"Hey! Where are you?"

"Here with J." He turned the phone towards Jazlyn and Nell's smile grew upon seeing her.

"Jazlyn!" Nell sang, her smooth brown face filling the screen. "What's up, girl?"

"Nothing at all; just taking a break from work. Your man brought me some lunch."

"Isn't he a sweetheart? What, you forgot to bring yourself something again?"

"Maybe." Jazlyn chuckled.

"I don't know how you got all that hips and booty when you forget to eat as much as you do."

"Girl, the hips and booty ain't the problem. Everything goes there and nothing goes up top. I'm barely a B-cup."

"At least you're not flat. And you'll be glad for those small titties when you don't have to spend a fortune on bras. Or have 'em hanging to your bellybutton."

"True enough."

"I love your nails," Nell commented, noting the red and gold shimmery colors on Jazlyn's customary long oval-shaped nails with an iridescent design painted on each. "I don't know how you do all that on yourself."

"Years of practice, girl."

"That's hot. I've never had the nerve to wear designs; I'm just plain and boring with my one-color-at-a-time self."

"Girl, as hot and fly as you are, you are *not-*"

"I guess y'all forgot I was here," Rome interjected, turning the screen back to him with a good-natured smile. "Y'all can pick up that girl talk another time. You home?"

"Not yet. I still have some running around to do. My dentist appointment is in a few minutes. You gonna hang out with Jazlyn tonight?"

"No, not tonight. Guess you're stuck with me."

"Aww, I'd better cancel the gigolo I requested from that app, then." The two of them shared a laugh.

Jazlyn stood there smiling, listening to them. At times she envied their relationship. Nell didn't trip about Jazlyn the way Marco tripped about Rome. Jazlyn wished that Marco was as secure as Nell, because Nell had never once been bothered by Jazlyn or her and Rome's friendship.

One thing Jazlyn hadn't told anyone was that she was wondering just how much longer she was going to hang in with Marco. Not just because of his insecurities, but because she just didn't see them going the distance. Not to mention, she wasn't as over his indiscretion with that model as she let on. Her man cheating with some random was embarrassing, and just about everyone thought she should've left him. She couldn't even explain why she didn't.

Her relationship with Marco might've been on shaky ground but she was glad that at least Rome had it together in that department. He and Nell had something good going and Jazlyn just hoped he appreciated it.

Chapter 2

"Ooh, that feels *so* good..."

Nell leaned her head back as Rome continued to rub her feet. They were on the couch in her apartment, half-watching the news.

"I like making you feel good. Is the remote over there by you? I wanted to turn it on the game."

"Oh, Rome, no...you know I don't love basketball."

"You don't have to pay attention to it. Focus on what I'm doing to you."

"Can we please just leave it on the news? You get so caught up in those games then you forget I'm here, half the time."

"Fine," Rome acquiesced, somewhat grudgingly. Nell never liked watching basketball with him and did a good bit of whining if he watched it when she was around. He tried to tell himself it wasn't that big a deal as he continued massaging her foot. "Is this a new toe ring?"

"Yeah. Got it the other day."

"It's hot. What else did you buy?"

"What makes you think I bought something else?"

"Because you know you have a shopping addiction and so do I, so I don't even know why we're doing this."

"It's not a shopping *addiction*; I just have a little problem with impulse buying."

"Pretty it up however you want. Every other day you're getting some kind of delivery or coming in with something else you bought..."

"I'm not that bad, Rome. And you're one to talk; don't you have like fifty pairs of sneakers?"

"Give or take. You gonna lecture me about that again?"

"I don't lecture; I simply don't think you need so many sneakers. And you were just talking about some pair the other day that you want to get, even though you already have plenty."

"Like you only have a few pairs, yourself."

"That's different. It's not just *one* type of shoe that I have. But anyway, I don't have a shopping addiction. And it's not like I don't buy *you* stuff, too."

"I don't think the credit card company cares either way." He winked at her and picked up her other foot. "You're cute, though."

She grinned her thanks. "As cute as you?"

"Well..."

"Uh-huh."

They laughed before Rome leaned in for a kiss, which she didn't hesitate to oblige. He grunted appreciatively as he lingered on her plump lips that were stained with the dark brick red tint that stayed put through eats and sips and smooches. Since he first saw her, Rome had been in love with Nell's lips. They were the kind people paid for, or tried to replicate through ridiculous lip-plumping exercises they saw on social media. But Nell's were all natural and Rome could never get enough of them.

"You being greedy again?" Nell giggled when Rome stopped her from pulling away.

"Can you blame me?"

"It's so wild that you love my lips so much. I used to get teased for them mercilessly back in the day."

"Like my freckles that you think are so adorable but made folks call me the Black Opie?"

"Yeah, like that." Nell grabbed his chin, intending to give a final kiss, but squealed when Rome dove on top of her. She laughed when he began playfully gnawing at her neck. "Why are you so silly?"

"Gotta keep you entertained, right?"

She shrieked with laughter when he started tickling her, squirming beneath him. "Rome!"

"What?"

"You *know* I'm ticklish!"

"Of course I know. That's why I'm doing it."

"You're gonna make me pee on myself!"

"It's your couch."

"Rome!" Nell let out a playful scream as she tried to slide from underneath Rome to the floor. "I will *pay* you to stop!"

"Yeah? Oh!"

Nell managed to buck him off of her and tried to crawl away, but he quickly caught up to her, grabbing her by the ankle. Flipping her onto her back, he momentarily buried his face in her exposed stomach before sliding up, both of them all smiles.

"What am I gonna do with you?" she panted, tweaking his chin before sliding her hands across his shoulders and back.

"Don't leave it up to me. You'll just say I'm being mannish again."

"Well, you're kind of a sex manic."

"I'm a man with a hot girlfriend that he can't keep his hands off of. If that makes me a sex maniac, then so be it."

"Sweet-talker. And...horn-dog."

"Only for you, though."

"I have no complaints, then." She pulled his face to hers and they shared a languid kiss before Rome pulled back slightly, taking in her dark coffee brown skin and sultry narrow eyes. He'd always thought she was gorgeous and often caught himself gazing at her, even if she was just humming while brushing her teeth or curled up with one of her comic books.

"I love you, Nell," he told her, looking right into her eyes as his smile faded slightly.

So did hers, and her eyes darted from his. She began to squirm uncomfortably. "Rome..."

He sighed. "Why do you always get like this when I say that?"

"Can we not do this, please?"

"You don't love me, Nell?"

She gently pushed against him. "I need to get up."

He looked at her for a moment but finally pushed himself up when he saw she wasn't going to meet his eyes. She scrambled to her feet, brushing her waist-length microbraids off her shoulder.

"Are you hungry?" she asked, still not looking at him.

Rome started to say something, but changed his mind. It was the same thing every time he mentioned feelings or anything too serious; Nell got uncomfortable and changed the subject. It had caused many an argument in the past, which Nell skirted even more. Anything intense or deeply personal sent her running, sex being the one exception. It always just left Rome frustrated and he wasn't in the mood for it tonight.

"No, I'm not," he finally responded, standing himself to his full six-foot-three height.

"You sure? I know I haven't cooked much lately but I did make some pasta salad yesterday."

"I'm good."

"I could toast some pita bread-"

"Nell." He leveled a look at her. "You can chill. I'm not gonna keep talking about feelings or anything else you clearly don't wanna hear."

She sighed, edging closer to him. "It's not like that. You *know* how I feel about you, Rome."

"It'd be nice to hear it sometimes. But whatever."

"Rome-"

"Let's drop it, all right? You're off the hook." He grabbed his sneakers and patted his pockets for his keys.

"Where are you going?" Nell asked in mild alarm.

"I need to make a run."

"Are you coming back?"

"I don't know."

"Can you? Please?"

Rome glanced at her. "Why?"

"I want you to stay with me tonight."

"Or do you just not want me to be upset with you?"

"Of course I don't." She moved over to him, gently removing his retro Jordans from his hand and placing them back on the carpeted floor. "And I don't want you to leave now, either. You don't *really* need to make a run, do you?"

Looking down into her pleading eyes, Rome told himself to calm down. He'd been with Nell for over nine months; her skittishness when it came to deep subjects or heated, sensitive topics wasn't anything new. And hearing some of the things his employees complained about with their women, he figured he should count his blessings, since this was the main issue he had with Nell.

"I guess not," he replied, letting her ease his keys out of his hand and drop them on the end table.

"Good." Nell's smile was back as she leaned up for a hug, holding him close. Rome couldn't stop his arms from encircling her just as tightly. He never could stay upset with her long.

"Hey," she began, pulling back to look up at him. "You gonna dance for me tonight?"

He smirked. "I'm sure you'd like that, huh?"

"Watching my adorably sexy boyfriend strip for me? Uhh, yeah."

"Oh, now it's *stripping*, huh?"

"Hey, just because you're not a background dancer anymore doesn't mean you can't still use the moves. Wouldn't want you to get rusty."

"I run a flooring installation business now, Nell. No dancing required for that."

"Whatever. As long as you end up naked."

He shook his head, unable to resist a smile. "What am I gonna do with *you*?"

Grinning, she took his hand and led him to her bedroom.

• • • •

A COUPLE OF HOURS LATER, Rome was sitting up in Nell's bed, shirtless and checking something on his phone. He looked up when she wandered into the doorway of the en suite, smearing her face with cleanser.

"You remember I'm gonna be going out of town soon, right?" she asked him.

"Oh, the work thing? Yeah. When are you leaving, again?"

"A couple of weeks."

"You're still going to be able to go to Asha's wedding, right?"

"Yeah. I won't be leaving until a couple of days after that."

"Good. It's still tripping me out that my little sister is getting married. She's not supposed to be old enough for that yet."

Nell moved back into the bathroom to remove the cleanser from her face. She took her time responding. "Is Jazlyn going?"

"Yep."

"Maybe you can hang out with her while I'm gone. She can keep you from getting lonely."

"I'm sure I'll see her. If her man Marco doesn't trip about it."

"Why would he?"

"He doesn't believe that men and women can be just friends, apparently."

"Really? That's silly. Of course men and women can be just friends."

"Well, he believes something will always happen eventually. Which just means he doesn't trust me around Jazlyn."

"But you and Jazlyn have been friends for years, though." Nell emerged from the bathroom, dewy-skinned and a scarf around her braids. "Like, what, six years?"

"Eight."

"And nothing has happened between you before, right?"

"Nothing at all. Jazlyn is my homie, that's it."

"So clearly, Marco is wrong." Nell hopped onto the bed, gently removing Rome's phone from his hand and placing it on the nightstand before straddling his lap. "I don't get why people have to be so pessimistic."

"Yeah, well..." He ran his hands up and down her smooth thighs. "I'm just glad *you're* not. And that you trust me."

"Of course I do." Her fingers traced his shoulders. "Nothing happens between people unless they want it to. And if you and Jazlyn wanted to go there with each other, you'd have done it by now. I have male friends *I've* never been intimate with."

"Well, between you and me, I hope Jazlyn drops that joker. He's not good for her. But she's all in love and shit."

"I'm sure if he's that bad, she'll realize it on her own sooner or later."

"Not soon enough. But we don't have to keep talking about them." He pulled down the strap of her camisole, biting his lip as he eyed her while exposing her lush breast. "You agree?"

There was a sharp intake of breath from Nell as Rome began slowly licking her dark nipple, moaning as he did so.

Her hands quickly gripped the back of his neck as her eyes slid closed, whimpering in pleasure.

"Rome..." she breathed, her head easing back.

His fingers grazed the length of her arm as he slid down her other strap. "Turn the light off."

She groped blindly for the lamp, Rome tackling her as soon as the light was out.

• • • •

ROME WAS GOING OVER some things in his small office a couple of days later when there was a soft knock on the door.

"Yeah," he called out.

His younger sister Asha poked her head in, all smiles. "Hey. Busy?"

"Yeah, but you know I make time for you." He pushed back and stood, smiling as he rounded his desk. He opened his arms for a hug, which Asha quickly stepped into. "What are you doing over here?"

"Just out running errands with Ashton, getting some things done for the wedding." She stepped back and swiveled from side to side, practically giddy.

"Yeah? Where is Ashton now?"

"Right here," Ashton announced, entering the office wearing as big a smile as his fiancée. He slid an arm around Asha's shoulders, planting a loud smooch on her cheek, which only made her smile grow even wider. "Good to see you, future bro-in-law."

"Yeah, you too." Rome bumped his fist to Ashton's before crossing his arms and peering at them. They both looked like they were about to burst from excitement. "Are...y'all all right?"

"Of course," Asha replied. "Why do you ask?"

"Because the both of you are grinning and vibrating like you're on something."

"We're just happy and excited about the wedding, that's all." Asha cast a dreamy glance up at her future husband. "I can't believe it's just a week away!"

"Yep, in just a few days, this beautiful soul is going to be my wife," Ashton added. "I can't wait."

Rome eyed them both, glad to see them so ecstatic but still wondering if they had taken some kind of drug. "Well, I'm happy for you two. I'm still tripping that my sister actually got with someone named Ashton."

"Asha and Ashton; it was just meant to be." Ashton leaned down to kiss Asha's lips before giving her shoulder a squeeze. His short locs were looking a little fuzzy and Rome hoped he was planning on taking care of that before the wedding.

Asha, who only held a vague resemblance to Rome due to her taking after their mother and Rome being almost the spitting image of their father, smoothed a hand over her auburn brown natural hair that was pulled back into a neat low puff. "Straight kismet."

"Check the t-shirts, future-bro."

Rome hadn't even noticed the matching t-shirts they were wearing that had a heart-shaped picture of the two of them hugged up on the front. He chuckled, unable to help it.

"Yeah, it's official...both of y'all are corny," he informed them.

Asha sucked her teeth. "Shut up, Rome. Like you and Nell wouldn't do the same thing if you got engaged."

His smile melted slightly. Marriage was a subject that he and Nell hadn't dug into much because she got skittish and uncomfortable whenever he even alluded to it. Rome was in no hurry to the altar but he certainly wanted to get married someday. But for all he knew, Nell didn't even want to marry him.

And if that was the case, their relationship was a waste of both of their time.

"I don't know about all that," he finally grumbled, managing to keep the frown off his face.

"She's still coming to the wedding with you, right?"

"Yeah. That's the plan, anyway."

"Is Jazlyn coming?"

"You know she wouldn't miss it. She's already looking forward to your bachelorette party."

"I'm thrilled she's gonna be there; Jazlyn always turns up. It's gonna be *so* much fun."

"Not *too* much fun, I hope," Ashton muttered.

"If y'all have strippers, I don't wanna hear about it," Rome told her.

"Same for the bachelor party," Asha immediately retorted, looking back and forth between them. "Because I already know there's going to be plenty of ridiculousness and debauchery going on in there. I'm just hoping my brother being in the room will help my man behave himself."

"Damn, baby, what do you think I'm gonna do?" Ashton asked, plastering a hand to his chest. He was a little on the wiry side, which Rome was surprised that Asha liked, but apparently she was too much in love to care about his lack of muscles. "I'd never do anything to disrespect you, whether Rome was there or not."

"You'd better not." She playfully nudged him before saying to Rome, "Anyway, we were just stopping by since we were over this way; we'll get out of your hair and let you get back to work."

"Thanks for coming by," Rome said, accepting her hug. He gave Ashton some dap before Asha stepped back and linked her fingers through her fiancé's. "And when I show up to the wedding, I hope y'all won't be wearing matching outfits."

"Shut up, Rome."

Asha and Ashton left, and Rome went back to what he'd been doing, the smile still lingering on his lips. He was glad that his little sister was so happy.

But when Jazlyn called a little later, she wasn't feeling as optimistic.

"I just have a bad feeling," she informed him.

Rome frowned slightly. "Why is that?"

"I don't know; I can't say exactly. Something just feels...off."

"About Asha and Ashton?"

"Could be. Hell, it might be about my own damn relationship; you know I haven't exactly been doodling Marco's name on my notebook lately."

"Which is why I, again, wonder why you stay with the dude."

She sighed. "Rome, don't start."

"Just saying."

"I never said I wanted to be Marco's wife. We're just...rolling along."

"Also known as wasting time..."

"Rome."

"Jazlyn. I know you're not super-romantic and sentimental but you can't tell me you don't want to spend your life with somebody. I just don't know why you're wasting time with a man you can't see yourself with down the line. A man who cheated on you, at that."

"You don't have to keep throwing that in my face. I already know."

"You don't seem like you know. You act like you forgot that."

"I haven't. I'm very well aware of what he did. But he apologized and promised not to do it again, so..."

"Yeah, so?"

"Anyway...back to what I was saying," Jazlyn diverted. "Something in my gut is telling me that something bad is coming. It's been eating at me for a couple of days, really."

"You're sounding paranoid, homie."

"You know I'm hardly ever wrong about this stuff. The last time I had one of these gut feelings, my girl Ginger got laid off. And the time before that, you twisted your ankle."

"I was playing ball and slipped. And that first one could have been avoided if Ginger had kept her mouth shut. She cussed her boss out."

"Still happened, regardless. Believe me, I'd love to be wrong."

"Well, if it *is* about you and Marco, I hope you're not."

"Now what if I said something like that about you and Nell?"

"You wouldn't unless you felt that strongly about it. And it's not like me and Nell are rock-solid ourselves, anyway."

There was a pause. "Did something happen?"

"Just more of the same. And me wondering if I need to make some kind of move or not. I love her, but...I'm not sure we're right for each other."

"Don't be too hasty, Rome. Not everybody is comfortable expressing their feelings but that doesn't mean they don't have any."

"I get that, but hell. *You're* quicker to tell me you love me than she is. And it's not just that; she runs from *any* kind of intense situation that's not sexual. I just don't know if I can see myself long-term with a woman who starts acting funny when things get deep."

"Maybe there's a reason she's like that."

"I wouldn't know because of course that would be a serious conversation, and those make her itch. If it's not laughing and joking and giggling, she's not with it."

"Just saying. This can't be anything new; she's *been* like she is and you got with her, anyway. So it couldn't have been that bad. Just remember all the good things instead of focusing on this *one* flaw of hers. That's what I try to do with Marco."

"Humph," Rome grunted, though he could see Jazlyn's point. Nell had been more happy-go-lucky than serious when he met her, but that hadn't stopped his pursuit. There were more things about Nell that he loved than he didn't, so he tried to check himself yet again. He just had to decide how big of a deal this main flaw of Nell's was to him.

In the meantime, he just wanted to be there for his little sister at her wedding and hope Jazlyn came to her senses about Marco because regardless of what she said, Rome knew his friend deserved better.

Chapter 3

It was a strange day for a wedding.

Jazlyn really wasn't in the mood for anything celebratory, but she knew she wasn't going to skip out on Asha's big day. And unfortunately, the bad feeling she'd been carrying around in her gut was still there.

Butting heads with Marco wasn't helping her mood, either.

"I'm not trying to argue with you this morning, Marco," she'd said to him earlier. They'd only been up a little over an hour and the issues had started already. "You really have a lot of nerve trying to tell me what to wear when you're half naked on social media every damn day."

"I'm a fitness influencer; people need to see *my* body," he retorted. "You don't have any reason to go out wearing something that revealing unless you're trying to draw attention to yourself."

"This dress is not revealing. It's just form-fitting."

"It's tight as hell. And I don't like it."

"Well, I don't know what to tell you, 'cause I'm wearing it."

"No matter what I say, huh?" He shook his head. "See, if I did some shit like that, you'd be going off."

"Oh, you do plenty of other stuff for me to go off about, believe me."

"You know what?" He held up his hands. "I'm can't with you today. Go to the wedding without me."

Jazlyn whirled around. "Excuse me?"

"I'm not going." He yanked a hoodie from the closet and pulled it over his head. "I'm not standing there while my woman struts around showing off how much hips and ass she got in front of everybody."

"Oh my gosh, are you serious with this?? So you're gonna bail on me just because you don't like my *dress*? A dress that doesn't even show anything?"

"I just told you what it shows."

"This is ridiculous." Jazlyn shook her head, Rome's declarations about how she was wasting her time with Marco blasting through her head. "Fine, take your ass on, then."

Without another word, Marco stormed out, slamming the door behind him.

Knowing Rome would only gloat, Jazlyn called her friend Ginger, who she was almost as close to as she was to Rome. She just needed to vent.

"What did he do now?" Ginger droned when she picked up the call.

Not bothering to feign ignorance, Jazlyn just launched into her latest round of frustrations.

"He just left here. Said he's not going to Asha's wedding with me today."

"Why not?"

"He doesn't like my dress."

Ginger paused, apparently waiting for more. "That's it?"

"He said it's too tight. I bought that dress especially for today."

"Is it showing off your boobs or something?"

"Girl, you know I hardly have any boobs. It's a form-fitting dress that he thinks is too tight. Thinks it draws too much attention to my hips and ass."

"Not that I'm defending him at all, but you *do* have the kind of hips and booty that people can't stop peeking at," Ginger informed her. "Hell, even *I* can't help but look at times. All the squats in the world won't give me what you got."

"You need to stop."

"Honestly, Jazlyn, I can't even say I'm surprised at Marco acting like a boy about that. How many other times has he shown how immature he is?"

"Several."

"You're being nice about it. I have to ask you again why the hell you put up with it. And please don't tell me anything about love."

"We don't have to do this part today, Ginger. I know Marco and I have been going at it a lot lately but that doesn't have to mean anything; every couple argues. It's just a rough patch."

"Now you're being delusional. You *know* you don't believe that."

"You just got married yourself. Are you going to question you and Zion's relationship the first time you butt heads?"

"Please! It's not like we haven't fussed. But we get along more than we don't. Can *you* say that? Not to mention, Zion never cheated on *me*."

Jazlyn sucked her teeth. "Everybody has to keep reminding me of that..."

"Because you deserve better. Someone like...Rome."

"What? Rome is my boy."

"Doesn't mean he's not tall, fine, and cute as hell. Not to mention a sweetheart that handles his business running that flooring company. You two are already ahead of the game, being best friends. Not sure why y'all are playing."

"For the millionth time, Rome and I are *just friends*. Not to mention him being in a committed relationship with Nell."

"I've seen the two of them. I don't see that going anywhere. But whatever. What are you gonna do about today?"

"I'm just gonna have to go to the wedding by myself and deal with Marco later. He's not messing up my day."

So Jazlyn got showered and dressed in her peach-colored halter dress, maroon heels, and wrangled her wild, bushy hair into a bun. When she showed up to the park where the wedding was being held, she wandered over to where Rome and Nell stood, subtly shaking her head at his questioning eyes as to why she was arriving alone.

The weather was borderline; the sun wasn't out, but it didn't feel like any rain would ruin everything. It was just...blah.

That didn't bother the bride, though. Asha was still floating on cloud nine just as she'd been since getting engaged seven months before, all smiles and anticipation. She stood with her parents and the minister in her knee-length white lace dress, clutching her bouquet in both hands as she chattered excitedly. Then she floated over to talk to a few of her friends, oblivious to or forcibly ignoring the steadily growing tension around her.

"He's late," Rome muttered, resisting the urge to look at his watch.

"It's only by a few minutes; I'm sure he'll be showing up any second," Nell insisted, keeping her voice low as she held onto Rome's arm. "He probably got stuck in traffic or something."

"I don't like this..."

"Yeah, I don't know what to think about this, either," Jazlyn chimed in, glancing around her. Several of the guests were periodically peeking at the time on their phones or watches and looking around them as if Ashton was hiding behind a bush or tree and would jump out at any moment. "*Told* you I had a bad feeling, Rome."

"Guys, let's not jump the gun," Nell insisted. "We wouldn't want any negative energy getting around to Asha. I'm sure there's a perfectly good reason why Ashton isn't here yet."

"There'd better be," Rome replied, glancing over at his sister.

"Excuse me a minute; I'll be right back," Nell whispered before easing away.

Rome looked at Jazlyn with an arched brow. "Flying solo today, huh?"

"Don't start."

"What happened this time?"

Jazlyn hesitated, not wanting to give Rome any more ammunition. "We...had a difference of opinion about something."

"Must be something stupid if you don't wanna say what it is."

"Rome-"

"Guys! Oh my god," Nell exclaimed, rushing over with her phone in her hand. "Turns out I was wrong. Ashton *isn't* coming."

"What??" Rome glanced around him, hating that he had drawn attention to himself. He lowered his voice and hissed, "What do you mean, he's not coming??"

Nell thrust her phone at him. "Look."

Rome took the phone and felt his whole body flame at what he saw. There on Instagram, in a picture posted just a few hours earlier, was Ashton grinning for the camera from some island beach. The caption said something about living his best life, and other stuff about following his gut. Rome couldn't believe his eyes.

"*Fucking* bastard," he growled under his breath, squeezing Nell's phone so hard his hand ached. He glanced over at Asha, who was looking around anxiously and trying to keep the tight smile on her face, but Rome could see the look in her eyes. She knew something was off.

Jazlyn took the phone from Rome's hand, her jaw dropping as she looked at the picture and caption. "Asshole!" she hissed. "How could he do that? *Why* would he do that??"

"Somebody has to tell Asha," Nell informed. "I can't; there's no way I could give her this kind of news. I feel funny even knowing about it before she does."

"*I'll* tell her," Jazlyn immediately volunteered, handing Nell her phone back and pulling her own from her purse.

She quickly pulled up Ashton's Instagram account. "I know she's probably over there losing her mind right now."

"Come on, we'll both tell her," Rome offered, his eyes already on his little sister.

Nell was visibly relieved as Rome and Jazlyn headed over towards where Asha was talking to a friend of hers, getting reassurance that nothing was wrong. Rome had to fight to keep his face even, knowing that wasn't true. He could just tear Ashton apart for this.

Jazlyn patted Rome's arm, motioning for him to stay put while she went over to get Asha. He appreciated this because it gave him another moment to compose himself.

"Hey, girl," Jazlyn greeted Asha, forcing a smile and placing a warm hand to her back.

"Hey, Jazlyn!" Asha's smile looked relieved, as if she was glad for the temporary distraction. "I love your nails. And that dress."

"Girl, not as much as I love yours. Hey, can I borrow you for a minute?"

"Sure, yeah."

Jazlyn winked at Asha's friend before linking her arm through Asha's and heading over to where Rome stood.

"What's going on?" Asha asked, noting the look on Rome's face. "I know everyone is getting a little antsy; I can't imagine what's keeping Ashton. He's usually late but you'd think that today of all days he'd be on time. But I'm sure he just-"

"Sis," Rome interjected, unable to stand hearing her delude herself. "There's something we've gotta tell you."

"What?"

Jazlyn handed her phone over to Rome as she kept a comforting hold on Asha's arm, already dreading this. Rome still didn't know the best way to come out with it and figured being straightforward was the only option.

"Ashton isn't coming, sis," he made himself say, keeping his voice low.

Asha frowned slightly. "What do you mean?"

Stepping closer, Rome handed Asha Jazlyn's phone, which was still open to Ashton's Instagram picture of him on the beach. He tried to keep his anger in check as he watched the horror slowly melt over Asha's face.

"This...this can't be," Asha whispered, her chest heaving more by the second. "This can't be for real...can it?"

She looked up at Rome, as if wanting him to assure her that there was some other explanation. Rome would have given anything to have been able to give her one.

"I wish it wasn't," he finally said, rubbing the back of his neck. "I hate having to show this to you..."

"Why, though?" Tears streamed down Asha's face, making Rome's chest tighten. "Why would he do this to me? We were so happy, I thought..."

"Baby, we wish there was something we could say to make this make sense," Jazlyn chimed in, putting an arm around Asha's trembling shoulders. "For whatever reason, he didn't have the balls to face you. I know my calling him a punk-ass won't ease your pain right now but that's what he is."

"He...oh my god!" Asha cried, unable to contain herself another second. She fell against Jazlyn, who immediately took her into her arms, holding her tightly. "This is *so* humiliating! How could I have been so *wrong*??"

"This is *not* your fault, girl," Jazlyn assured her. "This is on *his* punk ass, not you."

"I need to get out of here."

"Say no more."

Rome hurried over to his parents, who had been peering over at them curiously, and filled them in on what was going on. Their mother Georgia immediately rushed over to her daughter, pulling Asha from Jazlyn's arms into her own. Her and her husband Solomon ushered Asha away, Asha's loud sobs still piercing the air.

Rome informed the guests that the wedding was off, leaving out the reason but asking everyone to keep Asha in their prayers. He looked around and noticed Nell standing way off to the side, scrolling through her phone, and his frown only deepened.

He was just wrapping up his announcement when Marco showed up out of nowhere, decked out in a black suit and partially unbuttoned shirt, heading straight over to Jazlyn.

"Hey baby," he greeted with a smile, pulling her to him for a kiss. "Glad to see me?"

Jazlyn looked anything but. "Marco, you picked a hell of a time to show up..."

"Why? I know I'm a little late but I went to the gym after I left the house earlier and when I was on the bench press – I hit a personal best today, by the way – I realized it wasn't cool of me to stand you up like that. I still think the dress is too tight but I admit you look damn good in it."

"Now really isn't the time, Marco-"

"You're right. I don't want to get into it again, either." He pulled his phone from his pocket, grabbing Jazlyn by the waist with his other hand. "Come on, let's take a picture together."

She tried to twist out of his grasp. "*Not* a good time for that. Look, the wedding is-"

"Is it running late or something? I know we're always on CP time. Well, while we're waiting on whoever to show up, we might as well get some pics in, right? We're looking too good not to. Plus my followers aren't used to seeing me suited up." He held up his phone and took a couple of selfies, oblivious to the astonished looks around him.

"Marco!" Jazlyn exclaimed, her face flaming in embarrassment. "Can you *stop*??"

"What's wrong with you? I tried to get you to take one with me, remember?"

"Hey man!" Rome stormed over, getting right in Marco's face. "I know you're not coming here with this disrespectful bullshit!"

"Nobody's being disrespectful," Marco retorted, his scowl matching Rome's. "And you need to back up outta my face."

"And *you* need to quit worrying about your damn social media content when my sister just got stood up at the altar!"

Marco's expression faltered slightly at this new information. "How was I supposed to know that?"

"Maybe if you had been on time-"

"You don't need to be worrying about me or my time. I'm here for Jazlyn."

"You don't need to be here *at all*."

"Y'all, chill out!" Jazlyn ordered, trying to wedge her way between them. "Now is *not* the time for this!"

"Yeah, Rome, calm down," Nell pleaded, appearing at his side. She grabbed his arm, trying to pull him away."Come on, let's just go."

Rome didn't budge. He and Marco just stood there facing off, glaring at each other. Rome might've been a little taller but Marco had him by probably twenty pounds of muscle, not that it mattered. As livid as he was, he was just itching for Marco to jump so he could go crazy on him.

"Rome," Nell persisted, tugging harder. "Please..."

"Yeah, this isn't making things any better," Jazlyn added. She managed to push Marco away, her hands braced against his hard chest. "We don't need to cause a scene on top of everything else. Let's *go*, Marco."

After a few more moments of mean-mugging, Marco let Jazlyn pull him away, glaring at Rome over his shoulder as he walked.

Jazlyn noticed and yanked hard on his hand. "Stop it!"

"I don't like him," Marco grunted.

"Nobody's asking you to like him."

"I'm serious, Jazlyn." He stopped walking, causing Jazlyn to stop with a sigh. "For him to step to me like that??"

"His little sister just got humiliated on her wedding day and you were up in here taking selfies, *after* waltzing in late. Were you expecting a hug?"

"There's no way I could've known what happened before I got here. You should've given me a heads-up."

"You weren't coming, remember? I tried to tell you what the deal was but you kept interrupting me. And honestly with everything going on, Marco, I really wasn't thinking about you. I was worried about Asha and Rome."

"Yeah, you're always worried about Rome," he muttered. "And I don't like it."

"Oh, well. Rome is my best friend so I don't know what to tell you."

"Well, I know what to tell *you*." He stepped closer to her, the expression in his eyes hard and unflinching. "I don't want you around him anymore."

She looked at him incredulously, placing a hand on her hip. "Excuse me?"

"You heard me."

"Are you seriously trying to give me an ultimatum?"

"Call it whatever you want to. *I'm* your man and I'm telling you that I don't like you giving so much of your time and attention to another man, best friend or not. And if you don't want me and you to have some big problems, you'll hear what I'm telling you and respect that."

He stomped off to his car, leaving Jazlyn standing there in disbelief.

Chapter 4

"This is some bullshit," Rome muttered, throwing the book he'd been trying to read next to him on the couch and running a hand down his face.

Nell looked over at him in concern. "What's wrong?"

He looked at her like she was crazy. "Seriously?"

"I mean, I know you're still upset about what happened to Asha..."

"Yes, Nell, I'm still upset about what happened to Asha," he snapped. "It's been a week since she found out about her bitch-ass fiancé skipping out on her and she's still crying day in and day out, according to Mama. She won't see anybody, she's barely eating..."

"Oh, that's too bad..."

"Then come to find out that not only did Ashton leave her hanging on their wedding day, he was cheating on her, too. Hooked up with one of the strippers from the bachelor party and they flew to Jamaica in the middle of the night. Can you believe that shit?"

"Wow...this sounds like something out of one of my romance novels."

He glared at her. "Excuse me?"

"I'm not trying to excuse how Ashton went about things, but maybe this was just a case of meeting the right person at the wrong time. I mean, you can't help who you fall for."

His frown was so deep it was starting to ache. "Are you kidding me right now??"

Nell immediately held up her hands. "I'm not defending Ashton in any way-"

"It damn sure sounds like you are."

"I'm not. He totally should have been honest with Asha if he changed his mind about getting married. I'm just saying, if you take the part about him ditching her *out* of it-"

"There is no *taking that part out of it*, Nell!" He shot off the couch. "That's kinda the main part, here! Did you not see how *devastated* Asha was? *Or* hear me just say how devastated she *still* is? And you're willing to brush that to the side??"

"That's not what I meant, Rome!" Nell stood, looking at him pleadingly. "That came out wrong...look, just forget I said anything, okay? Let's watch a movie or something."

"I don't want to watch a movie. I'm not in the mood."

"It might help get your mind off things for a while."

He cut his eyes at her. "I doubt that."

"Well...maybe you can hang out with Jazlyn," Nell suggested, grasping at straws. "She usually knows what to say to get you to feel better."

"Nell, what part of this don't you get? The only thing that would make me feel better is Asha feeling better. Or Ashton getting hit by a truck. And thinking about Jazlyn only makes me think about her idiot meathead boyfriend."

"I still can't believe you were going to fight him like that."

"Hell yeah, I was. I hate you and Jazlyn came over there and stopped it."

"Rome, that wasn't going to fix anything. Especially since Marco didn't know what had happened."

"Well, you're just giving everybody the benefit of the doubt today, huh?" He grabbed his keys. "I'm out."

"Rome! Come on, I'm just trying to get you to think rationally." She hesitantly moved over to him. "I don't mean to upset you. And anyway, this is *your* place, remember?"

"You're right." He glared down at her. "So maybe *you're* the one that needs to leave, then."

Her mouth fell open. "Are you serious?"

"Yes, Nell, I'm serious. Because the way you're pissing me off right now, I might say something to you that I can't come back from. And we both know you can't handle tense situations or anything serious; I'm surprised you haven't made up a reason to leave here on your own by now."

Her narrow brown eyes looked hurt. "Rome, I'm sorry for upsetting you, but I want to be with you through this. And I wish you would stop saying that I can't handle serious stuff. That's kind of insulting, you know."

"Oh yeah?" Rome folded his arms. "So if I asked if you thought about *us* getting married one day, what would you say?"

She immediately averted her eyes, her fingers tangling together. "Oh..."

Rome leaned a little closer, looking at her pointedly. "Yes?"

"I mean...sure, I've *thought* about it, but..."

"But?"

"I don't know, Rome. I don't think we're at the place where we should be talking about that yet. We've only been together nine months."

"Hmm." Rome shook his head. "Well, you haven't bolted for the door or suddenly remembered something you have to do, so that's progress, I guess. What, should I check back at the one-year mark? Maybe we can talk about it then?"

Nell sighed. "Rome, don't be like that."

"If we're not on the same page, Nell, let me know now," he stated strongly. "Because otherwise, I'm not sure what we're doing together."

Her eyes widened. "What are you saying??"

"You heard what I said. It was pretty clear. If you're just trying to date for the hell of it, then we have a problem."

"That's not it," she quickly insisted, tentatively grasping the front of his shirt. "This isn't...this is real for me, Rome. Regardless of how it may seem, I hope you believe that."

Rome just looked at her, not knowing what to believe.

· · · ·

OVER THE NEXT FEW DAYS, Rome's mood didn't improve much. He went about work and whatever else he had to do on autopilot, going straight home afterwards. Usually he spent a couple of nights at Nell's, or she stayed with him, but she wasn't high on his favorites list for the time being. Wondering if their relationship was nothing but a dead end plagued his mind more and more every day.

And of course, he was still worried about Asha. He could still see the look on her face when she saw the picture of Ashton on the beach when he was supposed to be there marrying her. Rome still couldn't believe Ashton had played his sister like that and every time he thought of it, it just reignited his anger.

Rome and his crew were just finishing a job installing some new hardwood floors when his phone rang. He breathed a sigh of relief when he saw it wasn't Nell. Getting into his truck and slamming the door, he answered.

"What up?"

"Hey, what are you doing?" Jazlyn asked him.

"Just finished a job. About to head back to the office."

"How'd it go?"

Shrugging, Rome took a quick swig from his water bottle. "It was work."

"Since you still sound pissed off, I take it Asha isn't feeling any better?"

"No. I tried to go by and check on her but she's still holed up in her old room at our folks', not wanting to see anybody. Mama said she'll give her another day or two before she starts trying to get her up and about again."

"Damn. I was hoping she'd have made at least a little progress by now but I get it. Your man skipping town the night before your wedding with some thot has to be a hard pill to swallow."

"My thing is, he *still* hasn't had the balls to reach out to her and explain himself or apologize. And I know he hasn't because Asha definitely would've said something about that to Mama. I *swear*, if I knew where this joker lived..."

"I'm glad you don't, 'cause I don't have bail money. Though I'd be down for some minor vandalizing."

Rome couldn't resist a small smile at that. "Minor?"

"Hell, I'm not trying to get arrested behind that punk. But if I *accidentally* bumped my car door into his or dropped some broken glass in his driveway..."

"That's why you're my dawg."

"You know it. Things any better with Nell?"

"Probably about as good as they are with you and Marco."

"Oh, your girl gave you an ultimatum, too?"

Rome sat up straighter. "He what?"

"Yeah, after you two faced off the other day, he told me he didn't want me to be around you anymore."

"And why the hell are you just now telling me this?"

"You were too worried about Asha and your stuff with Nell for me to bring up this nonsense."

"Your man telling you he doesn't want you dealing with me is a big deal, J. What did you say?"

"Besides to kiss my ass? That he can't tell me what to do or who I hang with, especially since you haven't done anything wrong. He's been in his feelings since, hardly saying anything to me."

"And how much longer are you gonna let stuff keep going like that?"

"Me? *He's* the one acting like a spoiled brat. I'm over it. And if I'm being all the way real about it, Rome, I'm kinda over *him*."

"For real?"

"I love him and everything but I've been wondering what the hell I'm doing with him more and more often lately. It just feels like we're going through the motions; like we're together just because."

"I know that feeling," Rome muttered.

"I'm not trying to be his wife. We hardly have any fun together anymore; all he wants to do is work out and try to up his Instagram following. Sometimes I feel like he only needs me there to take his freaking pictures."

"Sounds like the two of you need to have a talk, then."

"Please. You don't think I've brought this up already? He doesn't think anything's wrong; 'we're good' is all he ever says. Basically giving me the brush-off."

"Why are you still there, then, J? One thing you're not is shy or desperate; if you're not feeling it anymore, then leave."

There was a pause. "I could say the same thing to you, homie. It's easier said than done."

Rome knew she had a point. There had been several times where he thought about just ending things with Nell because he didn't think they would work long-term, but she'd manage to smooth things over enough to get him to hold off. And he *did* love her; ending their relationship wasn't something he was gung-ho about. He just wasn't as sure about them as he thought he should've been by then, regardless of how often he tried to rationalize things.

Rome and Jazlyn talked for a few more minutes before Rome headed home. Nell was supposed to be coming by, having sweet-talked him into having dinner with her since they hadn't seen much of each other in days. He stopped by the grocery store to get a few things, and was almost home when he got a call from his father, Solomon.

"What's up, Dad?" he greeted, pulling up to his house.

"Hey, son. You home?"

"Just pulled up. Did something happen with Asha?"

"Nah, she's still devastated and crying up in the room. Listening to a bunch of sad music. Georgia is tending to her. Do you know if her punk ex-fiancé is back in town yet?"

"I wish I did, 'cause I'd surely be going to see him."

"You're not going without me. It still burns me up that he did that to my baby girl. But that's not why I'm calling. You heard about the blizzard that's supposed to be coming in a few days, right?"

"I heard but didn't pay much attention to it. The last time they said it was supposed to snow around here, it ended up being damn near seventy degrees."

"Yeah, well, still. They're thinking this is supposed to be a big one, so make sure you're stocked up. Non-perishables, flashlights, batteries..."

"I know the drill, Dad. I just replaced my generator and whatever supplies I don't have already, I'll get."

"You'd better get on it. You know how folks hoard stuff when they think bad weather is coming."

"Yeah, I'm one of 'em, which is how I know I'm good." They shared a laugh. "But for real, thanks for the reminder. I'd better make sure Jazlyn is good on that, too."

"What about Nell?"

"She'll be out of town by then, probably. She was supposed to leave a couple of days after the wedding but postponed it. We're meeting up tonight."

"Well, tell her I said hello, regardless. And my girl Jazlyn, too."

"Will do."

Rome got the groceries in the house and glanced at his watch, a little surprised that Nell wasn't there already. She'd been rather eager for them to spend time together so he thought she might be there waiting on him, though her car hadn't been in the driveway.

Shrugging, he just finished putting away the groceries, leaving out the fixings for the dinner he'd get started on after his shower. He figured Nell would be there by the time he got out.

But she wasn't, and there were no missed calls or messages from her on his phone. He frowned. They hadn't said a specific time, but usually she was pretty regular.

Even though he hadn't been hyped about them spending the evening together, he hoped nothing was wrong. He pulled on some basketball shorts and called her.

"Hey," she greeted after a couple of rings, sounding almost hesitant.

"Hey, you good? I thought you'd be here by now."

"Yeah, um...there's been a change in plans on that. I know I should've told you already..."

"What kind of change in plans? You want me to come to your place?"

"No, that's not it. I'm not there, either."

Rome frowned. "Where are you, then?"

"I'm out of town. I left for my conference this morning."

"Hold up..." He stood from where he'd been sitting on his bed. "You left town when you knew we were supposed to be meeting up and didn't say anything? What, was there some kind of emergency or something?"

"No. I just felt like we needed a break. You haven't wanted to be around me much lately and when we *have* been together, we're butting heads. I thought some time apart would do us both some good."

"So...you just decide that and stand me up?"

"Come on, Rome, you know we need this."

"Not the damn point, Nell. You could've at least let me know that, especially since you're the one that was hounding me about hanging out tonight."

"Hounding you? Wow, I didn't think us spending time together was such a burden. Now I *know* I made the right decision. Because we certainly can't keep going like we have been."

"We finally agree on something. Have a nice trip." He shook his head and hung up.

Chapter 5

Jazlyn was trying to concentrate on the nail art she was working on for her client at work and not think about the crappy state her relationship was in. Marco was still hanging onto the ultimatum he proposed, and Jazlyn was still refusing it. So they were at an impasse and Jazlyn wasn't sure how much longer she could deal with things like they were.

"I'm kinda tripping about this blizzard, y'all," one of her coworkers, Sammi, admitted as she massaged lotion onto her client's hand. "They said it's supposed to be really bad."

Her client sucked her teeth. "Didn't they say that last time and it ended up being picnic weather?"

"Yeah, but they swear they're more certain this time. They're predicting six inches of snow."

"I'll believe that when I see it," Jazlyn muttered, painting a perfect white diagonal line across her client's nail. "It's almost never as bad as they think it'll be."

"Don't brush this off, Jazlyn. It's better to be safe than sorry," Sammi advised. "I went and stocked up on stuff last night and once I get home after I leave here, I'm not going anywhere until all of this passes."

"My man made sure I had everything I needed, too," Rena, who was nearby doing a pedicure, chimed in. "He might have to work late tonight and in case he's not able to leave early, he wanted to be sure I was squared away. Which is good because I never know what to get in these situations."

Jazlyn frowned slightly. Marco hadn't even mentioned anything to her about the blizzard or tried to make sure she'd be good if it actually hit. For all she knew, he wouldn't even be there with her; he'd hardly been at her place since their (latest) fight. And she knew he probably heard the weather report; the fact that he was too stubborn to see about her at a time like this was upsetting.

Though, sadly, part of her wasn't surprised.

Jazlyn only had three clients that day and this was one time she was fine with that. There had been a couple of cancellations due to people being paranoid about the upcoming blizzard. So when she wrapped up her last client, Jazlyn started to head to the store, but instead went by to see Ginger.

"You're too pretty to frown like that," Ginger observed after Jazlyn plopped onto her couch with a sigh. She stood with a hand on her hip, her boy shorts showing off her long, toned brown legs. Her figure hadn't changed much since her college track star days. "What's going on? I didn't know you were coming by here."

"Yeah, I know." Jazlyn glanced around. "Where's the husband?"

"At his mama's house, making sure she has everything she'll need in case this blizzard actually hits."

"Yeah, that's all folks seem to be worried about."

"Kind of a big deal. Never know how long it might last. And god forbid the power goes out. I hope you're prepared for it, just in case."

"I have some stuff but I guess I should go and get some more before I head to the house. I probably need more batteries and I hardly have anything that's non-perishable..."

"Then you need to be out getting that instead of sitting over here. 'Cause you know how folks get; there's probably hardly any bread or milk left anywhere. I know it was tough finding stuff when I went out this morning."

"Great." Jazlyn let her head fall against the back of the couch. "That's just great. Maybe I can call Marco..."

"Oh, y'all made up, huh?" Ginger subtly rolled her eyes as she tucked some of her dyed dark blonde hair behind her ear, sliding into the other corner of the couch with a leg tucked under her.

"Not at all. But hopefully he's done a better job of preparing for this than I have."

"Well, then I guess it's a good thing this blizzard came up or else you might not have an excuse to put off doing what you know you wanna do."

Jazlyn glared at her. "Excuse me?"

"You know what I'm talking about. You've been bitching about Marco for months yet you still keep him around. And I know it's not because you're desperate."

"Excuse me for loving the bastard."

"Oh, that's it? That's the only reason you keep putting up with his bullshit? Especially when you have a man that would treat you a hundred times better right in your face?"

"Please tell me you're not talking about Rome."

"Of course I'm talking about Rome."

"We've had this conversation, Ginger. *Many* times. Rome is my friend and that's all."

"Uh-huh." Ginger leaned forward, looking at her intently. "So you're trying to tell me that you've *never* thought of him any other way? That he might as well be a chick with a mustache?"

"I didn't say all that. I'm not blind. Yes, Rome is cute as hell. But that doesn't mean I'm attracted to him."

"Oh, you aren't?"

Jazlyn immediately started to say no, but found herself hesitating. If she was honest with herself, there'd been a few times during the course of their friendship where she noticed certain things about Rome and felt parts of her wake up. But she always brushed it off, thinking it was nothing.

"Is he fine? Yes," she finally responded. "Is he a good guy? Absolutely. And have there been moments since I've known him that I looked at him that way? A couple. But that's where it ends. Even if I *did* see him like that, it's not mutual."

"So you're a mind reader? 'Cause I bet he didn't tell you that."

"I just know. He's committed to Nell and yeah, they have their issues, but he loves her. Just like I love Marco. He gets on my nerves but he's not terrible. And he's damn good in bed."

"Please tell me you're not still sexing him while y'all are supposed to be beefing."

"It would be a lie if I did. We don't have to talk to do that. Though it's been a little while, I admit, since he's still in his feelings over Rome."

"I don't get you at all," Ginger shook her head. "You're just wasting time, if you ask me. But you always think you know what you're doing so, hey, do your thing. Speaking of wasting time, though, you need to get out of here and get ready for this blizzard so you aren't sitting in your house freezing and starving."

"I guess." Jazlyn checked her watch and stood, Ginger following suit. They shared a hug before Jazlyn headed for the door.

"Take care of yourself," Ginger advised as Jazlyn headed out, grinning when a shiny black Tahoe pulled up in the driveway.

"Hubby is home, huh?" Jazlyn smirked, noting her friend's sudden giddiness.

"Yep yep. So you're leaving just in time 'cause our honeymoon phase definitely isn't over."

"Uh-huh. Well, enjoy." Jazlyn chuckled, waving at Ginger's husband as she got into her car and headed off.

She went to the store to try to grab some food and other items, but Ginger had been right; the shelves were practically bare. And it was the same at the other three stores she went to. She managed to scrounge up a few things, but she knew it wouldn't be enough if the blizzard turned out to be as bad as everyone thought.

"It's probably another false alarm, anyway," she told herself, heading to her house. Still, she tried to call Marco to see if she could just stay at his place, but the call went to voicemail. She went by his apartment, but no one answered and his car wasn't in the lot. And of course she didn't have a key because he took it back after one of their fights. She'd almost forgotten about that.

Frustrated, she headed home. As soon as she finished putting away the things she bought and started gathering her lone flashlight, blankets, and whatever candles she could find, the snow started. She rushed over to the window, her jaw dropping slightly.

"I'll be damned," she muttered, marveling at the light flakes falling from the sky. She honestly hadn't believed they would get any snow at all, and could only hope that it stayed as light as it was or that it wouldn't stick.

No such luck. Within the next half hour, the snow was falling at a much faster pace and was building up on the ground, not to mention the strong winds that she could actually hear from inside. Jazlyn kicked herself for not taking the forecast more seriously.

She changed into a hoodie and checked the thermostat, cranking it up a few degrees. It was already starting to feel colder. Her house was small and cute and homey, but it was also old. And she hadn't always heeded Rome's suggestions or warnings about upgrades or replacements she needed to make, thinking she could just get to it whenever. Rome often ended up just going ahead and taking care of it for her, if he could, and she admittedly ended up conceding how right he'd been.

"Yeah, I'm an idiot," she grunted to herself, grabbing her phone to call Rome. "He's surely gonna fuss at me for this one."

"Hello?" Rome's voice sounded distracted. "You there, big head?"

"Yeah, I'm here. I called you."

"I'm aware. But reception is kinda crazy right now. What's up? You good?"

"Uhh, kinda...where are you?"

"In my truck. Had to cut a job short when the snow started. Are you-" The line went dead.

Jazlyn glanced at the phone, then jammed it back against her ear. "Rome? Rome, you there??"

She tried to call him back but it went straight to voicemail.

"Damn," she muttered, dropping the phone to the couch. She figured he probably hit a dead spot, and couldn't help but worry a little about him being out on the road. The snow was falling faster by the minute, and people tended to drive crazy in bad weather. And she didn't see any city trucks out clearing or salting the roads, so apparently the city hadn't heeded the weather warnings any more than she had.

Sighing, she headed to the kitchen to get some crackers when there was a knock on the door. Part of her thought it might be Marco, but the relief upon seeing Rome standing there almost knocked her over.

"Whoa, glad to see me?" Rome joked when she threw her arms around his neck.

"I really am." She glanced at all of the bags in his hands. "What's all this?"

"I know how hard-headed you are and figured you hadn't gotten anything in case the snow hit." He entered the house, dusting his work boots off on the mat. "You hardly ever listen when I try to tell you about this stuff."

"That's not true."

He stopped and looked down at her. "So you don't need anything, then?"

Her chin quivered as she tried and failed to maintain her straight face. "Okay, you're right. Damn it."

"Yeah, that's what I thought." Rome continued into the living room, setting the bags either near or on the couch. "You'd better love the hell outta me, is all I know."

"Oh I do."

Jazlyn watched as he unloaded hand-crank lights, a kerosene space heater, a thermal blanket, a portable power bank, and extra batteries. He went about sealing her old windows (one of the things he kept telling her she needed to upgrade) with weather-seal tape. Jazlyn grabbed the bags with the food and took them to the kitchen, unable to resist a smile as she unloaded everything. Rome hurriedly went back to his truck to grab the cases of bottled water and juice that he'd gotten for her, plunking them on the tiny kitchen table.

"Is that what I think it is?" she asked, nodding towards the two lidded cups on the counter.

"Yep. Hot chocolate with a shot of vanilla."

"I love how you know what I need." She grabbed one of the cups, lifted the tab on the lid, and took a long sip. Her eyes closed as she swirled the sweet, rich, warm liquid in her mouth. When her eyes opened, Rome was watching her with an expression that she would mistake as longing if she didn't know better. He hurriedly went back to what he was doing.

"There," he said breathlessly a little while later, rubbing his gloved hands together. "You should be good now, whatever happens. You remember how to use the power bank, right?"

"Yeah. You've quizzed me several times."

"Well, at least you listened to *that*."

"Shut up, Rome. But for real, thank you so much for all this; thinking about me enough to bring this stuff over here. I admit I dropped the ball with not getting it myself."

"It's all good. You know I've got your back. Need me to do anything else before I head to the house?"

Unable to resist, she stepped forward to give him another hug, the gratitude overwhelming her. He had come through for her, as he had so many other times before, and it hit her just how fortunate she was to have a friend like him in her life.

Rome noted how tightly and how long she was holding onto him and smiled, his arms tightening around her. As stubborn as Jazlyn was, he could appreciate how she didn't let her pride keep her from admitting when she messed up.

"I appreciate you, Rome," she whispered, still holding onto him.

"Right back at you."

They separated and shared a lingering look before tearing their eyes away.

"I'd better go," he finally said, his hands slowly dropping from her waist. "It's really picking up out there."

"Yeah." Jazlyn stepped back, hating that he had to leave. She didn't want to go through all of this by herself, but for whatever reason, she felt weird about asking him to stay with her. "Call me when you get home."

"I will." His soft brown eyes roamed over her face. "You sure you're good?"

"Actually...I wouldn't mind it if you-"

The power went out, cloaking them in near-darkness.

Chapter 6

"Jazlyn, come on...you've gotta chill out."

"It's kinda hard for me to chill out when it's snowing like crazy outside and I have no clue where my man is. Haven't even heard from him."

"I get that you're worried..."

"Damn that. The bastard hasn't even tried to check on me or make sure I didn't need anything. I went by his place when I left work earlier and he wasn't even there."

Biting his tongue, Rome just continued his task of firing up the heater. The power had been out for almost a half hour, and it was getting increasingly colder in the house. The waning daylight coming in from the windows provided some light, and he was waiting for it to get darker before cranking up the lighting he brought. He chose not to fuss at Jazlyn again for not replacing her generator like he told her she needed to.

"Why are you being so quiet?" Jazlyn asked when he hadn't commented after several moments.

"I probably shouldn't say anything."

"Why not?"

"Don't wanna disrespect your man."

"That's never stopped you before."

"Come on, J. I'm not gonna act like I'm a Marco fan 'cause I'm not, but I haven't outright dogged him to you. You're choosing to stay with him for a reason, whatever the hell that reason is."

"I'm wondering what that is, myself," Jazlyn admitted, playing with the edge of the thermal blanket. "I'd be lying if I said I was happy with him. Certainly not like you are with Nell."

"Hmph, please." Rome grabbed a bottle of water and took a small sip. "Don't use me and Nell as a barometer for anything. She up and left town without telling me because we were going through a rough patch. Couldn't even tell me to my face. I know Marco fussing about stuff might get old, but at least he cares enough to do it. Nell acts like she's scared to butt heads with me."

"Sometimes I wish Marco was. He comes at me about *stupid* shit."

"So we're both having relationship issues." He kicked off his boots and sat on the couch, with Jazlyn joining him, close but not touching. "It'd be nice if at least one of us was satisfied in that area."

"You're not satisfied with Nell? I mean, I know y'all are going through a rough time, but..."

"I don't know. I'll admit that lately I've been questioning some things." He played with the cap of the water bottle. "Yeah, I love Nell, but that doesn't mean she's the right woman for me. It's hard to imagine a future with a woman who can't handle tough topics or situations. I thought I could deal with that, but...the more I think about it, the more I realize I'd be settling just because she's a good woman."

"Wow..." Jazlyn eyed him, noting the anguish on his face. "And she has no idea?"

"I can't talk to her about this stuff. The last time I brought up marriage, she said we haven't been together long enough to discuss it, basically."

"Damn, you wanna marry her?"

"It's not like I was about to propose right then. But I'd like to get married one day. And if she doesn't, or can't see herself marrying me, then we're just wasting each other's time."

"I guess I can understand that." Jazlyn chewed her lip for a moment before glancing over at Rome again. He seemed genuinely bothered by this. Hesitating, she sat forward slightly in her seat and asked, "Rome...if Nell walked through that door right now, would you end things with her?"

His eyebrows rising in thought, Rome slowly hunched his shoulders. "Honestly, J...it'd be so easy for me to just say yes. But I don't know. I'd definitely tell her we need to have a serious talk. If she fell back again and brushed me off, then...yeah. I'd probably go ahead and end it."

"So you really *are* unhappy, then."

"I'm not as happy as I'd like to be. That's not all on Nell, but she plays a part in it, for sure."

"You deserve to be genuinely happy, Rome. You're a good man."

"I appreciate that. You deserve the same, though. I mean, why keep spending time with someone who just doesn't get you?" He looked at her. "You know?"

Jazlyn returned his look, her head gently nodding at his question. She let her eyes roam over his face and settle on his lips, which sent a current through her that had her feeling guilty and good all at once. For the first time, she wondered what his lips felt like, and if he would stop her if she tried to find out.

Friends could kiss, right? It didn't have to mean anything...did it?

Rome was having similar thoughts. His hands were itching to slide into her bushy reddish-brown hair. He always loved her hair. And her skin looked so smooth and she smelled delicious...he started to lean closer but stopped himself. His eyes stayed on her face, though, as he unsuccessfully willed his body and mind to calm down.

This was Jazlyn. He wasn't supposed to be feeling like this about Jazlyn. They were best friends, buddies. In all the years of their friendship, they'd never so much as shared a forehead kiss. So why was the thought of tackling her on this couch and kissing that sugary lip gloss off her lips playing through his mind on a loop?

Shooting off the couch, he patted his pockets for his keys. Clearly, he needed to get out of there. All the drama from the past few days must have been getting to him.

"I should, um...I should probably go," he muttered, looking everywhere but at Jazlyn.

"The snow is pretty bad out there," Jazlyn informed, standing herself. She stepped closer, looking up at him anxiously. "You sure?"

He heard that *something* in her voice. "There's probably no ice yet; I should be able to make it."

"Rome..."

He went to the front door but as soon as he opened it, he knew he wasn't going anywhere. The snow was halfway up his tires already and still falling hard, not to mention the wind that had picked up. And there was already a line of traffic on the road in front of Jazlyn's house, barely inching along. It would be foolish for him to try to go out in all that.

I might do something equally as foolish if I stay here, the way I'm feeling, he thought to himself.

"Rome, close the door; you know you can't go anywhere," Jazlyn said from behind him. "It's just not safe."

"Yeah." He grudgingly shut the door and locked it, but took his time turning back around. "I guess it's not."

"And...I'd rather not have to be here alone during all this. I don't want you to leave."

Closing his eyes momentarily so he could let the unsettling feeling that shot through him after her comment pass, he assured her, "I'm not going anywhere. You know I got you."

Jazlyn grinned in relief. "Good. And you know you really couldn't have gone out there right now, anyway."

"Why not?"

"You don't have any shoes on."

Rome looked down at his socked feet, shocked to realize he'd forgotten to put his boots back on. He couldn't help but chuckle a little, with Jazlyn giggling, herself. They melted into quiet again, standing there as if awaiting further instruction.

"I should call to check on my folks," he said after a brief awkward silence, avoiding her eyes as he pulled out his phone.

"Yeah, I should check on Ginger."

They made their respective phone calls with their backs to each other, keeping the calls short since they weren't sure how long the power would be out and they wanted to conserve their phone batteries for as long as they could, in case something went wrong with the power bank.

Once that stall tactic was exhausted, the awkward silence returned. Rome tried to shake it off by loudly clapping his hands and throwing on a smile. "So, what's up? You wanna eat something? Play some cards? You have any of those board games?"

"Nah, Marco took them somewhere and never brought them back. I have some cards, though."

"Aight, grab those and I'll get some snacks."

A few minutes later, they were facing each other on the couch, wrapped up in blankets while they played gin and shared a big bowl of popcorn and granola bars. Pretty soon, the earlier awkwardness had faded and they were back to being buddies who laughed and talked junk and good-naturedly teased each other again. Rome wasn't thinking about Nell, and Marco was the furthest thing from Jazlyn's mind. They were just glad to be there together.

"Damn, it's really getting cold in here," Rome commented, pulling the blanket tighter around him. "Even with that heater on."

"We can go back to my room; it's usually a little warmer in the back of the house," Jazlyn suggested. "Plus, this long day is catching up to me and I kinda want to get comfortable and stretch out."

"Um, okay yeah, let's do that," Rome agreed, some of the assuredness leaving his voice.

Jazlyn immediately hopped up and started towards her bedroom. "Come on."

Rome followed, telling himself it was no big deal. They'd crashed together on beds before after late nights of partying or when one of them just didn't feel like driving home, or had too much alcohol. Nothing happened any of those times. And nothing had to happen now.

Still, he stopped in the bathroom first, closing the door and shrouding himself in the darkness as he took a few deep breaths. This feeling of nervousness around Jazlyn was totally new, and throwing him off. He thought it was just a momentary blip, but it returned as soon as she mentioned going to her bedroom. Of course he knew how attractive Jazlyn was, and might have admired certain parts of her at times, but he'd never been attracted to her to the point where he actually wanted to act on it. He didn't know what made this time so different; them being alone in her darkened house, him being upset with Nell...whatever it was, it was messing with him.

Telling himself to get it together, Rome took a few deep breaths before leaving the bathroom and easing into Jazlyn's bedroom. She was already curled up under her comforter, nothing visible but a cloud of hair. She lifted her head when Rome entered the room.

"You good?" she asked him.

"Yeah."

"Come on; get in." She pushed back the comforter. "I know you're probably exhausted by now, too."

Fatigue wasn't what Rome was worried about, but he didn't want to make a big deal out of what was probably nothing. This was Jazlyn; just because he was feeling some kind of way in the moment didn't mean she was, too. It was all in his own head.

He climbed into bed behind her, inching to where his front was just barely touching her back, snatching the comforter around his shoulders. Jazlyn immediately scooted back into him, groping for his arm so she could pull it around her.

"It's cold," she reminded him, shivering slightly. "Get closer to me."

Rome obliged, but stayed silent. Jazlyn reached back and smoothed her hair up and away from Rome's face. They laid there quietly, Jazlyn's hand still holding Rome's arm in place around her waist.

Some time passed before Rome remembered something. "I forgot about the heater," he reminded, leaning up slightly. "Lemme run and get it."

"No," Jazlyn quickly retorted, her grip on him tightening. She could only imagine the look he was giving her, and kept her face forward. "I mean...we're already in here. Might as well just stay like we are. I feel way better with you in, umm...I'm good."

She knew Rome was looking at her, but she stayed facing forward. The truth was, she was enjoying lying with Rome like they were, and wouldn't be able to justify them continuing it if he brought the heater in the room. She preferred Rome's body heat, getting to smell his fading soap-and-body oil mix up close, feeling his gentle warm breath on the back of her neck. Even if she had no idea *why*, she did.

Thankfully, Rome didn't fight her on it; he just wordlessly laid back down, settling in behind her. Jazlyn became very aware of his chest against her back, the weight of his arm around her waist...his crotch against her backside. She shifted as if she needed to adjust her position, but it was just an excuse to press into him. And when she felt the twitch in his groin, the whimper escaped from her lips before she could catch it. It took everything in her not to back into him again, because the urge to feel him was growing with each passing second. The reminder that they were supposed to be just friends was fading like the remaining heat in the house.

Rome felt like he was being tortured. Feeling Jazlyn's soft, ample butt wiggling against him was driving him crazy. He didn't know if she was doing it on purpose or not, and the little voice in the back of his mind was telling him to stop whatever this was, but he stayed put. He didn't *want* to move. And the little sound she just made was like a plug lighting up his arousal full force. His breathing deepened as he eyed the back of her neck, licking his lips as the urge to kiss her soft skin spread over him like a swarm of ants.

Jazlyn's fingers played with his. She closed her hand around his first two fingers and stroked them over and over as if she were imagining it was another part of him. Her body was starting to ache with wanting him to touch her, for them to finally cross that line. She had no idea that his desires matched hers as he laid behind her; all she knew was that she couldn't keep laying there, wanting him and doing nothing about it.

She eased his hand just beneath the hem of her hoodie, releasing a small breath when his fingertips touched her skin. Her fingers pressed his hand flush against her stomach, wanting to slide it both up to her breasts and down to her crotch.

"Rome..." she whispered, not even trying to hide what she wanted.

He got the message. Rome began slowly pushing his hardened manhood against her, working up to a slow grind. Any lingering doubts about what they were doing melted as Jazlyn wound against him. He was done trying to talk himself out of anything.

"Shit, Jazlyn..."

She slid his hand further up underneath her hoodie until it was on her breast, the usual self-consciousness about their size nowhere to be found. She just wanted him to touch her.

And that he did, moving her bra cup to the side and rolling her nipple between his fingers.

"Oh *god*!" she moaned, loudly, reaching back to grab his dick through his pants. She loved hearing the sharp intake of breath from him. "Pull it out."

He immediately pulled her onto her back, hovering over her, his hand still fondling her breasts. He looked square into her eyes. "You sure?"

"Yes, Rome." She eyed his lips. "I'm totally sure."

He bit his lip before leaning down to brush his lips over hers, their chests heaving almost in unison. The coldness in the room was forgotten, the heat from their arousal giving them everything they needed.

She rubbed her leg against him. "Please..."

His lips crashed onto hers, not needing any more assurance. He lowered himself on top of her, kissing her deeply. He loved how her tongue felt against his, how her hands felt as they pulled him closer to her, how it felt to be on top of her like this. It felt like the most natural thing, and it only fueled him as he pushed up her hoodie and helped himself to her hardened nipples, earning a gasp of pleasure.

He licked down the middle of her stomach, tugging the side of her leggings down so he could gently nip the skin on her hip with his teeth. His hand slid along the waistline of her leggings with his lips following, placing wet kisses over the areas he was exposing, before taking both hands and yanking the leggings the rest of the way down.

Jazlyn writhed impatiently in anticipation. When she finally felt Rome's tongue on her clit, she thought she was going to lose it. She released a string of curse words as she sat up and leaned on her elbow so she could watch him, holding his head in place with her other hand as she grinded against his face.

"That feels so *fucking good*," she whimpered almost in disbelief, her head falling back briefly. "*Shit!* How are you so good at-*ahhhh*..."

Rome moaned in response, wanting to let her know how good she tasted but not wanting to stop even for the few seconds it would take to do it. He continued to feast on her, slow-licking and sucking, coaxing her onto her back as he pushed her legs open wider, making her scream louder than he'd ever heard her scream for anything. And he'd heard several of her screaming matches with Marco.

Remembering that she was in a relationship led to remembering he was in one, too, but in the moment, it wasn't the deterrent it should've been. If anything, it only reminded him of the headache their respective relationships had brought them recently, and he was determined to make Jazlyn feel as good as she deserved to feel.

He pulled her leggings and thong completely off, and she quickly sat up, eager to help him out of his jeans, as well. As soon as they were off, she took his dick into her hand, stroking a few times before leaning down to swirl her tongue around the head.

"Fuck!" Rome grunted, grabbing a fistful of her hair. He was on his knees, and Jazlyn pushed him onto his back, taking him into her mouth again for a few moments before the urge to feel him inside of her became too great. She grabbed a condom from the nightstand before straddling him, bracing her hands against his chest, sliding up and down his length.

"I promise I'm gonna break you off before the night is over with, but I can't wait anymore," she informed him, her voice breathless. "I need it *now*."

"Take it, then."

He covered himself before she took over, stroking him a few times before sliding down onto him. She paused to adjust to his size before working her hips, almost wanting to cry at how good it felt. Rome's hands slid up and down her thighs as they traded erotic banter, urging each other on as the pace increased to one where they were both panting and sweaty.

Rome flipped her onto her back and pounded into her, pushing her left leg up and hooking it over his shoulder. Jazlyn welcomed what he was bringing, feeling the orgasm about to steamroll her.

"I'm coming," she breathed, momentarily biting her bottom lip. "Don't stop, I'm coming!"

Encouraged, Rome grunted and went harder, concentrating his strokes, gripping and caressing her thick hips as he focused on giving her the best orgasm of her life. His thumb began working her clit, which only sent her over the edge.

"*Rome!!*"

"Jazlyn, *yes*...I need you to come for me...come for me, J..."

Her body convulsed as the pleasure train slammed into her full force. She actually saw light flash before he eyes before she went into orgasm-aftershock, her skin tingling so much that she jumped and twitched when Rome touched her. She eventually opened her eyes, looking at him in amazement.

He gently eased her leg from his shoulder, extracting himself before lying down beside her. She glanced over at him and found his eyes already on her, his expression unreadable.

"I'll be right back," she muttered, rolling off the bed. Her legs still felt a little shaky as she headed for the en suite bathroom, closing the door behind her.

By the time she relieved herself and replayed what just happened with Rome a few times in her mind, Rome had gotten the heater from the living room and had it fired back up, warming the room considerably. He'd also plugged both of their phones into the power bank, giving them some much-needed charging, something Jazlyn had forgotten about. He was curled up on one side of the bed, his eyes closed. Jazlyn couldn't help but wonder if his pants were still off.

Without a word, she eased into bed, staying on the other side. She started to wonder if he'd gotten the heater so they wouldn't have to cuddle up anymore, but she pushed the thought out of her mind. No need in letting paranoia start to creep in.

As soon as she was settled in, Rome's eyes opened. He turned his head slightly in her direction, starting to say something but changing his mind. There wasn't anything he could think of to say that wouldn't sound stupid in the moment. Really, he was still trying to make himself believe he wasn't dreaming.

Eventually, both of them drifted off to sleep, the exhaustion from their respective long days and impromptu sexual romp finally catching up to them.

It was late the next morning when Jazlyn's eyes eased open. There was still a chill in the air and her bedside clock was blank, so the power was still out. She turned to look at Rome, who was still sound asleep. He shifted, ending up on his back, his head turning towards her. She marveled at how cute he looked even as he slept, reaching out to touch his freckled face but stopping herself.

She turned her body to face his, adjusting her pillow under her head as she eyed him intently. Her mind replayed him kissing her and touching her the night before, and how it felt to do the same to him. Surprisingly, guilt was nowhere to be found. What happened with Rome felt like something that was supposed to happen, not something that she should regret the day after.

And as for Marco...she figured they were even now.

The more Jazlyn laid there gazing at Rome and recalling what they did the previous night, the more her body remembered it, too. She began to feel that ache again. Part of her worried that he wouldn't feel the same as she did in the light of day, but that didn't stop her from moving closer to him and gently pressing her lips to his.

His eyes opened and they stared at each other for a moment. Just as Jazlyn's uncertainty began to creep in, Rome grabbed the front of her shirt and pulled her closer, burying his face against her neck. Her eyes slid closed as she bit her lip, enjoying how he licked and gently sucked her skin. She gripped his arm, leaning her head back to give him better access.

She was pulling him on top of her when he suddenly stopped, bracing his hands on the bed as he looked down at her with a troubled expression.

"What?" Jazlyn asked, though she already knew.

"What are we doing, J.?"

"I think it's pretty clear. Let me guess, you're regretting it."

"Not because I'm not enjoying it," he quickly assured. "I...love being with you like this, J. I'm enjoying it now and I damn sure enjoyed last night, as weird as that is to say."

"Why is it weird?"

He gave her a pointed look. "Come on, Jazlyn, you know why. It's you and me...we've never gone there before; haven't even come close to it. There's no way things don't change after what we did."

"It doesn't have to change in a *bad* way, though, Rome."

"Maybe not. But let's not try to act like we're the only ones affected in this. We're both in relationships and while I'd love to forget about that right now, I can't."

"Rome..."

"Come on, J., this isn't us. We're not foul like that."

"I'm not gonna try to act like this is something to be proud of, but at the same time, I have to admit I don't feel all that guilty," Jazlyn stated, sitting up slightly. She played with the front of his shirt. "Maybe I should, but...really, I haven't felt so good about anything in a long, long time, Rome."

His hand closed over hers. "Jazlyn...if we were both single, believe me, I'd be all good right now. Last night was amazing and the way I'm feeling right now...it's something I want to keep feeling with you. But I can't make myself forget that I have a girlfriend. And that you have a man."

"I know, Rome. And maybe this makes me a bad person but I'm not worried about them. Marco and I are just running out the clock, you know that."

"There's a reason you haven't gone ahead and ended it."

"Hell, give me the phone; I'll call him and end it now."

"Be for real, J. You know you're not gonna do that. You've been fussing about him for weeks and haven't done it yet."

"Rome," Jazlyn sat up, causing Rome to shift. They sat facing each other, adjusting the comforter and sheets around them. "Do you know what Ginger asks me just about every time we talk?"

"What?"

"When you and I are gonna hook up."

Rome's eyebrows shot up. "For real?"

"And not just her. Every time you come to the salon, everybody comments on how cute you are and how you seem to take better care of me than Marco does, and how we'd make such a good couple. Partially because we're best friends first and also because we just vibe better than I do with Marco, and people can see that."

"And how do you respond when they say all this?"

"My automatic response is that we're just friends and that's it. And honestly, before last night, that's the only way I've thought of you, other than a few random moments. But clearly, that's not the case now. And I'm not mad at it."

He eyed her.

"Do you regret what happened that much?" she pressed, dreading the answer. "Do you wish we hadn't gone there last night?"

Taking a moment before responding, Rome placed a hand on her knee. "Whatever it says about me to admit this, I don't. I already know I'm gonna be playing that back in my head over and over after we leave here."

She smiled.

"It's just...I'm not a cheater, J. At least, I wasn't. That's the part of all this that's jamming me up 'cause as much as I enjoyed being with you..."

"I know, Rome. I know what kind of man you are. But...do you honestly think that if you and Nell were on good terms, that you would've let anything happen last night? You two are no better off than me and Marco."

"I get that…"

"And you've *never* thought about me like that? Be straight up."

Hesitating, Rome hunched his shoulders. "A few times, yeah…"

"Again, I'm not gonna front like us having sex was the honorable thing to do. But I think the fact that we're still feeling something for each other right now says something. We're not terrible people. It wasn't just sex, Rome…it goes deeper than that, for me. And I know that's only because it's *you*."

Rome couldn't help but feel something when she said that. Right or wrong, it touched him that Jazlyn felt so deeply about what they did. And if he was honest with himself, he felt the same way.

"It was deeper than that for me, too," he admitted, taking her hand. His eyes roamed her face, feeling something wash over him. "And to be real, I don't want it to be a one-time thing."

Jazlyn grinned, relieved. "Neither do I."

"We're gonna have to handle things with Nell and Marco."

"Yeah, of course. Later."

"Jazlyn…"

She pulled the sheets from his lap. "I believe I made you a promise last night that I didn't come through on."

Rome couldn't help the sly smile that came at the reminder. He bit his lip as she got on her knees and slowly began stroking his manhood, and whatever protest he felt he should launch fizzled out. "I like that you're a woman of your word."

"Oh, I most definitely am." She pushed him onto his back before running her tongue up the length of him, their moans in tandem. "But don't think this is all we're gonna do."

Chapter 7

A couple of days later, the blizzard had passed. But the memory of the night Rome and Jazlyn shared hadn't.

Jazlyn couldn't get it out of her head, often catching herself smiling or biting her lip when she remembered certain things Rome did to her body. Every time she thought about how he sexed her, it sent a jolt through her that only made her want a repeat. Even after a couple of days and a clear head, she still couldn't make herself feel guilty about what happened. Especially since she and Marco still had barely talked, even since the blizzard ended.

It wasn't until a full day later that he even called, making no mention of where he'd been or why he'd gone scarce. Jazlyn realized she didn't even care. Between that and the constant comparisons she couldn't help making between his and Rome's sexual skills (where Rome came out on top in practically every category), it was even more proof that she needed to put their relationship out of its misery. Maybe it was time for her and Rome to take things to another level; explore this new romantic side of things and be a couple instead of just best friends.

The only problem was, Rome wasn't feeling as sure about things as Jazlyn was. He absolutely enjoyed their time together at her house, and it was true that the majority of him didn't feel all that bad about it. But that's what bothered him. He wasn't the kind of guy that cheated on his girlfriend, regardless of what issues they having. Whenever he was with someone, he just ended it if he felt things weren't working; he didn't get with someone else. He couldn't even blame his night with Jazlyn on alcohol or emotion; he'd known full well what he was doing. And he loved it. Which was what had his brain so scrambled.

In all the years he and Jazlyn had been friends and as many times as they'd been alone together, why then? What was so different about that night? If there had been no blizzard that had them stuck together and they were just hanging out as they usually did, with the option to get up and leave whenever, would that have happened?

The only thing Rome was sure of was that things between him and Jazlyn were different now, and he didn't know if that was a good or bad thing. He felt a small pang of guilt every time he went back and thought about what they did at her house, because he enjoyed thinking about it. They'd spent most of the following day in her bed, naked and exploring each other's bodies, neither able to get enough. They only got up for food and for the bathroom. Neither of them even bothered to check their phones, and when Rome finally did, there was a text from Nell, checking on him.

He needed to have a talk with her. *And* with Jazlyn. But he honestly didn't know what he'd say to either of them.

• • • •

JAZLYN WAS WRAPPING things up at work, wondering if she should call Rome or not. She knew he was feeling conflicted about what happened, and wanted to at least try to put his mind at ease. She just didn't want him to talk himself into separating from her, or worse, ending their friendship.

The last thing she expected when she walked out to her car was to see Marco leaning against it, holding flowers.

"What are you doing here?" she asked, approaching him.

"I wanted to see you."

"Why? You haven't cared about seeing me the past week or so."

He sighed. "Come on, don't be like that..."

"Don't be like what? Truthful? 'Cause that's all it is."

"Look, I'm sorry for disappearing like that," Marco admitted, holding the flowers out to her. She just glanced at them with an arched brow, but made no move to take them. He sighed again. "I get now how jacked up it was that I didn't even check to make sure you were good when the blizzard was coming."

"You're *just* getting that now, huh?"

"I guess I knew it then, too, but I was being spiteful. I was still tripping about you and Rome."

Jazlyn fought to keep her face even. "Mmm-hmm."

"It bothers me, how close y'all are," Marco continued. "Hell, you probably love him more than you love me. And when you refused to stop talking to him and hanging with him like I asked-"

"*Asked*? You gave me a damn ultimatum."

"Whatever. The point is, you basically told me to kiss your ass and I got in my feelings about it. But that was fucked up. If you say you and Rome are just friends, I should take your word on that."

The image of Rome on top of her flashed through her mind. "Yes, you should've."

"Well, I'm apologizing for that now." He held the flowers out to her again. "Can you take these?"

"Marco, do you really think a day-late apology and some partially-wilted flowers are going to make up for how much of an asshole you were? And not just about the whole Rome thing; we've been butting heads for a minute now. And I'm tired of fighting with you."

He pushed off the car, standing upright. "What are you saying?"

"I'm saying that this clearly isn't working. We're not right for each other."

"What?" He stepped closer to her. "Now you're ending this?"

"Let's not act shocked about it. You had to see this coming."

"Hell *no*, I didn't see it coming! Jazlyn, just because we fuss doesn't mean we shouldn't be together. Do you know how much my folks argued when I was growing up? Damn near every day. And they're *still* together now."

"Good for them. But I'm not living like that."

"Jazlyn, no," he protested when she tried to step around him. "I'm not trying to lose you. Especially not over some shit we can fix."

"I don't think we can-"

"Yes, we *can* fix it," he interjected, pulling her to him. He looked at her with pleading eyes. "You know I love you. And you love me."

Sighing, Jazlyn shook her head. "That's not all that's needed to make this fly, Marco."

"At least give a brotha a chance to do better. I know I can be difficult and stubborn but...I'll work on that. I don't want this to be over, Jazlyn."

"Marco-"

"At least think about it." His arm tightened around her waist. "Please?"

She glanced up at him. He looked as sincere as she'd ever seen him. Even though she still thought they should just cut their losses and part ways, there was the tiny voice in the back of her mind reminding her that she wasn't blameless, even before she slept with Rome. When it came to her and Marco's arguing, she gave as good as she got. And she had let things drag on probably eight months longer than she should have.

"Fine, I'll think about it," she finally relented.

Marco smiled, relieved. "Good."

He grabbed the back of her neck, pulling her to him for a kiss. She let it happen, kissing him back as she tried to stop comparing Marco's technique to Rome's.

"Now can you take these damn flowers, please?" he asked with a smile when she ended the kiss.

She wordlessly accepted them as she stepped back, his other arm preventing her from going too far.

"Thanks," she made herself say.

"You going home? Can I come through?"

"No, Marco. I just want to be by myself right now."

He started to say something, but thought better of it. Instead, he just gave a conceding nod. "All right."

"I'll talk to you later." Moving out of his embrace, she went to open her car door.

Marco just stood and watched as she got into her car and drove off.

• • • •

JAZLYN WENT ABOUT DOING her laundry and throwing something together for dinner, the flowers from Marco stashed on the kitchen counter. She didn't want to give any more thought to the things he said, but she wasn't able to totally push it out of her mind, try as she might. Marco had never been so humble as he'd been earlier, and it was frustratingly endearing. She still didn't think they needed to stay together for the long run, but she couldn't help being touched.

She wanted to talk to Rome so they could figure out what was going on with them, but he'd become difficult to reach. Usually, unless he was working or asleep, he was quick to respond to her texts. But since they slept together, the replies were more and more delayed. He was clearly avoiding her, and Jazlyn had to remind herself to be patient. Apparently he was saddled with all the guilt she had yet to feel any of.

Still, she grabbed her phone to call him, hoping she'd hit pay dirt this time. When it went to voicemail, she sucked her teeth and sent him a text:

Hey. How much longer are we gonna do this? You know we need to talk.

She put her phone down and proceeded to wash her dinner dishes. To her surprise, her phone chimed with a response from Rome just a couple of minutes later.

I know. Not trying to ghost you; I just need a minute.

All right. I guess.

She waited for him to say something else but he never did. As much as she told herself not to be, Jazlyn couldn't help being a little frustrated. She could understand him feeling guilty about cheating on Nell, but she also felt some kind of way about being shut out like this. It was the first time in their friendship that they'd gone more than a couple of days without speaking. Jazlyn could only hope that this wasn't the start of their decline.

Figuring there wasn't anything she could do about it, she went on about her evening. After taking a shower and talking to Ginger for a while (*not* telling her about the night with Rome), she grabbed some juice and curled up on the couch to watch Food Network.

"Ooh, honey, that is too much work," she muttered as she watched a chef make their own sausage. When another one started making pasta from scratch, she shook her head. "They have all kinds of perfectly good pasta right in the box; why in the world would I do all that?"

Jazlyn was enjoying noting all of the things the chefs were doing that she wouldn't do when there was a knock on the door. She sat up eagerly and immediately adjusted the scarf that was covering her hair, checking her clothes as she stood up. Juice in hand (one of the ones Rome had brought for her), she went to answer the door.

"Who is it?" she called out.

"It's me."

Her enthusiasm deflated upon hearing that it was Marco and not Rome. Taking her time, she trudged to the door and opened it, her posture slouched and her expression unwelcoming.

"Why are you here, Marco?"

"I had to see you."

"You *just* saw me a few hours ago. And I distinctly remember telling you I wanted to be alone."

"Yeah, and I'm sorry about that..."

"See, this is part of our problem. You don't listen to me."

"It's not that. I'm not trying to get on your nerves, though it seems like damn near everything I do does exactly that lately."

Jazlyn eyed him. "What? Are you really trying to paint me as the 'Black woman with the attitude' right now?"

"Are you gonna try to act like you're not? Look, baby, I know can be a pain in the ass; I'm not trying to act like I'm flawless. But the reason we're in the place we're in is because of *both* of us, not just me."

"I was a lot more of a sweetheart before you cheated on me last year."

"And I've apologized a hundred times for that. And we're still together a year later so I'm not understanding why that is if you're just gonna hold a grudge about it."

Jazlyn started to retort, but realized he had a point. She'd chosen to stay with him after she found out about him meeting up with some model that sent him a direct message on Instagram, claiming she wanted him to train her, and they ended up sleeping together. His guilt drove him to confess a couple days after it happened. That he'd admitted it proactively had gone a long way with Jazlyn at the time, but she still couldn't help but look at him differently after that, and treat him differently.

Did she sleep with Rome as some kind of subconscious revenge? That hadn't been on her mind at the time, but maybe that was why she didn't feel any guilt afterwards. Marco had stepped out on her, and now she'd done the same to him.

The only difference was, she wasn't planning on confessing anything.

"Okay, fine," she finally conceded with a sigh. "You might have a point. I'm clearly not as over that as I thought I was."

"And I get it. I know I'd probably have a chip on my shoulder if you got with somebody else."

Jazlyn took a swig of Rome's juice and stayed quiet.

"Look..." Marco hedged, stepping closer as he looked at her earnestly, "I'm not gonna trip about you and Rome anymore. You say you're just friends, so that's what it is. I just wanna put my energy into making us better instead of fighting about insignificant shit. Can we do that? Can we try to get back to how we were before I fucked up last year, when things were good between us?"

It was on the tip of her tongue to say no; that they were wasting their time and should just end it and go on about their business. But Marco was willing to eliminate what had been the main subject of most of their arguments, which was his jealousy over her and Rome's friendship. And the truth was, they'd never *really* discussed her anger over what he did the year before; he confessed, she cussed him out, *said* she forgave him (after a few days of stewing), then they just continued on without really dealing with it. And any time he wanted to talk about it, she shut him down.

Maybe she hadn't been fair to him. If she was honest about it, Jazlyn could think of a few times since he cheated that she deliberately did things to mess with him, namely taking Rome's calls during their dates or throwing what Marco did back in his face every chance she got. There were times when she got an attitude with him and blamed it on what he did, even though it had nothing to do with that. Instead of really trying to get past his mistake or just move on, she just continued to hold his indiscretion over his head, just because she could.

"I love you, Jazlyn," Marco continued, tentatively taking her hand. "And I'm willing to do my part to make things better."

"I appreciate that, Marco," she couldn't help but respond. "That means a lot, to hear you say that."

"You love me?" he asked, taking a step closer and linking his fingers through hers.

A smile tugged at her lips. "Yeah. I love you."

His free arm grabbed her around the waist and pulled her close. "A lot?"

She chuckled. "Yes, Marco, a lot."

"So," he gently took the juice from her hand and set it on the ground before placing her arm around his neck, "You gonna let me come in?"

Jazlyn really wished she could talk to Rome first and see where his head was, because she still believed what they shared meant something. But there was no telling when Rome would get around to talking to her. And since he was feeling so guilty, he'd likely want to put his focus on fixing things with Nell, despite his previous doubts about their relationship. So maybe Jazlyn should do the same.

"Yeah." She bit her lip as he pressed his forehead to hers. "Come in."

"Can I kiss you?"

She nodded. Marco wasted no time claiming her lips, and the kiss quickly escalated to the intense, frenzied, erotic level that always made Jazlyn forget everything else. The tip of his tongue played with hers before sliding down the side of her neck and to her chest and back up again, earning a moan from her lips and a rush to her panties. Her hands squeezed his large biceps before sliding to the back of his neck, giving in. He grabbed the back of her thighs and lifted her off the ground, her legs wrapping around his waist, and entered the house, kicking the door closed with his foot. They didn't even make it to the bedroom.

Chapter 8

Rome was glad to finally get in touch with his sister, Asha. He hoped it meant that she was finally starting to feel better but also, he wanted to get her perspective on his conflicting feelings for Jazlyn. Asha had been around for the entirety of their friendship and was as much a fan of hers as Rome was; maybe she could shine a light on things he hadn't discovered yet.

"He called," Asha told him, referring to her runaway groom, Ashton. "Said he was sorry."

"He's sorry? That's it?"

"He admitted he freaked out about getting married; some of the horror stories his friends told about what they went through got to him. They put it in his head that his bachelor party was the last time he'd get to have any fun so he needed to take advantage of it."

"And he fell for that?"

"Apparently. These friends of his also thought it was totally fine to pay the stripper extra to sleep with him."

"So she was a prostitute."

"I guess. She was willing to be one that night, at least. All this clearly went down after you left."

"How in the world did they end up going away together?"

"A drunken impulse, he said."

"Wow. I know him ditching you hurt but it sounds like you dodged a bullet, sis."

"I really did. Can you believe he had the nerve to ask if I'd give him another chance? That was the first laugh I've had in weeks."

"So you're done? There's *no* chance for reconciliation at all?"

"After what he did?" Asha scoffed. "Maybe if he'd *just* gotten cold feet, I could understand it. But he cheated on me the night before we were supposed to get married, then left in the middle of the night with this woman without so much as a word . He told his social media followers before he told me. I didn't hear from him until more than two weeks later. He's not only a coward, he's a *cheating* coward. There's no way I could trust him after that."

"Right..."

"I have no respect for cheaters at all," Asha continued strongly. "If people are that unhappy or unfulfilled in a relationship, they should just end it. Hurting someone you made a commitment to is just the lowest of the low."

So confiding in Asha was out. Rome knew there wasn't a reason or justification he could give that would get her to have any empathy for him. Even if he deserved it, he couldn't stand for his little sister to be disappointed in him like that.

Especially since his regret only went so far; he absolutely felt bad about cheating on Nell, but he also enjoyed the memory of what he and Jazlyn did the night of the blizzard. And it would be a lie to say there was no part of him that wished for a repeat experience. As much as he tried to, he just could not get Jazlyn out of his head.

She wasn't just his buddy anymore. Now when he thought of her, he imagined her lips, and what she could do with them; how her hands felt on his body; the way she moaned when he was inside of her; how she was both submissive and dominant with him. He wanted more, and that frustrated him. He didn't get how he could feel guilty for cheating with her, yet still want to do it again.

Which was why he needed some space. He needed to get his head together before he talked to Jazlyn, and especially before he saw her. He couldn't afford to mess things up more than he already had.

• • • •

NELL CAME HOME THE same way she left; without notice. She was waiting at his house when he got home from work.

"Shit!" he exclaimed when he saw her sitting on the couch. He frowned, willing himself to calm down. "I was about to reach for my damn gun, Nell. What the hell are you doing here?"

"I got back this morning," she informed him, putting down the magazine she'd been reading. "I wanted to surprise you."

"Not a good plan. Especially after your *last* surprise."

"I thought you would've seen my car out there."

"I didn't notice it," he muttered, removing his coat and hanging it on the hook by the door. "My mind was somewhere else."

She stood and started to head over to him but apparently thought better of it. "I missed you."

"Yeah?" He stood several feet from her, his expression a mix of indifference and skepticism. "Missed me so much you only sent one raggedy text while you were gone, huh? Nor did you acknowledge any of my calls or the texts I sent *you*."

"I'm sorry about that. But I figured since I said we needed some distance..."

"And you get to decide when that starts and stops, huh? And I just have to deal with it?"

"Rome..." Nell briefly covered her face with her hands before pressing them together in front of her, looking at him pleadingly. "Can we please not fight? Didn't we do enough of that before I left?"

He started to reply, then shook his head with a sarcastic chuckle. "Yeah, we did. And I'm not in the mood to go back and forth with you, anyway."

"Can we just talk?"

"Nell, I've had a really long day and-"

"Please?"

He looked at her and sighed. She looked so contrite, he knew he couldn't refuse her. Especially knowing what he did while she was gone.

"Fine."

She walked over, stopping him before he could take a seat on the couch. "Can I get a hug first? We haven't seen each other in over a week."

Rome wordlessly let her pull him into an embrace. He thought he'd feel even more remorse over what he did when he saw her, but all he felt at the moment was frustration. He didn't want to deflect, but maybe if Nell hadn't been so skittish about discussing their relationship and then skipped out of town on him, he wouldn't have been so conflicted. And he wouldn't have let the night with Jazlyn happen.

His rational mind knew, though, that he was still in the wrong, regardless. And he would have to tell Nell what he did.

Easing away from her, he sat on the couch, gently tugging her hand to join him. "Look, Nell, there are some things I need to say to you-"

"Rome, please, let me go first, okay?" She kept her hold on his hand as she turned towards him. "I want to explain why I always get so nervous when you want to talk about our relationship."

Rome wanted to unburden himself, but he also needed to hear this. "I'm listening."

"The truth is...I'm scared of you."

He frowned. "What do you mean, you're scared of me?"

"You've been practically the perfect boyfriend," Nell explained. "Everything I always said I wanted. But there's a part of me that always wondered if I was the same for you."

"I don't expect perfection, Nell. I'm damn sure not perfect, either."

"You know what I mean, though. There's really nothing I can complain about with you, Rome. And when you start talking about love and our future and all of that, it freaks me out. I just wonder how long it'll be before you realize that I'm not good enough for you."

"Are you serious?"

"I know I'm sounding very insecure right now and that's probably not making me look any better to you. But it's the truth. Especially when I see you and Jazlyn together."

A cold shot jolted Rome's body, and he deepened his frown to mask it. "What does Jazlyn have to do with it?"

"I see the bond you two have. You're so in synch with each other. The way you tag-teamed that whole situation at Asha's wedding, while I stood over to the side like a coward? I know there's no way I could ever get to the level Jazlyn is on with you."

"Nell..." He rubbed the back of his neck, hoping he didn't look as guilty as he was starting to feel. "What Jazlyn and I have is different than what you and I have. She's...she's just my friend."

"She's your *best* friend."

"Yeah, but still-"

"Rome, don't get me wrong; I *love* Jazlyn," Nell insisted with a hand to her chest. "I adore her. But there's also a part of me that's a little jealous of her. You literally brighten up when she calls you, and times stops when the two of you hang out. It's hard not to be intimidated by that."

"You don't want me to hang with her anymore?" Rome asked, part of him wishing she would say no.

"I'd never ask you to do that. She was your friend before I came into the picture and I truly believe that what you two have is a beautiful thing. This is all in my own head and I know that."

"I guess I still don't really get what you're telling me with this."

"Rome, as long as things are light and fun with us, I don't have to worry about measuring up. It's when things get heavy that all these insecurities start plaguing me. Really, I never thought about marriage or any of that before you and I got together. And to be honest, I *still* don't know how I feel about it. But I figured if I admitted that to you, you'd leave."

His eyebrows lifting at this new information, Rome glanced at their joined hands. "I see."

"I'm rethinking a lot of things, and my mind is all over the place," Nell admitted. "You're sure about what you want, and I'm not. I'm scared of the love I have for you, because I don't know what to do with it. And I know you deserve someone who does."

Understanding things a little better now, Rome sat forward in his seat. His brown eyes roamed her face. "I hate that you felt you couldn't tell me all this."

"I know I should have. I just didn't want you to question being with me."

"I get it, but didn't you think shying away from the subject every time it came up would do the same thing?"

Slumping a little, Nell hunched a shoulder. "I guess I didn't consider that."

"Nell, look...you don't have to want what I want. If you don't want to go deep with me and get married and have a family sometime down the line, that's your right. That just means we're not right for each other long-term. So we should just-"

"No, Rome, that's what I'm saying!" Nell desperately interrupted, sensing where he was going. She inched closer to him on the couch, her knee resting on his leg. "I *want* to see if I can get on the same page you're on. You mean that much to me."

"If you're not feeling it, you're just not feeling it," Rome replied as he looked away from her, wishing she'd let him take this out that had fallen into his lap. He loved Nell, but if they didn't want the same things in their relationship, what was the point? "And I don't want you trying to force anything to please me. You'll only resent me down the line and that's not fair to either of us."

"Can you just...be a little more patient with me?" she requested, turning his face to hers before caressing his cheek with her hand. "I'm telling you I'm willing to try, here. It's not like I'm *against* marriage; I just never thought I needed it for myself. And no one before you has even made me consider it. I don't want to lose you, Rome." She leaned forward and touched her lips to his. "I love you. And I'm sorry that it took me so long to tell you that."

Confliction had Rome in a vice grip again. Part of him wanted to admit to what he did with Jazlyn, and part of him wanted to just cut things off with Nell and keep his mouth shut about it. He didn't know what would have to happen to get Nell to realize she wanted the same things in their relationship as he did. And he didn't know how much patience he had to stick around and find out.

Especially when he knew Jazlyn *did* want the all the things he wanted.

His conscience not letting him take the easy way out, he ran a hand down his face. "Nell, I love you, too. But there's something I need to tell you about me and Jazlyn..."

She held up a hand, shaking her head. "No, there isn't."

"What?"

"I already know."

"You *do*??"

"You and Jazlyn are soul mates and we're not. I get that."

Rome wondered if Nell could hear his heart beating, it was going so hard and fast. He sighed in both frustration and relief. "That's not what I was gonna-"

"Rome, I'm only worried about you and me right now," Nell interrupted him again, leaning forward to cup his face in both hands. "Whatever you and Jazlyn share is between the two of you; I've never interfered in your friendship and I don't want to start now. All I want is for you to tell me that we can move forward together. That's all I want to hear you say."

Is this some kind of divine intervention? Rome marveled to himself. He was trying to confess his indiscretion and kept getting shut down. Part of him wondered if maybe Nell sensed that something had happened and just didn't want to hear it, but he made himself dismiss that. There was no way he could get away with what he did that easily.

Figuring he'd just have to admit to what happened with Jazlyn another time, Rome nodded and simply said, "All right."

Grinning, Nell squealed and threw her arms around his neck. "I'm *so* glad; thank you!"

Rome just silently hugged her back, his eyes floating up towards the ceiling. He wished his enthusiasm matched hers but he was feeling like he'd just signed a contract locking him in to something he wasn't hyped about.

Nell pulled back and reclaimed his face in her hands, helping herself to a kiss. She moaned immediately while it took several moments for Rome to even close his eyes. This didn't feel right. Usually he loved when she slid onto his lap as she was doing now, kissing and slowly grinding on him, enveloping him with her customary orange blossom scent, but the usual automatic fire he had for Nell wasn't lighting like it usually did. Any other time, he was all over her, but now, this was the last thing he felt like doing.

"I missed you so much," she whispered against his lips, grazing her short nails down the side of his neck. An image of Jazlyn's hand sliding up his thigh flashed through his mind, her long oval nails painted in a sexy matte black. That was right before she gave him some of the best head of his life. His dick jumped and hardened at the memory, which Nell mistook for encouragement.

"Take this off," she ordered between kisses, reaching for the hem of his shirt.

"Nell, hold up..." He tore his lips from hers and grabbed her hand, stopping her. "Maybe we should cool out."

She frowned, confused. "Why?"

"We're in this strange place right now...maybe sex isn't what we need to be focusing on."

Sitting back slightly, she peered at him. He wondered if her suspicion radar was going off. He'd never refused sex with her; if anything, she was always teasing *him* about being a horndog. Him not wanting to get down had to be setting off an alarm for her.

"You don't want me?" she finally asked.

I want Jazlyn.

Rome blinked, startled at the automatic thought. He started to brush it off, but the more he gazed at Nell, the more he wished it was his best friend there on his lap instead of her. How had things shifted there so fast? Did one passionate night cloud his mind *that* much? Was that all this was about, the sex? Rome didn't want to think so, but he had no way of being sure right then.

And he'd been unfair to Nell enough; he wasn't going to have her share her body with him while his mind was on another woman.

"It's not about that," he finally responded, not wanting to lie to her. "I just...can't be all the way into it with all this stuff on my mind. I'm glad you finally broke everything down for me and I know I said we could try to work things out, but I need a minute, Nell. You don't have to leave or anything, but I...I can't do this with you right now. I'm sorry."

Without waiting for a response, he gently moved her off of his lap and stood. Running his hands over his head, he made himself look at her. She was still looking at him with questioning and confused eyes. "Are you pissed?"

Brushing her long braids from her shoulder, she gazed down at her tangling fingers for a moment before looking back up at him.

"I suppose not," she answered in a low voice. "I'm disappointed, but I get it. I guess I was just hoping we could forget about all of that for a while and just enjoy each other. I miss being with you."

Another pang of guilt shot through him. "I...I'm sorry. Maybe once I get some rest and have time to process everything, I'll be more into it." He looked away. "Um, I'm gonna go take a shower."

"Okay."

He headed to his room, feeling like the scum of the earth. He'd only said that part about rest possibly being all he needed to appease her but he knew it would take way more than that. He could sleep for ten hours and still feel the same way, and he knew it. He was just too confused.

It was time for him to finally talk to Jazlyn.

Chapter 9

B oth Jazlyn and Rome were nervous wrecks as they met up at the drive-in movie. They opted to meet in public since neither wanted to risk their respective mates showing up at either of their houses or jobs. They'd gone to the movies countless times together, but they both knew this time had nothing to do with entertainment. Rome didn't even know what movie it was; he just bought tickets for the first one he saw with a start time closest to when they agreed to meet.

Jazlyn parked her car and eased over to Rome's truck, rubbing her gloved hands together anxiously. She took a calming breath before opening the door and climbing in.

"Hey," she greeted, closing the door. Her hands immediately clasped on her lap.

"Hey." Rome swallowed before glancing over at her, a swirl of feelings overtaking him. Her bushy hair was stuffed underneath a colorful knit hat, and he tried not to focus on how good she looked in her green wool jacket and hip-hugging jeans. Silver hoop earrings hung from her ears and her usual sugar-scented lip gloss gleamed as if calling for him. He stuffed his hand underneath his thigh to avoid reaching for her like he wanted to. "You, uh, you hungry? Want some candy or some nachos or something?"

"No, I'm good, thanks."

"I did get you some hot chocolate, though." He motioned towards the lidded cup in the holder between them. "With a shot of vanilla."

"I appreciate that."

She bit her lip, looking at him with what she hoped was a casual expression. Her internal reaction to him was anything but casual, though. He smelled *so* good. And the way he looked in his navy blue baseball cap and hoodie made her want to dive on him. She'd been hoping that things would be back to normal when she saw him again; that the night of the blizzard and the rapidly-changing feelings since had all just been a phase that had to run its course. But being this close to Rome again only intensified them.

"Okay. Um, the blanket is back there, if you need it. I know it's kinda chilly..."

"Oh yeah. I'll...I'm okay right now."

They sat in awkward silence, each wanting to get to what they were there to talk about but neither really knowing how to jump in with it. Jazlyn didn't know how to tell Rome that she'd agreed to work on things with Marco, despite already regretting it. And Rome didn't know how to tell Jazlyn that all she had to do was say the word and he'd end his strained relationship with Nell.

"Before I forget, Ginger invited us over for game night," Jazlyn informed him. She grabbed the cup of hot chocolate and fiddled with the lid. "I mean, you and Nell. And me and Marco. If you can make it."

Rome wasn't hyped about the idea of a couples' event where he had to pretend to be glad to be there with Nell while watching the woman he'd rather be with hugged up with someone else. "I'm not sure...I can check with Nell. When is it?"

"This Saturday night. Eight o'clock. Do you have any jobs going on that day?"

"Yeah but we should be done by then. I'll let you know."

"Cool."

It was quiet again as they both mindlessly turned their eyes to the movie screen. Jazlyn anxiously gulped her hot chocolate, wishing it was spiked with something stronger than just vanilla. She hated feeling awkward like this, and around Rome, of all people. He was always the one she could be herself around the most, but now, she had no idea what to say. She knew what she *wanted* to say, but she couldn't make herself come out with it. Part of her felt that Rome had taken so long to talk to her because he felt that what they'd done had been a mistake, and he was just working up the nerve to find a nice way to tell her that. So she needed him to go first so she wouldn't embarrass herself by admitting feelings that he didn't reciprocate.

Rome *did* reciprocate them, but had managed to convince himself in the days leading up to this that Jazlyn was going to tell him that they should go back to being just friends. And he tried to talk himself into believing that would be for the best. He tried to force his mind and heart to stay on Nell, and light that fire between them again. But he could never get it going. Everything in him wanted to go to the next level with Jazlyn, but he needed her to give him *some* indication that that's what she wanted, too, so he wouldn't get his face cracked.

So they sat there, each wanting the other to make their admissions first. Each itching for a touch and aching even harder for a kiss. Their usual easy rapport and banter was nowhere to be found. They both hated this tension, but neither had the courage to do anything to break it.

Ninety minutes later, they said goodnight and Jazlyn got out of Rome's truck with nothing being said or resolved.

• • • •

BY THE TIME SHE GOT home, Jazlyn was still kicking herself. She hated that she'd punked out like she had with Rome. Everything in her wanted to ask him how he was feeling and tell him how she felt, but she kept losing her nerve. Being outspoken was usually her calling card but this was different. She didn't know how she would take it if Rome told her that he regretted what they shared, or worse, that he thought they should put a pause on their friendship. It would devastate her.

She hoped Marco wasn't at her place when she got there, but no such luck. Ever since the night she agreed to stay in their relationship, he hardly wanted to leave her side. Jazlyn had managed to convince herself that staying with Marco was a good thing, but it only took a day for the novelty to wear off. She was settling; it wasn't what her heart wanted. She tried to convince herself it was just in case Rome didn't tell her what she wanted to hear, although she knew that wasn't fair to Marco. Or herself.

"Hey baby," Marco greeted when she entered her bedroom. He was lounging on the bed, scrolling through his phone. Jazlyn tried not to picture Rome lying in that very same spot...naked. "How was the movie?"

"It was all right," Jazlyn replied with a shrug, pulling her gloves off. "Nothing mind-blowing."

"And how's Rome?" Marco made himself ask.

Jazlyn glanced at him, trying to detect some sarcasm but surprisingly, finding none. "He's fine."

"I'm surprised you're back so early; kinda thought y'all would go get some grub or something afterwards."

"Oh, no...he had some stuff to do and I was kinda tired, so..." She shrugged out of her jacket and hung it in the closet, keeping her eyes averted. "We just called it a night."

"I was about to make this video real quick; some of my followers have been asking how I wind down in the evening so I'm gonna do a reel about it."

"Oh. Okay, well...enjoy."

"Hold up," he called out as she started for the bathroom. He slid off the bed and reached for her, giving her a smooch on her sugar-scented lips. "That lip gloss reminds me of stuff I can't eat. It tastes good on you, though."

"Thanks."

"You gonna watch me make this video?"

Resisting the urge to say *hell no* like she wanted to, she shook her head. "I just wanna take a shower real quick and lay it down, Marco. I have a headache."

"Sorry to hear that. I can bring you some aspirin. But it would *really* help me out if you could hold the phone for me while I do this; it'll be faster than me getting the tripod and all that stuff. It won't take that long, I promise."

Sighing, Jazlyn stepped back and removed the hat from her head, revealing the silk bonnet she wore underneath to protect her hair. Sliding that off, as well, she ran a hand over her cornrowed tresses. She hadn't felt like doing her hair the last couple of days.

Telling herself to be nice, she made herself say, "Fine. But let's make it quick, if we can, please."

"Bet."

Marco yanked his shirt off and headed to the second bedroom, with Jazlyn grudgingly following. He handed her his phone and got in position, waiting for her to attach the mini ring light and start filming before launching into his spiel about what he liked to do at the end of his long days, including a mention of the green juice concoction he discussed in a previous video that he swore burned belly fat. Then he proceeded to do a series of stretches, narrating the whole time.

"One of the two things people don't do enough of is stretch. The other is get enough rest," he commented, lowering himself to the ground before leaning forward into Child's Pose. Jazlyn moved closer to get an aerial view of his tattooed back as he moved into Cobra. She knew he looked hot, and no doubt his followers would think so, too.

Once he was done with the stretching, he headed to the bathroom where he went through his nightly ablutions. Jazlyn wished they were doing this at his place instead of hers, but after they reconciled, he'd brought all of his stuff back to her house. They usually stayed there more because it was bigger.

"Don't think I'm metrosexual or some shit, but your boy *does* have a nighttime face routine," he admitted with a sly smile to the camera. "Gotta keep it smooth and sexy for the ladies."

Jazlyn quirked a brow.

"It's nothing fancy; here's my cleanser," Marco presented, holding up his tube of face wash. "Here's the facial scrub...and this here is the skin butter. Has a brotha's skin feeling like silk. And no, this is not an ad, but if the company wants to do business, hit a brother up." He winked.

He went through the rest of his nighttime routine, making a couple more mentions of things that he does for 'the ladies' benefit, before they were finally done. Jazlyn stewed as she handed him his phone and waited for him to give his okay with the videos, debating whether or not she was going to say what was on her mind.

"This is good; thanks, baby," he told her. "I'll edit it later so I can post it tomorrow."

"Awesome. Umm, Marco?"

"Yeah?"

"What was all that talk about doing this and that for the *ladies*?"

"Oh," he shrugged, turning his eyes back to his phone. "That didn't mean anything. It's just something you say, you know?"

"Uh-huh." She snatched his phone from him and scrolled through his timeline. "You really don't mention the fact that you're in a relationship at all and now that I'm thinking about it, you never have. You don't even hint at it."

"Don't start tripping about that, Jazlyn," he warned, taking his phone back. "I'm not trying to hide you, if that's what you're getting at. A lot of my followers are women and I get more response when I let them think I'm available, that's all."

"I've seen plenty of fitness influencers who show their spouses and get plenty of engagement. If a woman unfollows you because you're spoken for, then she clearly wasn't following you for your fitness shit, anyway. I would think that wouldn't be that big of a problem for you, seeing as how you're supposedly not interested in meeting any of them like that."

"I'm not. I'm not on here to get dates, baby. Just 'cause they flirt with me doesn't mean I flirt back."

"Oh? So if I looked in your DMs right now, there wouldn't be *any* exchanges between you and any women?"

"Yeah, there are *exchanges*. Nothing foul, though. It's not like I'm sending out dick pics or asking for anyone's number. This all comes with the territory, baby, but you don't have anything to worry about. I told you I'm not gonna step out on you again."

Jazlyn just stood there with her arms crossed, eyeing him. After a moment, though, she was over it. Marco could sleep with another woman tomorrow and instead of upsetting her, it would just give Jazlyn a concrete reason to finally leave him...other than having feelings for her best friend that were compounding by the day, of course.

"All right, whatever," she shrugged, turning to head back into the bedroom. "If you say so."

"Jazlyn, come on, don't be like that," Marco pleaded, grabbing her arm. He turned her around to face him and tilted her chin upwards, waiting for her eyes to meet his. "This shit online is just to bring in the money. Let 'em fantasize; *you've* got the real thing."

He held her chin in his hand as he leaned down to kiss her. Setting his phone on the counter, he squeezed her in his arms, deepening the kiss before backing her into the bedroom and onto the bed. He slid down her body and lifted the bottom of her sweater, swirling his tongue in her bellybutton. Jazlyn squirmed beneath him, but stayed silent. Marco either didn't notice or didn't mind as he unbuttoned her jeans and pulled them down over her hips along with her underwear, tossing them aside before lifting her right leg and leisurely licking her inner thigh. When he made his way to her center, she emitted a small whimper but largely kept quiet, doing more heavy breathing than anything else.

It was only when she began picturing Rome that she got more into it. Marco was muscular and tattooed and sexy beyond belief, but he wasn't doing it for her like he used to. One night with Rome had spoiled her. His skills below the waist were unmatched, certainly by anyone she'd ever been with, including Marco.

But Jazlyn let it happen, her mind on Rome while Marco's mouth was between her legs. She kept her eyes closed as she imagined that it was Rome's face down there, Rome's hands gripping her thighs, Rome's whispers urging her to come.

And when she did, she had to stop herself from calling out Rome's name.

• • • •

GAME NIGHT CAME MUCH quicker than either Jazlyn or Rome was ready for. They'd talked a few times since the movie, but still didn't address the elephant in the room. Both of them were still trudging through relationships with people they loved but no longer wanted to be with.

Jazlyn was eager to have a chance to talk to Ginger, even though she knew what she'd say. Ginger had been rooting for her and Rome to get together for a while. Jazlyn just needed to get all of this off her chest to someone.

She was a ball of anxiety as soon as she and Marco got to Ginger's. Part of her worried that Rome would back out, but he had assured her that he and Nell would be there, even though she got the sense that he wasn't looking forward to it.

"You two want something to drink?" Zion, Ginger's husband asked. "We have beer, wine, soda..."

"Any bottled water?" Marco asked.

"I think we have a few bottles in there, yeah."

"If you don't, I can just get my jug from the car."

Jazlyn subtly rolled her eyes. Marco was always carrying that gallon jug of water with him just about everywhere they went. She knew it was only because he didn't want an elbow to the ribs that he didn't request the water be alkaline.

"We have chicken sliders, pasta salad, fruit, teriyaki meatballs, and assorted cake pops in the kitchen," Ginger announced, taking Jazlyn and Marco's coats. "The meatballs are my grandmama's recipe, so you'd better like 'em. Help yourselves."

Rome and Nell arrived while they were in the kitchen and Jazlyn felt her body tense as soon as he entered the room.

Why did he have to look so good??

He had a fresh haircut and wore a black v-neck sweater, dark jeans, and retro Jordans. It was taking *all* of her effort for Jazlyn not to bite her lip and let her eyes linger up and down his frame like she wanted to.

"What's up, y'all?" he greeted, lifting his hand in a wave. Nell grinned from her spot beside him, holding on to his other arm like she couldn't stand up on her own. "Sorry we're a little late."

"You're good, man," Zion assured, waving off his comment before giving him some dap.

To keep up appearances, Jazlyn made herself go over and hug them both, playfully nudging Rome in the stomach.

"What's up?" she greeted, forcing a smile. "Nice of you to finally show up."

Playing along, Rome nudged her shoulder. "Shut up, big head. We got caught by one of those super-long trains."

"Hey, man," Marco greeted from his space at the counter where he was spearing watermelon onto his plate.

Rome lifted his chin briefly. "Hey."

"Come on, y'all, and get something to eat," Ginger instructed to Rome and Nell, casting a curious glance at Jazlyn. "And don't be shy 'cause I don't want a bunch of leftovers."

They all piled their plates with food and stood around the kitchen island talking and laughing about various things. Nell sidled up to Jazlyn, giving her a good-natured shoulder bump before grabbing one of her hands.

"Girl, your nails are always so *fire*...I need to come let you do something to mine one day. Think you could squeeze me onto your schedule? I know you stay booked."

"Anytime; just let me know," Jazlyn replied, stuffing half a slider into her mouth with her free hand. "You know I'll hook you up."

"I'd appreciate it. It would be good for me to try something new. Gotta stay looking good for our men, right?"

Taking her time chewing, Jazlyn made herself nod. "Yep."

Ginger eyed them with interest as she bit into her cake pop.

After everyone was done eating, they all caravanned into the living room to kick off the games. They played charades, Uno, and a surprisingly intense game of Heads Up. Jazlyn tried to keep her eyes from straying to Rome, but he was like a magnet for her attention. He just looked *so* sexy, and it didn't help that he was sitting right across from her. Every time Nell put her hand on his knee or hugged him when he got an answer right, jealously flashed through Jazlyn like lightning. She tried to hide it by stuffing cake pops into her mouth, one time biting the stick so hard she was surprised she didn't snap it in two.

Rome wasn't doing much better. It burned him up to see Jazlyn there with Marco. When she had hugged him earlier, Rome wanted to hold her tighter and longer, burying his face in her neck. He wished he could taste that sugary lip gloss. But instead he had to sit there across from her, slyly eying her body in a green jersey dress that was hugging her everywhere he wished he could, and watch Marco possessively put his arm around her and kiss the side of her neck. His jaw clenched so many times that it was starting to ache.

"You okay?" Nell murmured, leaning closer.

"Yeah." He took a swig of his beer.

"You just seem a little...tense. You've been on edge all day, really."

"I've just got some stuff on my mind; nothing for you to worry about." His eyes flicked to Jazlyn, the quick look taking in the large afro puff on top of her head, the swirly baby hairs around her hairline, the eyeliner and mascara she wore to bring out her brown eyes. If he could've snapped his fingers and gotten rid of everyone in the room except them, he would've. He needed to be alone with her.

Jazlyn wanted to get Rome alone, too. She needed to tell him all the things she'd been too much of a coward to tell him at the drive-in. It had been eating at her in the days since. She'd actually been nervous, knowing she was going to see him tonight, and put extra care into how she looked. And it went right to her middle whenever she caught him looking at her.

She was fantasizing about pulling Rome into the closet when Marco nudged her, causing her to almost drop her cards.

"It's your turn, baby," he informed.

"Oh yeah, sorry." She mindlessly tossed a card onto the coffee table and adjusted the collar of her dress.

Everyone looked at the card she threw, then back at her.

"You good, girl?" Ginger asked her.

"Of course, why?"

"We're playing Spades and you just put down a Draw Four."

"I what??" When had she picked the Uno cards back up? "Damn, my bad...guess my head is somewhere else. Nell, come take my place; you and Marco can finish playing Ginger and Zion. I'm gonna go get some more of these cake pops."

Without waiting for a response, she hopped up and headed for the kitchen. Instead of going for the sweets, though, she just pressed a hand to her stomach and paced around the kitchen island, trying to calm herself down. Tingles were still shooting all over her body from her attraction to Rome, and she knew it wasn't going to subside as long as she was in the same space with him.

Of course, it only intensified with Rome showed up in the kitchen.

"What are you doing in here?" she breathed, backing against the counter and grabbing the edge with both hands.

His eyes were on her as he approached. "The same thing you're doing."

"Cake pops?"

"Don't play. You know what it is. And it's not about no damn cake pops."

"We shouldn't be in here...*together*," she whispered, making herself inch away when he stood next to her. "Somebody could come in here."

"We're just talking. It's not like I'm about to kiss you." He moved to stand in front of her, looking at her intently. "Though I want to."

Her breath hitched. "You do?"

"I miss you, Jazlyn," he forged ahead, his voice low. "Ever since...*that* night, my head has been jacked up. I haven't been able to get you out of my mind, or stop wishing that I could be with you. And I don't just mean sexually. I want you, J., in *every* way."

Jazlyn couldn't remember the last time she'd been so happy. She started to grab him, but caught herself. "Rome..."

"I wanted to tell you the other night at the movies but I..."

"I know, me too," Jazlyn jumped in, taking a tiny step forward. She briefly placed a hand to his chest but made herself retract it, because it only made her want to touch more of him. "You're not the only one whose head has been messed up. It's all I've been able to think about."

His eyes widened slightly. "For real?"

"For real, Rome. This...I feel the same way you do. I knew the next *day* that I didn't want us to just be friends anymore."

He glanced over his shoulder before turning back to her, a gleam of excitement in his eyes. "Why didn't you say something??"

"The same reason you didn't. I didn't know where your head was, plus Marco and Nell..."

"I know," Rome sighed, rubbing the back of his neck. He stood next to her, leaning against the counter. They were quiet for a few moments, their hands inching closer on the counter's edge but stopping short of touching. "I want us to get outta here."

"Me too. But there's no way we'd be able to explain that."

"Shit." He sighed.

"I know." She glanced at him, finally unleashing the longing she'd been keeping at bay all evening. It frustrated her to be this close to him and smell him and feel his heat and not be able to touch him like she wanted. "What are we gonna do about this?"

"The answer is easy," he replied, nodding his head towards the living room and the sounds of their significant others laughing with Ginger and Zion, as they exchanged friendly trash talk. "But that doesn't mean doing it is."

"Yeah." Jazlyn could only imagine the hell Marco would raise when she told him the truth. She kicked herself for giving in to him when he came to her house that night. He wasn't the man for her and that would've been true whether Rome returned her feelings or not.

"We're gonna figure it out, though," Rome assured, grabbing her hand and bringing it to his lips. Jazlyn released a shaky breath as she eyed him while biting her lip. He took his time putting her hand down. Rome knew it was wrong, but he couldn't keep standing this close to Jazlyn and not feel her some kind of way. "At least now we both know how the other feels."

"Yeah." She rubbed her hand where he kissed it. "We need to figure it out quick, though, 'cause now that we know, I don't want to keep waiting."

Chapter 10

"You have some explaining to do."

Ginger wasted no time calling Jazlyn the day after game night. Jazlyn hadn't even gotten up yet.

Yawning, Jazlyn sat up in bed. "What time is it?"

"Doesn't matter. Spill it."

"Spill what?"

"Jazlyn. I hope you don't think I didn't see the way you and Rome kept looking at each other last night."

Jazlyn was glad she was alone; she'd convinced Marco to go back to his place when they left Ginger's, saying her stomach was hurting from eating too many cake pops.

She started to act like she didn't know what Ginger was talking about, but remembered she wanted to talk to her friend about this, anyway. Not to mention, Ginger wasn't an idiot. And Jazlyn could imagine that she and Rome seemed off, what with all the delicious tension between them.

"Okay," she conceded, adjusting the covers around her waist. "The truth is...something happened between me and Rome a little while back."

"*What* happened?"

"We...had sex."

Ginger screamed so loud Jazlyn had to pull the phone from her ear. "Are you fucking kidding me?? *When* was this?!?"

"The night the blizzard hit. Rome had come over to bring me food and supplies and make sure the house was prepared, and ended up getting stuck here. We were in my room and it just...went there."

"Oh my *gosh*, Jazlyn!"

"I know! It wasn't anything planned, certainly not on my part and I'm willing to bet not on Rome's, either. But we were here alone and I was looking at him and it just felt...different. I started really noticing Rome *the man* and not just Rome my friend. It freaked me out because it was the first time that had ever happened."

"Who made the first move?"

Jazlyn paused. "I don't even know, to be honest. I could see the way he was looking at me; something told me he was feeling it, too. When we were cuddled up in my room after the power went out, it just escalated. I swear, Ginger, I've never wanted anybody as much as I wanted Rome that night."

"Oooh girl..."

"And to top it off, the sex was some of the best I've had, if not *the* best," Jazlyn continued. "And ever since then, it's all I've been able to think about. *He's* all I've been able to think about."

"Are you telling me what I think you're telling me? In other words, are you finally going to admit to what I've been saying all along about you and Rome?"

"Ginger, before then, Rome and I had never even come *close* to that. I don't know what was so different about that night...I thought maybe it was the whole scene of us being stuck together in a cold dark house during a blizzard, but it feels deeper than that. Especially since my desire for him has only multiplied since then."

"The sex was that good, huh?"

"I'm not just talking about the sex. I'm talking about Rome, period. It didn't take long for me to know I didn't want us to forget what happened and go back to being just friends. But I didn't know where Rome's head was; last night was when he admitted he wanted me like I want him."

"Just last night? So all this time since the blizzard, the two of you have been going on with Marco and Nell like that night never happened?"

"Basically."

"Are you feeling guilty?"

"I *should* be but...not really. Not sure what that says about the kind of person I am, but that's the real."

"Hell, you know I'm not gonna judge. I never liked Marco's ass, anyway. What I want to know now is, when are you gonna dump him and get your man?"

"It's not that easy, Ginger. Marco humbled himself to me and I agreed to try to make things work. And I imagine something similar happened with Rome and Nell, seeing as how they're still together. These are people we care about, even if we know they're not right for us. It's not the easiest thing to just dump them."

"I get that but there's no need in dragging it out. If you want to be with Rome and he wants to be with you..."

"Marco is gonna pitch a *fit*, especially since I've said so many times that Rome and I were just friends and nothing was happening between us."

"Well, that *was* the case up until recently. Look, girl, things change. *Feelings* change. You have feelings for Rome that you didn't have before, and there's nothing wrong with that, but you need to be honest with Marco about it. You at least owe him that much. And the longer you drag it out, the worse it's gonna be, for everybody."

Jazlyn knew Ginger had a point. She wasn't looking forward to telling Marco the truth, but she also didn't want to prolong the inevitable. It was past time to put their relationship in her rearview mirror.

"You're right," she admitted. "I *do* need to go ahead and let Marco know what the deal is. I'm sure he wouldn't love knowing that I can't even get aroused when we're together unless I'm thinking about Rome."

Ginger laughed loudly, causing Jazlyn to move the phone from her ear again.

"Jazlyn, girl, I really, *really* want to clown about that but I'm gonna refrain. That is too funny, though."

"Yeah, it's hilarious."

"Do you know how *dope* it is that you and your best friend fell for each other after one passionate night while stuck together during a blizzard?? This is like one of those movies off that greeting card channel. Or those novels in the grocery store."

Jazlyn chuckled.

"I always knew you and Rome were gonna find your way to each other eventually. I expect a shout-out in the wedding vows."

"Ginger."

"Okay fine, I'll settle for being the matron of honor."

"I need you to stop. You are *majorly* jumping the gun."

"Like you haven't thought about that."

Jazlyn was glad this conversation was over the phone instead of in person because her face would've surely given her away. Her imagination had wandered to her and Rome holding hands in front of a minister a few times. A fantasy she never once had about her and Marco.

"Regardless," she finally deflected. "I need to focus on this conversation I need to have with Marco first. I'm *not* looking forward to it."

"I know. But the sooner you do, the sooner you can focus on Rome. *Without* having to sneak off to the kitchen just to get a minute with him."

"That's not...what I went to the kitchen for," Jazlyn replied, though it was weak. She knew Ginger thought so, too. "I went for cake pops."

"Uh-huh. But that's not why *Rome* went."

Jazlyn didn't bother trying to refute that. She was just glad he had because that's when he confirmed that his feelings matched hers. The thought alone made her giddy.

But she had to deal with Marco first. She just hoped that it didn't get ugly...and that she didn't punk out again.

• • • •

ROME WAS HEADING TO see his parents. Partly because it had been over a week since his last visit, but also to avoid having the inevitable conversation with Nell. He knew he needed to tell her the truth about his feelings for Jazlyn, but he dreaded hurting her. Especially since she had been so trusting of him and their friendship the entire time. He hated the thought of disappointing her, but he also knew it would be unfair to keep putting it off.

His mother and Asha were out when he got to his parents' house, and part of him was relieved. He needed some fatherly advice.

"Hey, son," Solomon, greeted when Rome let himself in. They shared a warm embrace, giving each other a few hearty pats on the back. "You had to work today? How's the business going?"

"Yes, we had a big one this morning that we've been working on for a couple of days; a mansion that's being renovated. Lots of stripping and sanding and sealing, not to mention the kitchen tile that was a monster to get up. We got it done, though. Business is going really well; been getting a lot of referrals lately."

"I'm glad to hear that. Though I still think it's hilarious that you went from dancing to running a flooring business. Of all things."

"Yeah, I don't know how it worked out like that, either," Rome chuckled, accepting the bottle of apple juice that Solomon handed him from the fridge before trailing him to the sun porch. Solomon liked to sit out there and smoke his cigars, since his wife hated the smell of it in the house.

"So what's on your mind?"

"Can still read me like a book, huh?" Rome shook his head with a wry smile before sipping his juice.

"Course I can."

"Well, I'm in a situation that doesn't shine me in the best light, and it's not something I can talk to Mama or Asha about. Well, *maybe* Mama, but definitely not Asha. Not yet."

Solomon looked at him with concern. "What's going on?"

"So..." Rome set the juice on the floor between his feet and rubbed his hands together. "Nell and I have been together for a while now. And I love her."

"Yeah..."

"For the most part, I've been happy with her. But recently I started wondering if she's the right one for me."

Solomon just nodded encouragingly as he lit his cigar.

Not knowing how long they had before his mother and Asha returned, Rome figured he'd better get to the point. "Jazlyn and I have been tight for years, and I've never looked at her as anything other than my friend. I swear. But the night the blizzard hit and I got snowed in at her house...that changed."

"Oh really?"

"*Everything* changed that night," Rome emphasized, leaving his father to put two and two together. "And ever since then, she's all I think about. And *not* in a platonic way."

Releasing a puff of smoke between his mustached lips, Solomon kicked his feet up on the wicker ottoman in front of him. "And now you're confused?"

"I was, but I became sure once Nell got back to town. I thought maybe I'd be reminded of everything I felt for her before when I saw her, but it was just the opposite. It only confirmed what I'd been suspecting; that she's not it for me. Everything in me wants Jazlyn, which still feels wild to admit."

"I figured that would happen sooner or later."

Rome looked surprised for a moment before shaking his head. "Seems like everybody thought that but us."

"Hell, me and your mama were close friends for a long while before the sparks started to fly."

"Really? I didn't know that. What made you decide you wanted more than just friendship with her?"

"She got sick with the flu one time and I went over to see about her. Realized I didn't wanna leave; that I always wanted to be the one to take care of her. Took her temperature and then kissed her; couldn't wait anymore."

Rome sat forward, intrigued. "And what did she do?"

"Oh, she kissed me back. We talked about how we were seeing each other differently and all of that. That's the good part."

"What was the bad part?"

"I ended up sick right along with her. But we were together, at least."

Rome laughed. "Dad."

"Son, I've been seeing you and Jazlyn together for years. I've caught you giving her that look a couple of times here and there when you thought nobody was watching. I tried to bet your mama how long it would take the two of you to link up but she wouldn't do it. Though she saw this coming, too."

"Well, if my falling for Jazlyn was the only thing, it'd be fine. But I fell for her while I'm with someone else. Hell, I was *with* her while I'm with someone else. I feel guilty enough about that part, but even more so that it didn't take long for me to want more of it. Stepping out on my woman...that's not who I am, Dad. This is the first time I've cheated on anybody and I hate that I did that to Nell."

"I understand. You did a bad thing but that doesn't make you a bad person, son."

"Does it make me a bad person that I'm considering *not* telling Nell what happened with Jazlyn?"

Solomon looked over at him with a quirked brow.

"It's gonna be hard enough breaking up with her," Rome quickly justified. "Do I *really* need to-"

"Yes," Solomon interjected strongly. "If the shoe were on the other foot, you would want the whole story and you know it. There's nothing wrong with your feelings changing, but you can't step out on Nell then try to hide your footprints. She deserves to know the whole truth."

"Yeah." Rome slumped in his chair.

"You knew that. But I get that you felt you needed someone to hammer it home for ya."

"I guess. Was just hoping there was some kind of loophole."

"Not this time, son. You've just gotta man up and own what you did. No other way around it."

Rome figured that's what his father would tell him. But it still felt good to confide in him about it, even if he didn't give Rome the out he hoped for.

"Thanks for listening, Dad. But I need this to stay between us. You know Mama loves Nell; I can't stand to admit that I stepped out on her. She was dropping mad hints about Nell becoming her daughter-in-law."

"Understood."

"And I *definitely* can't tell Asha. She's still pissed off about getting jilted and will automatically just put me in the same category as her cheating fiancé. I can't take that."

"How long do you expect to keep all this under wraps? The truth always comes out sooner or later."

"Well, it's gonna have to be later. At least until she comes down off all that anger and can think more rationally."

"She won't hear about it from me."

Rome left a little while later, suddenly feeling eager to start cleaning up the mess he was in. Nothing could really happen between him and Jazlyn while they were each still linked to other people, and he didn't want Nell to keep thinking their relationship was something it wasn't. He needed to bite the bullet and have the hard conversation.

He called Nell, wanting to take advantage of his momentary surge of courage.

"Hey," she greeted, sounding distracted. "Thank *god* you called."

Rome frowned in alarm. "Why, what's wrong?"

"It's just been such a crappy day; one thing after another since I got to work this morning. I *really* need to hear some good news."

Oh hell. His mind whirled for what to say. "Uhh..."

"What are you up to?"

"Just coming from hanging with Dad for a little bit."

"Oh yeah? How's he doing? I need to get over to see your parents; I admit I've been kind of avoiding them ever since your mother mentioned that stuff about us getting married one day. But I'm gonna get past that," she quickly assured.

Rome felt like the lowest of the low. He couldn't tell her what he had to tell her, not now. And he knew it would be a punk move to do it over the phone, anyway.

Promising himself he'd tell her before the clock struck midnight, he changed the subject. They made mindless small talk as Rome headed home, mostly with Nell just venting about her work day; she was a human resources manager. Before ending the call, he made sure to ask her to come by when she got off, giving no indication of the heavy conversation they needed to have. He didn't want to give her any reason to not show up.

Unfortunately, Nell called barely an hour later while he was out making a quick run to the store saying she wouldn't be able to make it; she was going to have to work late and wasn't sure when she'd be done. Rome tried to tell her that he didn't care what time it was when she came by, but she insisted that all she wanted when she got off was a stiff drink, her bed, and a Netflix comedy special. It was almost as if she sensed that he was about to drop a bomb on her.

Frustrated, he pulled up to his house. He had just killed the engine when he got a call from Jazlyn.

"What's up, big head?" he greeted, smiling like a schoolboy with a crush.

"I'm gonna need you to come up with a cuter nickname than that," Jazlyn greeted. He could hear the smile in her voice, too. "You've seen me naked."

The reminder made Rome's stomach clench; what he wouldn't give to see her like that again. To even *kiss* her again; it had been too long.

"I have," he finally concurred in a low voice. He adjusted the now-awakened bulge in his pants. "And I miss it."

There was a sharp intake of breath before she let out a small yearning sound. "Oh believe me, the feeling is mutual. And I'm sick of waiting. Have you gotten a chance to talk to Nell yet?"

"I was planning on telling her today but she can't come by like I asked her to; working late. And it's not something I should tell her over the phone or in a text."

"True."

"I'm not looking forward to it but I also just want to get it over with," Rome admitted. "It's gonna be worse the more time we let pass."

"Exactly. Which is why I'm getting ready to tell Marco now."

Rome's back straightened. "For real?"

"He's on his way here."

"You told him you wanted to talk to him about something or he's just coming over for the hell of it?"

"I told him there was something we needed to discuss. He tried to pry it out of me over the phone but I told him I needed to tell him in person."

"Oh hell. You think he suspects anything?"

"Who knows. I just know I need to get this off my chest; I can't keep pretending things are good with us when they're not. That's when I'm not trying to avoid him altogether so he won't try to get in my pants."

The thought of Marco touching Jazlyn made Rome's skin burn. "Good 'cause the only hands I want on that body are mine."

"You better stop. You know I get turned on by that shit."

"We're kinda in the same boat, because I've been keeping Nell at arm's length since she got back to town. I know she's has to be at least a little suspicious; I used to be all over her every chance I got."

"Uh-huh. Well, now you don't need to be all over anybody but me. So we *both* need to-"

There was a loud pounding sound in the background. "What the hell? What's that?" Rome asked with a frown.

There was a pause, and Rome figured that Jazlyn was checking the peephole or the window. "Ugh, it's Marco."

"Why's he banging on the door? Doesn't he have a key?"

"He used to until I took it back."

"When did you do that?"

"A few days ago. He's had an attitude about it ever si-"

"Jazlyn!" Rome could hear Marco's voice in the background. "Open the damn door!"

"Stop yelling! I'm coming!"

"Do I need to come over there?" Rome asked, already revving his engine back up.

"No, no, I'm good. He's just-"

"I don't like how he's yelling at you like that, J."

"I can handle it, Rome. I'll call you when he leaves."

"He must know something if he's sounding like that already."

"Don't see how he could. I've only told Ginger and I don't have a diary he could've snuck and read."

"Still, J.-"

"Rome." Her voice was strong. There was more pounding on her door. "I've got this. Marco is a bunch of bark with no bite; he's not gonna do anything. I'll let you know when he's gone, okay? Don't worry." She hung up.

Rome was already backing out of his driveway. He didn't care what Jazlyn said; there was no way he wasn't going to go check on her with Marco there yelling and banging on the door like a lunatic. There had to be a reason he was so angry already, and Rome didn't put anything past anybody. Just because he'd never laid a hand on Jazlyn before didn't mean he wouldn't, especially if she included the part about sleeping with Rome in her breakup speech. Marco hadn't liked or trusted Rome since he started dating Jazlyn and Rome wasn't about to take any chances.

By the time he made it to Jazlyn's and hurriedly parked his truck, he could hear the two of them yelling as he ran towards the front door. He pulled out his emergency key to Jazlyn's house and let himself in, finding Marco in Jazlyn's face, which made Rome want to tear his head off.

Rushing over, he grabbed Marco by the back of his collar and yanked him away from Jazlyn before pushing him further back with both hands to the chest, sending Marco reeling several steps.

"What the hell?" Marco yelled, completely caught off guard.

"Rome!" Jazlyn exclaimed, startled.

"Why the *fuck* are you in her face like that??" Rome demanded, almost nose-to-nose with Marco. His fists were clenched and ready.

"This ain't got nothing to do with you, bruh, so you need to roll," Marco angrily advised, breathing fire and clenching his own fists. "This is between me and my woman; it's none of your business."

"When you came over here yelling at her, you *made* it my business," Rome informed him. "And I ain't your *bruh*."

"Y'all, stop!" Jazlyn ordered, trying to pull Marco back.

"How the hell did you even get in here? He has a key and I don't??" Marco asked Jazlyn accusingly, shrugging off her hand and pointing a finger tauntingly close to Rome's face. "You took *my* key but let him-"

Rome batted Marco's hand away, his scowl deepening. "Don't push it, man."

"I'll push whatever I want to." He shoved Rome in the chest. "And if you're not out of my face in the next three seconds, I'm gonna start swinging, too. And believe me, you don't want that!"

"Bring that shit then!" Rome countered, charging at Marco again. Jazlyn scurried to block his path, bracing both hands against his chest. "*Move*, Jazlyn!"

"No! Y'all are not about to be fighting in here!"

"Tell him to leave, then!" Marco demanded, eyes blazing at Rome. "'Cause we got shit to deal with!"

"Marco-"

"I'm not leaving her in here alone with you so you can forget *that*," Rome informed defiantly, unflinching.

"Jazlyn!" Marco barked, looking at her incredulously, as if he didn't understand what was taking her so long to put Rome out.

Jazlyn turned to face Marco, her arms extended back to keep Rome in place. She could feel the heat from his body behind her and him shifting from one foot to the other, itching for the slightest excuse to barrel forward and finally have it out with Marco. Jazlyn's hand closed around his wrist.

Marco noticed. His eyes dropped to the action before looking back up at Rome, then Jazlyn, his eyes narrowing slightly.

"Marco," Jazlyn hedged wearily, sucking in a fortifying breath. "That's enough. I need you to leave."

"Me? Why not *him*?? You asked me to come over here, remember?"

"I *want* him here." She looked at Marco pointedly, hoping he got the message. "And...I need you to leave. You and me...we're done, Marco."

Rome could see the realization melt over Marco's face. And when the hand of the wrist Jazlyn was holding came around to rest on her stomach from behind, Marco's face tightened so much Rome thought it might rip. A flash of hurt crossed his eyes before the anger returned, his chest heaving harder with each second that passed. Jazlyn looked at him warily and pleadingly before Rome stepped in front of her, putting himself between her and the explosion it seemed Marco was building up to.

But Marco just grunted, his lip curled in a furious sneer. He nodded, as if his suspicions were finally confirmed.

"Okay, I see what it is," he snarled, his angry glare bouncing back and forth between the two of them before landing on Jazlyn. The sadness flashed again. "Just friends, huh? Yeah, fuck *both* of y'all."

He stormed past them and out of the house, slamming the door so hard the windows shook.

Chapter 11

"What the hell are you doing here??"

Thrown, Rome blinked several times. "Are you seriously mad at *me*??"

"Rome, I specifically told you I could handle it!" Jazlyn exclaimed, hands flailing, her long blue ombre nails slicing through the air. "I didn't need you to come over here!"

"If you're expecting me to apologize, you've got another thing coming, Jazlyn."

Her nostrils flared. "You should've respected my wishes, Rome."

"So I was just supposed to act like I didn't hear him screaming and hollering and trying to pound your door in? I'm not supposed to see about you when I think you might be in danger? That's not how this goes, J.!"

"Clearly! So I guess how it goes is that you ignore me when I tell you something. Well, I guess it's a good thing I find this out now, isn't it?"

"What the hell? You act like this is something new! I've had your back for *eight damn years*, Jazlyn, and that damn sure isn't gonna stop now! Even if we were still just friends I'd have done the same thing!"

"Oh really? Maybe we should walk this whole thing back, then, 'cause if you're not gonna-"

Rome snatched her to him by the front of her shirt with one hand and grabbed the back of her neck with the other, slamming his lips down on hers. Jazlyn immediately grabbed the sides of his jacket, her tongue welcoming his. She jumped into his arms, her limbs encircling his neck and waist. Rome's hands cupped her bottom as he plunked her against the nearest bare wall, their urgent breathy kiss only intensifying.

He pushed his hardened bulge against her, causing her to grunt in delicious frustration. She angled her hips to where she could feel him better, holding the back of his neck with both hands as his hand crept up the front of her shirt.

"Get those pants off," she ordered, her voice breathless and her eyes lustful.

Rome started to comply, then slowed down, looking troubled. He cursed under his breath as he reluctantly set Jazlyn back onto her feet.

"What's wrong?" she asked, alarmed.

"I can't do this yet, J." He placed his fist to his lips as he tried to gather himself.

"Why not? Oh." Her eyes brightened in realization. "Nell."

"Yeah." Rome cleared his throat. "You're in the clear but I'm not. And I know we've already done it before, but-"

"I get it, Rome," Jazlyn assured, placing a hand to his chest. "I understand."

"I'm sorry."

"Stop. You don't have anything to apologize for. I just wish you could go ahead and tell her so we could really jump in this thing together."

"You and me both, trust." Rome ran a hand down his face before grabbing her hand, leading her to the couch. "If I could've told her today, I would have. Hell, I tried to tell her after she came back to town but she kept stopping me, then I admit I just caved in and stayed with her. But I don't want to keep wasting her time. You're who I want. And I'm as anxious to take our finger off the pause button as you are."

"You still think she has no idea?"

"Not really. Though with the way she shut me down, it felt like she could sense she wouldn't like whatever I had to tell her."

"Maybe she could. Sometimes we women have a sixth sense about this kind of stuff."

"Hmph. Well, regardless, part of me wants to go to her office and just blurt it out but I know that's not the move. I don't wanna embarrass her on top of everything else."

"Yeah. I don't want you to do that, either; she doesn't deserve that. I kinda lucked up with how everything went down with Marco."

A few quiet moments passed as Rome played with her slim fingers. He finally looked at her. "What was happening when I got here? What were you two fighting about?"

"Ugh," Jazlyn grunted with a slight shake of her head. "At first, he was fussing about me taking my key back again. Then I said that I wasn't happy with how things were going between us, and he started yelling about how I'm never satisfied and I'm difficult to please and all that, and I admitted that part of me still didn't totally trust him, and that's when he *really* blew up. Then you came in."

"Wow."

"I'm glad you were here," Jazlyn admitted, squeezing his hand. "It means a lot that you came rushing over like that."

"You know I got you." He gazed at her adoringly, briefly cupping her chin. "I've *always* got you, Jazlyn."

She exhaled a short breath at his words, touched. Her finger reached out to trace his lips as her eyes slid up and down his face. "You are such a sweetheart."

"For people that deserve it."

"Well, I hope I always stay in that category with you. You...you mean so much to me, Rome. I want this...I want *us*."

"I want us, too." He brought her face to his, indulging in a kiss that stretched for several leisurely seconds. "More than I can tell you."

They shared a look they'd never shared before, conveying feelings they weren't sure they should be feeling yet but that they couldn't deny. Both of them were still floored that they were seeing each other in this light after so many years of strictly platonic friendship, but now that they were, there was no running from it.

She laid her head on his chest, curling into him and sliding her hand across his stomach. Her bent knees rested against his thigh. He wrapped his arm around her, occasionally sliding his hand down her arm or back. A tingly warmth spread over his body as he held her, speeding up the beat of his heart. This was where he needed to be, and Jazlyn was who he needed to be with. He knew it. With everything in him, he knew it.

But he also knew he had to speak to Nell. He had to tell her the truth. Not just so he could move forward with Jazlyn but because Nell simply deserved that. Despite the frustrations he'd had with her and their relationship, she was a good woman who had been good to him.

He and Jazlyn stayed cuddled up on the couch for a while longer before he made himself leave. He hated to, but when another of their lingering kisses started to escalate into something more heated again, they agreed they should pump the brakes while they still could.

Promising to call her later, Rome headed home. He thought about calling Nell and insisting that they see each other that night, now even more anxious to let her know their relationship was over.

But it turned out he didn't have to wait as long as he thought.

When he got home, Nell was in his room, clearing her clothes from the drawer he'd designated for her a while back and placing them in the open leather duffel on his bed. Tears streamed down her face. He paused in the doorway, his stomach tightening.

She turned to look at him, the hand holding the pair of shorts she'd just removed from the drawer falling to her side. Her lips trembled as she peered at him, sniffling. Rome swallowed, his expression pained.

"What..."

"Marco called me," she informed, her voice barely above a whisper. "About an hour ago."

Cursing under his breath, Rome cautiously entered the room. "Nell...I am *so* sorry. You might not believe it, but I really am. I never meant to-"

She held up a trembling hand, her eyes dropping to the floor. "Please don't."

He pursed his lips, still feeling compelled to give some kind of explanation. "I hate that I hurt you. That's the *last* thing I wanted to do. This wasn't...this wasn't something we planned at all. It just..." His shoulders hunched as he tried to find the words. "This just hit out of the blue."

Nell gave a sad chuckle as she slowly wrung the shorts in her hands. "It wasn't out of the blue, Rome. Not really. Something told me this would happen eventually; I've seen how you two are together. The energy you two have...it was bound to shift sooner or later. But I kept telling myself that I could be wrong; that you and Jazlyn really *were* just friends."

"We *were*," Rome insisted, stepping further into the room, his hands clawed in emphasis. "Until recently, nothing at all had ever gone down between me and Jazlyn. I *swear*."

"Until recently." She dropped the shorts into the bag and stood straight, looking at him. "*How* recently?"

He hesitated, not wanting to say it but knowing he needed to. "The night we had that blizzard. When...when you were out of town."

She nodded, not surprised. "I figured."

"You did?"

"Yes. You were different when I got back," she reminded, taking the last balled-up pair of socks from the drawer and passing it back and forth between her hands. "I used to be able to see the love in your eyes when you looked at me but it wasn't there anymore. You didn't speak to me the same, touch me the same; you wouldn't make love to me. I tried to make myself believe that you just needed time to process the things I told you about my feelings, but..." She mindlessly pinched the socks between her fingers. "I didn't know who had taken your attention but I knew *someone* had."

"I'm so sorry."

"Yeah. Well," she sniffled again and dropped the socks into the bag. "I guess I played a part in this too, with how skittish I was."

He immediately shook his head. "This isn't on you, Nell."

"Yes, it is." She zipped the bag. "At least part of it. You let me know more than once that you were unhappy with how I got whenever you tried to talk about us. I wouldn't tell you I loved you. There's only so long a person can deal with that, and I know it."

"Nell, this was not about spite or revenge. I need you to know that. It just-"

She held up her hands, the sloppy top knot her microbraids were wound into at the top of her head wobbling. "Please stop trying to make me feel better. I just want to get the rest of my things and leave."

"I'm sorry that you found out like this. I wanted to tell you myself; it was what I wanted to talk to you about tonight."

"It doesn't matter, Rome." She swiped her fingertips underneath her reddened eyes, smudging the eyeliner rimming the bottom. Pulling her plump bottom lip between her teeth, she picked up her jacket that was lying next to her bag and slid her arm into it. "I know now."

He watched wearily as her eyes pinged around the room, either to check to make sure she hadn't forgotten anything or to get last looks before she walked out. Either way, she picked up the bag and slung it over her shoulder, not even bothering to zip it closed. Moving towards the door, she hesitantly paused in front of him, looking up into his remorseful eyes.

Her mouth opened and then closed, unsure what to say. "I got a job offer out of state," she informed him, her voice cracking. "I wasn't going to take it but now...I don't know if I'll be able to handle being around here knowing I could run into the two of you. Or even just you. It would just be too much for me, seeing the man I love and having to keep my distance."

Rome started to tell her that she wouldn't have to do that, but he wasn't going to insult her with the 'let's be friends' platitude. He always hated that. And he wouldn't want to seem like he was flaunting his relationship with Jazlyn in her face.

"I'm sorry," was all he could say.

Her hand came up to touch his face, but stopped short and curled into a reluctant fist, hesitating before dropping back to her side. Finally, she just cleared her throat and whispered, "Bye, Rome."

She walked out.

Rome stayed in the same spot until he heard his front door close, then his eyes fell to the key he'd given Nell laying on the dresser. He flopped onto the bed, his head falling into his hands.

• • • •

THEIR PREVIOUS ATTACHMENTS now severed, Jazlyn and Rome could now fully claim each other.

Now that they were officially together, they had to adjust to thinking of each other as boyfriend and girlfriend instead of just best friends. It was a strange but exhilarating change. There was a period of awkward adjustment as they shifted from platonic to romantic, getting used to things like holding hands in public or calling each other by endearing pet names instead of (or along with) the teasing ones they'd exchanged over the years. They were both happy with the turn their relationship had taken, but each harbored a simmering nervousness about doing something to mess it up.

Rome drummed his fingers excitedly on the steering wheel as he went to pick up Jazlyn for their first official date as a couple. As many times as they'd gone out together as friends, he still felt that first-date nervousness and anxiety. It brought an automatic smile every time he thought about the fact that Jazlyn was his woman now. She was *his*. Just as it felt like she should've been all along. He'd never been as at peace as he felt once he let her know that things were over with Nell and they could finally be together.

Jazlyn was equally as sure about Rome. Just like that, she craved his presence, his embrace, his lips, his laugh, his *everything*. Rome gave her butterflies. He made her giddy, just by thinking of him and remembering that he was her man now. And she wanted it to stay that way.

She knew he was still feeling a string of guilt about Nell and how she found out about them. Jazlyn could just kick Marco in the nuts for being petty and telling Nell before Rome could. But being petty was Marco's specialty when he wanted it to be. He'd been hurt, so he had to bring someone down with him. He certainly didn't blab to Nell out of any particular concern for her; they hardly knew each other. The four of them hadn't hung together *that* much and when they did, his interaction with Nell was minimal. No, this was all about bringing someone else onto his misery train and making Rome look like the bad guy.

As much as Rome hated how that whole scene went down, he insisted that it was for the best. At least it was out in the open now and there were no more secrets. Nell had been understandably hurt, but she'd handled it like an adult. Marco, on the other hand, had proceeded to leave Jazlyn a bunch of angry messages and texts. She blocked his number, but then started getting calls from an unknown one and knew that was also likely Marco. She blocked that too, but knew it was only a matter of time before he tried something else. His bruised ego wouldn't let him just walk away and let it go.

She was putting on her earrings when Rome knocked on the door. Grinning, she quickly gave herself a once-over in the mirror before scurrying to the door, feeling like she did on her high school prom night when the fine fullback she was dating came to pick her up. Half the girls in her class wanted him but he was there to take *her*. She'd felt like the proudest thing walking.

Just like she felt when she opened her door now and saw Rome standing there.

Her heart surged upon seeing him. He had a way of looking at her and making every nerve and cell in her body wake up.

Damn, he's so fucking cute.

"Hey, sweets," he greeted.

Her grin widened. She loved when he called her that. Her top lip dragged under her teeth as she eyed him up and down.

"There's my baby," she purred.

Rome ducked his head, blushing, his own grin stretching across his face. Jazlyn thought it was adorable how he reacted when she said stuff like that to him.

She held out her hand and he quickly grabbed it, stepping inside the house. They slid into a tight embrace, their bodies molding together. Rome's hands slid down to just above her behind and up to the back of her neck, pulling back to kiss her. Her mouth immediately opened for him and they sank into each other, moaning concurrently. Jazlyn's hand gripped the back of Rome's head as if to keep it in place, in no hurry for the kiss to end. She loved kissing him; it felt like she was getting rewarded for doing something really, really good.

"You look amazing," he murmured, resting his cheek against hers once they finally pulled their lips apart.

"So do you." She took his hand and led him back to her bedroom so she could finish getting ready. "I'll just be another couple of minutes and then we can go."

"Cool." Rome sat on her bed, adjusting his dark gray button-down shirt. He wore a stark white t-shirt underneath, black jeans, and black KD16 custom sneakers. He grabbed the copy of *Essence* that she had lying there and leaned on his elbow, flipping through it. "You know what you want to eat?"

"Hmm, I'm kinda craving steak and potatoes, believe it or not."

"Oh, I believe it. With your greedy ass," Rome joked.

"Hush!" Jazlyn playfully chucked her mascara at him. "I haven't eaten much today."

"Why am I not surprised."

"I wanted to be good and hungry for you."

"For me or for the steak?"

She turned to peer at him with tightened eyes. "I'll forget all about the damn steak if you strip and lay out right there like a sexy T-bone."

His eyes met hers, challenging. "Don't think I won't."

She wanted to dive on him, but her stomach reminded her of how hungry for food she was. "We'll be getting to that later on, trust me."

"Yes, we will. I want to feed you first so you're good and fortified; can't have you tuckering out on me."

"Never that." She braced her knuckles on the bed and gave him a quick kiss before shuffling to the bathroom. "One second; forgot to put on my body spray."

Rome didn't bother telling her that she smelled good enough to devour already. He just nodded and turned his eyes back to the magazine.

Jazlyn's phone buzzed from beside him on the bed. He glanced at it, seeing it was some random number. "Hey, your phone is ringing."

"Just ignore it."

The buzzing stopped but immediately started again. "Seems like whoever it is really wants to talk to you, sweets."

A beat passed. "Is there a name on the ID?"

"No."

There were a few whispered curses before Jazlyn stomped out of the bathroom and snatched up the phone. She silenced the call before furiously swiping the pad of her finger across the screen, a slight frown puckering her brows.

"What's up?" Rome asked, noting her apparent frustration. "Telemarketers been hounding you or something?"

Jazlyn shook her head, her eyes flitting to him. "I wish."

Rome sat up. "Nobody *wishes* for telemarketers, so what's going on?"

Hesitating slightly, Jazlyn sighed. "I think it's Marco. He was blowing my phone up, leaving all these messages, until I blocked him. Then I started getting a bunch of calls from unknown or private numbers constantly, when I rarely got them before. It's probably him calling from another number."

"Shit, Jazlyn. Why are you just now telling me this?"

"It's not a big deal, Rome. And I knew it would just piss you off."

"You're damn right. What did he say on the messages?"

"Just talking about bunch of junk."

"Was he threatening you?"

"No. Just a bunch of angry rants, telling me I'm gonna reap what I sow and all that. Don't worry about it."

"You know better than that. Of course I'm gonna worry about it. I *knew* when he left outta here that day, it wasn't gonna be as easy as that. You need to let me know if you hear from him again."

She started to insist that wasn't necessary, but the look in Rome's eyes made it clear he wasn't taking no for an answer.

"Fine," she conceded with a sigh.

He stood, pulling her into his arms and tilting her chin up until her eyes met his. "I know you wanna tell me that you can take care of yourself. I know you can. But I take care of you, too. Not because you can't, but because I want to. I want you safe, sweets. I *need* you safe."

She melted. "Oh, Rome..."

"People do crazy shit when they're scorned and have time to sit and replay all the ways they feel they've been wronged," Rome continued, his hand palming her face. "Marco might do that, he might not. All I'm saying is don't assume he won't just because. Don't be too cavalier about all this."

"I could say the same to you. He's pissed at *you*, too."

"I know. Let's hope he just needs to lash out so he can get it out of his system and move on."

"If only."

She proceeded to finish getting ready, and then they went to dinner. Rome was going to take her to an art walk afterwards, but the way Jazlyn was nibbling his ear and massaging his crotch as he drove caused a change in those plans. He headed to his house, both because it was closer and also because there was less chance of a Marco pop-up.

"I've been wanting to take this off of you all night," Rome murmured as he lowered the side zipper on Jazlyn's green backless dress.

Her hands were unzipping his pants. "Yeah?"

"Yeah."

"Well..." She stepped back and shimmied the dress to the floor, revealing a backless bra and no panties. Rome's jaw dropped. "Now it's off. What's next?"

"What's next?" Rome hurriedly removed his own clothes before sweeping Jazlyn into his arms and carrying her to his bedroom. "You're about to find out."

Jazlyn's moans and screams were loud as Rome moved inside of her, varying his thrusts between smooth to achingly slow and teasing to breasts-bouncing banging. She loved how he flipped her around and kept her guessing, switching positions just as her fire reached the boiling point and switching it again before it spilled over, prolonging the pleasure. Her hands gripped the sheets as he stroked her from behind, their left legs bent and spread out, loving the weight of him on her back. Rapid pants escaped her open mouth before Rome grabbed her face and turned it towards him for a sloppy kiss. Then he braced himself on his fists and changed the angle of his hips, causing Jazlyn to throw her head back and release a string of obscenities.

"So fucking sexy," Rome whispered from behind her, sliding a hand up and down her sweaty back before giving a hard slap to her butt, which she loved. "I *love* making you scream like that, sweets."

"I-oooh, *Rome!*" she grunted when he switched to a smooth, firm thrust. He moved just as good in bed as he used to on the dance floor; better even. Jazlyn reached back to try to grab his thigh but her hand fell back to the rumpled sheets, fisting and even pulling them between her teeth when Rome pulled her by the waist to her knees and started fucking her in a way that she knew meant he was getting close. Which was good because she was super close, too.

"Turn around," he ordered, his voice raspy, turning her onto her back. "I want to be looking in your eyes when I make you come."

It didn't take long. His words pushed down the accelerator and sent her over the edge, barely ten focused strokes in before her breath caught in her throat, her body seized up, and her back arched so hard that she was actually balancing by the top of her head on the bed. Rome's arms encircled her, gently guiding her back onto the sheets, painting long licks across her chest and up her neck.

"Kiss me," she panted, eyes closed and biting her lip.

As soon as she turned her head the slightest bit, his lips were on hers. They kissed deeply and slowly, their dragged-out moans indicative of the absence of urgency. Their sweaty bodies molded together as Rome's arms framed her head, one hand tangled in her wild hair, and Jazlyn's oval nails lazily raking up and down his back. Their hunter green polish with the rhinestone at the tip of each one provided a striking contrast against Rome's nutty brown skin.

"I could get used to this," she purred between kisses. She smiled when he smoothed a smattering of sweaty hair from her forehead.

"You should." His hand kept smoothing her hair repeatedly as he gazed down at her, the adoration in his big brown eyes unflinching. "'Cause it's not stopping."

"I'm gonna hold you to that."

"I hope you do."

He was going for another kiss when the doorbell rang. They both looked towards the direction of the front door, annoyed frowns overtaking their relaxed smiles.

"I'm not answering that," Rome declared, gently tugging Jazlyn's earlobe with his teeth. "Whoever it is will get the hint and leave eventually."

But when the doorbell kept ringing, he cursed loudly and pushed himself up, slamming a fist into the mattress. He noticed one corner of the fitted sheet had come undone during their lovemaking, and a smirk graced his lips for a second before it disappeared. He threw on his pants from earlier, zipped but unbuttoned, and stalked towards the door with every intention of telling this unwanted and unannounced visitor to get the hell on.

But he wasn't expecting to see his sister when he whipped the door open.

"Asha?" He hurriedly buttoned his pants, wishing he'd put on a shirt. "What are you doing over here? You okay?"

"I'm sorry for just showing up like this." She smiled timidly. "I tried calling but it kept going to voicemail."

You don't wanna know why. Rome glanced towards his bedroom nervously. "Oh, ummm..."

"Oh!" Realization hit, as if Asha suddenly noticed he was shirtless. Her fingertips flew to her lips, eyes apologetic. "I'm so sorry; it didn't even occur to me that Nell might be here."

Groaning inwardly, Rome kicked himself for forgetting that he still hadn't gotten Asha up to speed on the change in his relationship. He didn't want to lie to her, but it wasn't exactly an ideal time to tell her about him and-

"Who the hell is it??"

Rome's eyes squeezed shut. *Shit*.

Asha's eyes grew wider by the second. "Wait...is that-"

Jazlyn appeared in nothing but Rome's shirt, her hand hastily holding the sides closed. Her reddish-brown hair was all over the place and her face was still flushed. It didn't take a genius to know from what. Her frown quickly gave way to an *oh shit* expression of panic, fully aware that Asha didn't know about her and Rome yet.

Until now, of course.

Rome sighed. When he finally looked back at Asha, her accusing eyes were already shooting daggers at him. Her hands squeezed the long strap of her purse so hard Rome wouldn't have been surprised if she broke it in two.

"Well, well," she finally droned through tight lips and a clenched jaw. "So you're one of *them*, huh?"

Chapter 12

"Asha, before you start tripping," Rome began, making himself shake off her hurtful comment, "You don't know everything. So don't go jumping to conclusions."

The siblings were now faced off in the living room, glaring at each other. Jazlyn started to slink back to the bedroom, but she didn't want to leave Rome to deal with whatever wrath Asha wanted to unleash alone. She was as much a party to everything as Rome was. And she wasn't about to leave her man hanging out to dry.

"What's not to know?" Asha retorted. "Last *I* heard, you were committed to Nell. You even mentioned thinking about *marrying* her one day. And, oh yeah, Jazlyn was with that meathead Instagram model," she added, shooting a glare at Jazlyn. "But now here you two are...together. Which I might not think anything of except that you've *clearly* been doing more than just hanging out."

Reminding himself to keep his cool, Rome took a beat before responding. "Asha. Nell and I aren't together anymore, and-"

"I bet you're not, seeing as how you're banging your best friend behind her back. What, did she catch you two in another compromising position like I just did?"

"No," Rome replied, tamping down his ire. "It wasn't anything like that."

"Yeah, right," Asha scoffed, shaking her head. Her accusing eyes turned to Jazlyn. "I'm really surprised at you, Jazlyn. I thought you were better than this."

Jazlyn didn't want to go off, but she didn't have the patience Rome had. Her nostrils flared as she immediately stomped over and got in Asha's face, shrugging off Rome's attempt to grab her arm.

"Asha, girl, you know I love you," she began, her voice firm. "But you really need to check yourself. Don't come up in here making assumptions and throwing jabs when you don't know all the facts."

"You're standing in my brother's house practically naked. What more do I need to know?"

"If you ask *me*, nothing, because this really isn't any of your business. Think whatever you want about *me*; I don't give a damn. But Rome deserves better than that. You didn't even ask him what the deal was before jumping to your damn conclusions. He is not your ex, Asha." Jazlyn's eyes softened a tiny bit as Asha's hard expression faltered. "Don't be one of those women that thinks all men are shit just because you got dogged. You're gonna have to find a way to let go of that anger, girl."

Asha's chin quivered as she and Jazlyn continued to stare each other down. Rome stood quietly, wondering what was going through his little sister's mind. They'd always been close. And while nothing would change between him and Jazlyn if Asha kept up this attitude, he certainly wished she would give him the benefit of the doubt. Even though he hadn't exactly been a choir boy, he still didn't think he deserved to be put into the same category as runaway groom Ashton.

He thought Jazlyn's words were getting to her when Asha finally turned her glistening eyes to him. "So are you telling me that *nothing* happened between you two while you were still with Nell? If that's the case, I'll take back everything I said. Did it?"

Jazlyn glanced back at Rome. They shared a brief look before Rome gave a subtle nod, standing straighter. It would've been easy to just tell her what she wanted to hear, but he wasn't going to lie.

"I can't say that, Asha," he admitted, looking right at her. "I'm not proud of it, but yes, something did happen between me and Jazlyn while we were both still with other people."

Asha's hopeful expression crumbled at his admission.

"Even saying that, though, you *still* don't know everything," Rome continued pointedly. "And yeah, we could've handled things better. But everything isn't so cut-and-dry. And I really hope that you can get over this anger you have right now and find a way to be happy for us." He grabbed Jazlyn's hand in his, shooting her a loving gaze. "Because I'm happy where I'm at. And however we got here, I'm not gonna apologize for that."

Jazlyn grinned, squeezing his hand. Relief washed over her at his words. There'd been a tiny part of her that worried that Rome's feelings about her might change or shift due to Asha's scorn, because she knew how close they were. It made her feel good to know that not even his sister's opinion would change anything between them.

Asha's eyed flitted between the two of them for a moment before she shook her head. "You can try to justify it all you want to," she seethed. "If you started feeling Jazlyn like that, you should've kept it in your pants until you did the *respectable* thing and dealt with Nell *first*. When it comes down to it, Rome, you're just another cheater. And you should be ashamed of yourself. I know *I'm* ashamed of you."

His face tightening, Rome fought to keep his emotions in check. Her words hurt but they also pissed him off. And he knew that he needed to get her out of his house before he said something he wouldn't be able to retract.

"Well, that's too bad, Asha," he growled, clearing his throat. Releasing Jazlyn's hand, he moved towards the door. "You need to leave. Now."

Asha's jaw dropped, genuinely shocked. "You actually have the nerve to put me out??"

"Yes, I'm putting you out." His hand grabbed the doorknob. "Because you're not about to stand here in my house and in my face downtalking me. I hate that Ashton poisoned you like he has, because now every man you encounter is gonna have to be damn near perfect in order to stay off your shit list. And I love you, Asha, but I'm not jumping through those kinds of hoops for you. Like Jazlyn said, you're gonna have to find a way to let go of that anger, sis. And until you do, it's probably best that we keep our distance from each other."

Rome opened the door and looked at her, hoping that she would recant at least some of what she'd said. He could take her being disappointed in him for cheating. He fully acknowledged he was wrong for that and he was anything but proud of it. But he wasn't going to be treated like he was the worst person alive because he realized feelings for one woman while he was still with another.

Asha looked at him incredulously before turning to Jazlyn, as if expecting her to come to her defense. But Jazlyn just folded her arms and arched a brow, silently making it known whose side she was on.

After a few moments, Asha jutted a stubborn chin and stood up straighter. "Fine. Kick me out instead of just facing the truth. It won't change anything."

Rome blew out a breath as he shook his head and looked at the floor. "Just go, Asha."

With a huff, Asha stomped towards the door. When she was just over the threshold, she turned to give a parting shot but Rome slammed the door in her face, not giving her the chance. He'd heard enough.

Jazlyn immediately went over to him, placing her hands on his chest. Her eyes tried to find his. "I'm sorry."

"It's not your fault."

"Still. We're *both* in this. It's not all on you."

"At least it's out in the open now. I hate that it went down like this but it is what it is."

"Rome-"

"I'm good, Jazlyn." He reached for her. "We don't have to talk about it. Let's go back to the room and pick up where we left off."

Jazlyn's hands slid along his arms but her feet stayed planted when he tried to walk her backwards. "You can't tell me you're able to brush it off just like that. It's okay to be upset about it, Rome. Hell, I'm upset too."

Sighing, Rome stepped back and dropped his arms. "I'm not trying to let her ruin our whole evening. This was our first date night and it's not gonna end on some bullshit." His reached for her again, trying to open her shirt. "Now take this off..."

Her hands grabbed his. "You're avoiding, baby."

He released a frustrated groan and threw his hands up. "Maybe I just don't wanna talk about this, Jazlyn! Do you not *get* that??"

"Yes, I get it, but you can't just act like it didn't happen."

"Why can't I? Asha feeling some kind of way about us doesn't change a damn thing. I'd rather just put that whole scene out of my mind and get back to *us*, but I'm not in the mood for no therapy session. So if you're gonna just spend the rest of the night hounding me, then maybe you need to roll, too."

"Hey, stop; come here!" Jazlyn grabbed his arm as he started to storm past her.

"I'm good on all this. You're not listening to me and I've had enough of that for one night. Let me go!"

"*No*, Rome." She knew he was lashing out and reminded herself to be patient. She'd known Rome long enough to know he needed time to process things before he dealt with them, and she needed to let him do that. "Look, I'm sorry, okay?"

"Why do you keep apologizing for shit?"

"Because I'm pushing you and I realize I shouldn't do that. I won't say anything else about Asha or what just happened; you know I'm here whenever you want to unleash about it."

"Like I said, it's not gonna change anything."

"Regardless, you'll need to get it off your chest at some point. I saw the look in your eyes when she said the shit she said, Rome; that cut deep, whether you admit it out loud or not. It's understandable to be pissed about it. But don't let it sit there and grow or else you'll be walking around here mad at the world like Asha is."

He looked at her, his scowl still in place. But it eased the more he looked into her understanding eyes. She had a point, and he knew it.

"And for the record, thank you for standing up for me and for us the way you did," Jazlyn continued, leaning into him. Her arms slid around his waist. "You could've tried to downplay what we have going on to appease Asha but you didn't. That means a lot to me."

The rest of his frown disappeared completely as he pulled her closer to him, tightening his hold. "I'm never gonna be ashamed of us, sweets. No matter *who* doesn't like it."

She grinned, feeling the warmth of his words spread over her. She didn't think she could get much closer to him than she was, but in that moment, she knew her life *had* to have Rome in it, regardless.

"I promise to be worth all the trouble," she assured him. "This won't all be for nothing."

His hand cupped her chin. "You're already worth everything, Jazlyn."

She whimpered as she accepted his kiss, sliding her arms around his neck. If she hadn't been sure before, she was sure now; she was officially in love.

• • • •

IT ONLY TOOK A COUPLE of days for Rome to finally unload the frustration about the things Asha said to him. He and Jazlyn were heading back to her house after grabbing something to eat after work when he just blurted out how frustrated he was with his sister.

"I mean, I get that she's still feeling it from getting stood up at the altar," Rome ranted, jerking his truck around a turn. Jazlyn grabbed the dashboard but didn't comment. "And that it might be a while before she's over it. But does that mean she gets to just say whatever she wants to me, just because I did something she didn't like?"

"Nope."

"What if it was reversed and I said that shit to her, huh? Even if she was in the wrong, she'd have been crying and fussing and probably would've gone and told Mama on me."

"True."

"You and I both acknowledge that we could've handled all of this better," he kept on, swinging into Jazlyn's driveway and killing the engine. He turned towards her. "It's not like I feel good about cheating on Nell. I know she's a good woman that didn't deserve that. But am I supposed to feel bad for realizing I have feelings for you, even if it was at an inopportune time?"

"Of course not."

"Exactly. I love Asha and I get her being pissed at Ashton still, but I didn't deserve that. Being put in the same category as his bitch ass, I didn't deserve that."

"No, you didn't."

"And you know she still hasn't walked any of that back? I thought she would've sobered up from all that adrenaline and realized she was doing the most, even if she was still disappointed in me. But she hasn't called, hasn't texted, hasn't sent any messages through our parents, hasn't said a damn thing."

"That's jacked up."

"It's *beyond* jacked up." He blew out a long breath, wearily rubbing his forehead as he leaned his head against the window. Jazlyn just reached over and rubbed his thigh. She was responding in short answers because she knew Rome didn't need her input; he just needed to vent. He'd been stewing about that showdown with Asha since it happened and now the frustration was finally coming out. Jazlyn knew she just needed to let it happen.

After several moments, Rome's tense shoulders began to relax and his rapid breathing eased. Jazlyn just kept rubbing his leg, eying the cars moving up and down the street. She waited patiently, letting him process how he needed to.

Finally, his hand grabbed hers. When she looked over at him, he smiled at her. "Thanks, sweets."

She winked at him. "You know I got you."

They went inside, with only a tiny part of Jazlyn wondering if Marco was going to show up and see Rome's truck in her driveway. It was one time she wished she had a garage.

"You wanna play some cards?" she asked, pushing those thoughts aside. "Or there's a couple of good games on we can watch."

He looked at her. "I'll just catch the highlights later. I want us to get undressed and get in the bed so I can hold you the rest of the night."

Jazlyn immediately headed towards her bedroom, grabbing Rome's hand as she passed him. "Sounds like a plan to me."

Once they were each down to their underwear and under the covers in Jazlyn's queen-sized bed, Rome pulled Jazlyn to him, her back against his chest, and kissed her shoulder.

"I could get used to ending my days like this with you," he murmured, lazily trailing his lips along her skin. When she purred in response, he planted a slow, wet kiss to the side of her neck and held her tighter. "You're spoiling me, sweets."

"That's what I'm supposed to do, right?" She turned to grin at him, and he grabbed her chin to give a quick peck to her lips. "And it's certainly not one-sided."

"Good. It shouldn't be."

"Do you ever feel like this was how it was always supposed to be with us?" She swirled her nail around his wrist. "This just feels so natural and right...doesn't it seem hard to think that we were ever *just* friends?"

"No doubt," Rome didn't hesitate to reply. "I've thought about that a few times since we got together. It's hard to think of us as any other way than we are right now."

"So before we hooked up, you never looked at me and thought, 'damn I wanna hit that'?"

Rome laughed. "I didn't have those exact thoughts."

"What thoughts did you have, then?" she asked, giggling. "Or did you not look at me like that at all?"

"I mean, I noticed you; I knew you were attractive. And there were times here and there when I'd pay a little more attention to your pretty face or your ass than usual. But I loved our friendship so much I was satisfied just leaving it at that."

"Yeah, I know what you mean. It was the same with me; I absolutely noticed how cute you are, and a few times when you took your shirt off around me, it was a little hard to look away. But like you said; we were so tight that I wasn't going to do anything to mess things up or make it weird."

"So what do you think changed the night of the blizzard?"

"I don't know; it just felt like something shifted that night. When you came through for me with the supplies and everything, I just knew I didn't want you to leave. And the more I looked at you and was around you, the more I stopped thinking *friend* and started thinking 'I want him.'"

"It's wild because that's part of the reason I said I needed to leave; I was starting to look at you that way, too, and thought I should get some distance before I did something that we'd both regret. But I don't regret anything about what we did. Well, I definitely regret hurting other people, but I don't regret what changed between us."

"So..." Jazlyn chewed her lip briefly before turning onto her back and looking up at him. "I don't want to jump the gun or anything, but do you...do you ever think about us long-term? Do you want to go the distance with me?"

Rome's lips tilted up. "You proposing to me?"

She chuckled. "Not quite. But I *have* thought about you being my husband one day. And having one of your little freckled-face babies. And the more I think about it, the more I want it to happen." Her brown eyes studied him for signs that she was freaking him out. "Too soon?"

Unable to help it, Rome slid his hand to her cheek and leaned down to kiss her, the intensity of it surprising both of them. Hearing her say she wanted a future with him made him feel even better than he already did about their relationship. It hit right in his chest to know that she felt so strongly about him, *and* that she wasn't running from it or afraid to express it. Knowing they were on the same page made Rome think they could get through anything that came up together.

"No," he replied when he finally eased back from the kiss, trailing a finger along her jawline, "Not too soon, J. Not too soon at all. I love hearing that you want that with me."

"Is it mutual?" There was a hopeful tilt to her voice.

"It's definitely mutual. This isn't a short-term thing for me. You're my best friend, now you're my woman...and one day you'll be my wife. I don't want us to rush it but I can definitely see it."

Jazlyn grinned and pulled him on top of her. She couldn't think of a time when she'd been happier than she was right then.

"I love you, Rome."

"I love you, too."

She slid her arms and legs around him, pulling him down for a kiss. Their lovey-dovey feelings quickly gave way to lustful ones and their underwear was shed as it escalated to something more, with their moans getting louder, their hips matching in rhythm, and after a long shared lustful gaze, Rome sliding inside of her. They moved together, totally engrossed in their lovemaking and having no idea that Marco was riding up and down the street in front of Jazlyn's house.

Chapter 13

Rome was at a job site, helping his workers unload boxes of floor tile when he got a call. Since his phone was in his pocket, he glanced at his smartwatch. His movements slowed when he saw it was from Nell.

"What could she want?" he muttered to himself, continuing into the house whose floors they were there to replace. Knowing he didn't have time to stop and talk to her, he told himself he'd call her when they wrapped up the job, though he couldn't imagine what she would want to talk to him about. They had ended on amicable-enough terms and he wanted to just leave it at that.

It wasn't until hours later that Rome was able to return Nell's call. He took his time doing it; first going home, calling Jazlyn, taking a shower, and having dinner. He was stalling but he couldn't make himself just ignore her. Especially since she hadn't left a voicemail; just sent a text saying 'please call me.' It left him with no clue what this was about and a little on edge. He just hoped she hadn't decided that she wanted him back because he'd hate to have to disappoint her a second time.

Out of ways to stall, Rome finally sighed and dialed Nell's number. Part of him hoped she wouldn't answer but no such luck.

"Hey, Rome."

"Hey, Nell. What's up?"

"I appreciate you calling me back."

"No problem. What's on your mind?'

"Okay, I...well, I know that things are different between us now but, um..."

"Yeah?"

"Do you think that maybe...well, I've been thinking a lot about how things ended between us and I wanted to know..."

Rome tried to be patient since whatever she had to say was clearly hard for her to get out.

"I'm sorry," she finally sighed, sounding defeated and timid. "I thought I had this together but it's harder than I thought it would be, now that I'm actually talking to you."

"Okay..." Rome was flummoxed. He didn't want to try to coax whatever it was out of her because he wasn't sure he wanted to hear it, anyway. "Well...I'm not sure what I'm supposed to say, Nell."

"I'm sorry I bothered you for nothing. You, um, have a good night, Rome." She hung up.

"That was weird," Rome muttered, glancing at his phone screen before sliding it into the pocket of his basketball shorts. He'd surely be telling Jazlyn about this later, but for the time being, he just wanted to have a beer, watch the basketball game, and turn his mind off.

• • • •

IT WAS ROME'S MOTHER'S birthday, and usually he'd be amped about that. He loved his parents and always enjoyed spoiling them on their birthdays or holidays, or just because. But this year wouldn't be as good a time as it usually was.

They had a tradition that Rome and Asha came over and made dinner for their parents on their birthdays, and Rome was not looking forward to the tension that he knew would be thick in the air, being around his little sister. They hadn't spoken or communicated since their showdown at his house when she called him 'just another cheater', and he wasn't in a hurry to see her now. He wasn't as angry about what she said anymore, but he still wasn't thrilled to share a kitchen with her and try to put on a happy face for their parents' benefit. He just hoped she left the snarky comments at the door.

"It'll be fine, baby," Jazlyn assured him as he was getting ready to go. She was sitting in the middle of his bed, in one of his hoodies and some shorts, flipping through a salon magazine. "No matter what Asha says tonight, just let it roll off your back. Be the bigger person. You know she's just trying to get a rise out of you."

"I can't promise that I'll just be able to stand there and let her take shots without saying anything back," Rome muttered, glancing at her over his shoulder before going back to buttoning his shirt. "I can only hope that she's chilled out since I saw her last."

"Maybe she has. Maybe she'll apologize for that bullshit she said as soon as she sees you."

"Hmph. I don't know about all that."

"You never know."

"I wish you would come with me," Rome commented, going to sit next to her on the bed and placing a hand on her knee. "It would help me keep my cool if there's any bullshit."

"You know I'd love to go with you; I've been to a few of these birthday dinners. But given that Asha is pissed at me, too, I just don't want to bring any more dissention."

"I get it. I'm almost ready to tell you that I don't care about that, though, and to get some clothes on and come anyway."

She smiled, tweaking his chin. "Just go, focus on your parents and what you're there for, hang with them for a while, and then come on back. Then we can finish binge-watching *Bridgerton*."

"I still can't believe you got me watching that."

"Says the one that bugged me not to watch any of it without him."

"Guess you got me there." He chuckled as he leaned over for a kiss, which she gladly obliged. With a heavy sigh, Rome stood. "All right, well I guess I'd better be out. I don't put it past Asha to make some kind of slick comment about why I was late."

"Think positively. You got my gift for your mama?"

"Yeah, it's out in the living room with mine."

"All right. I'll be here. Can you bring me back some birthday cake?"

"Do I get to decide what we do with the frosting?"

Jazlyn grinned. "I just love how freaky you are."

"I know you do." He winked at her. "I'm gone. Be naked when I get back."

She laughed and shook her head, though she knew he wasn't joking.

Rome told himself to take Jazlyn's advice and think positively as he headed to his parents' house. It was possible that Asha had cooled off since they last talked. Maybe she realized how foul the things she said to him were and just hadn't known how to apologize. For all he knew, she'd be ready for him with a big hug when he got there.

"I'm surprised you showed up," Asha sneered almost as soon as he walked through the door. "Thought maybe you'd be up under your new homie-lover-friend Jazlyn. You neglect people for her now, right?"

So much for the hug.

Rome started to respond, but thought better of it. He wasn't going to let her rile him, especially when he hadn't even been there two minutes yet. "Where's Mama?"

"Find her yourself."

Gritting his teeth, he just turned and headed for the den. Part of him just wanted to drop his and Jazlyn's gifts off, kiss his mama and promise to take her to dinner another day, and go home.

His parents were in the den, laughing at something amongst themselves. Rome couldn't help but smile at that. He could picture him and Jazlyn there years down the line, and the image warmed him. It still blew him away that he and Jazlyn were so in sync with where they wanted their relationship to go. As rapid as it seemed, it just felt right to Rome. That one night during the blizzard really changed everything.

"Hey lovebirds," he finally called out, causing both of them to turn and look over their shoulders.

"Hey, sweetheart!" his mother, Georgia, greeted him with a wide smile. "When did you get here?"

"Just now." Rome stashed the bag with the gifts on the other loveseat before going over to kiss her cheek and slap hands with his dad. "Happy birthday, pretty lady."

"Did you bring Jazlyn with you?" Solomon asked, glancing behind Rome as if he expected her to appear.

"No, she figured it would be less tense if she sat this one out."

"That's a shame. But I get it."

"Well, I *don't* get it," Georgia huffed. "I don't get how a brother and sister can be so ugly towards each other."

"*Me*?" Rome marveled incredulously. "Asha is the one that's acting like I'm the worst person walking because I did one bad thing. Did she tell y'all what she said to me??"

"She gave us the gist of it," Solomon replied. "Through I'm sure she only provided the PG version."

"Hmph."

"I just wish you two could get past this," Georgia lamented. "I don't like it when my babies are fighting."

"Well, it's not me that's keeping all this negativity up. As soon as I came in here tonight, she started in on me with the slick comments. I don't know how we're gonna make this dinner together without somebody's feelings getting hurt."

"You're the older brother; act like it," Solomon ordered. "Asha is still stinging over Ashton and is lashing out at you. What you did probably just makes her think of what Ashton did, even though the situations are different. If it wasn't for what happened to her, she'd probably have messed with you about Jazlyn but she wouldn't be anywhere near this upset. I'd bet anything on it."

"I guess."

"Just go on in there, make the dinner, and be the mature one. And hurry up, 'cause we're hungry."

Rome couldn't help but chuckle. "All right, all right. I'll try to be the bigger person. What are we making for you tonight?"

"We've got steak and shrimp in there, wild rice, vegetables for salad, and I think there's some broccoli that's on its last legs," Georgia replied. "I know you'll make something delicious, baby; Mama taught you well. And I already made the cookies for the ice cream sandwiches."

"Yes!" Rome pumped his fist, making his parents laugh. Georgia's homemade ice cream sandwiches were Rome and Asha's favorite when they were kids, and they never stopped loving them as adults. It was the dessert of choice at all of their family gatherings and birthday dinners, even if they usually also had a cake or something else for Rome and Asha to take home afterwards.

Rome headed back to the kitchen, where he hoped Asha was getting a jump on things. But she was just leaning against the counter, munching on a carrot stick.

Choosing not to comment on that, Rome just removed his jacket and went to the sink to wash his hands.

"I figured you were in there tattling on me to Mama and Daddy, so I didn't start anything," Asha said from behind him. "You weren't about to have me in here doing all the work."

Rome wanted to tell her to go somewhere and he'd just make the dinner himself. He didn't know how they were going to work together with her acting like she was.

"I can get started on the dinner if you want to assemble the ice cream sandwiches," he told her, his back still turned. "Then they can be ready by the time dessert rolls around."

He expected another smart comment, but Asha just wordlessly got the ice cream from the freezer and the chopped nuts and chocolate chips from the pantry. Georgia had left the cookies she baked earlier on the counter.

Rome decided that this was going to be a quick meal; he usually would do some kind of marinade on the steaks or roast them with an herbed butter, but that would take too long. Cut those steaks up, chop the vegetables, and throw it all together with the shrimp for a delicious stir fry over the wild rice; that was the new plan. He'd make some quick cornbread to go with it. The sooner he could get out of close quarters with Asha, the better. It was too bad, though, because they used to always enjoy making their parents' birthday dinners together.

The siblings worked in silence, to Rome's relief. Asha pressed healthy scoops of vanilla ice cream between the thick chocolate chip cookies before rolling the edges in the chopped nuts or the chocolate chips. Rome minced garlic and herbs to add to the butter before slicing up the steak and the vegetables. He could see Asha glance at him a few times. It wasn't lost on him how fast he was going; almost like he was on a timed competition show. He wanted to get this over with as soon as possible.

"What are you making?"

Rome cut his eyes in her direction but didn't turn his head. "Stir fry."

"Stir fry?? That's what you chose to make for our mother's birthday dinner?"

"Yep."

"That's not good enough."

"Feel free to do it your damn self if you have a problem with it," he couldn't resist saying. "They always buy the ingredients and leave what to make up to us; it's nothing new. And anyway, Mama loves stir fry."

"Hmph." He hoped she would shut up after that, but he should've known better. "Where's Jazlyn?"

"Don't worry about where Jazlyn is."

"Maybe she's out fooling around; she doesn't have any other male friends, does she?"

Rome felt his hand grip the knife handle and he had to make himself put it down. He just went to fish the wok from under the cabinet so he could hurry up and get the stir fry going; the cornbread was already in the oven. Asha clearly wasn't going to leave him alone.

"Look, Asha," he finally turned around. "You wanna stay mad about something that has nothing to do with you? Fine, whatever. If you wanna be childish and petty, that's your business. But I'm not joining in with you. All I'm trying to do is cook this dinner for Mama and have a nice evening. That's it. You and me, we don't have to talk. So throw all the jabs you want; just know *you'll* be the one messing up Mama's birthday, not me.'"

He turned back to what he was doing, fully expecting Asha to come back at him. But to his surprise and relief, she remained quiet.

They managed to finish the dinner without further incident, and when everything was ready, everyone sat down at the dining room table to eat. Georgia and Solomon raved about the surf and turf stir fry Rome made, which only made Asha's jaws clench tighter. Clearly, she wanted them to admonish Rome for not making something more complicated, but they were more than satisfied with that and the cheddar jalapeño cornbread he made. Really, all Asha did was assemble the ice cream sandwiches; she didn't *make* anything.

Thankfully, their parents knew not to mention Jazlyn or much of anything regarding relationships, not wanting to trigger Asha. She'd been quiet all through the dinner, picking at her food and slouching in her seat. Rome ignored her but their parents kept trying to engage her in the conversation. To appease his parents, he even tried to include her, asking her something about work. But Asha just rolled her eyes at him and said nothing.

Everyone gave Georgia her birthday gifts once they were done with dinner. Rome grinned at how excited she got when he gave her a gift certificate for a deluxe spa day, a cashmere sweater, and some of the chocolate-covered cherries that she loved. He opted to wait to give her Jazlyn's gift in private, not needing any more drama. Asha glared at Rome as she presented Georgia with a leather-bound journal.

"Thank you for this, baby," Georgia smiled at Asha as she ran her fingers over the personalized cover. "This is so sweet."

"I'm glad you like it. I just wanted to get you something *meaningful*," Asha said pointedly, cutting her eyes at Rome. "I actually put some thought into this."

Solomon shot his daughter a warning glance and she clammed up, taking a sip of her red wine. Rome just shook his head.

"I know *I'm* ready for dessert," Georgia announced, trying to ease the tension. "Let's get those ice cream sandwiches, huh?"

"I'll get them," Rome offered, starting to stand up.

"No, *I'll* get them," Asha insisted as she jumped out of her chair, actually knocking it over. Her face was flushed as she picked it up, keeping her eyes averted. "I'm the one that made them."

Rome just shrugged and sat back down. "Knock yourself out."

Asha stomped out of the room and Solomon got up to follow her. Moments later, Rome could hear his dad's voice in the kitchen, though he couldn't make out exactly what Solomon was saying. The tone was unmistakable, though, and Rome tried to suppress his smile at his sister getting reamed out by their dad right then.

"Stop that."

Rome looked at his mother in surprise. "Stop what?"

"You're smiling."

"I can't smile at my beautiful mama on her birthday?"

Georgia shook her head, her softly curled auburn hair swinging around her face before she tucked some behind her ear. Her light brown eyes narrowed slightly.

"We both know that's not what you're over there smiling about."

"You can't prove that."

She sighed, though Rome could see the tiniest hint of amusement in her eyes. Georgia was close to both of her children but she had a soft spot for Rome, and they often teased each other like buddies as well as being mother and son. Though that didn't mean she wouldn't admonish him.

"I'd like to talk to you when we're done eating," she informed him. "So don't be trying to run out of here."

"What did *I* do?" Rome screeched, plastering a hand to his chest.

"Just don't leave."

Asha and Solomon entered with the ice cream sandwiches, and after Georgia and Solomon got theirs, Rome looked for another one rolled in chocolate chips, which were his favorite. But apparently Asha had only made two of those; she knew their parents preferred them, too. All that was left were the ones rolled in chopped nuts, which Rome didn't care much for. He glared at Asha, who just smirked. She knew full well that the chocolate chip ones were his favorite, and had purposely only made enough for their parents.

Biting down on his lip to avoid saying something incredibly disrespectful, Rome sat back in his seat.

Georgia looked at him. "What's wrong, baby?"

"Nothing. I'm good, Mama."

"How come you're not eating?" Solomon asked him. "You usually dive on these things."

"Yeah, usually." Rome shot a glare at his petty sister before grabbing one of the remaining ice cream sandwiches, using his spoon to scrape off the chopped nuts.

"Wait, there were only two chocolate chip ones?" Solomon looked at the remaining ice cream sandwiches. "That's it?"

"Yep." Rome bit into his ice cream sandwich, which was still delicious but not as good as it would've been with the chocolate chips. "That's it. Apparently there was a limited amount of those this time."

"Who made 'em?"

Rome just jerked his head in Asha's direction. "Your daughter."

Solomon and Georgia both turned to look at Asha, who shrank a little under their glares.

"It wasn't on purpose," she insisted, though everyone knew that was baloney. "I guess I was moving on autopilot and wasn't paying attention to how many of each kind I was making."

"Girl, you think we're stupid?" Solomon barked at her. "You're being childish, like you've been all damn night. Sitting over there frowning and pouting and not having anything positive to say. You've barely smiled or laughed since you got here, just like you've barely smiled or laughed in the last few weeks. You're letting that dumb-ass ex of yours have too much power over you, baby girl."

Asha stared at the table as Solomon polished off his sandwich and stood up. He leaned down to whisper something in his wife's ear before grabbing another ice cream sandwich and leaving the room. Asha looked after him in surprise, looking like she wanted to say something but she stopped herself.

Georgia wiped her mouth with her napkin and stood, also. "Asha, clean up the dishes."

"Yes, ma'am," Asha replied meekly.

"Rome, come with me."

Rome ignored Asha as he got up to follow his mother out of the room, stuffing the rest of his melting sandwich into his mouth and grabbing a napkin to wipe his hands. He wanted to be petty and tease her for getting put on clean-up duty, especially since that was a job they usually shared, but he kept his mouth shut. He didn't want to get scolded, too.

Georgia went to the living room and sat on the couch, patting the spot next to her. Rome sat, hoping she wasn't going to tell him to be the bigger person again and cut Asha some slack for how she'd been acting all evening. He didn't care how much she was still hurting over what Ashton did; that didn't give her license to be a total brat.

"What's up, Mama?"

Georgia looked at him evenly. She didn't look angry, to his relief. "Rome, why didn't you tell me about what happened between you and Nell? I had to hear about it from somebody else."

Rome knew that *somebody else* was his spiteful sister. "It wasn't exactly something I was proud of, Mama."

"I get that. But you should know by now that you can talk to me about anything."

"Yeah, but I also know how much you loved Nell. And I felt bad enough for what I did to her without you getting onto me for leaving who you wanted for your daughter-in-law."

"What I'm really disappointed about is *why* you left who I wanted for my future daughter-in-law."

Rome briefly hung his head. "I know. I cheated on Nell. I love where I'm at with Jazlyn but I hate that's the route I took to get there."

Georgia paused as if gathering her words. "Rome, sweetie, you know I love Jazlyn. I always have; she's darling. But I can't help having a sweet spot for Nell. And honestly, I think she's a better fit for you than Jazlyn is. You and Jazlyn are too much alike."

"Probably why we're such good friends, then, huh?"

"Being best friends doesn't always translate to being compatible lovers."

"That's not a problem," Rome insisted, his mind flashing a quick montage of him and Jazlyn in various sexual entanglements. Though he would guess that his mother wasn't just referring to sex.

"You know good and well what I mean, Rome," Georgia admonished, swatting his arm. "Stop being mannish."

"I didn't say anything!"

"Rome. You're grown and have every right to choose who you want to be with. And you're a good man; I'm sure there had to be a reason other than lust why you let things go there with Jazlyn while you were still with Nell."

"Nell and I had our issues; I can't deny that. Not that it excuses what I did, but it's the truth. I was wondering if we needed to end things before anything even went down with Jazlyn."

"Really? Did Nell know that?"

"Yes, she did. And to her credit, she tried to make some changes. But by then it was too late."

"I don't think it is," Georgia commented, her voice strong. "I think you're just on a high with Jazlyn because you two have entered a different realm of your relationship. You're probably thinking she's the one for you and that you're so in love and all of this. But I'm willing to bet that it'll be only a matter of time before this high wears off and you start back seeing things how they really are, *without* the rose-colored glasses."

Rome just looked at his mother in mild alarm. He knew she loved Nell and wouldn't be happy about him ending things with her, but he didn't expect her to accuse him of being sex drunk and incapable of knowing his own feelings. It was like she thought he was a teenager who'd just gotten some for the first time and was sprung out of his mind.

"You have a right to your opinion, Mama," he finally replied. "And I get that you love Nell. Feel free to stay in touch with her, if it's like that. But as far as me and her go as a couple, it's a wrap. And that's not changing."

"Never say never," she warned, reaching over to cup his chin. "Only the Lord knows what's gonna happen for sure."

"Mama..."

"I'm just saying. I feel in my heart that your chapter with Nell isn't quite over yet."

"I thought only the Lord knew for sure."

"Hush, Rome. You can disregard it all you want but mark my words."

Rome remembered the call from Nell where she was so nervous that she couldn't verbalize what she called for. "Do you and Nell have something cooked up to try to lure me back to her? Is that what this is all about?"

"No! This is as far as my involvement goes; I've never meddled in your relationships and I'm not about to start now. I just want to put it on your mind, is all. Nell loves you and would make a wonderful wife."

"So would Jazlyn."

"I'm sure she would. And again, I love Jazlyn. But you and Nell have unfinished business." Georgia held up her hands. "I won't say anything else."

Rome shook his head but didn't comment any further. His mother could think whatever she wanted. He and Nell were over.

Chapter 14

"**I** saw your latest nail tutorial, Jazlyn. It's crazy how many views and comments you got."

Jazlyn smiled at Ginger over her shoulder as they snaked through the full coffee shop, cups and pastries in hand. "I know, right? I honestly didn't think anyone would be interested in watching me do my own nails but apparently I was wrong."

"You need to be teaching somewhere instead of just working at the salon."

"No, ma'am. I don't have the patience for people like that."

"I get it 'cause I damn sure couldn't do that, either. It would just be cool if you could spread your skills to more than just at Clipped. Not that there's anything wrong with working there and I know you stay booked and busy, but..."

"No, I feel you. I do work for private clients on occasion, which is cool. What I'd really like to do is have my own line of nail polish. I love experimenting with colors and mixing them to come up with funkier ones, and seeing what crazy designs I can come up with."

"Yeah, I always look at your hands to see what your nails are looking like from week to week," Ginger commented with a smile. She eyed the blue, orange and white tie dye design on Jazlyn's long oval nails and shook her head, marveling. "I still don't know how you do that, and on yourself. I make a mess painting my short little nails one color."

Jazlyn laughed. "Years of practice. Plus it's how I relax."

Ginger's smile faded as she looked at something over Jazlyn's shoulder. "Well, I hope you've loaded up on your polish."

"What?"

"Hi, Jazlyn."

Jazlyn froze and her eyes widened. She shot a look at Ginger before neutralizing her expression and turning in her seat.

"Nell, hey. What's up?"

"Nothing much. Hi, Ginger."

Ginger nodded. "Hey."

Nell turned her dark eyes back to Jazlyn, who was trying not to look as nervous as she felt. She never anticipated running into Nell around town, since Rome said that Nell was taking a job out of state. And while Jazlyn was thrilled to be with Rome, that didn't mean she was totally devoid of feeling for how Nell got hurt in the process.

"Can I sit for a minute?" Nell asked.

Jazlyn was stumped for a split second but quickly snapped out of it. She waved a hand towards the empty chair at the table. "Sure."

Nell graciously pulled the chair out, taking a moment to pull her waist-length microbraids over one shoulder before lowering herself onto it. She looked as cute and casual as she always did in a mustard yellow cropped sweater, navy duster, dark skinny jeans, and knee-high boots that matched her sweater. Large gold hoops hung from her ears and several gold necklaces adorned her neck.

"I've been wanting to talk to you," Nell informed Jazlyn, both hands holding her paper cup. She bit her wine-colored lips, looking as nervous as Jazlyn felt. "But I admit I didn't know how to approach you since...what happened."

Jazlyn nodded, her face flaming. She hated feeling so nervous and tense but there was no way she could help it. "Understandable."

"I, um...I've been having a rough time, dealing with the breakup," Nell admitted. "I thought I would be okay after some time, but I'm really no better now than I was when Marco told me about everything. While part of me wasn't terribly surprised that you and Rome realized you had feelings for each other, there's still the part of me that feels slighted; like I didn't totally get my fair shot with him."

Jazlyn wanted to remind Nell and she and Rome were together for over ten months, but she didn't want to be snarky. Nell seemed willing to be amicable and Jazlyn wanted to keep it that way.

"I'm sorry about that, Nell," is what she finally said. "I get that it might not mean much or you probably won't believe me, but I do wish things could've gone down without anyone getting hurt."

"I do believe you." Nell took a fortifying breath before taking a long sip from her cup. Her maroon-colored nails tapped the outside of it. "While I *am* hurt that Rome left me for you, there's a part of me that can't be too mad at you for it. I had my issues that probably helped drive Rome away. And I know that you and he are crazy compatible; way more than he and I could be."

Not knowing how to respond, Jazlyn just gave a small nod.

"I've been to therapy a couple of times. They suggested that part of the reason I'm so stuck in this place I'm in is that I feel like I didn't have any closure. And also why I put off leaving like I initially planned."

Jazlyn felt like Nell was trying to work up to something, though she wasn't sure what. "Okay..."

"So I have a request," Nell finally announced. "Or, more like a favor."

"What's that?"

"It's gonna sound crazy..."

"I'm sensing that."

"When I got back to town after the blizzard, I told Rome that I was going to work on the issues that were causing problems between us," Nell informed. "Not too long after that, we were over. I really feel like I got shorted; that maybe if I'd had time, I could've proven to Rome that he didn't make a mistake in choosing me."

Ginger made a noise and sat back in her seat, seeming to sense where Nell was going with this. Jazlyn and Nell glanced at her before turning their eyes back to each other.

"Jazlyn, what I'm asking is for you to send Rome back to me so I can get my fair shot at winning his heart."

Nell's words were nervously rushed but she looked right into Jazlyn's eyes as she said them. Jazlyn couldn't believe her ears.

"Are you serious?" she marveled. "You're actually asking me to just...*give* Rome back to you, just like that?"

"Temporarily," Nell specified. "Long enough for me to feel like I've had a real chance to do what I was starting to before he ended things."

Sitting back in her own seat, Jazlyn tried to process all of this. Part of her wondered if Nell might be joking, but there wasn't a hint of amusement on Nell's face. She just sat there eying Jazlyn, waiting for her response.

"Nell, I have to admit that I don't really know how to respond to this," Jazlyn managed. "I totally acknowledge that Rome and I didn't go about things the right way but...he's *my* man now. And I'm not trying to give him up."

"It might not even work, what I'm suggesting. And I know it's a crazy thing to ask. But I really need this."

"Nell-"

"You and I were always cool, Jazlyn. I considered you a friend. Hopefully you'll take some time to think about what I'm asking as a fellow Black woman, and not as Rome's girlfriend." Nell took another sip from her cup as she eyed Jazlyn. "I love your nails. They're so pretty. As usual."

Jazlyn's face tightened. Something about Nell's words pricked her with conviction. Still, it was on her lips to refuse but she felt like Nell had managed to back her into a corner.

"Even if I agreed to this," she hedged, "Rome would still have to. What about that?"

"I'll leave that up to you to convince him," Nell replied smoothly. "He'll listen to you, which is why I couldn't take this request to him myself. He'd just politely brush me off. But you're his best friend; he wouldn't do that to you."

Ginger was staring at Jazlyn, waiting for her to laugh in Nell's face and send her on her way. She just knew there was no way her friend would actually consider this and figured that Jazlyn's silence was simply feigned consideration before she finally let Nell down easy.

But to Ginger's surprise, Jazlyn muttered, "I'll think about it."

Ginger's jaw dropped, but Nell grinned like she'd just hit the jackpot. She reached over and grabbed Jazlyn's hand briefly.

"I appreciate it, girl," Nell gushed, standing. "I knew I could count on you."

"Right."

"I'll look forward to hearing from you." Nell told her, turning to leave. "Or from Rome."

Jazlyn and Ginger watched Nell stride out the door before Ginger slowly turned to look at Jazlyn incredulously. "Are you fucking kidding me? Did that really just happen?"

Taking a deep breath, Jazlyn nodded as she took a gulp of her barely-warm hot chocolate with vanilla. "Apparently so."

"You know I'm talking about the part where you actually agreed to consider sending your man back to his ex, right? I cannot *believe* you fell for that guilt trip."

"Part of me can't, either. But the other part couldn't say no. Believe it or not, I can see where she's coming from."

Ginger's expression skewed. "Excuse me?"

"I never felt great about how Nell came out in all this, you know that."

"But you didn't feel bad for Marco?"

"Hell no. He cheated on me first."

"Jazlyn. Look, I get it; Nell is a nice woman. And the two of you were cool before the whole Rome thing. But *still*..."

"Look, all I said was that I'd think about it," Jazlyn defended, standing. She roughly pushed her chair back under the table and grabbed her uneaten cinnamon roll. "Nothing is a done deal. And Rome wouldn't even agree to this shit, anyway."

"Yeah, but Nell is expecting you to *convince* him," Ginger reminded her, standing herself. "Remember? She totally put it on you to give your man back to her."

"You think she was scheming?"

"Hell, don't *you*?"

"I think she was sincere in the whole needing closure thing." At Ginger's arched brow, Jazlyn sighed. "Okay, maybe there was a little bit of scheming in there. But she was *mostly* sincere, I believe."

"Regardless, Jazlyn-"

"Ginger, girl, I'm still trying to process all of this myself, okay?" Jazlyn exclaimed, stopping just outside the door of the coffee house. "I don't feel guilty for falling for Rome but there's a part of me that *does* feel bad for stabbing another Black woman in the back. A woman I called a friend. So I figure the least I could do is *consider* what she's asking for."

"I just think it's a bad idea," Ginger warned, biting into her cranberry scone. "This could go left real quick. Just buy her a nice gift or something but tell her you're not able to do it."

"I don't think there's anything I could buy for her that would replace getting her 'fair shot' at getting Rome back."

"I'm telling you, girl; tell her *no*." They started towards Jazlyn's car. "She'll get over it eventually. People get dumped all the time; I'm sure she's not as fragile as she's trying to act like."

"It's not about her being fragile; she really loves Rome."

"And I'm not trying to be insensitive to that but like you told her, Rome is *your* man. He chose to leave her and be with you, just like you left Marco to be with him. How do you think it's gonna look for you to now go to him and suggest he go back to Nell, even if it is just 'temporary'? There's no way to make that make any sense."

"It makes sense." Jazlyn chewed her lip. "I don't love it, but it makes sense."

"All right, fine," Ginger conceded. "Guess there's nothing I can say to change your mind. I just hope you know what you're doing."

Jazlyn sighed as she deactivated the alarm on her car and opened the door. "You and me both."

• • • •

A FEW HOURS LATER, Jazlyn was with Rome at his house, trying to forget about her earlier conversation with Nell. And him recalling how things went at his mother's birthday dinner didn't help ease her sprouting guilt much. Rome had dove on Jazlyn when he got home that night so they didn't get a chance to talk about it then, since they were otherwise 'occupied'. Frosting included.

"It seems like Asha is making no progress towards getting over what Ashton did to her," Rome told her, stuffing half a slice of pizza into his mouth. "She started with the bullshit as soon as I walked through the door."

"Can't say I'm too surprised. It's good that you didn't let her bait you into an argument, though."

"Only because I didn't want to ruin Mama's birthday. I would've loved to cuss her out."

"She's apparently still hurting."

"It's one thing to still be hurting. It's another to turn all that anger onto me instead of just dealing with it. She clearly needs to talk to somebody about all this 'cause she's not handling it well at all."

Nell's earlier confession about going to therapy played through Jazlyn's mind. "I still can't believe she was so petty as to do that thing with the ice cream sandwiches. Everyone knows you don't like chopped nuts."

"Yeah, well. As stupid as that was, it wasn't as bad as what Mama pulled me aside to talk about later."

Jazlyn looked at him curiously as she plucked a piece of pepperoni from her pizza slice and popped it into her mouth. "What?"

"Believe it or not, she felt she had to let me know that she misses Nell. Said she loves you but she thinks we're 'too much alike.'"

"How is that a bad thing?"

"I guess she was trying to say that Nell balances me out. Whatever."

"Can't say it makes me feel good to know that your mama prefers Nell over me."

"She can prefer it all she wants. It won't change anything, sweets. Nell is out of the picture and everyone will have to live with it."

Jazlyn chewed her lip. "Are you sure?"

Rome looked at her, eyebrows raised. "What do you mean, am I sure?"

"I mean..." Jazlyn shrugged and averted her eyes. "Do you ever feel like things between you and Nell were left...*unfinished*?"

"No," Rome responded quickly. "I don't. Why, do you?"

Jazlyn usually could talk to Rome about anything, but she couldn't find a way to tell him that she was starting to feel bad about how they came together. She heard cheating stories almost every day when she was at the salon, and the cheaters always got dragged over the coals. Jazlyn never thought of herself as part of that group but regardless of how she twisted it, she was. She could only wonder what her coworkers would say about her if they knew the real story behind how she and Rome got together.

"I guess I can see how Nell would think they were," she finally replied, her voice low.

"Since when?"

"I always could, Rome. I mean, I *am* a woman..."

"Where is this coming from?" Rome turned to look at her, frowning. "You're feeling sorry for Nell now?"

"Not really that; it's just..." She looked at Rome's confused face and lost her nerve. She couldn't make herself mention Nell's request. It had only been a few hours; she hadn't even decided if she was going to agree to it yet. "Never mind. Forget it."

Rome thankfully changed the subject and they went on with their evening, and Jazlyn managed to put Nell and what she asked for out of her mind.

The next morning, Jazlyn's alarm blasted at eight o'clock. She blindly reached over to silence it before stretching and sitting up, resisting the urge to hit the snooze button and grab a few more minutes. She yawned as she checked the notifications on her phone, noting that Marco had tagged her on Instagram. When she clicked on the post, though, her jaw dropped.

We're all built differently, but for you ladies that are a little flat-chested, here are some moves that can take you from (no disrespect) 'man chest' to 'man, they can't stop *staring* at my chest!'

Rage bolted through Jazlyn. Marco knew that her small breasts were a somewhat sensitive issue. She used to get teased for them incessantly growing up, and even as an adult it took her a long time to get past the paranoia that whatever man she was dating was eyeing any big-breasted woman they came across. Rome was really the first man she'd been with that hadn't teased her about her small chest or made some flippant comment about how she should consider having them pumped up. He treated them as if they were one of the sexiest things about her.

Jazlyn wasn't surprised that Marco was still being petty. It was one thing to blow up her phone with calls and leave her angry messages, but now he was tagging her in subliminal disses on social media?

Throwing the covers from her legs, she jumped out of bed. She found an empty box in one of her closets and went around grabbing any and everything Marco left over there; gifts or trinkets, one of his old small ring lights, some t-shirts, a resistance band, some protein powder he was paid to promote but decided he didn't like. Once Jazlyn had stuffed all traces and reminders of Marco into the box, she taped it shut and set it aside to have it sent to Marco's later. It would've been quicker to take it herself, but she didn't want to take a chance on running into him.

Going on about her day, Jazlyn put Marco and his pettiness out of her mind. But he grabbed her attention back when he had flowers delivered to her the next day.

"What the hell?" Jazlyn muttered when she read the note inside the yellow roses, saying how he apologized for all the headache he caused her. He asked her to call him, saying he'd like for them to talk.

Jazlyn tossed the card in the trash and gave the roses to a neighbor who she knew was a flower nut. She had no intention of calling Marco. He was clearly trying to mess with her, sneak-dissing her on social media one day and then sweet talking her the next. She knew Marco to be a lot of things, but flaky usually wasn't one of them.

Then the gifts started. For the next few days, a different gift from Marco showed up on her doorstep; gift baskets, more flowers, other boxes she didn't bother opening. She just stuffed it all in a corner, having no intention of addressing them or Marco.

"He's playing with me," she groused to Ginger over the phone one evening. "I don't know what the end game is, but Marco is clearly on some bullshit."

"Why are you keeping all that stuff? Send it back."

"Too much trouble. I'm not using or opening any of it."

"*He* doesn't know that. He probably thinks he's wearing you down. By keeping it, you're just encouraging him to keep this going. Especially since you haven't bothered to tell him to stop sending them."

Jazlyn hadn't considered that. She was probably making things worse by accepting all the gifts, whether she enjoyed them or not.

"Shit," she mumbled.

"What did Rome say when Marco started sending all that stuff?"

"I haven't told Rome about it."

"Why not?"

"He's just gonna trip. You know he can't stand Marco as it is."

"So what? I bet he'd wanna know that another man is sending his woman gifts. You know you'd feel some kind of way if Nell started showering him with stuff and he kept it from you."

Another good point. Jazlyn blew out a long breath and groaned. "Damn, why does everything have to be so *difficult*??"

"It's designed that way. And believe me, it doesn't stop after you get married; Zion and I are *still* dealing with stuff. But it helps us appreciate the good shit when we get it."

"True."

"I'm telling you, Jazlyn; send that shit back to Marco and tell him to fuck off. Don't let him keep thinking he's buttering you up. Pretty soon he'll start trying to make some kind of move on you."

That was the last thing Jazlyn needed. She wished Marco would just get over it and leave her alone.

• • • •

JAZLYN WAS IN THE KITCHEN when Rome came over later that night.

"Hey, sweets," he greeted, going over to kiss her. He wrapped his arms around her from behind and briefly buried his face in her neck. "You in here trying to cook?"

She shot him a look. "I know you're not trying to clown when I'm making a romantic dinner for you."

Rome peered at the pots and pans on the stove. "This doesn't look like spaghetti."

"It's not spaghetti. I *do* make other stuff, you know."

"Yeah? Wasn't aware of that. I appreciate you doing all this. What's on the menu?"

"Shrimp scampi and garlic bread."

"Yum. What's the occasion? Celebrating our two-month anniversary?"

Jazlyn looked at him. "Is that today?"

Rome chuckled. "I was just messing with you. And anyway, anniversary celebrations are more of a yearly thing for me."

"Thank god." Jazlyn tried to focus on mincing the garlic without cutting herself. She started to buy it already minced but didn't want to take any shortcuts with this meal, for whatever reason. She wanted to go all out for Rome, even if it was a relatively simple meal for most other people.

"Need any help?"

"I've got it. Go watch TV or something; it shouldn't take too long. I've got the pasta boiling now."

"Cool."

Rome shrugged out of his jacket as he headed into the living room and turned on the television. Jazlyn's house wasn't open concept but her small galley kitchen opened right into the living room, and she could still hold conversations with any guests while she cooked. She could hear him change the channel to some entertainment show, where (of course) the first story they talked about was one celebrity committing adultery against another one. Two stories later, it was about some rapper who was reported to be creeping around with his girlfriend's assistant. Jazlyn threw back her head in disbelief. If she didn't know better, she'd think it was some kind of sign.

"Dammit!" She quickly turned the heat down on the stove when she realized the garlic and shallots were burning. She hurriedly fanned the smoke alarm with the dish towel before it started blaring, then remembered the pasta. It was boiling rather vigorously, splashing a little over the pot and a few scalding drops flying to her bare arm, causing her jump back some. She lifted the linguine with her tongs, and realized she'd forgotten to stir it when it came out in one big clump.

"Great," she muttered. "That's just *great*!"

"You say something, sweets?" Rome called from the living room.

"Oh...no," Jazlyn distractedly replied, trying to remember what she did with her colander. When she rambled around under her cabinets and couldn't find it, she just tried to shake most of the water out of the clump of pasta and then plunk it into the pan with the garlic butter sauce, which by then had reduced to practically nothing. And of course it was then that she remembered she had the shrimp over-cooking in another pan, and she hurried and turned that burner off, removing the pan from the stove and looking around at her limited counter space for a place to put it that was away from the stove.

"Is something burning?"

The garlic bread. Jazlyn shimmied her hand into the oven mitt and yanked the pan of burnt bread from the oven, pushing aside the toaster and the blender to set it on the counter. Defeated and over it, she clanked the pan with the shrimp on top of the one with the pasta and slunk against the counter with her face in her hands.

Rome appeared in the entrance to the kitchen. He surveyed the mess before calmly going over to turn off the stove burners and the oven. Jazlyn knew he was there but kept her face covered, thoroughly embarrassed.

"Chinese or Italian?" he asked, his voice giving no credence to the ruined food or the stench of burned garlic in the air.

"*Not* Italian," Jazlyn replied, her face still covered.

"I got you."

Rome opened a delivery app on his phone and placed the order before taking Jazlyn's hand and leading her into the living room. He pulled her down onto the couch with him, on his lap, and wrapped his arms around her. Jazlyn curled up against him, grateful that he was just being quiet for the moment. He could tell she was embarrassed and thankfully wasn't teasing her for her failed attempt at cooking for him, which she appreciated. She knew if it had been Marco, he would clown her incessantly.

Speaking of Marco, Jazlyn was sure to put away the gifts he'd been sending her, which she still hadn't opened or sent back. She'd been so busy at work and with editing her nail videos the past couple of days and just hadn't gotten around to it, but she knew she didn't want Rome to see them. He wouldn't be happy at all and Jazlyn didn't need the headache.

When their food arrived, they ate while they watched the next episode of *Bridgerton*. Jazlyn hated that she had messed up their evening, even though Rome wasn't upset about it at all. He had no idea that she had partially wanted to cook for him out of guilt. She had actually made pasta from scratch and cut up her own bread and mixed up garlic butter that she'd put way too much salt into because she was trying to work up the nerve to tell Rome about Nell's request. Jazlyn knew if too many more days went by, Nell would reach out to her for an update. And Jazlyn just didn't know how to bring this up to Rome, or how she was going to explain why she was beginning to think it wasn't that bad of an idea.

"You okay?" Rome asked her.

"Yeah." Jazlyn twirled lo mein around her fork but made no move to eat it. "Just feeling a little ridiculous."

"No need for that. I appreciate what you tried to do."

"I just can't believe I messed it up like that."

"Don't worry about it, sweets. You're certainly not the first person to burn stuff in the kitchen."

"Burned, overcooked, ruined..."

"I'm telling you, it's all good," Rome assured her with a smile. He reached over and rubbed the back of her neck. "How come you're beating yourself up like this? Usually you'd just brush it off and laugh about it."

"Yeah..." Jazlyn knew he was right. In just about any other instance, this wouldn't have been that big of a deal to her; she'd probably be making fun of herself for even trying to do all that. But everything that was weighing on her mind had her more emotional than usual, and she wasn't to the point where she could see the humor in it yet.

"Hey...what's up with you?" Rome asked, sensing there was something Jazlyn wasn't telling him. He peered at her, concerned. "You haven't seemed like yourself since I got here."

She hunched a shoulder. "Guess I've just got some stuff on my mind."

"Anything you wanna talk about?"

She looked over at him and felt her heart swell. It amazed her how much she loved this man. For eight years, he had just been her buddy but now, she looked at him and saw her future. Rome was it for her; she was sure of it.

This was her opening to tell him what she needed to tell him. She put her food on the coffee table and leaned into him, caressing his face with her hand. She opened her mouth to tell him but what came out was, "I appreciate you so much."

He smiled, pulling her closer. "I appreciate you too, sweets."

"I just don't want anything to...I don't want this to end."

He frowned slightly. "I'm not planning on it ending any time soon. It's you and me."

She climbed onto his lap and kissed him, taking his face in both hands. Her tongue stroked against his, moaning when his hands slid up the back of her shirt. Jazlyn broke the kiss to lean back and quickly yank her shirt off then reach back and unclasp her bra. Then she went for Rome's shirt. Once both of their tops were on the floor next to the couch, their hungry kiss resumed, Jazlyn grabbing one of Rome's hands and placing it on her breast. The way he caressed and pleasured it with his fingers and his mouth and tongue made her forget about everything else; Nell's unusual request, Marco's flip-flopping actions, and Ginger's warnings. Jazlyn was more than glad to let herself get distracted from all of that for the time being, ignoring the reality that she'd have to deal with it sooner rather than later.

Chapter 15

Jazlyn might have used seduction to delay telling Rome what she needed to tell him, but she knew that wouldn't work every time. She knew he could tell something was off with her, and instead of just coming clean, she distracted him with sex. She had punked out again when it came to speaking up about something to Rome, and it frustrated her.

And the more time passed without her telling Rome about Nell's request, the more reminders or examples of cheaters came to her attention. It amazed her that she felt so conflicted now when she had almost no guilt right after she slept with Rome the night of the blizzard. She didn't know what changed, but she did know she couldn't go on like this. Every time she heard or read about someone stepping out on their significant other, or heard a song about being in love with someone other than who they were with, or when her coworkers gossiped about it in some way (which seemed to be almost daily), Jazlyn felt more and more prickles of stinging guilt. She knew she'd drive herself crazy if she didn't go ahead and address it.

Especially since Nell seemed to be getting impatient. She sent Jazlyn a text full of question marks, clearly asking what the deal was with her request.

Thankfully, Rome got really busy with work and hadn't been able to come over for a couple of nights, to Jazlyn's relief. And Yvonne, Jazlyn's boss at Clipped, did her a favor she didn't even think she wanted towards the end of one work day.

"Hey Jazlyn, what do you think about teaching a couple of night classes?"

Jazlyn's head snapped up from where she was cleaning her work station. "Huh?"

"You know I also own a cosmetology school. It's small, but we stay full every term. The lady that was teaching the nails portion is about to have her first child, so she'll be gone for a while. What do you think about filling in for her while she's on leave?"

"Oh wow; I'm not sure how good I'd be. I've never taught anything."

"But you know your stuff. Not to mention you're *by far* my most requested nail tech here. I'm sure you'll get the hang of it. The current teacher has already said she'd be more than willing to get you up to speed and answer any questions you might have. And it won't be forever."

As much as Jazlyn hadn't been interested in teaching when Ginger suggested it, she was intrigued by the idea now. Mainly because preparing for that would help her avoid dealing with the whole Nell and Rome issue.

"Why not," she replied, shrugging a shoulder. "Sure, I'll do it."

"Great! You're saving me from having to go through the tedious process of finding someone and interviewing them and blah blah blah. I owe you one. We'll talk about the pay and the other particulars later."

Jazlyn was just relieved that she had something to distract her from her love life mess.

When she talked to Rome late that night, Jazlyn didn't even mention the teaching opportunity. She let him dominate the conversation. And he could clearly tell something was off with her.

"What's up with you, J? You seem off."

"What do you mean?" Jazlyn asked, managing to keep her voice even.

"Something is clearly on your mind. Usually you talk my ear off but lately I have to drag stuff out of you. What's going on?"

"Nothing, I'm sorry. It's...I just can't talk to you about it yet."

Rome was quiet. "Since when can't you talk to me about anything?"

"Don't take that the wrong way. I just have to finish wrapping my mind around it first. You'll find out eventually."

"If it's something bad, I'd rather you just tell me now. I'm not trying to be blindsided."

"You won't be, Rome. You'll know everything soon."

He let it go, but Jazlyn knew he was suspicious.

Rome *was* suspicious. He knew Jazlyn well enough to know when something was bothering her; she usually talked or fussed about it until it was dealt with or became a non-issue. But when something was *really* under her skin, she tended to shut down. And he could feel her pulling away from him, and the reasons swimming through his head as to why that might be worried him.

Was she having second thoughts about them? He thought they were good now that their previous relationships were over and they were in the clear, but maybe not. Or maybe there was something else going on that she hadn't told him about. Was Marco bothering her again? Rome hated not knowing what was going on.

And he sensed that she knew he wouldn't like whatever it was, otherwise she would have told him already. Sometimes Jazlyn tended to *over*-share with him so for her to be so tight-lipped, it had to be something big.

Rome hoped with everything in him that she wasn't starting to doubt their relationship. That she wasn't considering telling him they needed to go back to being just friends. Or worse, nothing at all.

He was glad when he got a much-needed distraction in the form of a call from his dad, Solomon.

"How's it going, son?"

"It's going." Rome poured too much sugar into his coffee. "Just doing my thing over here."

"How's Jazlyn?"

Rome didn't want to get into their issues, since he wasn't even sure what they were. "She's good."

"Now to ask you something I'm sure I already know the answer to: have you talked to your sister?"

Rome frowned as he picked up his cup and took a sip. "Of course not."

"That's what I figured. I was hoping I was wrong, but..."

"Dad, come on. You saw how she was acting towards me on Mama's birthday. And I didn't even tell you about the crap she said to me in the kitchen while we were making dinner. All she brings is negative energy lately and I don't have time for that."

"I get it, son...she hasn't been very pleasant to be around in general lately. But I'm hoping you can cut her a little slack."

"And why would I do that?"

"Because she just got hit with another blow on the Ashton front. She found out he's seeing someone. *And* it's someone she knows. Apparently the idiot has been telling his business on social media again and one of her friends showed it to her. She's been kind of a mess since."

"Damn." Rome set his coffee cup on the counter with a sigh. As upset as he was with his sister, he didn't like to hear that.

"Right."

"I can't believe Ashton is so insensitive. He had to know she'd see that at some point. It seems like he's just trying to rub it in her face now."

"He probably is. And if I catch him in person, I'm gonna be doing some stuff to *his* face. But I'm good in the meantime, though."

"Dad. What did you do?"

"Nothing you need to know about. But he'll be too busy dealing with that to worry about posting more of his crap any time soon, I'll tell you that."

Rome couldn't help but laugh. His dad was pretty low-key most of the time, but he could be vicious when pissed off. And when it came to his family, Solomon didn't play at all.

"Enough said," Rome conceded.

"So hopefully you'll consider going to see Asha," Solomon commented. "You know she's stubborn so she wouldn't admit this but she needs her big brother right now."

Rome knew it wouldn't be as simple as that, but he couldn't make himself ignore Asha, knowing what she was dealing with. He could push his frustration with her to the side to make sure she was okay. "All right. I'll go check on her."

"That's my boy."

• • • •

ROME KNEW JAZLYN WAS avoiding him. And just like she knew that he needed time to process things when he was upset, he knew that leaving her alone to deal with whatever was bugging her was the best thing. As long as he kept asking her what was wrong, she'd put more energy into denying it than dealing with it. He didn't love stepping back and giving her space because he missed her, but he wanted them to get past this weird place they were in. And it wasn't all that hard to do since she was avoiding him, anyway.

So Rome was glad when Jazlyn finally let him know she was ready to talk. She asked him to come over, and he could see the nervousness on her face when he arrived. Before they got into whatever was on her mind, Rome pulled her in for a long hug.

"It's good to see you," he murmured into her ear. "I've missed you.

"I've missed you, too." She held onto him a moment longer, realizing how much she missed being in his arms. She knew she had to put an end to this standstill they were on and finally come clean about what was bothering her. It was only fair to him, and she was tired of stressing over this Nell situation. She'd gone over every outcome she could conjure every which way in her mind, and mentally, she was drained. Whatever came of it, she wanted to finally just deal with it.

Taking his hand, Jazlyn led Rome back to her bedroom. She got settled on her bed and waited for Rome to kick off his shoes and follow suit. Once he was sitting across from her, she scooted a little closer to him and placed a hand on his knee, taking a fortifying breath.

"I'm sorry I've been acting so weird lately," she began. "But I had an encounter a little while back that I wasn't quite sure how to handle."

Rome frowned curiously. "What kind of encounter? With Marco?"

"No, that's not who I'm talking about." She still hadn't told him about Marco's subliminal Instagram diss and subsequent gifts. What she was about to tell him was bad enough without adding that to it. "It was with Nell."

"Nell? Where did you see her?"

"At the coffeehouse. Ginger and I were there and Nell approached us."

"Was she trying to start something? And what is she even still doing here? She said she was taking some job out of town."

"Yeah, well...there's a reason she's still here. It turns out she's having some trouble moving on from the breakup with you."

"Okay..."

"Rome, you remember that stuff she said about proving her love for you or whatever? Well, she feels like she didn't get a fair chance to do that."

"A fair chance? By then I already knew I wanted you; there really wasn't anything Nell could have done that would have made any difference."

"Well, still. She feels cheated."

"She said that?"

"That and more."

"Hell. What else? Not that I'm sure I wanna hear it."

"The humdinger is that she wants me to... to give her the chance she feels she missed out on. She wants me to let her try to finish what she set out to do before Marco told her about us."

"Wait a minute," Rome held up a hand. "Are you telling me that Nell actually asked you to break up with me?"

"Not exactly. She said it would only be temporary. Like a month or two. Enough time for her to-"

"What kind of crazy shit is this? She expects you to just *give* me back to her? And for me to agree to it??"

"She feels like she didn't get any closure, Rome. She's been to therapy and everything. That's why she hasn't left town; she feels you two have unfinished business."

"We don't have any unfinished business. I don't love the way things went down with Nell but she told *me* she accepted it; if she's changed her mind about that, it's just too bad."

"Come on, Rome..."

"Are you seriously falling for this? What did you tell her when she asked you this shit?"

Jazlyn looked away. "I told her I'd think about it."

"You what??"

"The way she broke it down, I admit I felt a little guilty," Jazlyn admitted. "And that's what's been so heavy on my mind ever since; it started eating at me that I stabbed her in the back the way I did, even if it wasn't on some scheming, malicious tip. Nell and I were mad cool and I got with her man; the more I thought about it, the more it got to me."

"It didn't seem to bother you when it happened."

"I know, but it does now. I've been getting that bad feeling again; that's another part of what's had me acting so weird. I feel like what we did is going to come back on us some kind of way. And we know how right I was the last time my gut said something was off."

"Okay, the Asha situation might've been spot-on but let's not act like your gut was accurate every other time."

" Rome. We hurt people with what we did; there's no way we just get away with that. It's not like I'm saying we should break up but if we can do anything to make things better for the people we used to be in love with, why not? I just...my guilt has been growing by the day and it's just gonna get worse if we don't do something. We both loved Nell. And I don't think it would be the worst thing if we gave her what she's asking for."

Rome reared back, incredulous. "Are you kidding me with this, J?"

"No, Rome. When you really think about it, it's not *that* crazy of a request."

"The hell it isn't! What does she think is gonna happen in a month?"

"Maybe nothing. But at least she'll feel like she got her shot."

"We were together ten months!"

"I know that. But she didn't tell you about her issues with her feelings and stuff until right before you two broke up, and had no idea that you were already halfway out the door by then. She was totally blindsided. Rome, look, I know this is unusual but can you please just do it?"

"Just do it. You can't be serious. I don't want to waste time acting with Nell, Jazlyn. My time with her is over; I only want you."

"I want you, too, Rome. I'm not asking you to *actually* go back to her; just grant her this so she'll have some peace of mind."

"Stop. This isn't about her peace of mind, Jazlyn; it's about relieving your guilt. You wanna do this for you, not for her."

"It can be both."

"But more for you."

"It's sixty-forty. But whatever. Regardless of how it turns out, we'll at least be able to say we gave her a chance to win you back, even if we both know it's not gonna happen. One month isn't that long, Rome. Can you please just do it? If not for Nell, for me? I hate feeling guilty like this and I know I won't be able to get past it until this is done."

"Well, you're gonna have to find another way to deal with it, J., 'cause that's not happening."

"What about if I give you back that hoodie I took that you've been bugging me about?"

"Are you seriously trying to bribe me? And with something that's already mine, at that?"

"Yes. Blatantly. That's how much I want you to agree to this. Look, baby, it's not that I enjoy the thought of...*handing* you off to another woman, regardless of what the reason is. But I don't see us being able to really move forward until we do her this solid. I know it's asking a lot but please, please do this."

Rome sighed and rubbed a hand over his hair.

"You know Nell is a good woman," Jazlyn continued, sensing that she was finally starting to get to him. "And she's not unreasonable. For her to even ask for something like this, to my face, it must mean a hell of a lot to her. And you said yourself that you hated how she came out in this situation."

"All right, all right, you can stop piling on. I got it."

"Where are you going?" Jazlyn asked when he slid off the bed and headed for the closet.

"To get my hoodie."

Jazlyn grinned, relieved. But her relief turned to horror when she remembered what she had stashed away in her closet.

"What's all this, J?"

Squeezing her eyes shut, Jazlyn cursed under her breath. She'd temporarily forgotten about putting the gifts from Marco in there.

"Nothing, really," she replied, trying to sound convincing. But with the way Rome was perusing all of the packages, she could tell he wasn't buying it. And she knew it was only a matter of seconds before he noticed who the packages were from.

"Wait...Marco's been sending you stuff?" Rome stepped halfway out of the closet, a deep scowl marring his face. "What the hell is going on? Are these gifts?"

Sighing, Jazlyn eased off the bed. "Yeah."

"Why is he buying you gifts? And why did you accept them?"

"I guess he calls himself trying to win me back. Or apologize for being such a jackass."

"He's always been a jackass. That still doesn't explain why you have shit he gave you piled up in your closet."

"Rome, it's not a big deal. You see they're not even open. I was going to send them back."

"Oh, you were gonna send them back before telling me anything about it, huh?" Rome shook his head, moving to put his shoes back on.

Jazlyn rushed over to him. "What are you doing? You're about to leave?"

"I guess now I see why you're pushing so hard for this bullshit with Nell," Rome snapped, stuffing his foot into his Jordans. "If I'm back with her, then you're free to go back to Marco, right?"

Her jaw dropped. "Are you fucking kidding me??"

"How else do you explain getting all this shit from him and not telling me about it? What else don't I know about, huh? If I had a closetful of gifts from some other woman, you wouldn't like that shit either, Jazlyn."

She took a breath. "Okay, I should've told you about the gifts. But it doesn't mean anything, Rome, come on! You know I don't want Marco; I only want you!"

"Right." Rome stopped and glared at her. "You sure haven't been acting like it lately. And now I see why."

"Rome!" Jazlyn hurried after him as he stormed out of her bedroom. She managed to catch up to him, grabbing his arm before he could reach for the doorknob on the front door. "You cannot be serious with this! The *only* reason I didn't say anything about those gifts from Marco was because I knew you'd fly off the handle about it like you're doing now. I told you why I've been acting so strange lately and it has *nothing* to do with Marco. But since you've finally agreed to this thing with Nell-"

"Yeah, you can dead that," Rome cut her off. "I'm not doing that shit."

"Rome. You were gonna agree to it a minute ago."

"Yeah, well that was then and this is now. If you don't like it, you've got a bunch of gifts you can open to make yourself feel better."

He stepped around her and walked out, slamming the door behind him.

Chapter 16

Jazlyn wanted to call Rome, but she figured the best thing to do would be to give him time to calm down. Once his anger subsided, he'd realize how ridiculous the idea of her wanting Marco back was.

After getting another question mark-filled text from Nell, Jazlyn headed over to Rome's early the next morning, wanting to catch him before he headed off to work. She didn't want to wait all day (or longer) for them to work this out.

To her surprise, though, he'd already left. So she headed to his office, hoping he wasn't out on a job.

He didn't look too surprised when she knocked and poked her head in. "Hey."

"Hey. Can I come in?"

He nodded, and she fully entered the office, closing the door behind her. She didn't want his employees hearing their drama.

"Are you ready to talk or are you still pissed like you were last night?"

He looked at her for a moment before sighing heavily. "I'm cool. When I thought about it, I realized how much I was tripping, about the gifts and stuff. I just wish you'd told me about it."

"I should have. That's my bad. I was just trying to avoid more drama but I guess I didn't consider how badly not telling you would come across. I'm sorry about that."

"I'm sorry, too."

She hesitated slightly. "What about the Nell issue?"

Rome sighed again. "I still don't wanna do that, Jazlyn."

"I get it. But can you understand why it's so important to me that you do?"

"I guess…"

"Rome, our romantic relationship didn't start off on the most honorable foot, and maybe it's paranoia, but I don't want that kind of energy to trail us forever. I'm hoping that giving Nell what she's asking for will help clear our relationship karma."

"Marco was affected by this, too. What about that part of it?"

"He cheated on me first. So he got his karma already."

Tapping his thumb on the arm of his chair, Rome looked at his desk thoughtfully. "And this is really important to you, huh?"

"Yeah. It is."

Standing, Rome rounded the desk and grabbed her hand, pulling her up from the chair she was perched on the edge of to stand between his legs as he sat on the edge of his desk. He leaned down and placed a soft kiss on her lips.

"I'm gonna seriously consider it, okay? And I'm not gonna take forever to do it; before this time tomorrow, I'll let you know one way or another."

Jazlyn had hoped he would just go ahead and agree, but she wasn't going to complain. At least he wasn't flat-out refusing.

"Okay," she acquiesced, sliding her arms around his waist. "That's fair. It *is* a weird request, after all."

"To say the least."

"I don't suppose some office head will help speed up the decision-making process, huh?"

Rome's eyes darkened. "Don't tease me."

"Does that door lock?"

Wasting no time, Rome stepped over and locked the door to the office, and Jazlyn yanked him to her by his waistband. She sat back down in the chair and swiftly but smoothly undid his pants, pushing them down to his ankles.

"You know you can't be loud, right?" she reminded him with a teasing smile as she gave him a few leisurely strokes.

"I can do what I want; I'm the boss up in here," Rome grunted, biting his lip as he watched her.

"Yeah, okay then, boss." She swirled her tongue around the head of his dick, earning a few whispered expletives. She blocked his hand when he tried to grab her hair. "You can't be messing my hair up. I have to go to work after this."

"You can't expect me not to touch you when -*shit*," Rome muttered as Jazlyn slid her mouth over him, taking as much of him in as she could. His hands gripped the edge of his desk as she proceeded to pleasure him, unable to resist her own moans from escaping. She loved sucking him and licking him and kissing him, making him feel amazing. She loved discovering new spots on his body that drove him crazy. And she loved making him lose his mind in the best way.

Needing to touch her, Rome grabbed the back of Jazlyn's neck as he pumped into her mouth, the momentum building. He threw his head back and bit his bottom lip to keep from letting anyone in the vicinity of his office know he was about to have a major orgasm.

"You like that?" Jazlyn asked, her lips releasing him with a loud pop.

"Hell yeah..."

"You about to come?"

"Mmm-hmm..."

"You gonna come in my mouth?"

"*Fuck*, Jazlyn..."

"I want you to."

"I'll come wherever you want me to. *Shit!*"

In the next few seconds, Rome was growling and shuddering as Jazlyn sucked him through his orgasm, knocking a few items off his desk with loud clanks because he couldn't control his hand in the moment. The other hand that was clamped to the back of Jazlyn's head held her in place as he released the last drops, his hips locked. It wasn't until Jazlyn slid her mouth off of him that he eased his hold on her.

"We good?" Jazlyn asked after a few breathy moments, standing.

"You sure you have to go to work? There's some more stuff I want to do with you on this desk."

Jazlyn bit her lip as she checked her watch. "I have appointments coming in about half an hour. But I can meet you back here later, at the end of the day."

"That's a bet." He pulled her to him, giving her a deep kiss. "Then we can both get as loud as we want."

• • • •

JAZLYN WAS TRYING UNSUCCESSFULLY to wipe the grin off her face as she worked on the material for her upcoming class. She had in fact gone back to Rome's office when they were both done with work, and he gave her twice the pleasure she had given him that morning. When she thought of how he had her laid out on top of his desk, naked and writhing as he buried his face between her legs, and how she then straddled him in the desk chair and they were going at it so hard that the chair banged against the wall behind the desk, a delicious ripple shot through her. It was only because Rome had to go see Asha that she didn't go home with him so they could continue the fun. Jazlyn had never felt addicted to anyone but she surely felt like that with Rome; she just couldn't get enough of him.

She tried to focus on the class materials that Yvonne had given her. Part of Jazlyn already regretted agreeing to teach a class, as she had never done anything like it before and never desired to, but at least Yvonne told her she could make the class her own and didn't have to follow the real teacher's lesson plans to the letter. And Jazlyn had already talked to the teacher a couple of times for tips and encouragement. Thankfully they were already past the stuff about nail anatomy and diseases and all that kind of stuff and were onto the practical part of the training, which was more up Jazlyn's alley.

Jazlyn was jotting down some notes when there was a knock on her door. She immediately wondered if it was Rome coming to get some more loving, but remembered he was going to see his sister, plus he would have texted or called first. And he had a key. Part of her felt bad for hoping that he and Asha got to arguing and Rome had come right over to vent and take his mind off of it. Jazlyn was more than willing to help him feel better, if that was the case.

Her good mood deflated, though, when she saw it was Marco.

"What the hell you want?" she called out.

"Can we talk?"

"Why didn't you just call, Marco?"

"Because you blocked me. And even if you didn't, you wouldn't have answered. You know it and I know it."

"Well, what does that tell you?"

"Jazlyn."

"What, Marco? We don't have anything to talk about."

"Look, if you're worried about me popping off, I promise I'm not. I'll keep my cool, regardless of what you say."

Jazlyn doubted that, but found herself opening the door, anyway. At least him showing up meant she could save herself the trouble of sending all of his gifts back.

"Make it quick; I'm busy," she ordered, leaving him standing in the doorway and going back to her small kitchen table where she'd been working.

"I appreciate the time," Marco stated, coming inside and closing the door behind him. He followed Jazlyn, eying the papers and books on the table. "What are you doing?"

"Let's not waste your limited time on information that doesn't concern you. Why are you here, Marco?"

"I wanted to apologize."

"For?"

"The shit I said online, when I tagged you. That was petty and uncalled for."

"Uh-huh. Did you take the post down?"

He hesitated. "No, but only because I didn't directly call you out. If I had actually said your name-"

"You can't be all that sorry, then. What about you blowing my phone up and stalking me, driving up and down the street? My neighbors *do* tell me when they see you lurking, you know."

"I got carried away 'cause I was still fucked up about you and Rome. But I'm past that; I know that's not the way to deal with it. Did you get the gifts I sent?"

"Yeah."

"Did you like 'em?"

"I haven't opened any of them."

Marco frowned. "Why not, Jazlyn?"

"Because, Marco, there's nothing you can send me that would change my mind about anything."

"I'm just trying to make things right."

"There *is* no making things right. We're over."

"I disagree." Marco shook his head, taking a seat in the chair across from Jazlyn. "I want you back, Jazlyn. And I'm willing to prove myself to you again."

"Marco." Jazlyn dropped the papers she'd been holding and sighed. "Look. Our relationship was far from ideal. We both made mistakes. I appreciate the apology but like I said, our time is over. I've moved on and I'm happy with who I'm with."

A frown flitted across Marco's brow but he made himself clear it. He wasn't going to let himself get riled up. "I know you're probably just trying to push my buttons right now so you'll have an excuse to put me out..."

"Just being real with you."

"I *will* have you again, Jazlyn. Rome might be your best friend or whatever but he's not half the man I am."

"Big talk from someone who needed me to come kill a spider."

"That was *one* time! And spiders creep me out!"

"Whatever. My point is, you're wasting your time. So how 'bout we just leave things to where we don't completely hate each other and be happy with that?"

Marco sighed in frustration, running a hand over his bald head. "What if I wasn't around anymore?"

Jazlyn frowned. "What do you mean? You moving? 'Cause I know you're not talking about killing yourself."

"*Hell* no. I just mean...what if I got with somebody else?"

"Please do. Then you won't have time to worry about what I'm doing."

"So if I told you that my old girlfriend hit me up and wanted to meet, you wouldn't care?"

"Not even a little bit."

"I'm for real, Jazlyn. I can show you the message in my phone."

"I don't need to see it. I'm sure you have all kinds of messages from women in your phone; you usually do. In fact, you can take the gifts that I haven't opened and give them to her. I'm sure she'd love 'em."

"Damn." He sat back in his chair. "I can't believe you're acting so cold towards me right now. We were together for two years and I thought we were in love with each other. And now it's like you don't give a shit *what* happens to me."

"Oh my gosh, Marco. Don't make it sound more dramatic than it is. I don't want anything bad to happen to you but as far as what you do and who you do it with, no, I *don't* care. We had our time and our time is over. I wish you would just accept that and move on."

"Because I don't *want* to move on. I still love you."

Jazlyn ran her hands down her face. They might not have been arguing but she still regretted letting him in. Marco was still as stubborn as ever.

"We're just going around in circles, here," she concluded, standing. She stomped back to her room.

"Where you going?"

Jazlyn wordlessly retrieved the gifts from Marco from her closet, moving quickly so he wouldn't be tempted to follow her. Having already put them in a huge plastic bag, Jazlyn just grabbed it and returned to the front of the house, where Marco had just stood from his chair.

"Here," Jazlyn said, plunking the bag at his feet. "Please take these and go. I need to get back to what I was doing so I can go to bed. I'm tired and like I said, us getting back together isn't happening."

Marco eyed her for a moment before slowly leaning down and grabbing the bag in his strong hand, slinging it over his shoulder like it was nothing. He finally turned for the door, stopping a few steps short of it and turning back to Jazlyn.

"I still say we're gonna end up back together," he stated, his voice strong.

"And I still say we're not. Rome is it for me. So..." Jazlyn shrugged, looking pointedly at the door. "Bye, Marco."

To her relief, Marco stalked out. Though she had the feeling she'd be hearing from him again at some point.

Marco had already proven he wasn't one to back down graciously.

Jazlyn tried to go back to her lesson plans, but couldn't concentrate. She hoped what she said about Rome being it for her didn't come back to bite her. As much as she believed in her and Rome's relationship, there was the tiny voice in the back of her head that reminded her she had no way of knowing how things would turn out if Rome agreed to give Nell the time she asked for. Who's to say that Nell *wouldn't* be able to remind him of why he'd been so in love with her in the first place? What if he changed his mind and decided to go back to her?

The thought made Jazlyn start to panic a little. What if she was pushing Rome right back into the arms of his ex? She believed in the strength of their relationship, but Jazlyn still couldn't help but worry. There was no telling what Nell had planned; knowing she was on limited time would surely make her pull out the big guns. And once upon a time, Rome had been crazy about Nell. It would gut Jazlyn if he went back to her.

"Stop it!" she admonished herself, placing both hands on her now-throbbing head. Freaking herself out conjuring up every negative scenario wouldn't do her any good. Rome was hers; he'd said many times that he was over Nell. Jazlyn needed to be secure in that and remind herself why she was pushing for Rome to do this; so they could continue their relationship with a clean slate and she could rid herself of the guilt she felt for hurting Nell they way they did. There was nothing Nell could do to take Rome from her.

By the time Jazlyn climbed into bed an hour later, she almost made herself believe that.

Chapter 17

While Jazlyn was fending off Marco and agonizing over possibly doing more harm than good to her relationship with Rome, Rome was paying a visit to Asha.

"What are *you* doing over here?" Asha asked when Rome showed up to her apartment.

"Came to check on you."

"I don't need you to check on me. I'm sure you have plenty of other things you can be worried about."

Rome didn't flinch. He expected this kind of behavior. "I'm not trying to argue with you, Asha. Can I come in?"

Asha sucked her teeth and stepped back. "I guess, or else you'll just tell Mama or Daddy on me."

She left him standing there and Rome stepped inside. By the time he closed the door, Asha had plopped onto the couch, stretching her legs across it. Rome noticed how that left no room for him to sit, but he told himself not to get annoyed. Perching himself on the arm, he glanced around the small living room, noting how uncharacteristically messy it was. A basket of unfolded laundry in the corner. Various shoes strewn about, as if she just kicked them off and left them wherever they landed. Takeout containers covering the end table and the floor near Asha's favorite corner of the couch. Books and magazines stacked on the mismatched armchair. Dirty dishes on the kitchen counters and in the sink. Asha must have really been hurting because she was usually quite anal about things being just so.

"I'd offer you something to drink, but I don't want to," Asha told him, adjusting her glasses. She usually wore contacts. Just like she usually did her hair but it was in a sloppy afro puff, with a good amount of hair having escaped from the elastic band. Any other time Rome might have teased her for her appearance, but that was the last thing on his mind at the moment.

"Asha." He leveled his gaze at her. "I know about Ashton."

Her eyes snapped to him. "What are you talking about?"

"I know he's dating somebody. And that's at least part of the reason for your attitude and..." He gestured around the messy apartment. "All this."

Asha's mouth fell open slightly before her chin began to quiver. She looked away, but not before Rome caught the tears glistening behind her glasses.

"I feel so stupid," she whispered, looking down at her hands. It was then that Rome noticed she was still wearing her engagement ring. As if realizing that herself, Asha quickly stuffed her left hand under her thigh.

"Why is that?" Rome asked, not commenting on the ring.

"Because he fooled me. I sincerely thought he loved me as much as I loved him. Hell, if I'm real about it, I thought he loved me *more* than I loved him. But he's just made a fool out of me over and over."

"I'm surprised to see you so upset about it. When you told me about how he said he wanted you back, you were acting like you were over him."

"I thought I was." Asha played with the drawstring on her pajama bottoms. "But then he started posting about being in another relationship already – *and* with a former friend of mine, at that - and it felt like someone had ripped my heart out. It was so humiliating. All my friends saw that..."

"I get it."

"But what's worse is...there's a part of me that still misses him. It makes me want to throw up to even say that...I hate him but I miss him. And I hate myself *for* missing him. And the fact that I'm over here such a mess while he's moved on already just makes me feel more ridiculous."

Rome stood and moved behind the couch, leaning over the back of it near Asha and placing a hand on her shoulder. "I understand, sis. You were in love with him; it's hard to just get over it, regardless of what he did."

"Yeah." She tugged at her haphazard afro puff. "But I wish I could."

"You will. It'll just take some time." His hand squeezed her shoulder. "And I'm here for you."

She finally looked up at him, pushing her glasses up with her index finger. Her nail polish was chipped. "Even after the way I've been acting?"

"Yeah. Even after that."

"Daddy told you to come over here?"

"He told me about Ashton and that I should come check on you, yeah. It wasn't until I heard about that part that I agreed 'cause I initially said no."

"Guess I can't blame you." She sighed. "I know I've been acting like a bitch lately."

"Your words."

"Well, thanks for coming. You can tell Daddy I'm fine and haven't drowned myself in ice cream or slit my wrists or anything."

"That's not funny, Asha."

"It was just hyperbole. I wouldn't go *that* far over that asshole Ashton."

"I'm glad to hear it but I still don't like you saying stuff like that."

"Okay, okay."

They were quiet for a few moments before Asha spoke up again.

"You know, I know this is a mean thing to say, but regarding Ashton and that heffah he got with…I really hope something happens to ruin their relationship. It wouldn't be fair if they got to sail off into the sunset after how he did me."

"Maybe it's not anything serious," Rome offered with a shrugged shoulder. "It could be just another fling, like with the stripper."

"Who knows. He was showing her off on Instagram like she meant something to him. I have to believe he only did that to rub it in my face; he knew I'd see it."

"Maybe he's just trying to make you jealous since you wouldn't take him back."

"Hmm. Maybe."

"Why don't you just unfollow or block him? Then you won't have to see whatever he's doing."

Asha turned her face away. "I guess there's a small part of me that *wants* to keep up with what he's doing. I can't explain it."

"Makes sense. You're mad at him but that doesn't mean you're over him. But it might be good for you to just cut yourself off from him completely; block him on social media, block his number, toss anything you still have of his. Especially if you still don't want to reconcile. You'll just keep torturing yourself if you're able to see what he's doing, 'cause you know he knows you can see it and he'll just keep doing stuff to antagonize you. Don't let him have that kind of power over your emotions."

"Guess I didn't think of it like that," Asha muttered. "That's something to consider. I just...I know it's petty, but I can't help but hope his relationship crashes and burns. Since I didn't get a chance at an amicable ending, he shouldn't get one, either."

That made Rome think of Nell. Their split had been amicable enough - considering - but who's to say she wasn't thinking such ill thoughts about him and Jazlyn? Like Asha, Nell thought her relationship was just fine before she got the rug pulled out from under her and ended up alone. She had decided to stay in town, and even went to therapy, according to Jazlyn, because she couldn't move past it. Nell was a kind woman, but everyone had their limits.

He began to see the reasoning behind her asking Jazlyn for more time with him, and Jazlyn's reasoning for wanting to grant it. Rome still didn't want to spend time with Nell knowing he really wanted to be with Jazlyn, but he felt himself warming to the idea for no other reason than obligation. And guilt. He supposed it wouldn't be the worst thing in the world to grant Nell a little more time, if that was what it would take for her to feel better and move on.

He stayed at Asha's a while longer, helping her clean up her place before they watched a couple episodes of *Living Single*. She never did apologize for how she'd been acting towards him since finding out about him and Jazlyn, but Rome decided not to trip about that. She was dealing with a lot.

When Rome got home and removed his jacket, he was hanging it up when he noticed a sweater of Nell's hanging in the back. She must have forgotten it when she was getting her things. Rome gently grabbed the sleeve of the dark purple sweater, mindlessly lifting it to his face. It still smelled of Nell's signature orange blossom scent. A pang of something hit his chest; he'd been with Nell when she bought that sweater.

Before he could talk himself out of it, he dug his phone out of his pocket and called Jazlyn.

"I'll do it," he blurted as soon as she answered. It sounded like she was in the bed but she perked up upon hearing his words.

"Oh?" Jazlyn didn't sound as glad as he thought she would, considering how much she'd been pushing him to agree to it. "What made you change your mind? Actually, you know what? It doesn't matter. I'm just glad you did."

"Yeah. I guess I could've called Nell myself and told her but figured since she brought the idea to you first…"

"Right. Well, I get it. You should call her and let her know, though. I certainly don't wanna be the go-between for this."

"I can understand that. I'll call her tomorrow, I guess."

"Why not call her tonight?"

Rome paused, frowning slightly. "What's the rush?"

"Believe me, I'm in no *rush* for you to spend time with another woman. But the sooner you two start all that, the sooner you'll be finished with it."

"Oh," Rome's face cleared. "True enough. I just want you to know that nothing has changed about my feelings towards you or Nell; this is just...doing her a solid, so to speak. I feel bad about how things went down and figure it wouldn't kill me to help her get past things."

"And also so we can get going on a good foot, right?"

"Of course. Though I think we'd be fine regardless, I can understand you being worried about that. So it couldn't hurt, I guess."

"Good. Well, I'm glad you changed your mind. Oh, and just so you know, Marco came over earlier. Wanted to apologize for the shit he did and also let me know he's gonna get me back."

"Get you back?"

"Yeah, like get back with me. I told him there wasn't a chance in hell but you know he's stubborn. And I gave those gifts back to him, too."

"Glad to hear it. I wish he'd meet somebody else and leave you alone."

"Oh, he tried to make me jealous by telling me his ex contacted him. Not that I cared."

"I don't even know what to say about that guy. Make sure you let me know if he tries anything else. Anyway, I know you're in the bed so I'll let you go; I'll hit Nell up tomorrow, since it's kinda late."

"All right. Just...Rome?"

"Yeah?"

"Can you keep me posted on what's happening with her? I just don't want-"

"Sweets," Rome gently interjected. "You don't have anything to worry about. This isn't about getting back with Nell; you know that. It's still me and you."

"I know," she said, though she didn't sound as sure as she should have. "And I know I bugged you about doing it, but now that it's happening I can't help but be a little nervous. That bad feeling in my gut hasn't disappeared like I thought it would if you agreed to this."

"You don't have to be nervous at all. At the end of it I'm gonna be coming right back to you."

"Okay."

"You believe me, right?"

"Yeah. And just know it's not *you* I'm worried about; it's Nell."

"Don't worry about Nell. But I'll let you know what the terms of this crazy agreement are after I talk to her tomorrow. All right?"

"Okay."

"Get some rest. Love you."

"I love you, too."

Not wanting to drag things out, Rome sent Nell a text the next morning, letting her know he was willing to grant her request for this curtain call on their relationship. She immediately asked for him to come see her when he got off work, and he agreed. He was actually a little nervous as he knocked on her door, already starting to feel a little silly about this whole thing. Was he really doing this?

Nell swung the door open, a huge smile already on her face. She flung her arms around his neck.

"I'm so glad you're here," she whispered, holding onto him tightly.

Not knowing what to say, Rome just gently held her waist. "It's good to see you, Nell."

"Gosh, you too." She kissed his cheek before pulling him inside the apartment. "Come on in."

Rome let her lead him inside, glancing around as if he hadn't been there in years. Now that he was there, he started to second-guess his decision. What if this went all the way left and Nell ended up even more hurt than she already was?

But he knew he needed to stick to what he decided and hope for the best.

"You want anything to drink?" Nell asked him. "Or I can fix you something to eat; I know you just got off work and are probably hungry."

"I'm okay. Thanks, though. How 'bout we go ahead and discuss why I'm here?"

"All right." Nell went and joined him where he was taking a seat on the couch. She looked at him anxiously as she rubbed her hands along her thighs. "I have to say, Rome, I was a little surprised to hear from you. I've been waiting for Jazlyn to get back to me."

"It only makes sense that I tell you myself. I don't understand why you took this to Jazlyn instead of me in the first place."

Nell briefly looked away. "I admit I chickened out about asking you. That was the reason I called a little while back, but once I heard your voice, I lost my nerve. I told myself that getting Jazlyn on board first would be best."

"So you could double-team me?"

"That wasn't my intention. At least, not in a negative way. Rome, please know I'm not scheming, here; I have no malicious intent. I understand that you're with Jazlyn and that's who you feel you still want. But like I told Jazlyn, I just want to be able to do what I said I was going to try to do before we broke up."

"Yeah, she mentioned that. Well, whatever you said to her worked because she did the most to get me to agree to this whole thing. And I admit that guilt is a big part of the reason I finally did. How things ended between us never did sit right with me."

Nell pursed her lips but just as quickly relaxed them. "I appreciate that, though I wish it wasn't just a guilty conscience that brought you here."

"Nell, come on...what do you expect? Like you said, I still want to be with Jazlyn, at the end of the day. I'm not trying to be an asshole about it but really, I'm just doing this 'cause I feel bad for stepping out on you; I don't expect anything to change at all."

"I understand." Nell looked at her hands, then impulsively reached over and grabbed Rome's. "But I'm still glad you're here. And hopefully over the next few months-"

"Whoa, whoa," Rome interjected, leaning away slightly. "Months? See, this is where we need to establish the parameters of all this because it can't be that long. I was thinking maybe a week or so."

"That's not much time at all, Rome."

"*One* month. That's all I can give you, Nell."

She looked like she wanted to protest, but she thankfully nodded graciously. "All right. One month. During that time, though, are you gonna be all in? I don't want you to just say you'll do this and then I barely see or hear from you, or I have to share you with everything else. It needs to be just like it was when we were together, otherwise there's no point."

Rome chewed his lip. He wished he had thought to discuss this with Jazlyn first; he was sure there were certain things she'd rather he *not* do with Nell during all this. But maybe since she hadn't mentioned it, she was good with everything. Because she surely would have let him know if she wanted him to bring up any 'restrictions.'

"All right," he conceded. "I get it. You'll have my full attention."

"Will you stay here?"

Rome immediately shook his head. "We weren't living together before, Nell. We don't need to do that now. We'll spend plenty of time together but I won't move in here with you."

"Couldn't hurt to ask." She gave him a small smile, scooting closer to him on the couch as she interlocked her fingers with his. "It really does mean a lot to me that you're doing this, Rome."

"I'm just glad I can make amends for what I did in some way. Although I do have to admit that this all feels weird."

"It's a strange request, I know. But I'm looking forward to getting this time with you." She ran her free hand up and down his arm, and Rome had to make himself not squirm uncomfortably. It didn't feel right, having another woman's hand on him other than Jazlyn's. Once again, he had to remind himself why he agreed to this. "And I know this is asking a lot, but can you do one more thing for me?"

Rome turned his eyes to her. "What's that?"

"Can you not think about Jazlyn when you're with me? I know you two are technically still together but I felt how you tensed up just now when I got close to you; this doesn't have to be awkward or forced. You and I had great chemistry and rapport before things ended; try to think about that. Can you give me that much?"

Rome hesitated. That would be a tall order, putting Jazlyn out of his mind when he was with Nell. Everything in him wanted to be with his woman right then instead of on his ex's couch.

But he guessed he could see Nell's point. It would be a long month if he didn't loosen up.

"I'll try," he assured her. "It might take me a minute, but I'll do my best."

"That's all I ask." Nell reached up and caressed his face, her dark eyes peering at him appreciatively. It thrilled her to be that close to him again. "Thank you, Rome."

"You're welcome."

She brought his face to hers, and Rome tried to steel himself. When Nell's lips met his, she emitted a small sigh and moved closer, her hold on him tightening. Rome tried to relax and ignore just how wrong this felt. It wasn't all that long ago that he loved Nell's hands and lips on him, but now, he had to force himself to respond to her. Nell was still a beautiful woman; gorgeous even. But she wasn't the woman he wanted. And he didn't know how the hell he was going to force any kind of intimacy for the next four weeks. Or even how much intimacy he should allow.

Nell didn't seem to be in any hurry to end their kiss, so Rome closed his eyes and conjured up Jazlyn's face in his mind. Despite what he'd just promised Nell, that was the only way he could make himself get into it. Thankfully Nell didn't try to take things too far; she was satisfied with just kissing him and being close to him again.

But Rome knew it was only a matter of time before she wanted more than that, and that's what made him nervous. But he figured he'd cross that bridge when he got to it and should just focus on taking this month with Nell one day at a time, and hope the days passed quickly. That way his conscience would be clear and he could focus on the woman he really wanted to be with.

Chapter 18

"Jazlyn, girl, I love you, but you're a dumb ass."

This was exactly why Jazlyn took her time admitting to Ginger that she'd decided to agree to Nell's request. She knew her friend wouldn't get it. "Ginger..."

"Why in the world would you *give* your man to another woman? There's not enough guilt in the world to make me do that shit."

Sighing, Jazlyn checked on the ramen noodles she had on the stove before glancing at the phone on the counter, where she was talking to Ginger on speakerphone. "I don't expect you to understand, Ginger. But it was something I felt needed to be done so...I did it."

"No, you mean you're letting *them* do it. Because as long as he's over there pretending with her, you're by yourself."

"Rome and I are still together."

"Might as well not be. 'Cause you know Nell isn't gonna want to share him with you while they're in the middle of this...whatever the hell you call it. She is going to take *full* advantage of having Rome back and you know it."

Jazlyn tried to shake her friend's words off. "Nell knows she's on limited time. And Rome only agreed out of guilt. He saw my point about wanting to clear our relationship karma and start things out on a good note."

"So why don't you get back with Marco while Rome is over there with Nell?"

"Why would I do that? Marco cheated on me first. And anyway, I trust Rome, so if you're trying to imply that he's going to betray me, you can keep that."

"Well, technically he wouldn't *be* betraying you, since he's Nell's man for the next month. Whatever he does with her is fair game."

The spoon in Jazlyn's hand clanked onto the stove. "Are you trying to piss me off?"

"I'm trying to wake you up. Look, I get where your head was and I can even say you had good intentions with all this, but have you even thought about all the ways this can go left?"

"No." Jazlyn's voice was strong. "I've been trying not to focus on any negative stuff."

"Well, I'll focus on it for you, then."

"Ginger, I don't need to hear-"

"What if Nell actually manages to remind Rome of why he used to be so into her? What if he starts second-guessing his relationship with you?"

"That won't happen."

"Hmph. All right, then. Did you even set any ground rules, like telling Rome what he can and can't do with her?"

Jazlyn didn't want to admit that hadn't crossed her mind until after the fact. "It's not my place to do that, Ginger."

"Not your place? So you don't care if they're intimate, then? If Nell gets Rome back in her bed, you're okay with that?"

Jazlyn's spoon dropped again, this time to the floor. She cursed under her breath as she stooped down to pick it up.

"Of course not. But like I said, I trust Rome. And I honestly don't believe that this is all about sex for Nell."

"It doesn't have to be all about it for her to want it or try to get some. I need you to stop being so trusting. Or stop lying to yourself. Nell might be a decent woman but she's also desperate, or she wouldn't have even had the nerve to ask for this shit. And knowing she only has so much time with Rome, she's surely not gonna waste any of it. She's gonna pull out all the stops, whatever that may be for her."

Jazlyn remained quiet. She just stood eyeing her noodles on the stove, knowing it was time to remove them from the heat but making no move to do so. Ginger's warnings had paralyzed her.

"Jazlyn," Ginger called out.

"What?"

"I'm only trying to make sure you're not deluding yourself, that's all. You know I love Rome. But he's still a man. And you've basically given him free reign to do whatever with another woman for a whole month. And I just want to make sure you're *really* aware of what you've agreed to, that's all. I don't want you to end up hurt in all this just because you tried to make up for the hurt you caused Nell."

As much as Jazlyn didn't want to admit it, her friend had a point. There were so many ways this could go, and maybe she hadn't considered them all like she thought. And while she did trust Rome, there was no guarantee that she would end up on the good side of it like she expected to.

What if it caused issues for them even after Rome came back to her? Jazlyn knew she would wonder what happened between Rome and Nell, especially after Ginger's warnings.

And if Rome didn't want to tell her, for whatever reason, that would just send Jazlyn's imagination into overdrive. Jazlyn certainly wasn't naïve enough to expect Nell to keep her hands to herself. Could she *really* handle it if Rome got down with Nell? Would she even want to know about it if he did?

Jazlyn itched to call Rome right then and call the whole thing off. She'd changed her mind, just like that; Nell would just have to deal with it. And she and Rome would just have to commit themselves that much more to each other to keep their relationship going and withstand anything that might come at them as a result of their dual infidelities.

But she knew she had to be a woman of her word, as much as she didn't like it. A month wasn't all that long; before she knew it, she'd have her man back and Nell would be a thing of the past. Maybe she and Rome would even laugh about this crazy arrangement at some point down the line.

Jazlyn forked her overcooked noodles into a bowl and tried to convince herself that everything would be fine. And also that she hadn't made an amazingly stupid mistake.

• • • •

IT WAS ONLY A COUPLE of days into Rome's month with Nell and Jazlyn was already extremely curious as to how things were going. Rome had called her once to let her know how the talk with Nell went, and they had exchanged a few texts, but she hadn't seen him since the night before he went to see Nell. Jazlyn's body tightened when she remembered how they'd made love on his desk and in his office chair.

She missed it; she missed *him* already. Hopefully he'd be able to squeeze in some time for her soon; surely Nell wouldn't expect to monopolize every second of Rome's free time for the next month.

At least she had work and her upcoming class to focus on, and she had more time to make nail art videos. It still amazed her how much response she was getting on those. She'd even gotten some new customers at the salon from that, with people wanting the specific designs she'd demonstrated online. And to think she'd only started making the videos because she was trying to take her mind off how annoyed she was with Marco one night.

Speaking of Marco, she thankfully hadn't heard from him since his last visit, and hoped that meant he'd finally gotten the message that she had no interest in rekindling anything with him and had moved on.

Unfortunately, she saw that wasn't the case when he tagged her in another Instagram post. It was only because she needed something to take her mind off of Rome that she even looked at it. At least it wasn't anything derogatory this time, though Jazlyn wished Marco would stop these juvenile ways of trying to get her attention. It was a picture of him with a honey-skinned woman with a super-short haircut styled into loose fingerwaves, dressed in an orange crop top and jean shorts. Marco, shirtless and in grey sweatpants, had his arm around her, holding her close. Jazlyn thought it was ironic that he didn't post one picture of the two of them when they were together, but he would tag her in a post where he was hugged up with another woman after claiming to want Jazlyn back. Men were so backwards sometimes.

She checked out the caption:

You know what they say about not missing or appreciating someone until they're gone? Sometimes people need to *see* what it is they're sleeping on to get the message.

Jazlyn shook her head. She didn't know if this woman in the picture was Marco's ex that he had dangled in her face or some random woman, but it didn't matter. Marco was really something else. Did he seriously think this was a good way to get back into her good graces?

She started to ignore it but changed her mind. If Marco wanted to keep poking at her, she was going to poke back.

This isn't what you were saying when you were at my house begging the other night.

She knew it was petty. But Jazlyn couldn't resist giggling as she hit 'send'. Or the excited squeals at the almost immediate likes and responses that started rolling in. She entertained herself by reading the comments for a couple of minutes before Marco sent her a direct message, no doubt to fuss about her calling him out. But she ignored it. They didn't have anything to talk about; he was the one that started it by tagging her and sending stupid subliminal messages. Part of her expected him to show up at her door, but thankfully he didn't.

Marco was good for one thing, and that was distracting her from obsessing over what Rome was doing, even for a little while. And she only had twenty-eight more days to go.

• • • •

IT WAS TIME FOR JAZLYN'S first nail class. She was a little nervous, especially when she walked into the room and ten eager students turned towards her.

"Uhh..." She froze for a moment before snapping out of it. "Hey, everybody."

"Hey," they all chorused.

"I'm Jazlyn Mackie and it looks like you're stuck with me for a while." Thankfully the students chuckled, and Jazlyn felt a little more at ease. She put her bag on the desk and smiled, placing her hands on her hips. "Hopefully you won't feel cheated at all while your real teacher is out dropping her new baby."

"If the nails you're wearing now are any indication of what you can do, I think we're in good hands," one woman spoke up, peering at Jazlyn's hands. "Is that gold leaf?"

"Yeah," Jazlyn concurred, glancing at her dark purple oval nails with the gold leaf accents before holding her hand up for the class. "This is just something I was playing around with."

"I've seen your videos," another woman announced. "You're like a nail design savant. There are at least three designs I want you to show me how to do. Though I already know it won't look as good as yours. My hands aren't all that steady yet."

"Mine weren't at first either, girl, but you'll get better the more you do it," Jazlyn assured her.

"I sure hope so. Otherwise my parents are straight wasting their money on this."

Everyone laughed and Jazlyn felt a lot better. At least her reputation had preceded her and they seemed confident that she knew what she was doing.

"So..." Jazlyn rubbed her hands together. "Let's get started, huh?"

The class ended up going way better than Jazlyn could have hoped. All of the students were attentive, engaged, and enthusiastic about learning what she was there to teach. They had just started learning how to apply acrylic nails with their regular instructor, which was right up Jazlyn's alley; those were requested so much at the salon she could practically do them in her sleep. Before she knew it, ninety minutes had flown by and it was time to dismiss.

"See y'all Thursday night," Jazlyn called out as the class dispersed. "Great job."

She noticed one student was still in her seat and Jazlyn went over to her. "You good, Vickie?"

"Oh, yeah," Vickie, a twenty-something woman with smooth light brown skin and blue cornrows, turned to look up at her. "I'm just waiting on my brother to come pick me up. He just texted me; he's running late."

"Oh okay."

"Am I holding you up?"

"I'm not in any rush. Plus, I still need to straighten up in here, anyway."

"I'll help you." Vickie hopped up from her seat and grabbed a broom.

"Oh girl, you don't have to do that. But I'm not gonna try to stop you," Jazlyn joked, winking at her. They shared a laugh as Jazlyn went about wiping down the work stations, then made small talk about how the class went. It was a boost to Jazlyn's ego when Vickie said she was looking forward to the next one.

A man in blue coveralls rushed in, looking around. When his eyes landed on Vickie, he headed over to where she was folding chairs. "Hey, here I am, sis. Sorry I'm late. I got held up helping out Tito at the garage."

"It's all right. I've just been talking to Jazlyn," Vickie replied, nodding her head in Jazlyn's direction. "Jazlyn, this is my brother, Kash."

Kash did a double-take when he glanced over his shoulder at Jazlyn. He immediately moved across the room to her, his eyes never straying. "Jazlyn...it's nice to meet you."

Jazlyn glanced up and gave a polite smile. "Hey, you too."

"I apologize for keeping you. Hope your man won't be too upset about you being late getting home."

Jazlyn gave a dry chuckle as she stuffed a folder into her crossbody bag a little harder than necessary. "Not a problem."

"Is there anything I can do to help?" Kash persisted, taking a step closer to the desk Jazlyn was standing behind. He was determined to get her attention. "I can take out some trash or something. It's the least I could do, considering."

"Oh no, we're good. Vickie and I handled everything. Thanks, though." Jazlyn shot him another empty smile as she slung her bag and purse over her shoulder. "Everything's done."

"I can carry your bags-"

"Kash, come on," Vickie interjected, coming over to grab his arm. "Let's get out of Jazlyn's hair now."

"I'll wait to walk you both out; there's no way I'm leaving you to walk out at night by yourself, Jazlyn," Kash insisted, resisting as Vickie tried to pull him out of the room. He'd hardly been able to take his eyes off Jazlyn since he first noticed her.

Jazlyn hadn't noticed, though. She just nodded and headed over to turn out the lights. "That's nice of you. I'm ready; let's go, y'all."

They all headed outside, with Kash making last-ditch efforts to engage Jazlyn in conversation. She just continued giving short replies, oblivious to his flirtations. As soon as they got outside, she immediately headed to her car, declining his offer to walk her right to her driver's side door. She just waved at them, got into her car, and drove off.

• • • •

GINGER INVITED JAZLYN over the next night, since she knew her friend was probably driving herself crazy thinking about Rome and Nell. Jazlyn appreciated the distraction.

"You like pork chops, right?" Ginger asked her, coming back into the kitchen where Jazlyn was sitting at the island, playing around on her phone. "Zion just put some on the grill."

"Yeah, that's fine."

"He has some veggies on there."

"Cool."

"He just got that grill so he'll probably try to put dessert on there, too." Ginger looked over at Jazlyn, who hadn't looked up from her phone. "Do I need to take that thing from you?"

Her eyebrows raised, Jazlyn finally looked up. "What?"

"You've barely said anything since you got here. If you want to call Rome, why don't you just go ahead and do it so you can snap out of this funk you're in?"

"I'm not in a funk; I'm just a little tired. And anyway, there's no point in me calling Rome right now; I already know he's with Nell." Jazlyn couldn't keep the distaste out of her voice. "I'll call him when I get home."

"Okay, well while you're here, can you at least pretend like you're having a nice time? You're hanging with your girl..."

"...And her husband. What fun being the third wheel."

"You're not a third wheel. We're not anywhere out in public; we're just hanging out at the house. So I'm gonna need you to cheer up, damn it."

"All right, all right."

"Look, I'm just gonna say this and then I'm leaving it alone. About the whole Rome and Nell thing...remember why you agreed to it in the first place. Otherwise, you're just gonna drive yourself crazy, worrying about what they're doing every second of the day."

"I know." Jazlyn sighed. "You're right."

"Like you said, you trust Rome, right?"

"Yeah. I do."

"Well, then. Trust him to handle all this the right way. There's still over three weeks left for this arrangement; just do your own thing. The less you focus on it, the faster it'll go by, trust me."

Jazlyn knew Ginger was right. She couldn't spend this time staring at the clock and the calendar, imagining various scenarios in her head about what Nell might be trying with her man at any given moment. She just needed to chill out.

Though that didn't stop her from getting Zion's perspective on it. When they were all sitting down in the living room in front of the television with their plates piled high with grilled pork chops and vegetables, getting ready to watch the latest episode of *Power*, Jazlyn couldn't resist saying, "So Zion, I already know Ginger has probably told you what's going on with me and Rome..."

"You mean the thing where you sent him back to his ex? Yeah, she mentioned something about that."

Cutting her eyes at Ginger, Jazlyn shook her head. "That's not what I did. I should've known she wouldn't be objective about it, since she's telling my business and already made it clear how she felt when she called and cussed me out."

"I didn't cuss you out," Ginger protested, taking a huge bite of her pork chop. "Not that I didn't want to."

"Anyway. Zion, what do *you* think about all this? If you were in Rome's shoes, how would you handle it? Would you even agree to what Nell asked for?"

Zion thoughtfully chewed his zucchini before taking a sip of his beer. His dark brown skin held a stark contrast to Ginger's sandy brown as they sat side by side. "Honestly, I don't think so, Jaz. It's just too much of a slippery slope."

Even though Jazlyn had an idea, she still pressed, "Meaning?"

"Meaning, it would be too easy to forget what the point is. Even one good night of reminiscing and alcohol can change the game."

"So you would be tempted to do something with your ex?"

"What man wouldn't? Rome is straight-up but he's still human, and you've basically given him permission to have a relationship within your relationship. And he's gonna be spending all that time with Nell for a few weeks? I'd be really surprised if nothing goes down between them before it's all over with."

Jazlyn didn't want to hear that. "So if you had cheated on your girl with Ginger and decided Ginger was who you wanted to be with, but you felt guilty and your ex asked for one last ride, that wouldn't be a good enough reason to do it?"

"Why, so I could turn around and feel even more guilty for whatever I ended up doing with her? Nah, I'd rather just apologize to my ex and leave it at that. Really, that should be enough, as long as I'm sincere. Anything else could just get messy."

Slumping in her seat, Jazlyn kicked herself yet again. She had been so sure that letting Nell have time with Rome was necessary, but now she wondered how she could've been so stupid. In fact, the more she thought about it, the more ridiculous she felt. What woman in her right mind would let another woman *borrow* her man, for any reason??

"Don't sit over there beating yourself up, girl," Ginger advised, reading Jazlyn's mind. "What's done is done. And just because something *could* happen between Rome and

Nell doesn't mean it will. I know we've been throwing a bunch of worst-case scenarios at you but it might not even be all that bad."

"Right," Jazlyn muttered, picking up her pork chop and taking a chunk out of it like a Neanderthal. "It might not be all that bad."

She managed to have a decent enough time while she was at Ginger's, with Ginger managing to steer the conversation towards non-relationship topics. Jazlyn put Rome and Nell out of her mind for a while, though it didn't help that she and her friends were watching a show where the man had an affair with his ex.

As soon as she got back home, Jazlyn called Rome. She needed to hear his voice and hear him assure her again that she had nothing to worry about. She knew he'd been with Nell earlier but she figured he was back home by then, seeing as how it was almost ten o'clock at night.

She was mistaken, though.

"Hey, I can't talk right now, sweets," he informed her, his voice low.

Alarmed, Jazlyn asked, "Why?"

"I'm still at Nell's."

"Oh..."

"I'm sorry; I was hoping to call you earlier but Nell asked me to stay so we could talk and have dinner together, though I didn't plan to be over here this long. I'll talk to you later, okay? Love you."

Before Jazlyn could respond, he hung up.

Chapter 19

Rome hated that he couldn't talk to Jazlyn when she called. He could hear the disappointment in her voice when he told her why. Without even asking her, he knew she was still worried.

And it probably didn't help that he wasn't able to talk to her when she called the next couple of times, though one of those times was because he was still working. He wanted to put her mind at ease but Nell was doing her best to keep his attention on her. Any time he wasn't working, she wanted to be with him and when that wasn't possible, she wanted them to be talking or texting. Rome was indulging her because he agreed to, but he was already ready for this month to be over.

Even though Rome didn't think a month would change anything, Nell clearly did. She was making a real effort to sway Rome back in her direction, and while Rome felt it was futile, he could appreciate the effort. She communicated everything with him, not only about current things but also going back to the beginning of their relationship and divulging things she couldn't or wouldn't at the time. At times, Rome felt it was a little much, but he let her get everything off her chest.

And most of the time, he was giving her his full attention as promised.

Then there was the intimacy issue. Thankfully Nell hadn't tried to get him into her bed yet, but he knew it was coming. She loved kissing him, kissing *on* him, touching and climbing onto his lap, and Rome still wasn't able to fully relax with her. He automatically stiffened whenever she touched him, and it took a lot of mind power to loosen back up. Usually he thought of Jazlyn, though it felt strange (and wrong) to fantasize about her while another woman was hugging up on him.

"Are you okay?" Nell asked him one night. She had coerced him back to her bedroom and onto her king-sized bed, and was draped on top of him as she languidly kissed his face and neck. Rome hadn't said much and was barely responding to her, his hands lightly resting on her waist.

"Yeah, I'm fine," Rome replied, neutralizing his troubled expression. "Go ahead."

"Go ahead." Nell actually chuckled. Resting a hand on his chest, she propped her head on her other hand as she slid to his side. "Rome, am I gonna have to tickle you to get you to loosen up?"

Rome's lips quirked with a smile. "You know *you're* the one that's ticklish, not me."

"I'm sure I could find a spot on you that's ticklish if I tried hard enough. Or I can pull out my old joke book. Some of those things are so corny, you can't help but laugh at least a little."

Chuckling himself, Rome shook his head. "No need in going through all that trouble. And there's no telling how old that book is. They still *make* joke books?"

"I'm not sure, but this one I've had since I was about eleven."

"Damn! Yeah, I'm sure whatever's in there *is* corny as hell. I'm good."

"Well, I'm gonna find it anyway and knock-knock joke you to death if you don't stop acting like a corpse around me."

Rome sighed, looking over at her. She didn't look angry at all; her eyes held compassion that he actually appreciated. It meant a lot to him that she wasn't catching an attitude because he wasn't responding to her the way she wanted; she was being patient, even on her limited time. That meant something to him.

"I'm sorry, Nell," he told her, sincere. "I'm trying to chill out, but..."

"I get it, Rome," she assured him, grazing her nails along his jawline. Her eyes shone with adoration. "This is a strange situation. And I know it can feel awkward, still being in a relationship with someone else while you're here with me. It means a lot to me that you're granting me this. I just hope that, if nothing else, we can at least enjoy this time together. I don't want it to feel like some kind of punishment you're suffering through."

Rome didn't want to admit that's how he'd thought of it at times. But it wasn't because of Nell; it was all in his own head. If he was going to make the best of these next three weeks, he needed to change his perspective.

"You're right," he admitted, placing his hand over hers. "You've been really patient and I appreciate it. I know I haven't been very receptive."

"And I get why. I just wish there was something I could say to make this more enjoyable for you."

Turning onto his side, Rome faced Nell, his eyes roaming over her face. He was reminded of how beautiful she was; his mind hadn't registered that since he fell for Jazlyn. But he realized being this close to Nell wasn't as bad as he made himself believe it was.

"You don't have to say anything," he told her. "You being so understanding is plenty."

"I care about you, Rome. Regardless of what's happened, I'm gonna always care about you."

He felt silly for blushing at that, but her words touched him. Nell was being more gracious to him than he deserved, considering how he'd hurt her. Remembering that was like releasing the tension valve on his body, and he felt at ease for the first time since their arrangement started.

"I care about you, too," he replied, his voice low. "And I'm so sorry for-"

"Shhh," she stopped him, placing a finger to his lips. "You don't have to keep apologizing. I already know. Positive thoughts only, okay?"

He nodded, smiling. "Okay."

She gently brought his face to hers and kissed him, and a tiny bit of the tension returned to his body, but not all of it. He let his lips move against hers, and after a few moments, his tongue against hers, too. The kiss was slow and exploratory, with Nell releasing occasional soft sighs or moans. Her hands gripped his shirt, and her bare feet tangled in his socked ones. She moved closer to him to where their bodies were touching, sliding her outside hand over his waist and up his back.

Rome hadn't even realized his eyes were closed until she pulled her lips from his. She snuggled up to him, resting her head on his chest. Hesitating only slightly, Rome slid his arms around her, and her hold on him instantly tightened. That was as far as things went that night, and Rome had to admit it wasn't that bad. And he'd be lying if he said he felt *nothing*; he wasn't a robot.

But he still wasn't looking forward to when Nell would want more, because he knew she would.

• • • •

ROME MANAGED TO BREAK away from Nell long enough to go see his dad a couple of days later. He didn't hate spending so much time with Nell, but he needed a break from her.

"What's been going on, son?" Solomon asked him. "You hungry? Make yourself a pizza."

"You're *making* pizzas?" Rome eyed the various bowls of pizza sauce and toppings; pepperoni, chopped bacon, mushrooms, peppers, sausage crumbles, olives. He pointed to one of the bowls. "Dad, since when do you put pineapple on your pizzas? Please tell me you don't do that."

"Unless you've tried it, don't knock it."

"I'm good. You made this dough from scratch?"

"Who I look like, G. Garvin? It's store-bought. I'm not doing all that."

"Where's Mama?"

"Out shopping with her sisters, then they're gonna have dinner. Which is why I can make what I want; you know your mama doesn't really care for pizza."

"True." Rome washed his hands before grabbing another pan from under the counter and one of the balls of dough.

"I kinda remember seeing someone do this one of the times Jazlyn had me watching Food Network with her."

"There's not much to it. And if you mess it up, no big deal. No judges here."

"Thankfully. And you surely don't have to worry about me messing with that pineapple for this."

"Good. More for me. Speaking of Jazlyn, how's she doing? Seems like it's been a minute since I've seen her."

Rome worked to stretch out his dough. "She's all right, though it might be a little while more before you see her again."

Solomon glanced over at him. "Why's that?"

"She and I are kinda on pause right now."

"You have a fight?"

"No, it's nothing like that. We're actually good, but we're in the middle of a...strange situation for the time being."

"Like what? Talk to me."

Rome told his dad about the whole agreement with Nell, and how it was going so far. When he said it out loud, he still felt a little silly. He surely hadn't told any of his friends about it.

"I had good intentions with it," he concluded, sighing as he spread pizza sauce over his unevenly-shaped dough. "But I'd be lying if I said I was enjoying this. Even though I don't *hate* hanging out with Nell, I already wish this month was over."

"It's that bad?" Solomon scattered mushrooms over his pizza.

"It's not that it's bad, it's just not what I really wanna do. I only agreed because I still felt guilty for stepping out on Nell. But whenever I'm with her, I'm wishing I was with Jazlyn."

"And you're doing this for a month?"

"Yep. Though Nell wanted it to be longer."

"Well, son, you surely know how to get yourself into some interesting situations," Solomon chuckled, wiping sauce from his hands with a paper towel. "I think this is a new one for me."

"Hell, for me, too."

"I'm surprised Jazlyn was on board with this. Not many women would be."

"She felt guilty, too. Thought we might be doomed if we didn't give Nell this time."

"And neither of you are worried about something happening between you and Nell? Feelings-wise, I mean."

"*I'm* certainly not. As soon as this month is over, I'm going right back to Jazlyn."

"You think so, huh?"

Rome looked over at his dad. "I know so. Why, what are you trying to say?"

"All I'm saying is, don't be so sure of yourself with that." Solomon slid his pizza into the oven, then stepped aside as Rome slid his onto the bottom rack. After closing the oven door, Solomon leaned against the counter and folded his arms over his chest. "Remember how quick your feelings changed after you slept with Jazlyn the first time."

"Yeah...but that was different."

"How is it different?"

"I...it just is." Rome busied himself gathering the ingredient dishes. The conviction from his father's words made him uncomfortable. "And Nell and I were having issues even before anything happened between me and Jazlyn."

"True enough. But who's to say that Nell *won't* succeed in proving herself to you and make you question your decision again? You and I both know Nell is a wonderful woman. And you were knee-deep over her before."

"I know, Dad, but that was then. It's me and Jazlyn now."

"If that's the case, son, I'd be nothing but happy for you. I love Jazlyn. I'm just telling you to be careful. Your feelings changed on a dime before; it's not impossible that they could change back. You're spending a lot of time with a woman you were in love with not too long ago, and you all only parted because of something *you* did, not her." He peered at Rome, who was starting the water for the dishes, eyes averted. "Feelings don't always act how we want them to, son. You ever consider that what you and Jazlyn have is just infatuation?"

"Nothing is going to change between me and Nell, Dad," Rome insisted, his back still turned. They both knew he was talking to himself as much as he was to Solomon. "And I know the difference between infatuation and actual feelings."

"Let me ask you this, son. If you hadn't gotten stuck over at Jazlyn's the night of the blizzard, would you two still be just friends? Or do you think something else would've happened to bring you where you are right now? Because you said yourself that the two of you never looked at each other that way before that night."

"I-I don't know." Rome wanted to say no, but he knew the likelihood was that he'd probably still be with Nell if not for that night. It changed everything. "Maybe."

"You love Jazlyn?"

"Of course I love her."

"You in love with her like you were with Nell?"

Rome hesitated. "Almost. I mean, I will be."

"You sure?"

Rome sighed and let his head fall back. "Dad..."

"Hey, I'm just asking." Solomon moved over and turned off the water, standing next to Rome and looking at him pointedly until he finally turned his eyes to him. "Know that I've got your back, all right? But like I said, I want you to be careful. Not just for the ladies' sake, but for yours, too. I don't want to see you get hurt, either."

"I appreciate it," Rome said, relaxing slightly. "And I get your point. I guess none of us *really* knows how all this will turn out."

"That's all I'm trying to say." He bumped his son's shoulder. "Leave this stuff here; we can clean up later. Let's have a beer while we wait for the pizzas to be ready."

• • • •

ROME'S HEAD WAS ALL over the place by the time he left his parents' house a couple of hours later. His dad had given him a lot to think about. Maybe he *was* naïve to think this arrangement with Nell would be so cut and dry, simply because he wanted it to be.

He missed Jazlyn something terrible, and wished he could spend the evening with her, but Nell had sent multiple texts, asking him to come over so she could make him dinner and he finally relented, despite having just eaten with his dad and the fact that he'd told himself he needed a break from Nell. Before he went to her place, though, he tried to call Jazlyn to see if they could meet up. The call went to voicemail, to his disappointment. He couldn't recall if she had her class that night, and he was tempted to swing by to check, especially after going by her house and not seeing her car in the driveway. He checked his watch and tried calling her again. When her voicemail message came on again, he sighed.

"Hey, sweets. I'm just leaving from hanging with Dad and wanted to see if we could link up real quick. I'm going to Nell's in a little while but I wanted to see you. I miss you, babe. But you're not answering and I see you're not at home, so I guess it can't happen. Hope everything's good; guess I'll talk to you later."

He hung up and checked his watch again, sitting there for a few more moments in case he saw Jazlyn's car appear on the street. When she never showed up, he sighed and started his truck, heading over to Nell's.

He tried to put his game face on when he arrived, especially since Nell was all smiles as soon as he walked through the door. She threw her arms around his neck in a tight hug before giving him a tender peck on the lips and taking his hand.

"Hope you're hungry," she told him, glancing over her shoulder at him with a smile as she pulled him towards the kitchen.

Not wanting to tell her he just ate not that long ago, he nodded. "I could eat."

"Good, 'cause I made your favorites. Homemade three-cheese lasagna, with plenty of meat."

Rome couldn't resist grinning. He loved homemade lasagna. "Damn, girl. You trying to butter me up, huh?"

"Making you smile like that is part of the reason. And I admit I wanted to show off a tiny bit. I think I perfected my pasta-making; this is definitely my best batch yet."

"Nell, you didn't have to go through all that trouble."

"Please, I was glad to do it. I love to cook, anyway. And I have a little surprise for you later."

"Nell..."

"It's not a sports car, Rome, calm down," Nell teased, bumping his shoulder. He chuckled. "Just something I knew you'd like. But we'll get to that later. How was your day? I missed you."

"It was cool. Hung out with Dad for a while."

"Oh? How's he doing?" Nell took his jacket and hung it in the closet.

"He's great. I think he liked having the house to himself while Mama was out with my aunts. He can smoke all the cigars he wants."

Nell giggled. "I still don't get how anybody can enjoy those things. But it's cool that you got to spend some time together. I love how close the two of you are."

"Yeah, me too."

"I wish I had that kind of relationship with *my* dad. We love each other but we've never been all that close."

Rome looked at her in mild surprise. It was the first time she proactively mentioned anything about her relationship with either of her parents; it was always a sore subject whenever he used to ask her about it. "Why is that?"

"Honestly, I think he resents me. It wasn't exactly good news when he and Mama discovered they were pregnant with me in their forties."

"How is that your fault, though? They're the ones that...made you."

Nell laughed. "Yeah, but it's easier to resent me for being made than to accept responsibility for conceiving me, I guess. Mama and I grew to get along great before she passed. But I don't think Daddy ever got over all of his plans being delayed or ruined because I came along when I did."

"Wow, Nell." Rome felt for her. He and his parents had always been close, especially him and his dad. He couldn't imagine being in Nell's shoes. "I'm so sorry you had to deal with that from him."

"It's gotten a little better in recent years," Nell admitted, grabbing a beer and a bottle of water from the refrigerator and holding them up to him with her eyebrows raised. Rome pointed to the water, having reached his one-bottle limit for beer when he was with Solomon. Nell handed him the water, and to Rome's surprise, opened the beer for herself. "I make sure to call and check on him, make sure he has what he needs and is doing okay. He'll indulge me in conversation for a few minutes if he's not watching one of his crime shows. He loves that stuff; I don't know how he watches such things. It's so depressing."

"Yeah, that's never been my thing, either."

"The two of you have something in common, though. Well, kind of. He used to work construction before he hurt his back."

"Word? Yeah, my first job was actually on a construction site, when I was eighteen. That was before that singer saw me dancing in the club one night and asked me to go on the road with him. Mama must've called me twice a day for the first month before Dad got her to chill out."

Nell laughed, grabbing the potholder and leaning down to check the lasagna in the oven. Rome eyed her long dark brown legs that seemed to shimmer from whatever moisturizer she had on them. He found himself enjoying the view of her, cute and casual in her fitted tank and cutoff shorts, her toenails painted a deep red, her usual orange blossom scent mingling with the spicy savory aromas from the lasagna. Her microbraids were in a high ponytail, and Rome actually felt himself move to catch them when they started to fall over her shoulder. Nell brushed them back herself and stood, sliding the oven mitt from her hand, and Rome swallowed, looking away. He suddenly wished he had that beer.

"Just another few minutes," Nell announced, setting the timer next to the stove. She looked at him, her eyes mischievous. "Any chance I can get you to put on a performance for me tonight?"

"Girl..." Rome shook his head, his smile widening. "You're always trying to get me to dance. I told you, I hung that up years ago. All that time on the road turned me off dancing. It was just something to do; I never loved it."

"Understandable. Can't blame a girl for trying, though. I've caught you a few times when you thought no one was looking." She moved over to him, sliding her arms around his waist. "You've still got the moves."

"Oh yeah?" Rome smiled down at her. He felt himself warm as he looked at her beautiful face and under no power of his own, he leaned closer and his arms encircled her. "That's good to know in case I ever need 'em, I guess."

Nell grinned. They stood there gazing at each other for several moments, all smiles, her fingers mindlessly tangling in his shirt and his gently grazing back and forth along her lower back. It was the first time Rome felt truly at ease with Nell since this arrangement started, and he couldn't deny it felt nice. It felt comfortable. He became aware of how Nell felt in his arms, and he didn't hate it.

Their faces had just started drifting closer together when the timer went off, making Rome jump. He cleared his throat and stepped back, running a hand down his face. Nell eyed him before moving to take the lasagna out of the oven.

His father's words flared through his head, and Rome tried to check himself. It was one thing to loosen up and enjoy himself with Nell, it was another to get carried away. He had to remember what the point of all of this was; to assuage his guilt. That was it. Jazlyn was his woman.

"You can go wash your hands while this cools off a little bit," Nell suggested, setting the piping hot lasagna on the stove. "Then we can dig in."

"Cool." Rome headed to the bathroom, taking his time as he relieved himself and washed his hands. He glanced in the mirror, smoothing a hand over his black hair and anticipating his upcoming haircut that weekend.

After another couple of minutes, he headed back to the kitchen, where Nell had already started plating up the food.

"Ready to eat?" she asked brightly.

Glad that she wasn't commenting on his awkward moment from earlier, Rome nodded. "Yeah. What can I do to help?"

"It's all done, thanks. You want some bread? I could make some buttered toast real quick; I didn't get any garlic bread and didn't have time to make rolls."

"The lasagna is plenty, thanks." He sat down at the table, his stomach growling at the sight of the heaping plate of hot food in front of him. Nell hadn't cooked all that much during the time they were together but when she did, he always enjoyed it. "Thanks for doing this."

"My pleasure. I know I slacked off with it when we were together."

"What do you mean? I never expected you to cook for me."

"No, but I started off doing it a lot and then fell off. Remember those times you mentioned missing when I used to make certain things and I said I didn't feel like it?"

"Yeah. I never tripped about it, though. And I wasn't with you for your cooking."

"My point is that I started out doing something and then got comfortable. It's just one of the ways I took you for granted. Like when I told myself it was okay that I never told you I loved you because you should know I do."

Rome pursed his lips. "We don't have to get into that, Nell..."

"We need to get into it because that's part of what this month is about, Rome; I don't want to keep avoiding these conversations. I just want you to know I recognize my part in things, that's all." She took a bite of her lasagna. "And I'm not making that mistake again, taking you for granted."

"I appreciate it." Rome blew on his steaming forkful of food. "I hope I don't take you for granted, either."

"I never felt like you did. You were wonderful to me."

"Wasn't *too* wonderful. Or else we wouldn't be where we are now."

She placed her hand on his arm and he looked up at her. She was smiling at him.

"I'm *grateful* for where we are," she assured softly. "You're here. And that's all I want."

Her eyes held onto his, and Rome marveled at this woman sitting across from him. Even with the way he'd hurt her, she was still the same sweetheart she'd always been. He might have been there to give her a chance to prove something to him, but he realized he could also prove how sorry he was to her. Despite everything, he still cared immensely for Nell. And he didn't want her thinking ill of him.

They continued to eat, their conversation thankfully smooth and effortless. By the time they'd eaten their fill, they were both laughing and feeling nothing but good vibes.

"You sure you don't want any more?" Nell asked him, standing. She reached over to grab his plate but he stopped her.

"I'm good. But you're not about to clean up this kitchen, I hope you know." He took her plate from her hands and carried it with his to the sink. "You made this bomb lasagna; the least I can do is clean up."

"That's sweet of you. But it can wait. And I'm sending the rest of this home with you, just so you know."

"So that'll be my lunch tomorrow. One less thing to worry about."

"Good."

Nell was putting the leftovers in a Tupperware container when Rome's cell phone rang. His smile faded a tiny bit when he saw it was Jazlyn calling him back.

"Oh..."

Nell glanced over at him. "What is it?"

"It's Jazlyn." Rome looked at her apologetically. "I called her earlier; let me just tell her that I'll talk to her later. One sec."

Rome hurried out of the kitchen before Nell could respond, going to the living room to answer the call.

"Hey, sweets."

"Rome!" Jazlyn sounded relieved to hear his voice, which made him smile. And miss her that much more. "I'm *so* sorry I missed you earlier. My phone died while I was at work and I didn't have my charger."

"It's time for you to upgrade that thing."

"Ugh. I heard your voicemail; I can't believe you came by and I wasn't here. Can you come back now?"

Rome hesitated. "I'm still at Nell's, sweets. I just wanted to answer to let you know I'd have to call you back. Plus I needed to hear your voice, even if it was just for a minute."

"Oh." The disappointment was evident, but when she spoke again, Jazlyn tried to sound brighter. "I get it. Call me back when you get home, though, okay? I don't care how late it is."

"All right. I miss you."

"I miss you, too."

They ended the call, and Rome ventured back into the kitchen, hoping Nell wasn't ticked off. She didn't look upset, but he knew better than to just assume she was fine.

"Sorry about that," he said, tucking his phone back in his jeans pocket.

"It's okay. Your leftovers are in the refrigerator...though I hope you're not about to leave."

"I wasn't. Not right now."

"Good." She smiled at him. "'Cause I thought we could watch the recording of the Usher concert."

He brightened. Usher was one of his favorite artists. "Yeah, you're trying to butter me up."

"Guilty." Nell winked at him as she grabbed his hand and pulled him back to her bedroom. Rome kicked his shoes off as she cued up the concert on her wall-mounted television and dimmed the lights. Rome settled himself on the bed with his back against the padded headboard, and Nell crawled over to sit between his legs, her back to his chest. She pulled his arms around her as the concert began, with Usher dancing his way onto the screen.

"Isn't this nice?" she sighed.

"Yeah." He closed his eyes, inhaling her scent. "It really is."

They didn't talk much as they watched the concert, only speaking occasionally to comment on something or sing along with some of the lyrics. Rome was enjoying himself so much that he didn't even think about how late it was getting.

"Oh my gosh, I *love* Usher," Nell gushed once the concert was over. She turned in his arms to look at him. "I know you wanted to go see him when he was in town but we weren't able to get tickets, so I thought this would be a nice alternative."

"This was great, Nell. Almost as good as being there."

"And I still say you dance better than him."

Rome scoffed. "You're already on my good side, Nell; no need to lie."

They shared a laugh. Nell patted his arms excitedly. "Remember that surprise I mentioned earlier? I'm about to run and get it."

"Nell..."

"You're gonna love it. Be right back."

She jumped off the bed and scurried out of the room, and Rome couldn't help but chuckle at her excitement. He definitely appreciated all of the effort she was putting into the evening. He had enjoyed watching the concert so much that he almost forgot that he still needed to call Jazlyn at some point.

Nell reappeared, both hands behind her back and an eager smile on her face.

"What are you up to, Nell?" Rome asked, still smiling himself.

"I hope you saved room for dessert." She produced two chocolate chip cookie ice cream sandwiches, rolled in chocolate chips. When Rome's jaw dropped, she grinned widely.

"*Hell* yeah!" Rome exclaimed, grabbing one of the sandwiches like a kid at the ice cream truck. Nell laughed. He took a huge bite, grunting his approval. "Damn, this almost tastes just like the ones Mama makes."

"I hope so. The cookies are her recipe."

Rome paused the bite he was about to take and looked at her. "You called Mama?"

"I actually asked her for the recipe back when we were still together because I know how much you love these, but I kept putting off making them." Nell took a small bite of her own ice cream sandwich. "So I wanted to do it tonight."

Choosing not to comment, Rome just continued to enjoy his dessert. He eyed Nell as she ate hers, that warm feeling spreading over him, despite him stuffing himself with ice cream. Where would he and Nell be by then if she was doing all of this when they were together?

"Thanks for that, Nell," he said, cleaning his hands with the baby wipe she handed him. She always kept a pack in her nightstand, which often came in handy after they engaged in certain sexual activities. Rome tried to suppress that remembrance. "You really spoiled me tonight."

"I'm glad you enjoyed it."

He looked at his watch. "Damn, it's getting late. I'll go clean up the kitchen and then head out."

"One second, Rome." Nell moved over to sit closer to him, her leg touching his. "There is one thing I want to discuss with you first."

"What's up?'

"Earlier, when Jazlyn called..."

"You're mad 'cause I stepped out to talk to her?"

"No, I'm not *mad*. But it did make me think of something. Rome, I know you're technically still with Jazlyn and I can't ask you to just forget about her. But what I *do* want to request of you is that during these last few weeks together, if you could...put her on pause."

Rome frowned slightly. "She kinda is, Nell. You've been getting most of my time and attention. I haven't even seen Jazlyn."

"And what I'm asking is that during this time with me, you *don't* see or talk to her."

He leaned away, his frown deepening. "Seriously?"

"I know it's a lot to ask," Nell quickly replied, sensing his shift in mood. "But our vibe changed a little bit when she called and I don't want that."

Rome looked down at his lap, wondering what to make of this.

"Rome, you've reminded me more than once that you'll be going back to Jazlyn once this is over," Nell continued. "And I accept that. But if that's the case, I need this time to be just for me. I just...I'm trying my best to express myself and open up to you and it's not easy to do that when you're distracted by someone else."

Her words made sense, as much as Rome hated to admit it. There wasn't much point in him being there if he was going to spend the time wishing he was with Jazlyn or jumping when she called. He did intend on going back to her after this was over but in the meantime, the least he could do was let Nell be front and center.

He knew Jazlyn wasn't going to see it that way, though.

"I get it," he finally acquiesced. "I guess I can see your point."

Nell smiled, relieved. "Thank you."

"I'll need to let her know that, though. I can't just fall off without letting her know what's up."

"Of course."

Rome went to wash the dishes, refusing Nell's multiple offers to help. She just hung out in the kitchen as he cleaned, and they talked and laughed as they recalled earlier times in their relationship. It was after one in the morning when Rome finally got ready to leave, with Nell telling him she loved him before giving him a long hug and a lingering kiss on the lips before he headed out with a Tupperware container full of leftover lasagna. His smile still lingered as he drove home, full, tired, and pleasantly surprised at how well the evening had gone.

When he got home, he remembered that he needed to let Jazlyn know the bad news. Not having the nerve to hear the disappointment in her voice again, Rome opted to text her.

Hey, sweets. I'm finally home. Look, I know you're not gonna like this but Nell asked that we not communicate until my month with her is up. I don't like it but I see her point. So...I'll talk to you when this is all over. Love you.

Chapter 20

Jazlyn couldn't believe her eyes. She must've read Rome's text ten times and every time, it said the same thing.

"So now we can't even talk *at all*??" she exclaimed to her empty bedroom, pounding her fist on the bed. Nell was really pushing it. And why would Rome actually agree to not being able to see or talk to her for almost three weeks?

This wasn't how this was supposed to go. The only reason Jazlyn agreed to this whole mess was because she wanted Nell to get some of her dignity back after Rome left her, and because Jazlyn felt guilty for her part in that. She didn't want the cloud of infidelity hanging over her and Rome's heads for the rest of their relationship. But she fully expected to still be able to talk to her man while he was serving his penance with Nell. She kicked herself yet again for not establishing ground rules up front for this whole thing.

Jazlyn didn't want to believe that her and Rome not communicating would make any difference; that he'd still come right back to her the second his time with Nell was up. But she had to keep it real. Nell was clearly pulling out all the stops. There was no telling what she would try with Rome while she was hogging all of his time. Or what she'd *already* tried. Jazlyn shuddered to think about her Rome and Nell doing things that Jazlyn only wanted him doing with her.

The whole thing plagued her mind, despite her repeated attempts at internal pep talks. As much as she tried not to be,

Jazlyn was worried. And it didn't help that all people wanted to talk about around her was relationships.

"Hey Jazlyn, how's that cute-ass boyfriend of yours?" one of her coworkers asked her at work a couple of days later.

Jazlyn hadn't said much all day and was trying to concentrate on the set of gels she was applying to her client's nails. She wasn't in the mood to engage in the usual salon banter and gossip, and she certainly wasn't up for discussing her own relationship.

"Oh, he's good. Working a lot, you know." Jazlyn kept her eyes on what she was doing, not wanting to risk giving away how upset she was.

"Did he hire a woman for his flooring business?"

Glancing at her coworker Robin, Jazlyn frowned curiously. "What?"

"I saw him having breakfast with a woman with long microbraids the other day. He looked like he was dressed for work. She was really pretty, too."

Knowing that was Nell, Jazlyn just shrugged a shoulder and tried to keep looking unbothered, even though she was anything but. "Nah, I know who that is. They're just...working on something together."

"Girl, you're way more secure than I am. There's no way I'd be cool with my man being out with another woman, working together or not. Especially if she looked like this woman did."

Jazlyn wished they'd talk about something else. "Well, I trust my man. And if you recall, he and I were best friends for years before we got together. So I'm not trippin'. Hey,

Sammi, whatever happened with that baseball player you met at Whole Foods?"

That thankfully got the attention off of her as her platinum-haired coworker excitedly launched into the latest updates about the pro ball player she met and had already claimed as hers as she continued the spa pedicure she was giving to the client in her chair. Jazlyn breathed a sigh of relief, praying that nobody else tried to engage her in any more conversation. She didn't even want to be there, but if she had to be, she just wanted to do her work and leave.

After a busy day of doing nails and brows, Jazlyn was glad when the work day was over several hours later. It still burned her that Rome and Nell were out and about town together. They were having breakfast, Robin said. Did that mean they'd spent the night together?

This was yet another thing that Jazlyn hadn't considered; that other people would see Rome and Nell together. Because of course, Jazlyn hadn't thought to insist that they keep their little meetups private.

But then she considered that if they were out in public, they couldn't be doing *private* things.

But, knowing that they were out sharing pancakes and giggles made Jazlyn wonder if *private* things had already been done. Rome had to know that he and Nell could be seen if they were out together, and that it might get back to Jazlyn. Their friends and family knew that Rome and Nell broke up and he was with Jazlyn now; how would it look for him to now be out with his ex? Jazlyn generally didn't care what other people thought, but she wasn't trying to look like a fool. It was bad enough that she felt like one.

She itched to call Rome and ask him about it, but it was against the stupid rules. There was nothing stopping her from calling Nell, but Jazlyn didn't want to give the impression that she felt threatened in any way. Nell might become even more emboldened if she knew Jazlyn was worried, and Jazlyn didn't need that. She couldn't help but wonder what Nell would ask for next.

"A little less than three weeks to go," she reminded herself.

· · · ·

THE LAST THING JAZLYN felt like doing was teaching, but she trudged through night class on autopilot. She had initially been grateful for the distraction of having something else to occupy her mind but now, it just felt like a burden. Her students were cool, but Jazlyn just wanted to go home and stew by herself while she wished for time to speed up.

Once again, her student Vickie was the last to leave, and this time Jazlyn hated that her brother was apparently running late again. Jazlyn tried not to keep checking the time as they waited while straightening up the room. About fifteen minutes after the class ended, Vickie's brother Kash rushed in.

"Ladies, I'm *so* sorry," he immediately expressed, looking back and forth between them. "Got hung up at work again."

"It's fine," Jazlyn made herself say, already grabbing her purse and bag. She moved over to turn out the light. "Vickie helped me get everything cleaned up, so we can go ahead and go."

"This is what I get for letting my license get suspended," Vickie muttered, glaring at her tardy brother. "Come on, Kash. I'm hungry."

"Yeah, all right," Kash replied absently, his eyes on Jazlyn. He waited for her to lock up the building before following her and Vickie to the parking lot. "You want to join us, Jazlyn? My treat. It's the least I can do for holding you up again."

"Oh," Jazlyn glanced at him briefly as she continued on to her car. He strode right alongside her, not noticing or caring that his sister had moved over to his car and was waiting on him to unlock the door. "I appreciate the offer, Chris-"

"It's Kash."

"Kash, I'm sorry. Thank you for offering but I need to get home."

"Well, maybe I can take you out another time, then."

Stopping, Jazlyn turned to him. He stood there, eying her with his bottom lip pulled between his teeth. Jazlyn finally realized that he was flirting with her.

"Umm...that's nice of you, but I can't."

"Don't tell me there's a rule about you dating a brother of one of your students."

"No, but there's a rule about me dating anyone other than my man."

"Oh." Kash's face fell slightly. "Guess I should've asked if you were spoken for or not, huh?"

Jazlyn noted he was rather cute, with his milky brown skin, piercing eyes and admittedly sexy lips. He was about average height, seeing as how he wasn't that much taller than her and she was only 5'6. That wouldn't have been a huge deal to her if she were single, but she had a man that was 6'3 and adorable and sexy and-

"Jazlyn?"

"Oh." Blushing, Jazlyn looked away. "Sorry; I'm a little preoccupied. But yeah, I'm flattered but I can't go out with you."

"I respect that," Kash replied with a nod. "At least I know now."

"Kash!" Vickie called out from across the lot. "Can you hurry up? Or at least unlock the door? It's not exactly warm out here."

"You should go," Jazlyn suggested. "Feed your sister. I need to get home, myself."

"All right." Kash's eyes roamed over her fondly, as if getting a last look. "Get home safe, Jazlyn."

"You, too."

Kash unlocked his car over his shoulder with his key fob for his sister as he waited for Jazlyn to get into hers. He backed up slowly as she cranked up her engine, waving at her before she pulled off.

Jazlyn's fingers dug into the steering wheel as she drove home. It was ironic that she told Kash she couldn't date him because she had a man, but her man could date his ex while he was still in a relationship with her. Kash was cute and seemed nice but Jazlyn wasn't interested. All she wanted was for Rome to stop parading around with Nell so they could go on about their business.

It bugged Jazlyn that she couldn't be cool and collected about all of this. She hated obsessing about anything. But

not knowing what was going on between Rome and Nell was driving her crazy. At least before, he was giving her mini updates on things, even if they were sporadic. But now Jazlyn knew nothing and she hated that.

She also hated being sexually frustrated and not being able to satisfy it with anything other than her own hands or her sex toys. That wasn't cutting it. Rome had spoiled her with the way he pleasured her body, and anything else just wasn't good enough.

Yet *another* thing she hadn't considered in all this.

She got home and looked for something to eat, but realized she hadn't gone grocery shopping, so dinner ended up being cereal out of the box. After taking a long, stinging-hot shower, Jazlyn talked to Ginger while she went about twisting her natural hair and removing her makeup. Thankfully, Ginger didn't ask her anything about Rome, sensing that Jazlyn was too frustrated for that subject, knowing she couldn't see or talk to him. Jazlyn appreciated her friend for that.

She was sprawled across her bed on her stomach, mindlessly scrolling through the TV channels with half her face mashed into the comforter. She hoped to find something to take her mind off things, but she knew that was a tall order. This whole situation with Rome was starting to consume her, and she knew she had to find a better way to deal with it before she drove herself nuts.

When her phone rang, she lunged for it, twisting her body to grab it from the nightstand. She sucked her teeth when she saw it was Marco. Or she figured it was Marco since it was an unfamiliar number. She wasn't in the mood for him tonight.

But then there was a knock on her door. Jazlyn groaned loudly as she rolled off her bed, adjusting the silk scarf on her head as she stomped towards the living room. It was no surprise at all when she looked through the peephole and saw Marco standing there.

She snatched open the door. "What?"

Marco immediately took a step towards her, a concerned frown on his face. "Hey, you okay?"

She reared back slightly. "Yeah. Why wouldn't I be?"

He started to respond but hesitated. "Can I come in? I need to talk to you about something. No bullshit."

Figuring she didn't have anything else to do, Jazlyn just shrugged and turned to head back into the living room.

Marco quickly closed the door and came to stand in front of her. His muscled body was draped in a dark blue sweatsuit. "Don't go off on me for what I'm about to ask you; I'm just asking because I care about you, Jazlyn. Did something happen between you and Rome?"

Her back straightened. "Why?"

"Because I just saw him and Nell out together."

Jazlyn fought to keep her expression from crumbling at hearing that her man was out on the town with Nell yet again. It almost felt like Nell was trying to rub it in her face, and Rome was letting it happen. Did he even protest when Nell suggested they go out? Why couldn't they just stay at her apartment and spend their time together there? Jazlyn didn't even bother asking where Marco had seen them. The fact that they were out together was enough.

"Yeah, umm...it's okay, Marco," she made herself say. "It's nothing to worry about."

He looked confused. "What? Did y'all break up?"

"I really don't want to talk about this with you."

"I'm not trying to get in your business. But I didn't want you sitting over here thinking the two of you are good and he's out there showboating with his ex. I wouldn't want you to get played like that."

She could feel the emotion building inside of her and she tried to tamp it down. The tears pushed against her eyes, threatening to bust through. "That's sweet, Marco. Though I'm surprised you would care, considering."

"Don't get me wrong, there was a part of me that wanted to clown you for this. But when I thought about it, I realized I cared about you too much to have you out here looking stupid over this chump. I wouldn't want that to happen to you."

Not being able to hold it in anymore, Jazlyn broke down, keeling over at the waist. Marco immediately reached out to catch her, wrapping her in his strong arms and pulling her close.

"Jazlyn, come on, don't do this." He held her to his chest, surprised at how she clung to him. "Don't cry over him like this. If he's stepping out on you-"

"That's not what this is," Jazlyn cut him off, sniffling. "I don't want to get into *what* it is, but it's not what you're thinking."

"Okay...so why are you crying, then?"

Jazlyn stepped back, wiping her eyes. She needed to get herself together. There was no telling what was going through Marco's mind right then. Usually she didn't care what he thought, but she didn't want him thinking Rome was doing her dirty when he was just trying to grant Nell a favor.

"My bad," she muttered, pressing her hands to her cheeks. "I lost it for a second but I'm okay now. Thanks for trying to have my back; I appreciate it."

Marco didn't budge. "Jazlyn, talk to me. What's going on?"

Immediately shaking her head, Jazlyn hastily wrapped her arms around herself. "I can't get into it, Marco. But I promise you it's not what you think it is."

"Are you sure?"

More tears came before Jazlyn could stop them, and she turned away. The truth was, she *wasn't* totally sure. Not as sure as she should've been. She had no way of knowing what was happening between Rome and Nell. It wasn't impossible that Rome could change his mind again and go back to his ex, and Jazlyn's assurances to herself that that wouldn't happen weren't as strong as they were when all of this started.

Marco's arms encircled her from behind, and Jazlyn welcomed the embrace. Her hands gripped his forearms, needing the comfort right then. It felt nice to get that instead of being told how much of an idiot she was for giving her man to his ex for a month.

Turning in his arms, Jazlyn looked up at Marco. His cologne wafted around her, enveloping her as firmly as his arms were.

"I'm sorry, Marco."

His eyebrows shot up. "You are?"

"Yeah, you cheated on me first. But it was still foul what I did to you. And I'm sorry."

Marco was floored. He never expected to hear any apologies from Jazlyn for getting with Rome. She hadn't shown one shred of guilt since it happened, at least not in front of him. Whatever was going on with Rome must have really shaken her up.

"It's cool of you to say that," he muttered, palming the side of her face as his thumb wiped her tears. "It means a lot to me, to hear that from you."

"Yeah."

"Jazlyn." His other hand came up to grab her other cheek. "I hate seeing you cry like this."

She just sniffed and looked at the ground.

"What can I do to help you feel better?"

Her eyes lifted, bouncing off his chest before landing on his face. He looked so sincere, so concerned about her. She felt something shift, and in that moment she was glad Marco was there. They weren't arguing or at each other's throats; he was the sweet man that she'd been attracted to when they met almost three years earlier.

She saw his face getting closer and made no move to stop it. When his lips touched hers, she let it happen. Their mouths immediately opened to each other, the kisses getting deep and breathy, sending bursts of arousal blasting around Jazlyn's body. Her hands gripped his sweatshirt as she leaned into him, loving how he held her close. She needed this. She just wanted to feel better, even if it was temporary.

Marco's hands slid down her shoulders and arms before resting on her waist. He slowly began walking her backwards towards the couch, and Jazlyn's hand drifted between them to grab his erection through his sweats, stroking him. He moaned against her lips as his fingers slid under the tie of her bathrobe. It was then that Jazlyn remembered that she was practically naked underneath, wearing only a pair of bikini-cut panties. Grunting appreciatively at the sight of this, Marco picked her up laid her on the couch, his lips only leaving hers when she was on her back. Jazlyn gasped when she felt his hand on one breast and his tongue on the other, her hand gripping the back of the couch.

"Aaahhhh..." Jazlyn almost didn't recognize her own voice as she squeezed her eyes shut, giving in to the pleasure. Her body rolled underneath Marco, unable to help it, grunting and groaning loudly as Marco licked and sucked her nipples the way he knew she liked it. She managed to trick her mind into thinking it was Rome's hands and tongue pleasuring her. "Yes..."

But that only lasted for a moment because if it *had* been Rome doing that to her, she'd have orgasmed already.

Marco kissed his way down her stomach and back up again, his lips crashing onto hers. He climbed on top of her, wasting no time pressing his rock-hard erection against her. He lifted her leg around his waist as his hips grinded against hers, sliding his tongue down her neck. She immediately matched his rhythm as she grinded desperately against him, grabbing his butt with both hands.

"Fuck, Jazlyn," he whispered, his fingers teasing her nipple again. "I love you so much, girl. You have no idea how much I wanna be inside you right now. You feel how hard I am for you, baby? I want you so bad, *shit*." He hooked a finger inside her panties. "Take these off. Let me make love to you. I'll make you forget all about Rome."

Jazlyn's eyes slid open. She saw the bald head and felt the bulky muscular body and suddenly remembered the man on top of her wasn't Rome. And regardless of their weird, jacked-up situation, he was still her man. No matter how horny she was or what he might be doing with Nell, she couldn't lose her head like this.

"I can't," she muttered, her body going limp. Her hands pushed against his shoulders. "Marco, I'm sorry but I can't do this. Get up."

He lifted his head, a mix of frustrated and confused. Jazlyn couldn't blame him because she was both of those things, too. "What's wrong?"

"I just...I can't. Please let me up."

Peering at her for several moments, Marco finally pushed himself off of her. Jazlyn immediately rolled off the couch, tying her robe tightly and fixing the scarf on her head. Her body was still buzzing with arousal, but she also felt the heat of embarrassment. Fooling around with Marco was the last thing she needed to be doing. Things were messed up enough as it was.

"What just happened, Jazlyn?" Marco asked, still kneeling on the couch. "We were good and now you can't even look at me."

She shook her head, making herself turn her eyes to his. "Marco...this was messed up. I'll own this one; I shouldn't have let myself get carried away like that. I swear I'm not trying to jerk you around, I just...my head is jacked up right now. And us getting down isn't going to make it better."

"You sure? 'Cause it damn sure seemed like it was making you feel better a minute ago."

"Okay yeah, it felt good but that doesn't mean I need to be doing it."

"Jazlyn-"

"Marco." She held up her hands, suddenly exhausted. "Please just let it go. And I appreciate you coming to check on me but I need you to roll. Like, now."

Sighing, Marco stood. Jazlyn slunked a few feet away from him, hugging herself on the outside and kicking herself on the inside.

Thankfully, Marco didn't say anything else. He just gave her a lingering look and then walked out, closing the door firmly behind him.

As soon as he was gone, Jazlyn sunk onto the couch with her head in her hands, muttering to herself.

"Way to make it worse, Jazlyn."

Chapter 21

Rome hadn't wanted to go out in public with Nell. He knew there was the possibility of running into Jazlyn, or someone else that knew he and Jazlyn were now together. He didn't want to give off the impression that he was flip-flopping between the two women when that was the furthest thing from the truth.

Nell persisted, though, and he gave in. They met for breakfast one morning and went to a Paint and Sip event that night. Rome didn't have a terrible time; in fact, once he got past the paranoia of being out with Nell, he actually enjoyed himself. They had a lot of fun bonding over their shared lack of painting talent, but the wine made it funnier and less embarrassing.

They were still laughing about their subpar paintings when they got back to Nell's place.

"You should hang that in your living room," Nell suggested, nodding towards Rome's painting of a jar of flowers. "I have the perfect spot for mine."

"Uh, that's a no. It's not really something I'm proud of. It looks like a child painted this."

"Oh, stop. It's not that bad at all."

"You're being nice."

"What are you going to do with it, then?"

"Stuff it in the back of my closet."

"Rome." Nell chuckled, setting her own jar of flowers painting on the couch. She grabbed his and placed it next to hers. "Well, if you don't want it, I'll keep it."

He looked at her. "What?"

"I'll hang it in my room. It'll be a constant reminder of you after...well, I'd gladly take it, if you seriously don't want it."

She wouldn't look at him, but he could see the forced smile on her face as she continued gazing longingly at the paintings, as if they somehow represented the two of them together. Then she must have caught herself, because she threw a sheepish glance at him before clearing her throat and removing her jacket. "Hungry?"

"Not really."

"Do you have to leave?"

"No, I can hang out for a while."

Nell grinned, which triggered his own smile. He didn't even check what time it was, but he wasn't in a hurry to leave. They were halfway through their month and at some point Rome had stopped counting down the days and started enjoying them. It almost felt like old times, when he and Nell were at their happiest. She was still the same sweetheart of a woman he had fallen in love with.

"I was hoping you'd say that," she replied. "I'll be right back."

"Okay..." Rome eyed her as she hurried to her bedroom, already grinning in anticipation. Moments later, he heard mellow saxophone music playing.

Nell returned to the living room, walking right over to him and taking his hand. "I'm so glad you're staying, sweetie. Otherwise I'd feel a little silly for this."

"For what?"

She led him back to her bedroom, turned on the light, and stepped aside. Rome's eyebrows shot up when he saw what was in front of him.

"Wow."

"You think it's corny?" Nell asked, looking up at him.

"Umm...kinda. But corny isn't always bad." He eyed the blanket fort that Nell had built at the foot of her bed, with pillows, flameless candles, and a blanket inside. That explained why she had rushed out of her room and insisted on keeping her bedroom door closed when he'd come to pick her up earlier. "It's kinda cute, actually."

"Really?"

"Yeah. Doesn't look like there's a ton of space in there, though."

"I might've done that on purpose so we would have to cuddle together."

"So you're being sneaky, huh?" Rome playfully flicked her microbraids.

"I prefer to think of it as efficient. The room only has so much space, so..." She stepped in front of him and slid her arms around his neck. "It's just smart, if you ask me."

"Right." Rome's hands took firm hold of her waist.

They shared a long comfortable smile before their faces came together, meeting in a kiss. The first moan came from Rome this time, surprising them both. Nell pushed Rome's jacket from his shoulders, yanking the cuffs off his wrists and tossing it aside before reclaiming her hold around his neck, tighter this time. Rome's arms around her tightened, as well, and when she pressed her body closer to his, his hands slid down to just above her butt, flexing and pressing.

"You wanna come inside?" Nell asked, pressing her thick lips to his neck. She looked up at him with half-lidded eyes. Her hand eased underneath his sweater. "We can get more comfortable..."

Rome looked down at her and felt the threads of desire weave through him at high speed. Nell's company, her spirit, her effort, not to mention her scent, her moist lips, and her brown eyes that were looking at him with darkened desire were all scrambling his brain. In that moment, it was just the two of them. And he didn't mind it at all.

"Yeah," he nodded, gazing back at her, momentarily transfixed. He sucked in a breath when he felt her fingertips brush over his nipple under his shirt. "Yeah, let's do that."

Nell's eyes never left his as she stepped back, her bottom lip between her teeth. She toed her boots off before lowering her long body into the fort, sliding over to the side. Rome watched as she pulled off her chest-hugging white sweater, tossing it near his feet. He felt his dick jump at the sight of her in her cream push-up bra that looked amazing against her dark skin. His eyes roaming her, he kicked off his own boots and, after a brief pause, lifted his sweater over his head. The white t-shirt he wore underneath remained, and Nell didn't comment when it stayed in place as he knelt down and joined her inside the fort.

Nell immediately pulled him on top of her and their kiss resumed. It was hungry and intense, neither of them holding back how good they felt in the moment. Nell's hands were all over Rome, her grunts of sexual frustration filling the small fort along with their pants and moans and loud kisses.

"Rome," she breathed, lifting her hips to feel his erection. Her mouth fell open when he licked behind her ear then down her neck, and her fingers that were gripping the back of his head tightened. "Rome, please..."

"Please, what?" he whispered, kissing her chin. His hips began to move with hers, earning a tortuous whimper from her. "What is it you want?"

She placed his hand on her breast, pulling back to look at him pleadingly. "I want you to spend the night. And I want you inside of me when you do."

Rome looked down at her, his fire cooling ever so slightly. He was enjoying this. His body certainly responded to Nell. But fooling around was one thing; sexing her was another.

Sensing his hesitation, Nell gently pushed at his shoulders, silently requesting him to get up. Rome thought she was going to tell him off or start crying, and his eyes widened when she just sat up and unhooked the front clasp on her bra. She tossed it out of the fort near her sweater.

"Can we at least do this, then?" she whispered, straddling his lap. She gathered his t-shirt in her hands and lifted, easing it over his head and tossing it over her shoulder. Her hands roamed appreciatively around his shoulders and down to his chest before pressing her bare breasts to him. She gave a lingering kiss to his lips. "Is this okay? I just want to get as close to you as I can, Rome. And my body is screaming for you right now...please at least give me this."

Rome let her place his hands on her breasts, and she held them there as she began slowly grinding on him. Their hands squeezed and rotated on her breasts in unison, starting a sensual rhythm that caused hitched breaths and escaped gasps. Rome pinched her nipples before leaning forward and kissing one of them gently, causing Nell's head to fall back. His tongue eased out and began teasing, then sucking, a grunt of appreciation erupting from his throat. Nell cried out in pleasure, gripping the back of his neck in both hands as Rome's hand slid around to her butt. The grind of her hips became more focused and concentrated, and she wished to high heaven that their pants could be on the floor next to their shirts.

The intensity inside the blanket fort heightened as their kisses got deeper and sloppier, Rome sucked and teased her breasts to the point of Nell literally screaming his name, and her grinding on his lap so hard and so fast that she was working up a sweat. Rome held onto her, knowing what the goal was, and wanting to oblige her. His hands gripped her ass as she bucked on him, matching her movements and feverishly bringing his hips to meet hers. He urged her along with whispers to keep going, which only emboldened her. Before too long they were both going at it like crazy, Nell's lush breasts bouncing wildly in Rome's face, her face pinched in concentrated effort.

"I wanna come, Rome," she whimpered. "Please make me come, baby."

"I got you," Rome panted, grabbing one of her breasts and squeezing while his other hand pulled her against his bulging erection faster. "Do your thing; I got you."

"Oh my god...I'm close, Rome, don't stop..." She let out a long wavering noise before Rome took her nipple into his mouth again, sucking so hard that she yelped in painful pleasure. "Rome!"

She screamed so loud that Rome was sure her neighbors heard it, the orgasm hitting her full force. Rome held onto her as she shuddered on his lap, her fingertips gripping his strong shoulders, her face going lax with satisfaction.

Her eyes opened and settled on him, the post-orgasm glaze evident. She leaned forward and kissed him, stroking her tongue against his with a relaxed moan.

"I love you so much, Rome," she muttered against his lips. Her hand slid up to his face. "Do you still love me?"

Rome hesitated. "I still have love for you, Nell. But-"

"No. Please," She pressed her fingertips to his lips before kissing him again. "Can we just leave it at that?"

Rome didn't want to leave it that. "Nell...this might be a jacked-up thing to say after what just went down, but I have to keep it real with you. I'm still-"

"It's just you and me for now, remember?" She gripped his face in both hands, her pleasured gaze morphing into a pleading one. "For two more weeks, it's just us."

He sighed, acquiescing. "All right."

"And for the record, you must still feel something for me, or else we wouldn't be here like this." Nell looked at him pointedly. "I refuse to believe that this was meaningless for you. You're not that kind of guy and we both know it."

His eyes drifted up to hers.

"Just because you came into this believing one thing doesn't mean you can't change your mind." She caressed the side of his face. "We're good together, Rome. You might not want to admit it out loud, but you're enjoying this as much as I am. And I believe in my heart of hearts that you won't be able to just walk away as easily as you think you will. You still love me."

She pressed another kiss to his lips before he could respond, sliding her arms around his neck. Rome returned her kiss, choosing to let her believe what she wanted. Yes, he was having a good time with her. No, he wasn't counting down the days until their month was over like he was doing initially. And he was clearly still attracted to her.

Nell was a good woman. She was a sexy woman. But that didn't mean she should be *his* woman.

Did it?

The question stayed on Rome's mind after he left her apartment a couple of hours later and into the next day. He had begun feeling the slight pangs of guilt for the intimacy he'd shared with Nell, even though he and Jazlyn hadn't set up any parameters regarding that, not that Nell would have agreed to those, anyway. Rome had to ask himself why his attraction and desire for Nell was reigniting like it was, and he didn't think it was just physical. Before they broke up, she had tried to make moves on him a few times and he rebuffed her. Rome had never been one to just share his body with no feeling behind it; meaningless sex had never been his thing, even when he was on the road as a backup dancer. And when Nell was grinding on his lap the night before, bare-breasted and willing, it certainly had crossed his mind to just give her what she wanted. But that had been the one time during the evening when Jazlyn's face flashed through his mind.

Rome wasn't trying to have his cake and eat it, too. He'd always been a one-woman man, and the fact that his actions were belying that was as confusing as it was frustrating. Nell's words the night before had struck him whether he wanted to admit it or not. *Would* it be as easy to just walk away from her as he thought? His guilt over letting her touch him and them acting like a couple had faded without him even realizing it, and he didn't like how that realization made him feel.

Had Asha been right about him? Maybe he hadn't left someone standing at the altar like Ashton had done, but Rome still cheated on Nell. And now he was essentially cheating on Jazlyn, even though she knew about it and had encouraged him to spend the time with Nell. Everyone had entered this weird situation with their eyes wide open, but that didn't mean much when feelings were involved. There were just some things you couldn't control, like the one-eighty his feelings for Jazlyn had taken after the night of the blizzard.

Speaking of Asha, she called him when he was at work the next day, sitting in his office mindlessly flipping through flooring samples. He was supposed to be going through some invoices, but he had read the same ones several times without registering anything. He wasn't exactly thrilled to see his sister's name on his phone screen.

He let the call go to voicemail, not in the mood for any of her snippy comments. They had come to a semi-truce when he went to see about her a couple of weeks earlier, but she hadn't returned any of his calls since then. He figured she was back to her resentful attitude and he didn't have time for that.

When she immediately called back, Rome cursed under his breath and snatched up the phone. If she started something with him, he wouldn't be responsible for what she got back.

"Yes, Asha?"

"Hey, you busy?"

"I'm at work."

"I'll get right to it, then. Rome, I want to apologize to you."

He sat up in his chair. "What?"

"I owe you an apology for all those things I said after finding out about you and Jazlyn, and how I've been acting towards you since then. I was hurt and angry about Ashton but that's no excuse. And I hope you'll accept my apology."

Floored, Rome's eyes pinged around his small office as if someone was going to jump out at him, letting him know he was being pranked. He honestly never expected Asha to swallow her pride and apologize to him; at the most, he figured she'd eventually get over the anger and just start treating him like she used to without a word.

"I appreciate it," he told her. "Thanks for saying that."

"You accept my apology? We're cool now, right?"

"Sure, yeah." Rome didn't have the energy to make her sweat about it.

"Good," Asha replied, sounding relieved. "And I want you to know that I fully support your relationship with Jazlyn. My problem was never with her; you know I've loved her like a sister since you two became friends years ago."

"Good to know."

There was a pause. "Are you okay? Or are you just saying we're good even though you're still ticked at me?"

Sighing, Rome plopped back in his chair. "I have a lot on my mind, Asha. It has nothing to do with you."

"Anything I can help with?"

"I doubt it."

"I can at least listen, if you want to get something off your chest. It's the least I can do."

Rome wasn't sure he wanted to tell Asha about what was going on with him and Nell. He didn't know what happened to make Asha let go of her anger towards him, but he couldn't imagine her holding her tongue about him agreeing to give Nell a last hurrah while he was still with Jazlyn.

Figuring she'd probably find out at some point, he decided to just come out with it. The last thing he needed to worry about on top of everything else was fearing more judgment from his little sister.

"Well, if you must know, I'm in the middle of an unusual...*thing* with Jazlyn and Nell," he admitted, his voice gruff. "And it's messing with me."

"What do you mean? What thing?"

Rome explained Nell's request for a chance to prove her love for him, Jazlyn's reasoning for encouraging him to do it, and his recent confusing feelings about it. Asha didn't say a word as he spoke and he could just imagine her on the other end fuming.

"Go ahead and go off, if you want," he said when he finished. "But be ready for me to come back at you, with the mood I'm in."

"I'm not gonna do that, Rome," Asha assured, surprising him. "Believe it or not, I understand why you agreed to that."

Rome paused. "Are you messing with me?"

"Wow, I've really been that bad with you lately, huh? No, I'm not messing with you. I get it; you felt bad for what you did to Nell and wanted to leave her with a little dignity."

"Basically. Though now I'm wondering if it was a good idea, seeing as how I'm so jacked up over it. I wasn't expecting to enjoy myself with Nell as much as I have been recently."

"It makes sense, though, Rome. Nell is great. And you *were* in love with her. Even though you realized you had feelings for Jazlyn, that doesn't just disappear, just like that. It's not much different than my lingering feelings for Ashton; I might not want them, but they're still there."

"I just feel like things will never be the same between me and Jazlyn after this," Rome admitted, anguished. "And that I'm just gonna end up hurting Nell all over again. That's the last thing I want."

"Nell knew what she was getting into when she requested this," Asha stated strongly. "She knew the risk, so if she gets hurt when you walk away, that's too bad. And as for Jazlyn, you just need to be honest with her about whatever happened between you and Nell, if she wants to know. Remember, she agreed to this, too."

"Yeah. Still, though..."

"I really believe your relationship is strong enough to withstand this, Rome. Even though I acted like an ass when I saw the two of you at your house that night, I could see the way you looked at each other. Not to mention, you put me out; you weren't backing down from how you felt about her then, not even to your sister. What you have is the real deal."

Rome hoped so. Everything in him hoped that this whole experiment would have the desired effect and he and Jazlyn would continue on with their relationship, stronger than ever.

Though he couldn't imagine Jazlyn taking it in stride that he'd allowed anything physical to happen with Nell while she sat at home waiting for the month to be over.

"I hope you're right," he stated with a sigh. "We're halfway through this mess so we'll see how it goes, I guess."

"Just be honest with both of them about your feelings, whatever they may be. And be honest with yourself. If you decide you ultimately want to be with Nell and you and Jazlyn are better off as friends, then hey; it is what it is. If you go right back to Jazlyn and Nell ends up by herself again, so be it. I know as well as anybody that sometimes things just aren't fair when it comes to love. But at least have the courtesy to be honest with both of them like I wish Ashton had been with me."

"Yeah. I will; they deserve that."

"I know you'll do the right thing, Rome. And not that it matters, but I'm pulling for Jazlyn in all this."

"Nice to know."

Rome tried to go on about his day, managing to put his relationship issues out of his mind for a little while. But that relief ended when his mother Georgia called later in the day, having heard about his warped love triangle.

"I swear, Asha never could keep her big mouth shut," he muttered.

"She wasn't telling me for the sake of gossip; she's worried about you, sweetheart."

"That's all well and good but she still doesn't need to be telling my business."

"I wish you had told me yourself. Because I'm willing to bet you've told your father already."

"No offense, Mama, but this is one of those things it's just easier to talk to Dad about."

"I don't see why. You have to know I'd be thrilled about you giving Nell another chance."

"That's not exactly what I'm doing."

"Sounds like it to me."

"See, this is part of the reason why I didn't want you to know about this. You're getting your hopes up."

"Well, I can't help it. I love Nell."

"I understand that, Mama, but I can't take that into account, here."

"Okay, fine. How are things going, then?"

Rome hesitated, not knowing exactly how much Asha had shared with their mother. "It's good, considering. I'd be lying if I said I was *hating* my time with Nell."

"Is that right?" Georgia replied, a smug tilt to her voice. Rome was going to get Asha for this. "So her mission is working, I take it."

"I didn't say all that. I still plan on going back to Jazlyn when these next two weeks are over."

"Hmm. But you and Jazlyn haven't been communicating. And Nell must have worked her way back into your heart or else you wouldn't be so confused about your feelings."

"Mama…"

"Face it, sweetheart, if your feelings for Jazlyn were real, there would be nothing that could shake them. It's okay if you were mistaken; it happens. And please don't take this as disparagement towards Jazlyn; she's wonderful. But have you at least considered that your…*lust* for each other has fooled you into believing it was something deeper?"

"No, Mama, I haven't."

"Well, you should. Because that's what seems to be going on, here. I truly believe that if you felt that strongly for Jazlyn, in *that* way, there would've been nothing anyone could've said to get you to parade around with another woman, guilt or no guilt."

Rome thought about that. He hadn't wanted to agree to this at first but let himself get talked into it. Was that because, on some level, he wasn't as against it as he thought? Was guilt *really* the only reason he granted Nell what she asked for?

Keeping his musings to himself, Rome got up to find some aspirin for the headache he suddenly had. "I respect your opinion, Mama, but I need to handle this how I need to handle it. And I hope you'll be able to deal with it when I'm back with Jazlyn at the end of all this."

"All right, sweetheart. I'll leave it alone. But you're conflicted for a reason. You might not want to talk about it with me, but you'll have to face up to it at some point. There are two wonderful young ladies you're dealing with, here; I hate that one of them is going to be left heartbroken."

"I don't love that, either, but…I guess it can't be helped in this situation."

"Well, I know I'm clearly biased towards one of them, but please know that I'm here for you, regardless of who you choose," Georgia assured. "At the end of the day, I just want my handsome son to be happy."

"Thanks, Mama."

Rome ended the call, more confused than ever.

• • • •

THE NEXT NIGHT, ROME had another date with Nell. He would've preferred to spend the night alone, needing time to get his head together. But Nell again wore him down, insisting that she had a surprise for him.

What he really wanted to do was call Jazlyn. He needed to hear her voice and check on her. He could only imagine what she was going through, unable to talk to him, not knowing what was going on with him and Nell, just totally left in the dark about everything. How was she dealing with all of this?

Rome took a shower and headed over to Nell's, hoping she wouldn't want to go out anywhere. He didn't have the energy. When he arrived to her place and saw it decorated with sports memorabilia and her coffee table full of wings, pizza, and beer, he looked at her curiously.

"What's all this?" he asked as she excitedly pulled him further into the living room.

"It's the last night of the basketball season, right? I thought we could spend the evening watching it."

Rome had been so preoccupied that he'd forgotten all about that. "You never cared to sit and watch basketball with me before. And you don't like wings."

"But *you* do. And I want to watch the games with you now. Oh, and I have something else for you." She grabbed a red envelope from the end table and held it out to him. "Here."

"What's this?" Rome warily eyed the envelope.

"Open it. It's just a little gift."

Slowly taking the envelope from her, he peeked inside. His eyebrows shot up when he saw a Nike gift card. He looked at Nell, who was practically giddy with excitement.

"Nell, what's up with this?"

Her smile wilted slightly. "What do you mean?"

"This," he emphasized, holding up the envelope before waving his arm around the room. "All this you're doing. What's the end game, here?"

She frowned in confusion. "You...know the answer to that, Rome. I thought it was understood what this time together was about; to get a chance to prove how much I love you. To show you how much I want us to be together."

"Yeah, but is this even something you can keep up? Let's be real, Nell; you're pulling out all the stops because you know you're on borrowed time, but what if I were to decide to stay with you after this? Would all this continue, or would things go back to how they were before? You said yourself that you stopped doing stuff that you used to do in the beginning the first time. Why would I think this time would be any different?'

"Because I've already lost you once." Nell stepped towards him. "And I don't want to lose you again."

"Nell. You're giving me gift cards to get more sneakers when you used to always fuss about how many I already have.

You invited me over here to watch a sport you never wanted to watch when I asked you while eating food that you don't like. You don't see how this is coming off as disingenuous?'

"I...I guess I wasn't thinking about it like that. I'm just trying to make you happy."

"It seems to me this isn't about you proving anything to me; it's just about you trying to win back what you think Jazlyn took from you."

Her face tightened. "I thought we agreed not to talk about her."

"We can't act like she doesn't exist, Nell. She's as real now as she was when you went to her asking to *borrow* me so you could do all this. And you might not want to hear it, but one thing I don't have to worry about with Jazlyn is whether she's keeping it real with me or not."

"Wow." Nell turned away from him, her face crumbling. "Are you trying to hurt me now? Is this you trying to push me away?"

"The last thing I want to do is hurt you, Nell. But I'm not trying to get hurt, either. This affects me, too."

She whirled towards him. "Of course it does. I know that."

"And I'm not trying to get used to one thing only to have the rug pulled out from under me again."

"What are you saying?"

"It's been cool hanging out with you, Nell. But...maybe we should quit while we're ahead. I don't want to continue with these last couple of weeks and get your hopes up only for you to end up hating me in the end."

"So you're giving up already?"

"It's just hitting me that this isn't any good for anybody; you, me, or Jazlyn. We all might've had good intentions with it, but I have a feeling how this is going to end up. So we might as well just-"

"No!" Nell exclaimed, shaking her head. She stepped over to him, gripping the sides of his jacket. "Maybe I've been a little eager but it's only because I don't want to waste this chance I have with you. Even if you're not, I'm keeping hope alive. And you owe me two more weeks."

Rome figured she wouldn't give up that easily. "Nell, look...I just think we went about this all wrong. And I don't know what the *right* way would've been but...this wasn't it."

She peered up at him for a moment. "You know what I think? I think my efforts are working and it's freaking you out. You still love me, Rome, whether you want to or not." She slid her arms around his waist, her eyes taking a different slant. "Or else the other night in my little blanket fort wouldn't have happened."

He swallowed, hating that her words had merit. He *did* still have feelings for Nell, and should've figured that she wouldn't let him run from that like he was trying to do.

"I'll admit I've been a little confused," he told her.

"That's why we need to finish out these two weeks, so things can become clear for you."

"I don't see it like that. I think it'll just make it worse."

"Only one way to find out."

"Nell, come on. This little bubble we're in isn't how it's always gonna be. At some point, Jazlyn will be back in the picture. And I'd like to think that if what we had was strong enough, you wouldn't be so consumed with me not talking to her while you're trying to 'prove yourself'."

Her expression faltered but she quickly righted it. "Maybe you have a point with that. But I want my two weeks, Rome. I'm willing to do whatever I need to. And you promised me."

He sighed. "I know, but-"

She grabbed the back of his neck and brought his face to hers, taking a kiss. She pulled him to her desperately, both of them well aware of what she was doing. But Rome chose not to call her on her blatant distraction attempt. He just let the kiss continue for a few moments before they finally settled down to watch the basketball games, not that he could enjoy them. Between his jumbled feelings about Nell, missing Jazlyn, and now his family's opinions bouncing around his head, Rome was as frustrated as ever.

There was a small part of him that wished he could go back to before the night of the blizzard, before everything got so jacked up.

Chapter 22

Seven days couldn't pass fast enough for Jazlyn.

She was still missing Rome, still sexually frustrated, and still kicking herself for losing her head with Marco. He'd caught her in a weak moment, but that didn't mean she felt any better about it. The last thing she needed to do was give him the impression that he had a shot with her, as he was now thinking. He had left several notes in her mailbox and sent flowers to her at work, which annoyed Jazlyn more than endeared her. She just hated that she had reopened that can of worms just because she was horny.

The only man she wanted pleasing her body and spoiling her and sharing time with her was Rome. She just hoped that he still wanted the same things with her.

It was driving her crazy, not being able to talk to him. Every day she flirted with the idea of stopping by his office. She might have cruised by his house a couple of times, but his truck was never there; she figured all of the *quality time* was being spent at Nell's place. Jazlyn was doing her best to respect the boundaries Nell had set up and Rome had agreed to, but she wished she had insisted on some of her own.

She tried to keep herself occupied with work, her class, hanging with Ginger and messing up new spaghetti recipes, and it only marginally worked. It wasn't lost on her that eying the calendar wasn't going to make it go any faster. Rome was doing his thing and she needed to do hers.

One pleasant surprise came during a conversation with Kash. He was still picking up his sister after every class, thankfully now showing up on time, but he still hung around to help Jazlyn get everything cleaned up and walk her out. She realized he really was very nice, and while he still flirted with her a little, he thankfully hadn't asked her out again.

"You know, Vickie has been raving about you since you took the class over," he revealed, glancing towards his sister who had already gotten into his car. "You really know your stuff, she said."

"Yeah? Well, that's flattering," Jazlyn replied with a smile. "Students like her make it fun."

"You think you're gonna keep teaching after the regular one comes back?"

"Oh, I don't know. Probably not. This is cool but it's not what I wanna do. I'm really just helping out until the baby drops."

"What is it you really wanna do, if you don't mind me asking?"

"I'd actually like to have my own nail polish brand," Jazlyn revealed. "And maybe one day, a salon. But having my own line of nail polish would be dope. I'm always mixing colors, trying to see what I can come up with. Maybe I could even do nail kits, with special colors and everything else you'd need to do some of my most popular designs."

"And you're not worried about losing business because people would be learning to do their own nails?"

"Not at all. There will always be a demand for what I do. Not everybody likes or wants to do their own nails. And not to sound arrogant, but even with all the tools, they still won't have my skills; I stay booked for a reason. But that's why I'm trying to expand and not just do nails and lashes and brows at the salon, and the occasional private clients."

He looked impressed. "Oh, you do lashes and brows, too?"

"Yeah. But probably eighty percent of what I do is nails. That's my main thing, and what I love the most."

"I must say, you've got some skills," Kash commented, glancing at her nails. Each one had a different variation of the same color scheme of red and silver, a couple of them adorned with lines of nail glitter for extra pop. "How do you even come up with all that?"

"It's just what I love to do," Jazlyn shrugged. "Some of its imagination, sometimes it's a jumpoff of something I've seen somewhere else. I love it when a client just picks the colors and lets me do my thing. That's when the fun *really* kicks in."

"Wow." He folded his arms over his chest. This time he was dressed in a white Henley and dark jeans. "I always love to see it when people enjoy what they do. I kinda settled for my career."

"You're a mechanic, right?"

"Oh, no. I just help out at my cousin's garage sometimes when his mechanics don't show up. But I'm actually a geologist."

"You study rocks?"

Kash chuckled. "To put it succinctly, yes. I thought I would enjoy it but if I'm honest, I let my mother pressure me into that. It's cool but I can't say I love it."

"Wow. I've never met any geologists before."

"And I've never met anyone that wants their own line of nail polish. In fact, I might be able to help you out with that."

Jazlyn's eyes widened, then narrowed warily. "Help me how?"

"A buddy of mine I went to school with; he's in the science field, also, and has connections with that kind of thing. I'd be happy to talk to him for you, set up a meeting."

Excitement pinged through Jazlyn, but she hesitated. She didn't want Kash thinking that she owed him something just because he helped her out. "I appreciate that, but..."

"If you're worried I have an ulterior motive, I swear I don't," Kash insisted, holding up his hands. "I'm just trying to help a sister do her own thing, if I can. Once I make the introduction, I'd be out of it; I don't know the first thing about nail polish and honestly have no desire to."

Jazlyn couldn't help but chuckle at that. "I respect your honesty."

"And I respect that you're in a relationship; I already know what's up. Getting declined once was enough." Kash glanced over his shoulder towards his car, where Vickie was in the passenger seat on her phone. "I'd better go. Think about it and let me know."

"I'll do that. Thanks, Kash." Jazlyn got into her car, a little thrown by his offer. Kash waited for her to pull off, waving as she did.

"I think you should do it," Ginger said later, after Jazlyn told her about Kash's suggestion. They were hanging out at Jazlyn's, digging into the chicken dinners Ginger had brought. "At least talk to the guy and see what he says. Maybe he can give you a nudge in the right direction, if nothing else."

"I guess. I've looked into it myself to get an idea of what I'd need to do, and have been putting away money for the last couple of years to go towards it. I really just need someone to help me with the science part, 'cause I want the good shit; no chip, fast-drying, long-lasting gel-like polish."

"Exactly, so you might as well see what he can tell you. Can't hurt, right?"

"I guess not."

They continued to eat as they watched an episode of *Iron Chef*. Ginger began talking about her recent visit to her in-laws, and how she and Zion were contemplating when they were going to start their family.

"I think we're gonna wait another year," she commented, taking a bite of her biscuit. "A lot of people freak out about getting pregnant, but I'm looking forward to it, really. I'm gonna be an *awesome* mother."

"That's great for y'all. Though with the way you two are always going at it, I'd be surprised if you lasted another year before a bun goes in that oven. You know you're not on the pill anymore."

"Well, if it happens before then, it happens. It wouldn't be the worst thing it the world."

"You dealing with pregnancy hormones will be pure comedy, I already know. *That's* the part I'm waiting for."

"Shut up. What about you? You want kids, right?"

Jazlyn shrugged. "Sure, one day."

"With Rome?"

Taking her time chewing the bite of chicken leg she'd just bitten off, Jazlyn kept her eyes on the television screen. "I've thought about it. Rome would make a great dad."

"He would." Ginger paused, wondering if she should ask what she wanted to ask. "I've tried not to bring him up too much 'cause I know you're missing him but, how are you holding up?"

"As well as I can be for someone who can't see or talk to her man even though he's ten minutes from her, and is missing him like crazy. I've been hoping he would ignore Nell's wishes and call or text me or *something*. Just to see how I'm doing."

"Girl, I bet he's missing you, too."

"Well, I have no way of knowing, do I?" Jazlyn threw her chicken bone back to her plate with more aggression than necessary. "He's still shutting me out."

"He's not shutting you out, Jazlyn. He's just giving his attention to Nell. *Like you all agreed*."

"I didn't think she was going to ask him to ignore me this whole time. And I certainly didn't think he'd agree to something like that."

"Well, think of it this way; Nell must be mighty insecure if she felt the need to ask him to stay away from you."

"That doesn't make me feel any better."

"Well, there's no need in catching an attitude now. I tried to tell you that this wasn't a good idea but you were *so* set on clearing your conscience by letting Nell get a last lap with Rome."

"I remember, Ginger. You don't have to start with the 'I told you so' stuff."

"I'm just reminding you that this is what you agreed to. How did you think you were going to feel during all this?

Even if Rome was still able contact you, you still wouldn't feel good about him being over there with Nell."

"Yeah, but at least I'd get to hear his voice, or get some kind of reassurance from him. I'd have some idea of what was going on between them, even if he didn't tell me every little thing. But I don't know *anything* and it's driving me nuts."

"You're past the halfway point, now," Ginger reminded, setting her plate on the coffee table. "It'll be over before you know it."

"Not soon enough."

Ginger hesitated slightly before speaking again. "Is there any part of you that's worried that what Nell is doing might work? That Rome might decide to stay with her?"

Jazlyn winced at the words. Of course the thought had crossed her mind, even though she tried to squelch it every time. She didn't want to entertain the thought, regardless of how possible it was.

"I have to keep believing we're going to pick up right where we left off," Jazlyn responded, her eyes on her plate. "Yeah, it's possible that he...I can't let myself think like that. Rome is mine."

"If you're so sure about that, then why are you sweating any of this? Even if you can't communicate with him, it shouldn't matter, right?"

"It's easier to say that from the sidelines, Ginger. It's different when you're in it."

"I'm not trying to be insensitive. I'm just keeping that mirror on you, that's all. You've been in a mood ever since this month kicked off."

"Okay, so?" Jazlyn shot off the couch, frowning at her friend. She picked up her plate, then put it down again before pacing in front of the couch. "Excuse me for being human. And my agreeing to all this doesn't mean I'm not gonna still be affected by it. I can admit that I didn't expect things to go this way."

"I get that." Ginger stood herself, eying her troubled friend. "And even though I didn't agree with you doing it, I get why you wanted to. I just don't think you should keep stressing yourself out over all this. We've had this conversation more than a few times, Jazlyn. It's gonna end up how it ends up."

As true as she knew that was, Jazlyn wanted to press the fast-forward button and skip to the end of this torture. She just needed some kind of assurance from Rome that they were still going to be fine after all of this; that there wasn't anything Nell could do that would take him away from her. If she could at least get that much from him, it would make getting through these next few days way easier.

Sighing, Jazlyn trudged back over to the couch and flopped down onto it. She was tired of talking about this. Thankfully, Ginger left it alone and opted to take their empty plates to the kitchen. Jazlyn grabbed her phone and pulled up Twitter, which she only used every now and then. She was more of a lurker than a poster; most of her social media activity was on Instagram and YouTube. She didn't even follow that many people on Twitter.

One of the people she did follow was Nell, and when she saw Nell's tweet from a couple of days before, Jazlyn sat up in her seat.

Don't tell me prayer doesn't work. I'm enjoying the blessing I was graced with. And I'm NOT losing it again.

Jazlyn's jaw dropped. What did *that* mean? Nell's 'blessing' could have been anything, but every part of Jazlyn knew she was referring to Rome. And if that was the case, Jazlyn had to wonder if Nell was speaking on what had actually happened or what she just hoped would happen.

Had Rome already chosen Nell and he was just waiting for the right time to break it to her?

"Fuck this," she muttered, shooting back off the couch. She grabbed her shoes, stuffing her feet into them as she looked around for her purse.

"Where are you going??" Ginger asked, alarmed, coming back from the kitchen.

"To Rome's." Jazlyn grabbed her keys.

"But what about-"

"I don't care. Nell will just have to get over it. I'm sick of sitting over here in the dark while she does whatever with my man. I need to know *something*." She hurried towards the door and yanked it open, not allowing herself to stop and think about what she was doing. She glanced back at her stunned friend. "I'll be back."

She was out the door before Ginger could respond.

Adrenaline had Jazlyn's body buzzing with a tingling energy as she zoomed to Rome's house. She hoped he was home and not out with Nell. Her fingers alternated between gripping and tapping the steering wheel, and loud groans and curses filled her car every time she got caught at a red light or behind a slow-moving vehicle. She needed everyone to get out of her way because the closer she got to Rome's, the more anxiety ballooned within her.

Jazlyn caught a break when she saw Rome's truck in front of his house. It occurred to her that Nell might be there, but she decided she didn't care. When it came down to it, Jazlyn wasn't above throwing hands if Nell tried to step to her. That's just how over it she was.

She rang the doorbell, then banged on the door when she didn't hear anything. Lights beamed behind the window curtains and she hoped Rome wasn't asleep. She was prepared to stand there pounding on his door until he woke up, if he was.

Finally, the door swung open and Rome was standing in front of her. His angry expression quickly morphed into surprise when he saw Jazlyn standing there.

"Babe," he glanced up the street before turning his eyes back to her. "What are you doing here?"

"We need to talk, Rome."

"What's wrong?"

"What do you mean what's wrong? I'm sitting at home alone while you're doing god knows what with Nell and I'm *over* it." She stormed past him into the house, listening for any signs that Nell might be holed up in another room. "I need some answers."

Rome hesitantly closed the door. "Look, sweets, I get how tough this has to be for you. I don't love it, either. But you really shouldn't be here right now."

"Why not?" Jazlyn demanded loudly, turning in the direction of Rome's bedroom. "Why can't I be here right now, Rome?"

"Nell isn't here, J. I'm alone because I needed a break from her to get my head together."

"So my being here shouldn't be an issue, then, should it?"

"Come on. We promised Nell..."

"I don't give a damn about Nell! Do you care about her feelings more than mine now?"

He stepped towards her. "Don't do that. You know better than that."

"Then why are you trying to put me out? Rome, do you know how difficult this has been for me? Not knowing if your ex is actually getting her hooks back into you or not? Having no idea what the two of you are doing or if you've changed your mind about us?"

"I get it, babe, but I only agreed to this because you wanted me to. Because you said it would be good for us going forward."

"I know that, Rome. And I meant that. But I didn't know I was going to get shut out completely during it."

"That wasn't my idea. I don't like it any more than you do."

"But you had no problem agreeing to it. You don't seem to mind agreeing to anything Nell asks you for now, all because you feel guilty. And she's milking the hell out of it."

"I don't think that's what she's doing."

"Wow." Jazlyn placed a hand to her hip. "You're defending her now?"

"I'm not...look," Rome wearily ran his hands down his face. "I can understand you being paranoid. But my feelings for you haven't changed. I need you to be secure in that."

"How can I be, Rome? The more I think about it, the more I realize how stupid it was of me to agree to this. I *know* Nell has been all over you, and the thought makes me want to break something. Is she even doing anything to *prove her love for you* or has she just spent the last three weeks jacking your dick?"

"Oh my god..."

"What have the two of you been doing, Rome? I need to know. I already know you've been parading around town together, causing folks to ask me what's going on and making me feel even more foolish than I already do."

He winced, hating that Jazlyn knew about him being out in public with Nell. The only thing worse would have been her running into them herself. "I'm so sorry about that, sweets. I hoped that wouldn't happen. Nell begged me to go out and I wasn't crazy about it, but..."

"But you caved. Again. I guess you just lose *all* your backbone if you feel guilty enough, huh? Poor little Nell just gets anything she wants, doesn't she?"

"Jazlyn!"

"Has anything changed between you? Have your feelings for her changed? Or are you just letting her take advantage of you? 'Cause she surely pulled one over on me, and my dumb ass fell for it."

Rome's head fell back briefly, closing his eyes to gather himself. Jazlyn could tell he was agitated, and she wondered if it was because of the situation they were in or because of her.

Crossing over to her, he grabbed her shoulders before bringing his hands to her face. He looked right into her expectant eyes.

"I didn't keep my word to Nell when I promised to stay faithful to her," he began, choosing his words carefully. "I at least want to keep my word about this. That's the *only* reason I'm being so tight-lipped right now, and the only reason I'm asking you to please go home."

Jazlyn's blinked, floored. She honestly hadn't expected that from him.

"You're actually putting me out?" she verified. Tears glistened in her eyes.

The anguish on Rome's face was clear, and when he saw her tearing up, he looked even more pained.

"Babe, please don't think of it like that," he pleaded, gently wiping her tears with his thumbs. "This isn't easy for me, either. But I meant it when I said I needed to get my head together. So that's another reason I can't be around you...I'm just, I'm too confused right now."

Her breath quickening, Jazlyn stepped back. Rome's hands fell from her face. "Confused? About us?"

"About everything, J. All of this...it's a lot."

"What is there to be confused about? I thought we were *in* this. You said you wanted us as much as I did. And now after three weeks with your ex, you're confused about that?"

"It's not that simple, babe. I still love you. But I loved Nell, too. And I..." He rubbed his tired eyes. "I just want to be sure I know what I'm doing, here. I don't want to hurt anybody again."

"I see." Jazlyn stared at him, feeling like someone had kicked her square in the gut. "So now you're not even sure I'm the one you want to be with. Is that what I'm hearing? And what, you think that if you go back to Nell, you and me will go right back to being just friends like it's nothing? I couldn't take that, Rome."

His eyes snapped to her. "I don't want to lose you, Jazlyn. If I'm not sure of anything, I'm sure of that."

"Well, forgive me if that doesn't bring me a lot of comfort. Because it sounds to me like I've fallen in love with my best friend and now he's having second thoughts."

"I don't wanna leave you. I need you in my life, sweets; you *know* that."

"But you're not sure if you want me to be your woman anymore. Right?"

Rome stepped towards her, but she stepped back. She couldn't take him touching her when it seemed like he was slipping away from her.

"Jazlyn, please," He pressed his hands together in front of his chest, looking at her pleadingly. "We only have seven days left. Let's just ride out this last week. Please just give me that. I'm trying to do the right thing by everybody but you *have* to know that it would absolutely gut me to see you get hurt. Or to lose you out of my life."

She peered at him. She could see the torment on his face. Clearly, this wasn't any easier for him than it was for her. But what pained her was that they were evidently hurting for different reasons. She was missing her man, while her man was apparently debating if he wanted her or his ex. That wasn't a good feeling.

"This is the first time I've ever doubted anything you've said to me," she mumbled painfully, the tears free-flowing down her face. "I just can't believe we're here, after everything."

"Jazlyn, don't talk like that, please. I just-"

"You know what? Just stay with Nell." She hastily swiped at her tears with one hand as she turned for the door. She couldn't stand to look at him anymore. "Maybe that'll make it *easier* for you."

"Jazlyn!" Rome grabbed her arm, turning her to face him. "Are you serious??"

"Let me go, Rome!"

"I'm not letting you walk out of here like this!"

"Oh no! You *wanted* me to leave a minute ago, remember?" She pushed against his chest, even though most of her wanted to press herself to it. She yearned to jump into his arms, but she needed to get away from him before she totally lost it. "I'm just giving you want you want!"

"This is *not* what I want, sweets! You crying and hurt and doubting me...that's not what I want! Babe, I understand your position in all of this but can you please try to understand mine??"

"No, the only thing I *understand* is that you were sure about us before we started this stupid arrangement but now you're not. And I'm not going to just sit around waiting for you to find some way to let me down easy. So get your damn head together all you want." She snatched her arms free of his grasp then pushed him away from her. "I'm *done*!"

She yanked the door open and ran out, dodging his attempt to grab her again.

"Jazlyn, stop! Babe, don't leave like this, *please*!"

The tears were practically blinding her by the time she made it to her car, and she cried loudly as she fumbled her way inside and pulled off, speeding past Rome as he stood in his driveway calling her name.

Chapter 23

R ome hated himself.

He didn't think he would ever get Jazlyn telling him she was done and running from him crying out of his head. Turning her away was the last thing he wanted to do. He ached to hug her and kiss her and spend the rest of the night giving her all the reassurance she needed. Anything to erase the heartbroken look she had when she ran out of his house.

As soon as she sped off, he tried to call her but of course, she didn't answer. He hurried back inside to get his keys and follow her. She was so emotional and probably wasn't thinking clearly; he just needed to be sure she made it home safely. When he saw her car pull into her driveway without incident, he breathed a sigh of relief. He sat and watched as she went into the house, yearning to go in after her and make things right. But he made himself pull off and go back home.

It was no lie when he told her he was confused. He absolutely loved Jazlyn, but the previous three weeks with Nell had him rethinking some things. Nell opened up to him more in that short time than she did in the ten months they were together, and while he wasn't sold on whether her recent efforts were temporary or something she could maintain long-term, that didn't mean they were meaningless to him. She'd managed to remind him of how good things were between them, and why he'd initially fallen for her.

Then there was Jazlyn. His best friend in the world, and outside of his dad, the person he trusted the most. Ever since he kissed her and touched her intimately and shared his body with her the night of the blizzard, his feelings for her transformed at warp speed. She became everything to him; there was no way he could go back to looking at her as just a friend. He didn't want to. The thought of Jazlyn not being in his life made his chest ache.

But he remembered his dad's question about whether his romantic feelings for Jazlyn were mere infatuation. And his mother's assessment that his entertaining Nell meant that he still felt something for her, and what he felt for Jazlyn didn't run as deep as he thought. Then of course there was Asha, insisting that either woman would be okay regardless as long as he was honest with them both. Rome wasn't so sure. It wasn't that he thought super highly of himself, but Nell had already gone to therapy when they broke up and postponed taking a job out of state that she'd agreed to take. She clearly didn't take their breakup well before; why would this time be any better? Even if she did go into it knowing he could disappoint her again, that didn't mean she would just take it in stride. He worried about her.

And of course his mother and sister were both in his ear, constantly asking for updates and putting their bids in for who they wanted him to choose, and that wasn't helping at all. He had to stop taking their calls because this whole situation was consuming him and stressing him out. It was just getting to be too much.

He was glad that there were only a few days left of his obligation to Nell. Even though he still wasn't totally sure what he was going to do at the end of it, it gave him some relief knowing he'd *have* to decide something in just a matter of days. He'd managed to spend a couple of nights away from Nell to try to clear his head, but she only let that go for so long.

"I miss you," she whined over the phone to him. It had been two days since Jazlyn showed up at Rome's house and he was still messed up over it, and hadn't had the energy to deal with Nell. "You know we have less than a week left before our month is up."

"I know. I'm not trying to ghost you, Nell; I just have a lot on my mind."

"Does it have anything to do with me?"

"In large part. And Jazlyn."

"Rome-"

"Yeah, I know you want me to act like Jazlyn isn't a factor but she just is, Nell. All this time I've spent with you hasn't made me forget about her, as much as I'm sure you'd like that."

Nell got quiet for a moment and he wondered if he'd hurt her feelings, but he wasn't sorry. He hadn't intended on biting her head off but he was feeling testy and irritable, and wasn't in the mood to be told what he could and couldn't talk about.

"I know I've asked a lot of you these past few weeks," Nell finally stated. "Yes, I've wanted your mind and attention to be on me but I'm certainly aware that Jazlyn is still in the picture. And I know it hasn't been easy for you to stay away from her."

"No. It hasn't."

"You should know that I appreciate you doing that for me, Rome. It means a lot that you would grant me this time. I know you didn't have to."

"Yeah, well. I figured I could at least do that."

"Rome...is this *still* all about you relieving your guilt? I'd hoped it would've moved beyond that by now."

"Nell, I can admit that I've had a better time with you than I thought I would going into this. And now I'm questioning things I never thought I would. That might be good news for you but it's not for me."

"Maybe you don't want to hear it but I'm thrilled to hear that, Rome. You were so sure that none of this would make any difference; it feels good to know it has."

Rome just grunted.

"I have an idea. How about, for our last weekend together, we go away somewhere?"

"Oh, I don't know about that, Nell," Rome quickly refuted. "Not sure that's the best idea."

"Why not? Come on, it'll be beautiful. We don't have to go that far; maybe down to the beach or something. That's just a couple of hours away."

"Nell, going away together is a whole other thing. And that's not what we agreed to."

"We agreed to spend time together," Nell persisted firmly. "And I thought it was important to you that we do that. I just want us to get away alone before you make your decision. It would mean a lot to me. Especially now that I know you're conflicted about Jazlyn. While I understand it, I want to get your mind back on me."

Rome sighed. "Nell..."

"You said you didn't want to hurt me again. And it hurts every time you bring up Jazlyn's name and feel the need to remind me that she's still on your mind. I don't think a weekend at the beach with me would be asking too much in light of that, do you?"

Feeling his frustration rise like an overbaked soufflé, Rome gripped the phone. Jazlyn's words about Nell taking advantage of the situation rang through his head. "Nell, I wish you'd chill with the guilt trips. You've pulled that a few times and I've let it go, but I'm not trying to hear it now. I've gone above and beyond what I *have* to do because I felt bad for what I did to you, but don't try to take advantage of it. 'Cause we can call this whole thing off *now* and be done with it."

"I'm sorry; that's not what I was doing-"

"Yes it was. You know it was."

"All right, fine. Maybe I got carried away with that; I apologize. But I still maintain that I want us to go away this weekend. What's the harm in that?"

Knowing that she wasn't going to let it go and also that it would be rude to hang up on her like part of him wanted to do, Rome decided to counteroffer. "All right, Nell. If it's that important to you, fine. But there *will* be conditions."

"Conditions?"

"Separate beds. Don't expect sex. None of these damn guilt trips when I say or do something that you think threatens your position. You can't pout to get your way anymore."

"Wow, Rome. Is that what you think of me? And is all of this really necessary? You're making this sound like some kind of business proposition. I just want us to have a romantic weekend-"

"Nell, I'm not trying to be rude, but spare me, okay? I've conceded to all of your requests these last three weeks. So it shouldn't be too much for you to grant one of mine now."

"I don't want it to be like this."

"Well, we don't have to go, then."

"Why are you changing things now that we're at the end? Is this your way of running from your feelings? Are you afraid that if we sleep in the same bed and make love that it'll confirm for you what I already know? We're meant to be together, Rome, and I think you're starting to realize that. I could feel it in the way you kissed me, when you touched and pleasured me. The good time you've been having with me wasn't an act."

"Maybe not but that doesn't change anything."

"How can you say that?"

"Because I'm still in love with Jazlyn!"

Nell gasped. Rome hadn't meant to blurt that out; he hadn't even been sure that his feelings for Jazlyn had yet gotten to that point. He definitely loved her, but he hadn't been sure if he was *in* love with her yet. But in that moment, he knew he was.

Rome could hear sniffling, and he was glad that they were having this conversation over the phone. He didn't enjoy making Nell cry, even though he meant every word he said.

"All right," she mumbled, her voice cracking. "I get it. But as crazy as it sounds, I still want us to go. Whatever your terms are, I'll accept them."

Rome still wasn't sure going away with Nell was a good idea. He still had some things he needed to work out, mostly because he wanted to be absolutely sure of what he was doing. His energy for this whole agreement with Nell had dwindled significantly in the past couple of days and he really just wanted it to be over with so he could get on with his life.

"I'll see what I have on my schedule for the weekend," he told her, his voice devoid of any enthusiasm or energy. "We'll see."

"Thank you." Nell sniffed. "And, foolish or not, I'm still thinking positively about us."

Not knowing how to respond to that, he just said he'd talk to her later and ended the call, getting up to see if he had any more aspirin.

• • • •

JAZLYN DIDN'T WANT to be bothered with anyone or anything. The realization that she'd probably lost Rome sucked all of the energy out of her.

She might've told him to stay with Nell, but she didn't mean it. That was her anger and pride talking. As soon as she got back home, she regretted saying those words. It might've hurt to hear him say he had any confusion about them, but on some back shelf level, she could understand it. Things turned very quickly between them; they went from best friends to lovers to being in a relationship with no time to catch their breaths. And Rome had considered marriage with Nell not long before things changed between them.

Jazlyn knew it was unreasonable to expect him to have just forgotten about all that.

She wanted to call him, if only to tell him that she took back what she said. But she didn't. Instead, she sulked and moped, dragging through work and her classes. When Ginger came to check on her, Jazlyn both appreciated and resented it.

"Ginger, girl, I appreciate you checking on me and everything, but I'm all right," Jazlyn droned, leaving her friend at the door and shuffling back to the couch, where she was eating the wings and fries she'd had delivered. She was supposed to be practicing some more nail art designs but kept messing up, so she stopped. Her concentration wasn't good enough for that. "You were just over here yesterday."

"And I'm going to be over here tomorrow and the next day, too," Ginger insisted, closing the door and moving over to the couch. She stood there in a pink cropped hoodie, white leggings, and gray Uggs, her wild curly hair pulled back in a high ponytail. "Until this whole mess with Rome and Nell is over with."

"Yeah, well. Three more days."

"And I suppose you still haven't talked to him since you left his house the other day, huh?"

"No." Jazlyn picked up a buffalo wing but only brought it halfway to her mouth before dropping it back to the takeout container. "He wants to stick to the agreement so that's what I'm letting him do."

"You're still worried about him going back to Nell, huh?" Ginger sat next to Jazlyn, snagging one of her fries.

"Of course I am."

"Girl, I get it, but I really believe that Rome will be right back here with you at the end of the day. I can understand his head being all over the place; there's no telling what Nell is over there doing and saying to him. You know she's desperate."

"Humph. Which means she'll probably do damn near anything to sway him."

"If you recognize that, Rome does, too. He's not an idiot."

"He's still a man, Ginger. And it doesn't give me a lot of confidence when I hear him tell me that he's confused and that he didn't want to see me."

"It wasn't that he didn't want to see you; he just wanted to respect Nell's stupid wishes."

"Yeah, I bet he's been over there respecting *all* of her wishes," Jazlyn grunted, stuffing some fries into her mouth.

"You might as well not even think about that; if you do, it'll just piss you off. Whatever he does while he's over there is between them. You just need to worry about what the two of you will do when he comes back to you."

"*If* he comes back to me."

"Jazlyn, if he doesn't, you'll be all right," Ginger strongly assured. "Yes, it'll suck and it'll hurt and I'm not saying you'll get over it just like that. But when it's all said and done, you'll be fine. Because you're a strong woman and there's more to you than just being Rome's girlfriend."

Jazlyn appreciated Ginger's encouragement, but to her ears, it felt like she was trying to prepare Jazlyn for the possibility of Rome leaving. Jazlyn would move past it, but she knew it wouldn't be any time soon. Because she'd meant what she told Rome when she said she was in love with him, and that she wouldn't be able to stay friends with him if they split. If Rome went back to Nell, she couldn't have anything more to do with him. And that thought made her sick.

After Ginger left, Jazlyn went to bed early, feeling emotionally drained. The next night after she got off work and finished with her class, Jazlyn headed to the first bar she came to. She didn't want to go home and mope around anymore, worrying about things she had no control over.

Jazlyn drunk often enough, but she usually saved the heavy stuff for the weekends. But it was Thursday night and she heard herself order a vodka tonic, chugging it before the bartender had time to make his way down to the end of the bar. She immediately flagged him down to order another.

She wasn't sure how many drinks she'd had by the time someone sat down next to her. She didn't even bother looking to see who it was, until she felt a hand on her shoulder.

"Jazlyn?"

"I recognize that voice..." Jazlyn slowly turned her head, then frowned at the freckled-faced woman sitting next to her. "Oh, Asha."

Asha disregarded Jazlyn's apparent lack of enthusiasm for seeing her. "Are you all right?"

"I'm peachy."

"You don't seem peachy. Are you here by yourself?"

"All by myself. I can sing the song for you, if you like."

"I'm surprised Ginger isn't here with you."

"She had a thing with her in-laws." Jazlyn drained the rest of her vodka tonic and raised her hand for another, but

Asha gently blocked her, shaking her head at the bartender. "In-laws. Something it doesn't look like I'll get to have. It's too bad...I really liked your parents."

"Oh, Jazlyn...come on, let's get you home."

"I'm fine where I am. And I'm sure you need to get back to whoever you came with."

"I'm here with friends; they'll understand. Where are your keys? There's no way you're driving like this."

"I don't know."

Asha unzipped Jazlyn's purse that was still hanging from her shoulder and dug through it, finding the car keys at the bottom. "Come on, I'll take you home."

"Why? I thought you were mad at me."

"I'm not mad at you. Wait one second." Asha stepped away to pay Jazlyn's tab and let her friends know she was seeing a friend home before coming back to help Jazlyn off the bar stool. She didn't seem to be totally wasted, but was too inebriated to take more than a few steps without wavering, let alone drive.

Jazlyn didn't bother protesting anymore; she just allowed Asha to usher her to her car and into the passenger's seat. Thankfully Asha didn't try to engage her in any conversation as they headed to Jazlyn's house. It seemed they were pulling into her driveway in no time.

"Jazlyn, we're here," Asha announced, gently shaking her arm.

Not realizing she had dozed off, Jazlyn sat up with a start, looking around her. "This looks like my house."

"Yeah." Asha couldn't resist a smile as she got out and scurried around the car to help Jazlyn. As soon as they got into the house, Jazlyn stumbled towards her bedroom and flopped face-first onto her bed. After Asha was confident enough that Jazlyn wasn't going to hurl, she went to the kitchen and rummaged in the cabinets. A little later, she was heading back to Jazlyn's room with a tray laden with a bowl of chicken and stars soup, a box of Triscuits, and a bottle of water. Jazlyn was still in the exact same position.

"Jazlyn." Since there was nowhere to place the tray, Asha used her knee to nudge Jazlyn's foot that was hanging off the bed. "Jazlyn, wake up."

Stirring, Jazlyn pushed herself up slightly, looking at Asha through squinted eyes. "Asha? When did you get here?"

"Yeah, you're out of it. Here." Asha waited for Jazlyn to sit up before placing the tray on her lap. "Eat this. I can imagine you probably didn't have any food when you were tossing back all that vodka at the bar."

"I haven't eaten since lunch," Jazlyn admitted, picking up the spoon that was lying on a folded paper towel. "Or breakfast. Can't remember."

"Still doing that, huh? Go ahead and eat up."

Jazlyn ate most of the soup and a few crackers before drinking half the bottle of water. After Asha returned the tray to the kitchen, she came back and removed Jazlyn's sneakers from her feet and helped her out of her coat. Jazlyn hadn't even realized she was still wearing that stuff.

"You don't have to stay here," she muttered as Asha sat next to her on the bed. "I'm sure you have other stuff you'd rather be doing."

"I don't want to leave you alone like this. How are you feeling?"

"Still peachy." Jazlyn leaned her head against the headboard and closed her eyes. "And tired."

Asha started to respond but noticed Jazlyn had dozed off again. So she just pulled her phone from her pocket and opened a book on her Kindle app, kicking off her own shoes before she settled in to read.

When Jazlyn stirred a couple of hours later, Asha was still there. By then she had finished her book and was on her word find app, her phone plugged into the charger Jazlyn kept by the bed. She glanced at Jazlyn, who was looking around as if she didn't know where she was.

"You're still here," Jazlyn observed, sticking a hand in her flattened hair.

"Yep." Asha put her phone down and folded her hands in her lap. "So am I correct to assume that you chose to get drunk to forget about what's going on with Rome?"

Wincing at the reminder, Jazlyn turned her face away from Asha. "Something like that. Wait, how do you know about it?"

"Rome told me. After I apologized for how I'd been acting towards him."

"Oh."

"Are you seriously that worried about Nell?"

"Can't help it. It's hard to be confident when I don't even think *Rome* knows what he wants."

"I think he does. He's just trying to be the good guy. He'd love to find a way for everyone to come out of this thing unscathed."

"Not sure how that's gonna happen. Not unless he's thinking of some polyamorous shit and that's a *no*-go."

Asha chuckled. "You and I both know Rome is a one-woman man. He's just made some mistakes and is trying to atone for them, that's all. Even he realizes he's overcompensating for cheating on Nell, but wants to keep his word to her. I'm sure once he gets back from their weekend away, he's going to come straight to you."

It took a second, but Jazlyn finally registered what she said. "Weekend away? They're going somewhere?"

"Oh..." Asha looked regretful. "I forgot that you and Rome aren't speaking during this. Yeah, um...Nell asked him to go to the beach with her for this last weekend."

"Hmph. Of course she did. And of course he agreed."

"It's one last thing he's granting her. But he didn't agree until she accepted his ground rules."

That gave Jazlyn a sliver of hope. "What were they?"

"He wouldn't say. But what I'm all but sure of is that Rome is as fed up with this whole thing as you are. He's ready for it to be over; he said that flat out."

"I don't suppose he told you which way he was leaning, decision-wise, huh?"

"No...it seems like he's still only telling me so much. And I admit I've been kinda bugging him, asking for updates every other day. If it makes you feel any better, though, I told him I was team Jazlyn."

Jazlyn was strangely encouraged by that. She and Asha had been close before the blowup at Rome's. It was nice to know there was someone in her corner, whether or not it made any difference.

She didn't love hearing about Rome and Nell going off for some time alone at the beach. Nell really was going for the jugular. And while Jazlyn wanted to believe Ginger and Asha's assurances that she was who Rome wanted, Jazlyn wouldn't believe it until it happened.

Until then, she figured she couldn't do anything but wait.

Chapter 24

Rome and Nell were all checked in at the hotel by the beach, and while Nell marveled over the floor-to-ceiling windows overlooking the Atlantic Ocean, the breezy colors in aqua blue and yellow and light gray, and the pillowtop (double) beds, Rome mentally started the countdown to checkout time. He couldn't even appreciate the beauty of their surroundings because his mind was still back home.

His last conversation with Jazlyn was still heavy on his mind. He knew her well enough to know that she likely didn't mean it when she told him to stay with Nell, but that didn't mean he loved hearing it. Even if she'd been a hundred percent serious, it wouldn't have made things any easier on him. That was an out he didn't want. Jazlyn running out of his house in tears ran on a loop in his mind that he'd been unable to stop.

"Isn't this beautiful, Rome?" Nell asked him, turning from the window with a smile. She released a long exhale of content, raising her arms. "I'm so glad we picked this hotel."

"This is all you. I didn't have a hand in the decision," Rome drudged, still in the same spot as when he entered the room, his hands in his pockets. "Which bed do you want?"

Her arms dropped. "Are you going to be in this mood the whole time?"

"I'm not trying to be a grouch. I'm just a little stressed."

"How can you possibly be stressed in an environment like this? It just screams *relaxation*."

"I must be deaf to it, then, 'cause I'm feeling anything but relaxed."

"Rome." Nell crossed the room and slid her arms around his waist. His hands stayed where they were. "I get that you have a lot on your mind but can you please try to enjoy yourself? Just clear your mind of everything for the next couple of days. Think of it as a new beginning."

Rome didn't bother saying how that was a tall order for him. Nell clearly still had high hopes about the two of them and he didn't have the energy to refute her pep talk this time. She could think what she wanted. "Fine."

"Good." Apparently satisfied, Nell leaned up to give him a quick peck on the lips before stepping away. "After I run to the restroom and freshen up, you want to go get something to eat?"

"Sure."

After Nell grabbed her toiletry bag and closed herself inside the bathroom, Rome pulled out his phone. Part of him hoped Jazlyn would have defied the 'rules' again and sent him a message. He had missed her before, but after seeing her, he couldn't get her out of his head.

He sat on the stuffed chaise by the window and scrolled through some pictures of Jazlyn, not realizing just how many he had on his phone after all their years of friendship. He scrolled to the ones from early on, back when her hair was black and relaxed, hanging down around her shoulders. He came across one of them outside of the fair, both holding huge pink bundles of cotton candy. A smile finally came to his lips, remembering that day. They'd stayed there for hours, riding all the rides and pigging out. Jazlyn had teased him when his stomach started hurting from all the junk food they'd eaten, but she ended up being the one to throw up when they were racing to his car because it had started to rain.

Then there was the picture in Rome's old car when they were taking an impulsive road trip to the casino. She had a super-short haircut that she hated thanks to recently cutting off her relaxed hair, but Rome thought it was cute on her.

Rome remembered that was the trip where they were mistaken for a couple for the first time. They both had laughed it off, thinking nothing else of it. Now look at them.

He was so engrossed in Jazlyn's pictures and reminiscing that he didn't notice when Nell came back into the room.

"What are you smiling about?"

Rome's head snapped up. "Was I?"

"Yeah. Almost fondly."

"Oh." Rome turned his phone off and stood. "Didn't realize that. You ready?"

"You don't wanna change?"

"No. Let's just go."

They headed out to a nearby restaurant, and Rome tried to return his mind to the present. He was sure Nell could tell that he was preoccupied, but thankfully she didn't press him on it. She just engaged him in casual conversation that thankfully had nothing to do with their situation or relationship, and he felt himself thawing out because of it.

"How's the lasagna?" Nell asked him, cutting into her eggplant parmesan.

"It's good."

"As good as mine?"

Rome could see the playful glint in her eye. "They could use your help back there."

"Such a sweetheart. I don't even care that you're probably lying."

"This is pretty good, though," Rome mentioned, picking up his wine glass. "And I usually don't even get down with wine like that. You've got a brother drinking...what is this called, again?"

Nell giggled. "Chianti."

"Yeah, Chianti. It's not half bad, whatever it is."

"Better than beer?"

"Let's not push it."

Once they'd enjoyed their dinner and shared an order of tiramisu, Nell suggested a walk on the beach. The light conversation and the Chianti had him loose enough to agree. They strolled along, close but not touching, each holding their shoes in their hand.

"It's such a beautiful evening," Nell marveled, her eyes drifting upward. "I've wanted to make it down here for a while. I used to come all the time back in the day."

"Why'd you stop?"

Nell shrugged. "Life, I guess. Work. Just stopped making the time like I used to."

"I know how that is. There's plenty of things I used to do a lot of that I don't anymore."

"You remember the night we met? At that auto parts store, of all places. You were kind enough to help me pick out a set of windshield wipers."

"Yeah, I thought you were doing the damsel-in-distress bit but it turned out you really didn't know what you were doing in there," Rome chuckled. "You were all over the place."

"I was. I know nothing about cars. But you were sweet enough to help me out; even put them on my car for me after I bought them. And while you were doing that I was standing there wondering what I could ask you to help me with next, because I wasn't ready for you to leave. I thought you were *so* cute; I wanted us to stay in touch but didn't have the nerve to say so."

"Thankfully I had more guts than you had," Rome teased, winking at her. "But I already knew I was gonna ask for your number as soon as I saw you wandering up and down the aisles, looking like a lost puppy. It was on from there."

"Yes, it was." She slid her free hand into his, smiling up at him. "Best boyfriend ever."

"Come on now, you don't have to gas me up like that. I appreciate it but-"

"I'm serious, Rome. You've treated me better than any man I've been with."

"Up until-"

"No." Nell stopped walking, tugging on his hand. "We're not dwelling on that anymore, remember? This is a clean slate; the past doesn't matter."

Rome peered at her. Her eyes were unwavering and he could tell she meant what she was saying. "Just like that?"

"It's not just like that. I went through the devastation, the depression. I was angry, both at you and at myself. I went to therapy, for goodness sakes."

"Was it your therapist that suggested you ask for this time?"

"She said I needed to get closure. I wasn't sure how but it came to me during one of my sleepless nights when I was tossing and turning in bed. It took me a few days to work up the nerve. I'm glad I did, though, because look where we are now."

"And where is that?" Rome didn't want to kill the vibe by reminding Nell that them having a nice time together for a few weeks didn't mean they were back to where they were before the breakup, but he needed to pull Nell's head out of the clouds a little bit. "Where is it you think we are?"

Nell started to respond when there was a scream from nearby. They both whipped their heads around to see a woman running towards them, arms extended and grinning like she'd seen her favorite celebrity.

"Cornelia!"

Nell glanced at Rome with wide eyes that almost looked panicked. He just looked at her before returning his eyes to the approaching woman, thinking maybe she was addressing someone behind them. But they were the only ones in the area.

"Cornelia, I can't believe that's you!"

"Who?" Rome asked Nell, confused. "Is she talking to you?"

"Umm..."

"What are you doing down here?" The woman practically tackled Nell in a hug, knocking her back a few steps. "I haven't seen you in too long!"

"Yeah, I know. It's so good to see you; we just came down for the weekend," Nell told the grinning woman, motioning towards Rome. "Rome, this is my cousin, Miranda."

The woman looked at him excitedly. Rome could see a vague family resemblance. "Rome! So *you're* the one we've been hearing about all this time!"

Rome glanced at Nell, who he could swear was blushing. He held out his hand. "Nice meeting you, Miranda."

She waved off his hand. "Oh please, we're practically family. Give me a hug!" She lunged forward, wrapping her arms around him in a tight embrace that pinned his arms to his sides. "You were right, Cornelia, he *is* the definition of sexy-cute!"

Rome looked at Nell again, who averted her eyes. She briefly covered her flaming face with her hands before stepping forward and gently grabbing one of Miranda's arms. "Girl, let the man go. I know you love to hug, but..."

"Oh, I'm sorry; I know I get a little over-excited at times," Miranda acknowledged, glancing up at Rome apologetically. "It's just that I haven't seen my cousin here in so long. Are you two still engaged? Ooh, did you come down here to elope? Are you gonna invite your dad? I know y'all haven't talked much since he took that money from you but I'm telling you, he feels bad about that. He said y'all haven't talked in over a year-"

"Um, Miranda, girl, we really need to get going," Nell hastily interrupted, grabbing Rome's hand. "It was so good to see you; I'll call you soon, okay?"

"Okay, girl, call me. And let me know where to send your wedding gift! Congratulations, you two!"

Rome was still trying to process what he'd heard when Nell pulled him down the beach towards their hotel, her flushed face tilted towards the ground. He stayed quiet as they headed up to their room, awkwardness hovering over them like a rain cloud.

Once they were behind their hotel room door, Rome cleared his throat. "So...I don't know what to address first..."

Nell dropped onto the bed, her face in her hands. "Rome..."

"For starters, who the hell is Cornelia?"

Her hands fell to her lap. "That's my real name."

"Why am I just now learning this?"

"Because I hate it. I've always hated it. But my family insists on still calling me that, regardless of what I say."

"Hmm. And your dad stole money from you? You told *me* that your relationship with him had improved recently but now I hear that y'all haven't talked in over a *year*?"

"I...we don't have to get into that. There was a thing with Mama's life insurance money that he lied about...can we not? I'm kinda tired."

"Yeah, and apparently you need to be rested up for your wedding. *When* did we get engaged?"

She still wouldn't look at him, which only accelerated Rome's rising frustration. As nice of a time as he'd been having with Nell just a half hour before, now he felt like he was looking at a stranger.

"I'm sorry," she finally responded, her voice barely above a whisper. "I might've exaggerated the scope of our relationship to some members of my family. They don't know we broke up because I was too embarrassed to tell them, because then they would ask why, and that would be a whole other *thing*. It was just easier to tell them things were great between us."

"Easier for them or easier for you, Nell? Oh my bad; *Cornelia*."

"Rome, please don't call me that."

"Why not? That's your name, right?"

She sighed and looked at him pleadingly for a moment before standing. She started to move towards him, but his eyes warned her to stay where she was. "I'm so sorry. I didn't mean to...I wasn't trying to lie on you, Rome. Not in a bad way, at least. It just came out when I was talking to them and I felt too silly to take it back. I figured it was harmless enough-"

"Harmless?" Rome looked at her incredulously. "You seriously thought it was harmless to lie to your family about being engaged to me, without me knowing anything about it? And how ironic is it that you would lie about that considering how the mere subject of marriage sent you running whenever I brought it up when we were together."

"But I'm better about that now!"

"So what? Hell, *now* I'm not even sure who you are! We were together for ten months and I didn't even know your damn name!"

"I'm still the same person!" Nell insisted, plastering a hand to her chest. "I might have withheld a few things but that doesn't change who I am or what we've been through together. What we mean to each other!"

"No? So if you found out my name wasn't Rome Ellis, and on top of that, that I'd fronted about my relationship with you, didn't tell you some pretty major stuff about me, where I came from, or stuff I was dealing with, you'd be fine with that?"

"I..."

"I'll answer it for you; you wouldn't. And you'd be wondering what else I've lied about or kept from you, just like I'm wondering about you right now."

"Please don't start doubting me." Her eyes glistened with tears, which usually would have softened Rome's anger but it had no affect now. "After what we've been through together, please don't use this as an excuse to-"

"Are you fucking kidding?? You spent *months* using your issues as an excuse, though I didn't know what those issues were until after we'd broken up. Face it, Nell, you can't handle the tough shit. Not with me, not with your family, not period. You want stuff to be all peaches and candy and rainbows and when shit turns sour, you can't handle it."

"That's not true!"

"You can't even be woman enough to tell your family we broke up. Don't tell me that's not true."

"I don't want to argue," Nell replied, holding up her hands before wiping the tears from her cheeks. "Let's just table this until we've both cooled down, all right?"

What Rome wanted to do was get his bags, get in the car, and go home. He knew he wouldn't feel any differently about this in the morning, or even in a few days. Nell just didn't look like the same woman to him anymore.

"This is what you always do," he told her. "You always fall back when things get heated."

"Why wouldn't I, Rome? Why would I want us to go back and forth in anger? I'd rather we stop before either of us says something we don't mean or can't take back."

"Nell, damn, sometimes you just have to deal with shit!" he exploded, slapping the back of his right hand into his left palm. "You can't always put stuff on the shelf until you feel like it! Sometimes you've just gotta go in hot! And I need somebody next to me that's willing to handle stuff with me, not somebody that's too scared to get their hands dirty with the ugliness that sometimes comes up in a *grown* relationship. And," Rome sighed, shaking his head in disbelief that they were at this point, "I'm finally seeing that's not you."

Panic washed over Nell and she felt like her chest was caving in. Her hand went to her stomach, as if she felt nauseous. "So that's it?"

"That's it."

They faced off in the middle of their beautiful hotel room, looking at each other. The tension and emotion swirled between them like August heat. Both of them knew that nothing would ever be the same between them going forward.

. "Look," Rome finally droned, running his hands down his face, exhaustion taking over his anger. "I'm tired and out of energy for this. You do what you want; I'm going to bed."

Without looking at her, he grabbed his duffel bag, not even bothering to dig his toiletries or clothes out of it, and went to the bathroom. After a long hot shower, he only felt marginally better. Thankfully, by the time he emerged, Nell was in the bed closest to the window, still fully clothed. She was turned away from him, but he knew she wasn't asleep. He could hear the occasional sniffles and whimpers, and saw her wipe her eyes several times. But he wasn't going to try to make her feel better this time.

He just got in the other bed, turned out the light, and went to sleep.

The next morning, neither of them said very much. Rome was still quietly fuming about everything he learned the previous night, and wasn't interested in trying to find a way to give Nell the benefit of the doubt.

"Will you have breakfast with me?" Nell finally asked him.

Rome was sitting on his bed, his phone in his hand, looking at old text exchanges between him and Jazlyn. He had dreamed about her the night before and his desire for her shot through the roof.

"I'm good," he muttered, barely glancing up.

"Rome. We have to eat. I know you're still upset with me; all I'm asking is that we have a meal together. We don't even have to talk that much, if you don't want to."

Rome was over conceding to Nell's requests, but he realized he was hungry. So he wordlessly pushed off the bed and grabbed his shoes.

Once they were seated in the downstairs restaurant with their French toast and omelets and bacon, they proceeded to eat in tense silence. They were almost done with their meals when Nell finally took a hesitant breath.

"Rome, last night was intense and I know it changed your perception of me more than I'd like. But I hope you know that I never set out to be deceitful or misleading. As much as it hurt to hear what you said, I can't deny that sometimes I *do* run from heavy or difficult situations instead of just dealing with them. I guess I'd just managed to talk myself into believing it wasn't that bad."

Rome raised a brow as he sipped his orange juice, but didn't comment.

"You might be doubting a lot about me now but I hope one of those things isn't the love I have for you," Nell continued. "That's something that's a hundred percent sincere. And, crazy or not, I still hope you choose me. I sincerely believe we can make this work if we both put in the effort and are willing to leave the past in the past."

Actually chuckling, Rome put down his glass and sat back in his chair, leveling his eyes at her. His fingers laced over his full stomach. "Out of respect for you, Nell, I'll keep what I *really* think about what you just said to myself. But what I *will* say is that I can't do this with you anymore."

"This weekend?"

"This everything. We've run our course, Nell. Last night was the final straw for me. There's no way I can be with a woman I can't trust, and I'd always be wondering if you're telling me the whole story or if there's something you're hiding because you don't have the guts to deal with the consequences."

Nell had clearly been holding out hope and her face fell upon hearing Rome's words. "It's not gonna be like that, though."

"I don't believe you. But more than that, this is a problem I don't have to have, especially when there's a woman I love that I don't have these issues with."

"I see." Nell fiddled with the end of her napkin, eyes downcast. She fought to keep her emotions in check. "So you're going back to Jazlyn."

"Yeah, I am. That's where my heart is. If there's anything good that came from that mess last night, it was that it cemented what I already knew but had let myself question because guilt from stepping out on you had clouded my mind. It made me start questioning everything about myself and my relationship with Jazlyn. But that's over. *We're* over, Nell."

Rome felt a weight lift from him as soon as he said those words. Finally declaring his decision that he'd been struggling with for the previous few days felt amazing, and he was anxious to get home to the woman he really wanted.

Not trusting herself to speak, Nell was quiet for several moments. When she finally turned her brown eyes to him, they were shiny but no tears were falling.

"I don't suppose there's anything I can say to change your mind..."

"No."

"I was afraid of that."

"I'm ready to go home," Rome announced. "There's no need in us staying here together. I think we both need to get on with our lives."

Pursing her lips, Nell nodded. "That's going to be easier said than done for me, but I get it. I want to ask you to at least give me this last day and we can just hang out here as friends, but I suppose that's just prolonging the inevitable. You want to get back to Jazlyn and I...well, I need to have enough pride to not beg you to stay with me any longer. For what it's worth, I do appreciate you giving me these last few weeks. And I apologize for not having enough courage to be straight with you about so many things. When it comes down to it, I only have myself to blame for us getting to this point."

"No need in playing the blame game. We both played a part."

"Right. Well, I hope you'll understand that I can't handle a three-hour car ride with you after just being dumped. I'm going to call Miranda and see if I can stay with her for a couple of days, and then get my own way back home."

Rome tried not to outwardly show how relieved he was upon hearing that. He hadn't been looking forward to riding back with her, either. "I understand."

With nothing left to be said, they paid for their meal and headed back to the room to get their things together. Nell called her cousin and Rome was tempted to call Jazlyn and let her know he was coming home, but decided he wanted to surprise her. He wanted to see the look on her face when he told her that he was all hers, and for good this time.

He just hoped that was what she still wanted.

• • • •

JAZLYN HAD SPENT MOST of the morning in bed, too emotionally and physically tired to get up. She did something she rarely did and took the day off work, calling in sick. Saturdays were when she made most of her money, but she needed the break. Between work, teaching her classes, dealing with Marco, and stressing about Rome and Nell, she was feeling burned out.

It was almost noon by the time she finally got up. She shuffled to the kitchen, ate some cereal while leaning against the counter, then returned to the living room and collapsed on the couch, closing her eyes again. She didn't even feel like pretending to watch a movie; for the time being, she just wanted to do nothing.

The loud knocking on her door woke her. Shooting off the couch with a start, her head darted around the slightly darkened room with squinted eyes. She didn't have a clue what time it was, since she didn't have her phone in there with her. The sunlight from the brief time she was up earlier had already muted itself for the night.

"Shit," she muttered as she rolled off the couch and stumbled to the door. Her heart wished for one man to be on the other side of it but her head knew who it likely was.

"Marco," she droned, once she'd peeked through the peephole and opened the door. "What a surprise."

"I would've called first, but..."

"Why do I feel a sense of déjà vu?"

"What?"

"Why are you over here yet again, Marco? You're always popping up and I really, really wish you'd stop."

"I went by the salon and they said you called in sick," Marco informed, disregarding her statement. "And I thought maybe you were still tripping about what we did last time I was over here..."

"Barely even thought about it."

"But you must be sick for real, 'cause you look like shit."

"Thanks, Marco. You're such a blessing. Well, I can look like shit in my own house while I'm minding my own business. And once I close this door in your face, you won't have to see how I look anyway, so..."

"Jazlyn!" Marco stopped the door she was in fact starting to close in his face. "I shouldn't have said that. But you don't look like yourself right now, and I know it must be hitting you hard 'cause you never ditch work on a Saturday. Hell, you barely ditch work, period. Let me help you out."

"I don't need any help. I'm fine."

"So you're *not* still stressing over Rome and Nell being hugged up around town? Because I'm sure they are."

Jazlyn's eyes narrowed. "You wanna go there, huh? You're trying that?"

"Not trying to be an asshole; just saying."

"Bye, Marco." She closed the door in his face, but he opened it and stepped inside before she got a few steps away. She kicked herself for forgetting to lock the door. "Ugh, *what*?"

"I don't want to leave you alone like this."

"I'm not crying. Not gonna have another breakdown. I'm just fine. So you can go, 'cause I'm also *not* gonna fall for you trying anything with me again."

"I'm not gonna do that. But regardless of what you say, I *know* you're not as good as you're trying to act like. That whole Rome shit is still bugging you."

"So what if it is? It's not your business."

"*You're* my business, Jazlyn. Whether you like it or not."

"I don't know why you think that. We're *over*; you need to get that through your thick head." She headed back towards the bathroom. "Lock the door on your way out."

She closed herself in the bathroom and splashed some water on her face before quickly brushing her teeth. Of course, Marco had ignored her directive and was still there when she stepped out, not that Jazlyn was surprised. At least dealing with him was more entertaining than lying around on the couch.

"Still don't listen, huh?" she noted, looking at him with an arched brow. She brushed past him and headed to the spare bedroom, not wanting to be alone with him in her room. He was right on her heels.

"I just don't understand why you wanna sit over here depressed over somebody that's made it clear he doesn't want you," Marco said. "Rome and Nell weren't even trying to be discreet with it; they were out where anybody could see 'em. Yet you wanna act like *I'm* the bad guy."

"I'm not acting like you're the bad guy; I'm acting like you're somebody that I broke up with who won't leave me alone. It's almost like you're in some kind of bet or something that you don't want to lose. Is that what it is?"

"No!"

"It has to be something because I've never seen you this persistent about anything that didn't involve maintaining your body fat percentage. I already told you that you don't know everything about the Rome and Nell thing; it's not what it looks like so you really need to keep your opinions to yourself."

"How can it not be what it looks like, Jazlyn?"

"Again, none of your business."

"You sound like a fool, you know," Marco told her, shaking his head. "You're sitting over here in your house, depressed and skipping work over a dude that cheated on you-"

"Pot, meet kettle..."

"And Nell must be an idiot, too, 'cause he stepped out on her first. What, he's just gonna go back and forth between y'all? When is it gonna be your turn again?"

"You are *so* far off what you think you know, Marco. Is it *that* hard for you to accept that I just don't want you anymore? Are you not man enough to take someone dumping you? We had our time and now it's done. I'm in love with Rome. Get over it."

Marco scowled, clearly not liking the reminder. "Damn, I didn't think you were that desperate, to settle like that. Claiming you're in love with somebody that ain't even thinking 'bout you. I think Rome has made it clear he doesn't want you, Jazlyn."

"That's where you're wrong."

They both whipped around to see Rome standing in the doorway. Jazlyn gasped, almost wondering if she was dreaming.

"Rome?"

He stepped into the room, eyes on her. "Hey, sweets."

Her shock giving way to excitement, she rushed over and jumped into his arms, her legs wrapping his waist and her face buried in his neck. Rome held her tightly, loving having her in his arms again. His eyes were closed and his brow furrowed, the emotion of being with Jazlyn again overtaking him.

"Damn, I'm glad to see you, sweets," he whispered, tightening his hold on her.

"I'm glad to see *you*. You have no idea."

They stayed clamped to each other, forgetting all about Marco. He stood there frowning at them both before finally clearing his throat.

"I don't need to be here for this," he grudgingly muttered.

"No, you don't," Rome concurred, his eyes opening. He glared at Marco as he placed a lingering kiss to the side of Jazlyn's face. "And let this be the last time you come over here or bother Jazlyn. Like she said, y'all are over. This is *my* woman. And that's not changing any time soon."

"Or ever," Jazlyn amended, placing her own kisses to Rome's face. She repeatedly pecked his cheek before grabbing his face and turning it towards hers so she could kiss his lips, which he eagerly obliged. They melted into a deep, languid kiss that continued so long that they forgot Marco was still standing there.

"Yeah, okay. Whatever." Marco stomped towards the door, stopping to glance back at them. They were still going at it, Jazlyn holding Rome's face in both hands, Rome's hands underneath her butt to keep her hoisted off the ground. It burned Marco to see Jazlyn kissing another man like that in front of him, and he swallowed with the realization that it really *was* over between them, like she said. He'd hoped she was just giving him a hard time, or playing hard-to-get. But given how she forgot about him as soon as Rome came in, he saw that wasn't the case.

"I give it six months, if that," he spat, unable to resist a parting shot. "In fact, maybe I'll hit up Nell and show her what being with a *real* man is like."

They didn't even hear him. And when he saw he wasn't going to get the rise out of them that he wanted, Marco finally left them alone.

Chapter 25

After Marco left, Rome and Jazlyn migrated to her bedroom. Jazlyn didn't want to let go of Rome, almost as if he'd disappear if she did. She held onto his waist as they lay face-to-face on the bed, their legs tangled together.

"I thought you weren't going to be back until tomorrow," she said softly, her fingers tracing swirls across his chest.

Rome looked down at her. "You knew I was out of town?"

"I ran into Asha and she told me."

"Of course she did. Yeah, the plan was to stay until tomorrow but I didn't need to waste any more time there when I knew I wanted to be here with you."

A smile shot across Jazlyn's face. "You have no idea how glad I am to hear that. Though I can't help but be curious as to what happened with Nell."

"I realized she wasn't for me," Rome replied simply.

Jazlyn paused, waiting for him to elaborate. "And?"

"And what?"

"I know there's more to it than that. What happened?"

"She wasn't who I thought she was, basically. And I realized that I was letting my guilt over what I did to her influence things too much. And you were right; she was milking it. I knew before we even went that we'd veered into wasting-our-time territory. There was no need in trying to be polite and continuing to go through the motions with Cornelia."

"Who?"

"Long story. My point is, I knew I wanted you."

"I'm just glad you didn't take me seriously when I told you to stay with her."

"I know you," he reminded her, tilting her chin up for a kiss. "And I can't even blame you for being fed up over that whole situation. I'm so sorry for putting you through that."

"No, don't apologize. I'm the one that convinced you to do it. And you were just trying to keep your word to her. It was just hard waiting and not knowing anything."

"I get that."

"And I don't suppose you'll tell me-"

"No, Jazlyn," Rome interjected, a knowing smile on his lips. "Let's just be glad we're together now and done with all that. Besides, I don't think you really want to know details like you think you do."

Considering his words and what they implied, Jazlyn was inclined to agree. Though she still didn't like the idea of Rome and Nell sharing any kind of intimacy, she told herself that it wasn't important.

And when she remembered what happened with Marco on her couch, she knew she couldn't get *too* upset about anything Rome and Nell might've done.

"You're right," she finally conceded. "I don't want to spend any more time worrying about Nell. She got what she wanted, she had her chance...now we can just move forward without worrying about the past."

"My thoughts exactly. Nell and Marco are in the past." Rome caressed her face. "It's all about us from here on out. You're my future, Jazlyn."

Grinning, Jazlyn fisted his shirt, slinging her leg over his. "Promise?"

Rolling on top of her, Rome gave her a deep kiss. "Promise."

Their kiss resumed, steadily escalating until they were both panting and hurriedly pushing each other's clothes off, anxious to show how much they missed each other. They had four weeks to make up for.

• • • •

"DO THEY KNOW I'M COMING with you?" Jazlyn asked Rome as they headed to his parents' house the next morning. They had invited Rome over for brunch in an attempt to show support for whatever decision he made regarding the situation with Nell.

"No, I already told them I was coming before last night. As far as they know, it'll just be me. Though I'm sure Mama is hoping to see Nell."

"It still stings that she was rooting for Nell so hard. I thought me and your mama were cool."

"She loves you, sweets. She just had some kind of soft spot for Nell. They had a lot of the same interests and were like girlfriends from the jump; half the time, they'd forget I was even there."

"Nice. Well, I guess I'll just have to prepare myself for Ms. Georgia being disappointed when I walk in."

"She'll get over it. And not that it made any more difference, but Dad and Asha were pulling for you."

"Two to one. I'll take it."

They arrived to his parents' house and Rome let them in with his key. His parents were in the kitchen putting the finishing touches on everything when Rome and Jazlyn entered.

"Oh," Georgia marveled, clearly surprised. Her eyes drifted down to their joined hands. Jazlyn shot Rome a told-you-so look.

"Well, I'll be damned," Solomon commented with a smile. He wiped his hands on a dish towel and crossed over to them, his arms out. "It's so good to see you two here together."

"Thanks, Dad." Rome joined in on the group hug, patting his dad's back heartily.

Stepping back, Solomon briefly grasped Jazlyn's shoulders, the smile still on his face. "I'm glad to see you, sweetheart."

"I'm glad to see you, too." Jazlyn grinned up at him before looking over at Georgia. "Both of you."

Collecting herself, Georgia's surprised expression morphed into a pleasant smile as she went over to give her own hugs. "Of course it's wonderful to see you both. I guess I was just a little taken aback because of, you know..."

"Yeah, all that's over, Mama." Rome verified. "Nell is out of the picture and it's me and Jazlyn now. She's who I want to be with; there's not a doubt in my mind."

"Mine, either," Jazlyn added, rubbing his arm. They shared a smile before gazing at each other, their smiles fading slightly.

Georgia eyed them, recognizing that look. Her son was in love; she hadn't even seen him look at Nell like that in all the months they were together. She glanced over at her husband, who winked at her knowingly.

"Then I couldn't be happier for you, baby," Georgia insisted sincerely. She briefly reached up and cupped Rome's cheek in her left hand and Jazlyn's in her right before stepping back. "Hope you two are hungry. We made far too much, as usual."

"I'm starving," Rome replied, patting his stomach. He hadn't eaten since before going to Jazlyn's house the night before, and they'd been too busy making up for lost time to eat. After Jazlyn had woken him up with some morning fellatio, they'd almost lost track of time and Rome had been very close to just telling his parents he couldn't make it. He was already looking forward to when they could be alone again.

"Well, let's eat, then."

After washing their hands, the four of them piled their plates high with salmon croquettes, grits, waffles, eggs, smoked sausage and sausage patties, and fruit. Georgia had also made a cream cheese coffee cake, and Rome immediately called dibs on any leftovers.

To Rome and Jazlyn's relief, neither of Rome's parents tried to dig for any details on what happened with Nell. They mostly talked about Georgia and Solomon's upcoming trip to Italy, Asha's new obsession with making candles, and how things were going with Rome and Jazlyn's respective careers. Everyone expressed excitement and encouragement when Jazlyn revealed the news about the nail polish brand she was working on. Rome kissed her right there at the table, with Solomon having to throw a napkin at them when it went on a few moments too long. Georgia couldn't help but chuckle at her son and his girlfriend's flushed faces, Jazlyn briefly ducking her head against Rome's shoulder.

After they ate, Rome tried to think of an excuse for him and Jazlyn to get out of there but Jazlyn offered to help clean up. He usually would have offered to do that himself, but that's just how anxious he was to get Jazlyn alone again. Now that they were back together, he realized just how much he'd missed her and he wanted to get out of his parents' house so he wouldn't have to watch how he touched her and didn't have any time limits on their kisses.

"Rome, sweetie, I need to see you for a moment," Georgia informed when Rome and Jazlyn were carrying the dirty dishes to the kitchen.

He looked at her warily, remembering the last one-on-one talk they had.

"Don't give me that look," Georgia admonished, smiling. "Now come on here, before I change my mind about letting you take the rest of that coffee cake home."

Rome immediately plunked the plates in his hands on the counter and headed in her direction. "Coming, Mother."

Solomon and Jazlyn laughed, shaking their heads.

Georgia led her son to her and Solomon's bedroom and motioned for Rome to close the door behind him. The slight apprehension was still clear in his expression.

"What's up, Mama?"

"You and Jazlyn seem really happy."

"Yeah." He looked at her evenly. "We are."

"I'll admit that I thought what the two of you had was nothing more than lustful infatuation. But apparently I was wrong. I've never seen that look in your eyes that you had earlier when you were looking at Jazlyn. That's how your father started looking at me when our relationship moved beyond friendship. And I was as giddy over it as Jazlyn is."

"I tried to tell you."

"I know. And I know I gave you a hard time about Nell, but I hope you believe me when I say I am truly happy for you. Jazlyn is a wonderful young woman; I've always thought so. She's good for you."

"She really is. This is gonna work, Mama; she's it for me. I've never been more sure about anything."

"You've discussed marriage, then?"

"Here and there. We both want that. I'm not rushing into it but I absolutely plan on making Jazlyn my wife one day."

"I thought you'd say that." Georgia went over to one of the bedside tables and opened the drawer, pulling out a royal blue ring box. She held it out to Rome. "Here."

"What's this?"

"Open it and see."

Rome shot his mother a curious look before taking the box and easing it open. His eyebrows shot up when he saw the two-carat vintage diamond engagement ring with accents. Rome didn't know a lot about jewelry but he figured it was worth a pretty penny. He looked up at his mother curiously.

"When you're ready," Georgia said, grasping his arm. "I want you to give that to Jazlyn."

Blinking in surprise, Rome looked at the ring again. "Wow, Mama...are you sure?"

"I'm absolutely sure. This belonged to my grandmother and I've been saving it to give to you for when you were ready to settle down. And this would look gorgeous on Jazlyn. Do you think she'll like it?"

"She'll love it." Rome's eyes dropped back to the ring, already imagining himself presenting it to Jazlyn while he asked her to marry him. Excitement and anxiousness sprouted in his chest, and he was almost tempted to go out and propose to her right then just so he could get to see the look on her face as he slid the ring onto her pretty finger.

But he knew they weren't quite there yet. He wanted them to just enjoy each other and keep getting acclimated to being together in this capacity without all the drama of stubborn exes or spiteful siblings or biased parents or dormant guilt. He wasn't sure how long he was going to hold off but he figured he'd know when the time was right. And he already couldn't wait.

He pulled his mother into a tight hug. "Thank you for this, Mama."

"My pleasure, sweetie." She lovingly rubbed his back before they separated. "And I just have one more thing to say about Nell and that's it."

Managing to stop his sigh before he could release it, Rome just steeled himself. "And that is?"

"I'm proud of you."

He hadn't been expecting that at all. "Really?"

"Yes, really. For trying to do right by her. Even if I thought the way you did it was a little unorthodox, I respect that you cared about her enough to do it. I know it couldn't have been easy on you, or Jazlyn, for that matter."

"To say the least. Especially when Nell asked me not to talk to Jazlyn at all during the month I was spending with her."

"Goodness. I'm sure it must have been devastating for Nell when you decided to go back to Jazlyn but I'm sure she'll be all right. I'm just glad to see you so happy."

"Thanks, Mama." He leaned down for another hug, noticing her usual floral scent that she'd been wearing for as long as he could remember. It was Chanel and the main thing she splurged on for herself. "I love you."

"I love you too, baby."

They returned to the kitchen to find Jazlyn and Solomon laughing hysterically at something amongst themselves, Jazlyn's hands soapy from the dishwater and Solomon almost dropping the plate he was trying to dry.

"Mr. E, you are too *much*!" Jazlyn exclaimed, trying to catch her breath. "You almost made me pee on myself!"

"You started it!"

Rome and Georgia just stood and looked at them amusingly, now the ones shaking their heads.

• • • •

WHEN ROME AND JAZLYN were finally back at his place, he grabbed her as soon as they were inside, pushing her against the wall and kissing her deeply. Jazlyn's arms immediately wrapped around him, eagerly returning the kiss.

"Do you have *any* idea how much I've missed you, sweets?" he asked, resting his forehead against hers.

"I bet I do. Because I was missing the hell outta you."

They resumed their kiss, their hands beginning to slide around each other's bodies. When Rome's hand slid down to her breast, she covered it with hers, stopping him.

"What's wrong?" he asked.

"There's something I need to tell you." Jazlyn suddenly looked nervous, easing from her spot between him and the wall and edging over to the middle of the room. "It happened a little while ago and I don't feel right keeping it from you."

Rome frowned curiously. "Okay..."

"I was at home and feeling pretty down about you and Nell when Marco came over. Unannounced and uninvited, as usual, but he was telling me he'd seen you and Nell out somewhere. And I kinda broke down. He held me and we ended up...kissing."

Trying to keep his automatic ire in check, Rome took a breath to calm himself. "*Just* kissing?"

"There...was a little more than that. We fooled around some but that's as far as it went, and it didn't even last long. I came to my senses and put him out." Jazlyn looked at him with remorseful eyes. "I'm so sorry. It was in the middle of your time with Nell, but still. He caught me at a weak, sexually-frustrated moment."

"I see."

Jazlyn eyed him. "Are you mad?"

Rome was, but he knew he didn't have a right to be. He and Jazlyn were essentially on pause during that time, and it's not like he hadn't been intimate with Nell at all. It gave him marginal comfort to know that she hadn't let things go all the way.

"It's cool," he made himself say. "I'm glad you told me."

"Does that mean you're gonna tell me what went down with you and Nell?'

"Same. We fooled around but no sex. I didn't feel right going there with her."

A relieved grin broke out across Jazlyn's face. "Good. I'd been worried about that. Though I don't like the thought of her touching you at *all*..."

"You think I loved hearing about you letting Marco kiss on you?"

"Touché." Jazlyn held up her hands in concession. "We both did some stuff, but thankfully that's all behind us now."

"Yes, it is."

She strode over to him, with Rome's smile widening as he eyed her approach. She pushed his coat from his shoulders and tossed it somewhere near the vicinity of the couch. Taking his face in her hands, she looked right into his eyes.

"I love you *so* much, Rome," she stated, impassioned. "I'm in love with you. You know that, right?"

"I'm in love with you, too." Rome grabbed her waist and pulled her closer, his hands sliding up her back. "More than you know. I want this to be a permanent thing, J."

"It *is* a permanent thing. I'm all yours."

"You'd better be. Now take these damn clothes off so I can do what I've been fantasizing about all day."

"Oh?" Jazlyn bit her lip as she stepped back and kicked her chunky boots off, then unbuttoned her jeans. "And what's that?"

"Keep stripping. You'll see."

They each steadily removed their clothes, their eyes locked the whole time. Before too long Rome had Jazlyn perched on top of the back of the couch while he buried his face between her legs. Her back braced against the wall behind her, she held the back of his head with one hand as she grinded against his face, a frown of immeasurable pleasure twisting her expression. It amazed her how good, how *amazing*, Rome was when it came to pleasuring her body. He simply put his hands on her and it sent her tingling. No other man had such an effect on her.

She shrieked when Rome yanked her onto her back on the sheet he'd laid out on the couch, wasting no time sliding into her. His lips crashed onto hers as they moved together, their pace frenetic, neither having the patience to take their time.

"Jazlyn, *shit*," Rome moaned, his mouth falling open as an earthquake-level shudder rocked through him. His eyes slid closed when Jazlyn leaned up and began licking his nipples, her nails digging into his back. "Babe..."

"If you like it, go harder."

Rome lifted her leg over his shoulder and began pounding into her so hard that Jazlyn had to hold on to the back of the couch, calling out in unbridled pleasure. Then he pushed her legs back to where her knees were almost to her ears, and Jazlyn thought she was going to lose it. Especially when she saw the sexy frown on Rome's face as he sexed her orgasm out, encouraging her to come and scream out loud when she did. And mere moments later, she did exactly that.

"*Fuuuuuck!*"

Rome wasn't too far behind her, his thrusts getting more erratic the closer he got to his orgasm.

"Shit!"

He quickly pulled out and released all over her stomach, the sight so erotic that his other hand gripped her thigh and slid down to her hip, giving it a long squeeze.

"Next time, do that on my face," Jazlyn requested, sitting up on her elbows and looking at him with lingering hunger.

Rome looked at her. "Damn, I love how freaky you are."

"Only with you, baby."

"That's what I wanna hear."

He got up to get a washcloth. Once he cleaned the both of them up, she opened her arms to him and he eased his body back on top of hers. They laid in sated silence, sharing occasional kisses or nuzzles against each other's necks.

"Oh my god," Jazlyn suddenly muttered.

Sitting up slightly, Rome looked down at her with concern. "What? What's the matter?"

"Is that what I think it is?"

Rome followed her eyes and groaned inwardly. The ring box his mother had given him earlier had fallen out of his jacket pocket and was sitting on the floor next to Rome's Kyrie Infinity sneaker.

"Yeah," he finally confirmed. "It is. But don't freak out or anything...Mama gave me that earlier."

"Can I see it?"

Only hesitating for a second, Rome reached over and grabbed the ring box, but closed his hand around it tightly before handing it to her. "Wait..."

"What?"

"I kinda don't want you to see it yet. I want you to be surprised whenever I finally propose."

Jazlyn grinned. "Well, then maybe you should go ahead and do it."

"Don't play."

"Who's playing? Ask me."

"Jazlyn. You know I wanna marry you. But I don't want us to rush into it. Plus we *just* came out of all that bullshit with our exes..."

"And all that bullshit just cemented things for me, Rome." She gazed into his eyes, lovingly sliding a hand up to his face and behind his neck. "You are my best friend in the world. My heart is yours. There's nobody else I can imagine my life with and being without you these past few weeks only proved how much I want *us*. It's you and me, Rome, so whether you ask me right now or next year, the answer will still be the same."

Her words hit him right in the chest, and he felt the emotion building behind his eyes. The way Jazlyn felt about him, he felt the same way about her. Jazlyn was everything he wanted in a woman, and there wasn't a doubt in his mind that she was the one he wanted to grow old with. He wanted to have kids with her and grandkids and vacations and memories that carried them through their final days. He never wanted to be without her again.

Swallowing, he opened the ring box and turned it towards her, leaning on his elbow. She gasped upon seeing it, a hand clamping over her mouth.

"Rome, that is..." Her hand dropped to her chest, tears wetting her eyes. "That is *gorgeous*."

"It'll look even better on you." After removing the ring, he set the box on the arm of the couch above her head before pushing himself up slightly so Jazlyn could sit up. She rested her back against the corner of the couch, anxious anticipation in her eyes as she stared at him.

"Jazlyn," he took her left hand in his, kissing it. "I love you more than anything and I want you by my side for good. Everything you just said you felt about me, I feel the same way about you. And..." He slid the ring onto her finger. "Now I'm asking you to be my wife."

Already nodding vigorously, Jazlyn waited for Rome to fully put the ring on her before throwing her arms around his neck, grinning so hard her face hurt. "Absolutely yes!"

Rome grinned as he hugged her back tightly, feeling better than he had in years, if not ever. This was fast and not the way he planned it but as soon as he slid that ring onto her finger, any lingering doubt evaporated. This felt right. And he felt like the most blessed man in the world, to fall in love with his best friend.

He pulled back and they shared an urgent, intense kiss, his body sinking back down onto hers momentarily before he grabbed her and pulled her onto his lap. Their kiss resumed, Jazlyn's hands grasping his face, her engagement ring gleaming.

"We're crazy, aren't we?" Rome asked with a smile, his hands sliding up and down her back.

"Maybe." She tweaked his chin. "But I'm not mad at it."

"Me, either. I love you, big head."

She grinned. "I love you, too. With your cute self. Now, future hubby, I'm kinda thirsty..."

"Oh, you want some water or some juice? I'll get it."

"Nope, no need." Jazlyn slid off his lap and to her knees, taking his length into her hand and looking up at him hungrily. "I'm good right here."

Rome's head fell back as she proceeded to pleasure him, and he actually pinched himself to see if he was dreaming.

But he wasn't. He was really there, engaged to his best friend and woman of his dreams (who was giving him some top-level head), and he couldn't wait to see where this journey together took them next.

THE END

I had such a fun time writing Jazlyn and Rome's love story; I love friends-to-lovers so much. I hope you got some enjoyment reading about their journey. It all started with the blizzard; the image of them on Jazlyn's bed when they were stuck together is what sparked the idea for this story. It really doesn't take much sometimes. lol

Whatever you thought of this story, please leave a review on Amazon, Goodreads, or wherever you purchased it. Reviews mean so much and are vital to us indie authors. I appreciate your time and attention.

The social media stuff: you can find me on Instagram, Facebook, and TikTok under @AuthorJessicaTerry, and on Twitter/X at @ItsJessicaTerry. I *love* to see (positive) shout-outs for my books on there, so feel free to tag and show love, if you're so inclined. ☺ And you can get a free book when you subscribe to my email list at www.jessicaterry.com. It's a complete and total bribe.

<u>Also by Jessica Terry</u>

Some Like 'em *Thick*

It's All Right...Now

Not By a Long Shot

Get Right

Decisions and Consequences

Take One For the Team

When You Share Too Much

Backtalk

Emasculated

Restless

The Beginning of Again

Always and Nevers

She is Me

Split By the Bell

The Karma Call

Forehead Kiss

All Because of Ava

Love Intolerant

Mr. Time Waster

The Stubborn Kind

From Meltdown to Mistletoe

Mrs. Soul Crusher

<u>The Introvert Series</u>

An Introvert's Christmas

Wooing the Introvert

The Introvert Roast

I, Take Thee Introvert

The Introvert Series Compilation (paperback only)

Discussion Questions (heads up; contains mild spoilers)

• • • •

1. Do you think a friendship between a heterosexual man and woman will always eventually lead to something romantic or sexual, even if it's just a one-time thing?
2. Did you feel Jazlyn was disrespecting Marco?
3. Was Nell too trusting of Jazlyn and her friendship with Rome, even before anything happened between them? Did you find her naïve?
4. Everything changed the night of the blizzard. Jazlyn and Rome were each in relationships, however imperfect, when they took things to another level then realized they had feelings for each other. Were you rooting for them to make it, or were you against their romantic relationship?
5. How crazy did you think Nell's request was? Would you ever have agreed to something like that, even if you felt guilty?
6. Was Asha's anger towards Rome justified?
7. Marco couldn't seem to leave Jazlyn alone. Did you feel he just had a bruised ego from getting dumped, or that he sincerely wanted her back?
8. Did Rome go too far trying to make up for how he hurt Nell? Was he overcompensating?
9. Despite Rome's infidelity, do you feel Nell was at fault at all for the demise of their relationship, even

after the extra month? Did any of what was revealed about her at the beach surprise you?

10. Ginger tried to keep Jazlyn's head on straight while she waited for Rome to make his decision. Did you ever feel she was insensitive to what Jazlyn was going through?

11. What did you think of Rome's parents, Georgia and Solomon? Did you agree with their suspicions that Rome and Jazlyn's relationship was just infatuation, not love?

12. I didn't really set out for this to be a 'love triangle' story but I suppose that's kind of what it was, in a sense. So that leaves the question: Team Jazlyn or Team Nell? Who did you want Rome to end up with?

Did you love *I Want Us*? Then you should read *Love Intolerant*[1] by Jessica Terry!

[2]

Adele Mozley was used to the friend zone. Men liked hanging with her but when it came time to get romantic, she usually got the polite stiff-arm.

But so what, right? She had a job she liked, a loyal BFF, an amazing son and slightly-curmudgeonly father, and Friday nights with Jamaican takeout and her remote. That's not so bad.

Enter Kingston Ferrell, who is persistent, younger...and so hot it's almost intimidating. And he has eyes only for

1. https://books2read.com/u/bPNk9j

2. https://books2read.com/u/bPNk9j

her. Adele didn't lack self-esteem, but she couldn't quite let herself believe that this hunk would be interested in a 40-something widow with a teenage son. So will she get out of her own way and let him love her? Or will she go back to spending her nights alone with forbidden dairy and regrets?

Read more at https://www.jessicaterry.com/.

About the Author

Jessica Terry caught the writing bug at a young age and loves little more than holing up at home in Douglasville, GA, cranking out contemporary novels. And eating. www.jessicaterry.com

Read more at https://www.jessicaterry.com/.